LIFE IN THE FLAMES

CHRIS MORPHEW

LIFE IN THE FLAMES

THE PHOENIX FILES 3

hardie grant EGMONT

Life in the Flames
published in 2016 by
Hardie Grant Egmont
Ground Floor, Building 1, 658 Church Street
Richmond, Victoria 3121, Australia
www.hardiegrantegmont.com.au

A CiP record for this title is available from the National Library of Australia.

Cover design by Design By Committee
Typesetting by Bookhouse, Sydney

Printed in Australia by McPherson's Printing Group, Maryborough,
Victoria, an accredited ISO AS/NZS 14001 Environmental
Management System printer.

1 3 5 7 9 10 8 6 4 2

MIX
Paper from
responsible sources
FSC® C001695

The paper in this book is FSC® certified. FSC® promotes
environmentally responsible, socially beneficial and
economically viable management of the world's forests.

To Mum and Dad,
For more reasons than I could possibly list here.
Thank you.

book 5
fallout

Chapter 1

I didn't like being out here while it was still light.

Not that there was any ideal time to be standing out in the open, waiting for the Co-operative to come and find me, but the blood-coloured sunset dripping down between the trees wasn't exactly an encouraging sign.

The wind whipped around my face, stinging my ears and stirring up braids that had deteriorated almost completely by now into dreadlocks. I flicked my head back, clearing my line of sight, feet shifting on the asphalt to keep warm.

Waiting.

The road stretched out in front of me, slicing a narrow path through the bushland. It curved away to the right, almost imperceptibly, winding out from Phoenix in a spiral. Eventually, far out of sight, it bypassed the warehouse and petered out, dead-ending into the trees just short of the towering wall that sealed us off from the outside world.

The road was a lie, like almost everything else in this place. But those lies were starting to unravel.

It had been three weeks since Shackleton gave up the benevolent-leader act and turned the town centre into a concentration camp. Three weeks of scouring hijacked surveillance feeds, of searching the bushland for anything or anyone that might be able to put a dent in the Co-operative's plans, of watching the days slip out from under us.

And now our food was running out.

There were thirteen of us down in the Vattel Complex, getting by on food supplies originally meant for two, and things had only got worse when Kara's hydroponics bay finally bit the dust. Watered-down soup might trick the eyes, but it didn't trick the stomach, and it seemed like a waste to die of starvation when there were so many other, more interesting threats to my life – like getting gunned down by a Co-operative security officer, or disappearing into one of my visions of the past or future, either of which might happen at any minute.

I shivered, hugging myself through the same crusty jumper I'd been wearing for five days straight. It was one of Luke's, although we didn't really think like that anymore. It had been a long time since I'd worn anything properly clean or entirely mine.

The wind picked up and I glanced over to the side of the road. It was impossible to tell through the jostling leaves whether anyone was out there.

Mind on the job, Jordan, I ordered myself. *No time to start jumping at –*

My eyes snapped forward again as the low hum of

an engine cut through the noise of the bush. I took a breath, steeling myself.

The rumbling grew louder, and a black supply truck crested the rise in front of me. I held my ground in the middle of the road, fists clenched at my sides. The driver jolted in surprise and slammed on the brakes, screeching to a stop about five metres short of me.

The passenger door flew open. A black-uniformed security officer jumped out, raising the semi-automatic rifle that was apparently standard-issue now.

It was Officer Cohen. Formerly just *Mr* Cohen, the school cleaner.

'Down on the ground,' he ordered. His voice was hard, but his eyes flashed back and forth, like he already suspected he was being set up.

'Mr Cohen, please,' I said, refusing to let the nerves spill into my voice. 'You don't want to shoot me.'

'No,' he said, fingers tensing. 'No, Jordan, I don't. But I will if I have to.'

I glanced into the bush, opening my hands and slowly raising them into the air.

'Down on the ground,' Mr Cohen repeated, 'or I promise you, I will –'

There was a crash. A figure flew from the bushes, impossibly fast, hair streaming behind her like black fire. The figure collided with Mr Cohen. I heard a split second of his startled shout before it was drowned in gunfire. I dived to the asphalt, rolling clear of the torrent of bullets.

Mr Cohen fell to the ground, rifle slipping from his grip, putting an end to the firing. The black-haired figure – Amy – landed on top of him. She grabbed the rifle and jumped up, stumbling off again, and spun her gaze to the trees. 'Get out here!' she yelled in her weird, too-fast voice. 'Hurry!'

Luke and his dad burst out from their hiding places, wielding a rusty bit of pipe and one of Kara's pickaxes. Soren swept in from the other side of the road, carrying a rifle identical to Mr Cohen's. All three of them were as dirty and underfed as I was. They looked like a pack of survivors from a zombie movie.

I got up, ears still ringing from the blast of the gun. No way had they missed that, back at the warehouse. We had maybe five minutes before more trouble arrived.

Luke's dad bent down to disarm Mr Cohen. 'Nice work, girls.'

'Thanks,' I said, looking up at the driver, frozen in his seat. 'Hey, you! Get out here!'

The driver nodded shakily and cut the engine. He clambered down from the truck, and I recognised him as one of the old delivery guys from back when Phoenix was still a town. He glanced out at the bush, like he'd love to make a break for it, but he came around to kneel next to Mr Cohen.

'Please,' Mr Cohen whimpered, as Luke's dad stood up with his rifle. 'Shackleton – he'll kill me.'

'I will do it for him if you don't keep your mouth shut!' Soren snarled.

'No, you won't,' I said, wishing I'd fought harder to keep him from coming with us. 'And Shackleton won't either. Just let us pick up a few supplies and we'll be out of your hair.'

'Where are the keys?' asked Luke. The driver cocked his head in the direction of the truck, and Luke went to pull them from the ignition. I followed after him, leaving the others to handle the guard duty.

As soon as we got around the back of the truck, Luke dragged me into a hug. 'That was ridiculous. I thought he was going to –'

'We've done worse,' I said, squeezing him back, still dizzy with adrenalin.

'Yeah, but usually I don't have to sit there and *watch* it.'

'Good thing this is a one-off then,' I said. No way would we get away with it again.

Luke turned his attention to the truck. I watched him cycle through the keys, dirty fingers fumbling in the cold, and the low-grade dread I carried everywhere with me swirled up to the surface again, clawing holes in my stomach.

He was going to die.

If that old surveillance video of Kara's was to be believed, he'd *already* died.

Sometime in the next two weeks, Luke was going to find himself thrown twenty years into the past. We had no idea how that was even possible, but neither of

us doubted for a second that it was going to happen –
unless we did something about it.

And we *were* going to do something about it.

Because Luke wasn't the only one going back.
According to the video, Peter was going to follow
him back there, stab him to death in a blind rage, and
return to the present again.

And then came the final piece of the puzzle: as he
bled out on the floor, Luke was going to deliver – had
already delivered – a message.

Take Tobias to the release station.

Tobias. The anti-Tabitha. The cure for the end of
the world. The answer we'd been waiting so long, so
desperately for. At least, that's what we were hoping
it was. But for all our talking and searching and tying
ourselves up in knots about it, we were still no closer to
knowing what Tobias even *was.*

'Got it,' said Luke, popping open the padlock and
heaving the roller door into the air to reveal mountains
of neatly labelled boxes. A month ago, we might've
found pretty much anything in here – office stuff,
school uniforms, magazines – everything a town needed
to keep believing it was still connected to the outside
world. Now it just looked like food and a few other
basics. Exactly what we were after.

'All right,' I said, climbing into the back of the truck,
stomach grumbling in anticipation. 'Let's go shopping.'

My hands landed on the nearest box, and it took

all my self-control not to tear it open and start gorging myself.

Focus, I thought, hauling the box down to Luke. I dropped a second box on top of the first, and he ran them around to the front of the truck.

I could hear Soren threatening Mr Cohen again, shouting at him in the weird, stilted voice he'd picked up over a lifetime in isolation.

'Everything okay back there?' I asked as Luke returned.

'Hard to say,' said Luke. He grunted as I dumped a giant bag of rice into his arms. 'Shackleton's guys aren't giving us any trouble. Soren might be a different story, though.'

I gritted my teeth and ducked back into the truck. Theoretically, we were all on the same side now, but that didn't make Soren any less unstable. Sooner or later, he was going to become a real problem.

I heaved a box of soup tins down from the top of a pile, then froze as I heard the growl of another engine coming up behind us.

Luke jogged back. 'Already?'

'Yeah,' I said, passing the soup down to him. 'Time to go.' I grabbed one last box, and we raced to rejoin the others.

Amy and Mr Hunter were loaded up, ready to run. Soren's box was still at his feet. He was standing over Mr Cohen and the driver, waving his gun around like a crazy person. Luke tossed the keys out into the bush and looked down at the two men. 'Just stay where you are until your mates get here, okay?'

The driver nodded.

'I don't trust him,' said Soren, pointing the rifle in the driver's face.

The driver lurched. 'No! You can't!'

'Tell me about Tobias,' said Soren. 'Tell me where Tobias is being kept and I may let you live.'

'I don't know!' the driver moaned. 'I swear – please – I don't even know who that *is!*'

'Soren,' I snapped, over the growing engine noise behind us. 'Put it down. We're going.'

'Please,' said Mr Cohen. 'Please, just go.'

'Shut up,' Soren grunted. He pulled the trigger. *Click.*

The men on the ground shrieked and reeled out of the way, not registering at first that the weapon hadn't fired. Soren squeezed the trigger a few more times, shaking the rifle like that was going to fix it.

Click, click, click.

He shot me a furious look. 'You did this!'

Soren let the rifle drop to his waist. He growled in frustration and kicked the truck driver in the face, knocking him to the ground. Then he snatched up the box at his feet and followed the rest of us into the bush.

Chapter 2

Thursday, July 30
14 days

Soren lashed out at me as soon as the entrance to the Vattel Complex rolled shut above our heads. 'Never do that again!'

'Won't be an issue,' I muttered, moving ahead of him down the decaying stairs, fingernails digging into the box in my hands.

Soren swore. 'What is that supposed to mean?'

'Trust me,' I said, 'that's the last time you're going up with us.'

Soren charged into the hallway behind me. He dropped his box, grabbed me with both hands and shoved me up against the wall, sending my own box flying. I felt the rifle hanging between us, pressing into my stomach.

'Do not pretend you are in charge here,' he said. 'You do not decide –'

'You would have killed them!' I shouted. 'You would have *murdered* two people who weren't any threat to us!'

'Hey!' said Luke's dad, coming up behind us and grabbing Soren's shoulder. 'That's enough.'

Soren shrugged the hand off. 'Do you expect me to apologise? They are the enemy, Jordan! If you are not willing to do what is necessary –'

'You know what, Soren?' I said. 'You don't exactly have a brilliant track record of figuring out who the enemy is. How about you let someone else decide what's necessary?'

Soren opened his mouth and closed it again. He stormed off to the surveillance room, throwing his rifle to the ground.

'Yeah, that's right,' I said under my breath, 'go have a whinge to your mum.'

A thin face framed by matted black hair appeared in a doorway off the corridor, peering at Soren as he passed. Mike. Soren scowled at him and he shrank back inside.

Luke glanced sideways at me, checking if I was okay. 'Come on,' he said, grunting under the weight of the box in his hands, 'let's get this stuff to the kitchen.'

We headed up the corridor and I shoved past Mike into Kara and Soren's old lounge room, which was now set up as one of our main sleeping areas. Theoretically it was the boys' room, but I'd moved my bed in here too. I didn't care how 'safe' Peter was, locked in his cell at the other end of the Complex. I wasn't taking any chances when it came to keeping Luke alive.

'You should speak to Soren with more respect,' hissed Mike, following along behind us.

I glanced back at him, but didn't respond. Not worth the energy.

We'd picked up him and Cathryn about a week ago. Luke and I had been out past the eastern end of town, setting up a fake campsite to keep security looking for us on the surface, when the two of them burst out of the bushes, half-starved and begging us to take them in.

Turned out Kara had warned them. Two days before Shackleton took the rest of the town captive, she'd written to Mike, Cathryn and Tank, telling them to get out. A gesture of goodwill, I guess, after everything she and Soren had put them through.

She'd come clean with them about all of it. Who she and Soren really were. The whole elaborate deception they'd used to lure Mike and the others into kidnapping Peter. But one letter wasn't going to undo all the wrong that had been done – and it wasn't going to bring Mike's fingers back either.

He'd been badly injured when we found him, hand torn up by a bullet wound from a run-in with security a few nights earlier. They were separated from Tank that same night, and he hadn't been seen since. Kara did what she could for Mike, but the infection had already set in. His left thumb and forefinger ended up getting left behind on the operating table.

'Everyone okay?' asked Luke's mum, already waiting when we arrived in the kitchen.

Soren's furious voice echoed across the corridor. Luke raised an eyebrow. 'More or less.'

He dropped his box on the floor and gave his mum a hug. He seemed to be feeling a bit more sympathetic towards her these days, after what had happened to Dr Montag. Luke had hated his mum's new boyfriend all along, but that didn't make his murder any easier to stomach.

Managing the food supply was kind of Ms Hunter's thing now. Luke said it was good for her, that she needed something like this to help her deal with everything. He said she'd be fine with the end of the world, so long as she had a project to be in charge of.

Cathryn was in here too, sitting on the bench, picking the dirt out of her nails. She smiled at us as we piled into the room.

Amy squeezed in after us, deliberately slow again now that we were back underground. She glanced around anxiously. 'Hey, Ms Hunter? Um, could you …?'

Luke's mum nodded. She unlocked the cupboard above her head, pulled out two chocolate bars, and passed them down to Amy. My stomach growled again.

'Thanks,' Amy breathed, turning to leave.

Mike grabbed her with his good hand. 'Hey. Wait.'

'Problem, Mike?' I said, before he had time to do something stupid.

He ignored me, turning to Luke's mum. 'Seriously? *Two?*'

'You know she's entitled to extra rations,' Ms Hunter said evenly.

'That's crap. She doesn't need all that.'

'Mike,' I said. 'Let her go.'

Ms Hunter stared down at him. 'Would you like me to give her your dinner as well?'

Mike muttered under his breath. He threw down Amy's arm and pushed his way out of the room.

'Not your fault,' I told Amy, catching the look on her face.

'Yeah,' she sighed, and slipped off to her bedroom.

Cathryn dropped down from the bench and went after her. The two of them had struck up a bit of a friendship this past week. Something to fill the void for Cathryn now that she and Mike were barely speaking.

Luke's dad put his box down where Cathryn had been sitting. Ms Hunter tore it open and looked inside. 'What's this?'

'Cereal,' said Luke's dad, pointing to the label on the box.

'Does this look like cereal to you, Jack?' She pulled a smaller box out of the big one. It was a video camera. One of those little handheld ones, about as big a phone. Ms Hunter stared at her ex-husband, pursing her lips like it was his fault the box had been mislabelled.

'Sorry,' said Luke, moving quickly to head off another argument, 'should've checked inside before we took it.' He pulled another camera out of the box. 'It's not like the Co-operative to stuff up like this.'

'I'm going to have a shower,' said Luke's dad stiffly, walking out.

Too many people down here, I thought, not for the first time. Too many people and not enough space. Things had never exactly been friendly in this place, but now it was like you couldn't open a door without walking in on someone else's argument.

Luke stared at the ground, turning the camera box over in his hands. I felt a flicker of recognition, but the thought was pushed out of my mind as my mum appeared in the doorway. She walked into the kitchen, bleary-eyed, with Georgia trailing behind her.

'Oh, thank goodness,' said Mum, putting an arm around me. Her stomach bulged out in front of her, pushing up her shirt. We'd done our best to make sure everyone had enough clothes, but maternity wear options were pretty limited down here. 'Sorry, I didn't mean to fall asleep. I was just –'

'Mum, it's fine,' I said, crouching to put my hands on her stomach. 'How's she going in there?'

'She?' said Mum.

'Yeah, I changed my mind,' I said. 'I'm going with girl.'

Mum sighed, resting her hands on mine. 'Believe me, I will be only too happy whenever this kid decides to come out and settle it for us.'

According to Kara, that could happen any day now.

But given that Mum was carrying an almost full-term baby after less than three months of pregnancy, it wasn't much more than guesswork.

'We just have to ask him to come out,' said Georgia, nudging me aside and grabbing hold of Mum. 'Hey baby!' she shouted. 'Get out of there! We want to talk to you!' She collapsed against Mum's stomach, giggling.

'Hey, Georgia,' said Luke, holding a bright pink camera he'd pulled from the box. 'We got you a present.'

Georgia's face lit up. 'Cool!' She grabbed the camera and gave him a lung-collapsing hug. 'Thanks!'

'No worries,' Luke coughed.

'Thank you,' mouthed Mum, looking even more grateful than Georgia. It hadn't been easy keeping a six-year-old entertained in this place.

Georgia loosened her grip on Luke. She looked up, face twisted in concentration.

'What's wrong?' he asked.

Georgia frowned. 'You're trying to be happy, but you're not.'

Luke stepped away from her, suddenly uncomfortable, knowing as well as I did that this was beyond the scope of a normal six-year-old's perception skills. 'I'm fine,' he said. 'It was a bit scary going out to get the food, but I'm okay now.'

Georgia shook her head. 'I don't believe you.'

My stomach turned. We'd been protecting Georgia as much as we could from all the horrors of this place, but how are you supposed to keep anything from a kid who can read your mind?

'I'm going to go check on Kara and Soren,' said Luke, heading for the door.

'Yeah,' I said. 'I'll come with you.'

'You should kiss my sister some more!' Georgia shouted as we left the room. 'That's what makes you feel happy!'

She burst into another round of giggles, and I felt a smile creep across my face. I saw Cathryn re-emerging from the girls' bedroom and quickly wiped it away again. 'She okay?' I asked.

Cathryn shrugged. 'She said she just needs to rest.'

I didn't know what to do for Amy. She never complained about life down here, or about what was happening to her, but I could see she was struggling. And her body's need for extra food wasn't exactly helping her fit in.

Kara had done a few tests, trying to figure out what exactly was happening to Amy. The closest she could get was that the fallout had somehow 'sped her up'. Amy's whole body – heartbeat, nervous system, even her *mind* – was running three or four times faster than normal.

It should've killed her. That was Kara's diagnosis. But then, I could fill a warehouse with all the things in Phoenix that *should* have been true.

With practice, Amy was getting better at slowing her movement and her speech down to normal, but it was a big effort for her. It didn't surprise me that she was choosing to spend a lot of her time alone.

'You okay?' asked Luke, nodding at the surveillance room. 'You sure you want to go in there?'

'Don't worry,' I said, pushing the door open, 'I won't hurt him.'

Kara and Soren were across the room, setting up a row of computers along the wall that, until recently, had been covered in photos of Peter, Luke and me. Kara had been in here all afternoon, rearranging things.

Soren was lying under the table, plugging something in. Kara moved along the row, hitting the power buttons, and the laptops whirred to life.

'I'd like to apologise for my son's outburst,' she said, turning around.

Soren's head snapped up. 'It was not an *outburst*. I have nothing to –'

Kara stared at him over the top of her glasses. 'I am not interested in having this discussion again.'

Soren's hands twitched, like his first impulse was to throttle her. But whatever else he might be capable of, Soren was still not in the habit of standing up to his mum.

'Fine,' he growled. He got up and walked back out of the room. Kara pursed her lips, but let him go.

'Anything new in town?' I asked, turning to the main circle of surveillance computers in the middle of the room.

'There was another altercation at one of the meal

tables a little while ago,' said Kara. 'The men involved were disciplined.'

'Nothing unusual there,' said Luke, leaning in behind me as I sat down at a laptop looking in on the Shackleton Building. I punched the right arrow, cycling through the different camera angles.

By now, Shackleton's concentration camp was running with typical Phoenix precision. Everyone in town had been assigned their own seat in the town hall to sleep on. They even played movies on the big screen to keep the kids from getting too out of hand.

Outside, in the giant, sparkling foyer area that had once been Shackleton's 'welcome centre', security had set up a food line and a row of portable showers and toilets. They'd also erected a circle of razor-wire fence on the main street, stretching from the front doors of the Shackleton Building to the fountain in the centre of town, so that the prisoners could get out into the sun.

People seemed to be allowed to move freely around the camp, but there was no escaping the eye of security. Dozens of officers, all armed with rifles and capsicum spray, patrolled the building around the clock, quickly stamping out any hint of misbehaviour.

The whole thing was just a bit too clean for something the Co-operative had come up with on the fly. It seemed to be a contingency plan they'd had up their sleeves all along.

I kept scanning through the surveillance images,

hammering the button more quickly now, nerves starting to get the better of me. *'Where are you?'*

'There!' said Luke. I backtracked through a couple of images, hand freezing over the keyboard as I spotted him at a table in the welcome centre, hunched over an empty dinner plate. Dad.

He was deep in conversation with Peter's parents. It was hard to tell from this distance, but it didn't seem like anything too awful had happened to them while we were out. Maybe Calvin really had given up on them.

After they were captured, Calvin had dragged the three of them to the security centre every day for interrogation, trying to figure out where the rest of us were hiding. And every day I'd sat here, glued to the screen, watching. It had been horrible. Excruciating. At one point, Luke and his dad had needed to physically hold me back from running out there in a suicidal attempt to put an end to it. But no matter what Calvin did to them, Dad and the others never gave us up.

And now, it seemed like Calvin might have finally put an end to it himself. Today made it a full week since their last trip to the security centre.

Dad glanced up as a security officer approached the table. The officer jerked his head in the direction of the hall. Dad and the Weirs got up without arguing and joined the crowd that had started milling towards the doors.

Bedtime. They were shutting everyone in for the night.

Kara walked up behind us. 'Soren is still working on a way to circumvent the new restrictions on the surveillance network,' she said, in the closest she ever came to a sympathetic tone. 'Once we've established a way to disable –'

I rolled my eyes. 'No offense, Kara, but if Peter hasn't been able to figure that out, why on earth would you think Soren had any chance of …?'

I stopped talking, distracted by the grainy surveillance image that had just flashed into view in front of me. Kara's new row of computers – which I now realised were just the old surveillance monitors from the storeroom – had finished loading and were now relaying footage of the Complex's research module, or at least the few rooms that hadn't been blown up or concreted over.

Crazy Bill lay strapped to a bed in the room where I'd been held prisoner the night we first came down here. In the three weeks since we'd rescued him from the medical centre, Kara had kept him alive with an old I.V. unit that Soren had repaired and a feeding tube thing. She'd done everything she could think of to bring Bill around, but he hadn't even moved since we'd put him there. Hadn't even opened his eyes.

At least, not until about five seconds ago.

Chapter 3

We bolted into the corridor. Soren had just emerged from the toilet. He doubled back to follow us, guessing that something was up.

Mike had been waiting outside for him. 'Hey, boss –'

'Not now!' snapped Soren, shooing him away, and we raced through to the old research building, down a half-destroyed corridor strewn with debris.

'Have you been down to see him?' Luke glanced back at Kara. 'While we were up on the surface, did you do anything?' He ducked just in time to avoid smashing into a bit of pipe sticking out of the concrete.

'No,' said Kara, ducking under the pipe after him, 'no-one has gone near him.' And it was a sign of how far we'd come that I actually believed her.

The corridor opened up for a minute, and we shot past Peter's room, still barricaded from the outside. His face appeared behind the little hole in his door.

'Jordan! Jordan, get over here!'

'In a minute!' I called back.

We kept running, snaking past abandoned research

stations half-drowned in concrete. The destruction got steadily worse as we went along, closing in on the site of the explosion that had brought this place down.

I stopped as we reached a block in our path: a rusty old bookcase, pinned to the wall by two heavy lengths of pipe we'd wedged across the corridor. I kicked the bits of metal loose and they clattered to the ground, freeing the bookcase.

Luke pulled it aside, revealing a misshapen gap in the wall – the remains of an old doorway, leading into the remains of an old laboratory.

Kara slipped inside and I ducked in after her. I could still hear Peter shouting behind us. I tried to tune it out, tried not to let it get to me, but the dull dread was already creeping back into my stomach.

He was right here. Luke's future murderer, *right here* under our roof, and getting more unstable by the day. It was insane. An accident waiting to happen. But what choice did we have? We weren't about to kill Peter, couldn't let him loose on the outside, and didn't have enough sedatives to keep him knocked out for more than a few days. Our only option was to keep him here, keep him as calm as possible, and try to avoid giving the past any reason to repeat itself.

Not that *reason* was much of a priority for Peter anymore.

Bill's bed sat in the middle of the room, on the one bit of ground that still resembled a flat surface. Steel chairs littered the floor, cemented in at weird angles. I guessed this had been a meeting room back before the explosion. But given that my first experience of this place had been waking up strapped to one of those chairs, it was hard to picture it as anything other than a prison.

I crossed to the bed. Bill wasn't moving. His hair and beard had grown back a bit, and Kara had found a gown for him to wear, but apart from that he looked exactly the same as when we'd brought him down here.

'Who *are* you?' I whispered, staring down at his closed eyes.

Bill had been a piece of this puzzle since the very beginning. It had been *him* who'd dragged us into this fight. He knew – or *seemed* to know – more about what was going on in Phoenix than practically anyone. But since he'd spent most of the last few months either imprisoned or unconscious or both, we knew almost nothing more about him than the day we'd first met.

Kara frowned and reached down to take Bill's pulse.

'You saw it, right?' I said. 'You saw him moving on the monitor.'

Bill let out a groan, twisting away from her. Kara's hand snapped back. We'd warned her what Bill was capable of.

'I certainly saw *that*,' she said, as Bill settled back down. He didn't open his eyes again, but there was something different about the rhythm of his breathing. He seemed less comatose and more like he was just sleeping.

'Bill?' I said, ignoring the nervous shiver that ran up my spine as I leant over him. 'Bill, can you hear me?'

No response. I put a hand on his shoulder.

'Careful,' said Luke.

'Yeah,' I whispered. But if Bill knew something about Tobias, we couldn't afford not to know too. I bent down to try again. 'Bill. It's Jordan. Are you –?'

'Jordan,' Bill croaked.

I straightened up again, giving him space. Giving *myself* space, in case he decided to lash out or something. 'Yeah, that's right,' I said. 'Are you ready to wake up now, Bill?'

His mouth opened again. He murmured something but I couldn't make it out, especially not with Peter still yelling from up the corridor. I threw a frustrated glance behind me.

'I'll go see what he wants,' said Luke.

'No,' I said reflexively, wishing I hadn't let my irritation show. 'Leave him. Wait until –'

'Jordan, I'll be fine.'

'Soren, why don't you go with him?' Kara suggested.

'*No,*' said Soren and I at the same time.

'Don't worry,' said Luke, 'I won't open the door.'

He'll be okay, I told myself. But it was like this every time I wasn't with him. Because that was the thing that kept bugging me about the surveillance video Kara and Soren had shown us: I wasn't in it.

Where was I when Luke was getting stabbed to death?

I pushed the thought aside and bent over the bed again. 'Bill? Are you still there?'

If he was, he showed no sign of it.

'Waste of time,' Soren muttered under his breath. He grabbed Bill by the shoulders and started shaking him. 'Hey! Wake up!'

'Stop that!' I shoved him away and he staggered on the uneven concrete, almost knocking over the I.V.

Soren grabbed the back of a chair, finding his footing again. 'I am not afraid of –'

'*Soren*,' said Kara, silencing him. 'Why don't you take a seat, and I'll tell you if I need your assistance?'

'Mum, you cannot just –'

'Take a seat, Soren.'

Soren glared at her, but did what he was told. I circled around the bed to avoid having my back to him.

Outside, Peter's shouting came to a sudden stop. I tried to convince myself that meant he was calming down.

Bill was flat on his back again, like nothing had happened. Kara crouched down and opened the battered kit she kept under the bed. 'My kingdom for fifteen minutes in that medical centre,' she said under her breath, bobbing back up with a torch and a silver sedative pen. 'Only use it if you have to,' she said, handing me the pen. 'They're not going to last forever.'

She eased one of Bill's eyes open and flashed the torch inside. The pupil shrank a bit under the light. Kara let go of him and the eye snapped shut again.

'Is that good?' I asked, as she reached across to check the other one.

'It means he's alive,' said Kara. 'But given I have no idea what that "machine" you found him in was doing ...' She trailed off as Luke reappeared in the doorway.

'Is Peter okay?' I asked.

Luke shrugged, rolling his eyes. 'He only wants to talk to you.'

'Of course he does.' I sighed, looking to Kara. 'What's the story here?'

'He might wake up at any moment,' Kara told me, in a voice that said my guess was probably as good as hers, 'or he might never wake up at all. I'll send Soren for you if anything changes.'

'Don't worry,' said Luke. 'If Bill does wake up, I'm sure he'll let *everyone* know about it.'

By the time Luke and I got to his room, Peter was back to yelling again. 'JORDAN! JORD–!'

'Yeah,' I said, crossing to his door. 'I'm here. What's up?'

'Jordan! Quick, come in,' said Peter. 'I need to show you something.'

'Not now,' I said. 'Luke and I are –' I faltered, catching the flicker in Peter's eyes at the mention of Luke's name. 'It's Crazy Bill. Kara thinks he might be about to come around.'

'Oh,' said Peter. 'Crap. What are you going to do if he wakes up, you know, *crazy*?'

'Good question,' I said, mind already drawing up contingencies to get Mum and Georgia to safety. 'But that's why we need to get back there. What did you want to tell me?'

'Right,' said Peter. He grabbed his laptop from the bed. 'Thought you might want to know about this.'

Peter held the screen up in front of the gap in the door. It was a surveillance feed. The entrance above our heads. The sun had gone down on our way back from the supply truck, but I could still make out the dark form moving low across the ground.

There was someone up there, and they were trying to get in.

Chapter 4

The figure moved again, shifting through the grass on hands and knees. It was impossible to see much more than an outline, but there weren't many people in Phoenix with a silhouette that size.

'Tank,' I said.

'Alive,' Luke commented.

No-one had seen Tank since Mike and Cathryn lost him in that skirmish with security. All we'd known for sure was that he hadn't reappeared back in town. But then, neither had a bunch of others. There were at least thirty people who hadn't shown up on our feeds.

'Jordan!' said Peter. 'If you let me out, I can go up there and –'

'He's digging,' breathed Luke, as though Peter hadn't spoken. 'Look. He's trying to find the entrance.'

A shiver raced up my back. 'We need to get him down here.'

'Whoa, hang on, are you sure that's –?'

'Before someone *sees* him!' I said, running for the entrance.

Luke came sprinting up the corridor behind me. 'What if it's a trap?'

'A trap?' I said, ducking under a half-collapsed beam. 'If Shackleton knew we were here, you really think he'd send *Tank*?'

'That would be the "trap" part,' said Luke. 'Like in your vision. You *saw* security coming down here.'

'Yeah, but ...' I trailed off, realising I had no end to that sentence.

We shot out of the research module and up the hall through the living area. I poked my head into the lounge room on my way past. Mr Hunter was sitting on his bed, drying his hair with a towel. Mum and Georgia were still in the kitchen, helping Ms Hunter pack away the food.

'Get ready to run,' I said.

'Why?' said Mum, grabbing Georgia's hand. 'What's going on?'

'Probably nothing,' I said. 'But get ready.'

Way down in the bowels of the Complex, I'd set up a panic room to hide Mum and Georgia whenever my vision came true and Shackleton finally worked out where we were.

Not today, I thought. *Please don't let it be today.*

Luke's dad followed us into the surveillance room. 'What's happening?'

'Tank,' said Luke. 'He's up at the entrance.'

Mr Hunter glanced at the same feed Peter had

shown us. 'We need to get him down here before someone sees him.'

Luke threw up his hands like we were staging a mutiny.

I stopped at the control panel, fingers hovering over the button that would open the trapdoor. I could see the anxiety on Luke's face, and suddenly I wasn't so sure he was wrong. 'Are we doing this?' I asked.

Luke took another look at the feed. Tank was still clawing at the ground. How long before he hit concrete?

'All right,' said Luke, shaking his head. 'Yeah. Open –'

'Wait!' said Mr Hunter.

I jerked back from the control panel. 'What?'

Then I saw it. A second shadowy figure, shifting into view behind Tank. It turned slowly, peering around at the bush, sweeping a long, dark shape through the air at chest height.

'He's got a rifle,' said Mr Hunter.

'See?' said Luke, his face drained of colour.

Mr Hunter rubbed his face. 'Get the others. Get them as deep into the Complex as you can.'

'What? No! I'm not just going to leave you out here to get –'

'Hang on,' I said, watching the screen. The man with the gun crouched next to Tank. I moved closer, scrutinising the man's ragged outline. 'Look at him. Look at his clothes. I don't think – does that look like a security officer to you?'

Neither of them answered. My eyes stayed fixed

on the monitor. Something about this didn't add up. Either way, the image of security storming in and gutting this place was too fresh in my mind for me to feel sure of anything.

Finally, Mr Hunter turned and headed for the corridor. 'Whatever this is, we need to deal with it. Open the door.'

Luke started to answer, but his dad had disappeared.

I pushed the button. On the laptop screen, Tank and the other man scrambled out of the way as the ground opened up under them.

They knelt over the entrance, staring down into the blackness.

'What are you waiting for?' I hissed, hand resting on the control panel, ready to close the trapdoor as soon as they got inside. But still they didn't move.

I gave up waiting and dashed out after Luke's dad.

I could hear Tank calling down the stairs. 'Hello?'

'Shh!' I hissed. Even if this wasn't a trap, Tank was going to bring the whole Co-operative down on top of us if he didn't shut up.

Mr Hunter was standing at the bottom of the stairs, shoving a clip into the rifle Soren had abandoned before.

'Tank!' I snapped, cutting him off as he started calling out again. 'Get down here!'

Silence. Then: 'Jordan?'

'Hurry up! And tell your friend to put his gun down.'

My heart pounded. I heard a shuffling noise, feet on concrete, and then a dull hiss as Luke sealed the entrance.

'It's closing!' Tank panicked.

'Just get down here.' I said. My eyes flickered to Mr Hunter, kneeling to take aim up the stairs. 'Wait. The gun. Throw the gun down first.'

'No way!' said Tank. 'You think we're –?'

But he was drowned out by a sudden, noisy clattering as the other man did what I'd asked. I jumped out of the way as the rifle rocketed off the stairs and skittered across the floor.

'All yours, Jordan,' called a second voice, warm and familiar. 'But how about you let me come down and say hi before you start shooting?'

Relief exploded in my chest. Mr Hunter stood up, lowering his rifle. A huge smile broke across my face as the mysterious gunman slowly descended the last few steps, hands above his head, grinning. I ran forward and hugged him. 'Reeve!'

'Good to see you, kid,' he said, lowering his arms and patting me on the back.

'Reeve, where have you –? You're so *thin*,' I said, feeling the bumps of his spine poking up through his clothes. I stood back from him. He was wearing a tattered old hospital gown, the one he'd had on the night we'd rescued him from the medical centre. It was belted together with a bit of rope over a pair of jeans that might once have been the right size for him, but were now hanging off him like clown pants.

'Yeah,' said Reeve, bending to pick up his gun

again. 'It's been a rough few weeks.' He smiled again as Luke emerged from the surveillance room. 'Hey, mate.'

Tank came down the steps behind Reeve, mouth hanging open, dressed in the school uniform he must have been wearing the night Shackleton rounded everyone up. It was filthy, not much more than rags by now. His face was covered in patchy stubble.

A high-pitched shriek cut through the corridor behind me, and I almost jumped out of my skin. Cathryn came hurtling out of the girls' bedroom and threw herself at Tank.

'Guys,' said Luke urgently, over the sound of her sobbing. 'Did anyone –?'

But he was silenced mid-sentence as Mike came shoving past. 'What the *crap*, man?' he laughed, punching Tank in the arm. 'Where have you *been*? We thought you were –'

'HEY!' Luke boomed.

And it was such a shock to hear him demanding their attention that they all turned and gave it to him.

'Everyone, please, just shut up for a second,' said Luke. He turned to Reeve. 'Did anyone see you come down here?'

Reeve scratched at his ragged beard. 'No,' he said after a minute. 'No, I don't think so.'

Luke let out a long breath. 'Okay. Good.'

Tank was gazing around at the corridor again. 'What is this place?'

'This is *their* place,' said Mike. 'The overseers. This is where they live.'

And at that moment, like he'd been waiting for an introduction, Soren came tearing in from the other end of the corridor. 'Jordan! My mother says you have to come back –' He skidded to a stop, taking in the sudden crowd in the corridor. 'Why are they here?'

Tank strode towards him. 'You.'

'Stop!' Soren ordered. 'Stop right there!'

Tank kept walking. 'Screw you.'

'You should do what he says, man,' said Mike, weirdly nervous.

'No,' said Tank.

Huh, I thought, a smirk pulling at my lips. Since when did Tank start having independent thoughts?

'On your knees!' said Soren, glancing at Luke and me, like he expected us to back him up. 'Now!'

'You're not even real,' said Tank, closing in. 'Where's Peter? Tell me or I'll smash you.'

Soren turned and ran. Tank went to chase him, and I was tempted to let him go, but the last thing we needed down here was another fight.

'Tank, wait!' I called. 'Just stop for a second.'

Tank hesitated long enough for me to come over and grab his arm. 'Where's Peter?' he demanded again.

'He's here,' said Cathryn. 'Pete's here, but …'

'Trust me,' said Mike, 'you don't want to see him.'

After everything they'd put him through, Peter hadn't exactly welcomed Mike and Cathryn with open arms. Even with Phoenix's accelerated healing power, they'd only just lost the bruises from their last visit to Peter, and we'd kept them well away since.

'I'll take you to him,' said Cathryn.

'*I'll* take you to him,' I said. Better to keep Tank with me for now than to leave him here with these guys. 'But don't expect him to be happy to see you. And if you do anything stupid, I'll –'

'What's going on out here?' asked Luke's mum, appearing in the doorway.

'Nothing,' I said. 'Sorry, false alarm.'

'Who are they?' she asked.

'Friends,' said Luke, which was true of Reeve at least. 'Just give us a minute, all right?'

He turned back to his dad, cocking his head at Mike and Cathryn. 'Can you keep an eye on things out here?'

Mike scowled.

'Hey …' said Tank, eyes dropping to Mike's left hand, taking in his missing fingers for the first time. 'Mate … What happ–?'

'Go and see Pete,' said Mike, sticking the hand into his pocket.

'C'mon,' I said, nodding at Reeve to come too.

Luke and I guided the two of them deeper into the Complex, leaving Mr Hunter to hold the fort.

'They didn't tell us about any of this,' said Tank, awed.

'Yeah,' I said. 'There's a lot your overseers didn't tell you.'

Tank grunted, squeezing down the hall with more difficulty than Luke and me. 'They're not my overseers.'

'Okay, Peter's just through here,' said Luke, as a battered leather couch came into view up ahead. 'But listen, he's kind of sick. It doesn't take much to get him angry. You might want to keep your distance.'

'I just want to see him,' said Tank.

Peter was still standing at his little window.

'Pete?' Tank stopped a few metres short of him, eyeing the bars over his doorway. 'Mate, what are you doing in there?'

Peter's eyes went dark. 'Open the door.'

'Not a good idea,' said Luke in an undertone.

'Jordan!' said Peter. 'Bring him in here!'

'Hang on,' I said, keeping my voice level, suddenly remembering why we'd been down here before Tank and Reeve had arrived. 'Wait until we've checked on Bill, and then we'll work something out.'

'He kidnapped me out of my freaking *bed!*' Peter yelled. 'He held me down so Mike could beat the freaking crap out of me!'

'Settle down, mate,' said Tank. 'Let me –'

'BRING HIM IN HERE!'

WHAM!

Tank shot through the air, slamming into Peter's door like he'd been magnetised. He crumpled against the barricades, grunting as the impact knocked the wind out of him, then dropped to the floor in a heap.

Reeve gasped behind me.

Peter shouted and bashed his fists against the other side of the door.

Tank scrambled away from him. 'What –?' He stood up, wiping his nose, smearing blood across his face. 'What was *that?*'

'Wait over there,' I said, pointing Tank across the room and walking over to deal with Peter.

'Jordan, come on,' said Peter, eyes darting around. 'He should have just done what I said!'

'Listen,' I told him, 'this isn't how things get fixed. Just relax, okay? Give us time to deal with this properly.'

'But –' Peter glanced from Tank to his own hands, then back to me again, like he was struggling to figure out what had happened. His expression softened and his eyes dropped to the floor. 'Yeah.'

'All right. Good. I'll come and see you tomorrow, okay?' I started back to Bill's room, picking up Luke, Reeve and Tank on my way past. Moving on to the next thing, as though I hadn't just watched someone get levitated across a room.

'I think we might have a bit of catching up to do,' said Reeve, looking out the way we'd come.

Soren was waiting for us in the doorway. He ducked back inside as we approached.

Bill looked just the same as we'd left him.

'How is he?' I asked Kara, weaving between the chairs to the bed.

But her attention was fixed on Tank. He stopped in the doorway, like he was thinking about making a run for it. I couldn't figure out the expression on Kara's face, but it was the first time I'd seen her look at him like he was an actual human being. 'My letter. You saw it too?'

'Yeah,' said Tank, wiping his nose again, 'we got it.'

'Who's this?' asked Kara, eyeing Reeve with her usual cold scepticism.

Luke was looking at him too. 'Hey. You were with Bill in the medical centre. What were they doing to him? Did you ever see them wake him up?'

'Mate,' said Reeve, shaking his head at the bizarreness of it all – this weird huddle of people standing around a homeless guy's bed in a secret underground hide-out. 'I've got no bloody idea about *any* of –'

There was a groan from the bed.

Bill's eyes snapped open. He rose up from the mattress to look at me, arms tugging at his restraints. He snorted absently as the feeding tube moved in his nose, face breaking into a smile filled with swelling gums and mangled teeth.

And then suddenly, his expression shifted. 'NO!' he snarled. 'No, no, no! You're not right! You are not mine!'

'It's okay,' I said, backing off a bit. 'Bill, listen to me. Just take it slow, all right?'

'No! I need … Please …' He mouthed soundlessly, seeming to lose his train of thought. He gazed around the room and his face lit up again. 'We're here,' he said breathlessly. 'We are here. Yes, yes, it's almost –' He turned to Luke. 'How many days?'

'Until Tabitha?' said Luke.

'HOW MANY DAYS?'

'Fourteen,' I said. 'We've got two weeks left. Bill, what do you know about Tobias? Do you know what –?'

'It's time!' he shouted, falling back against the mattress. 'Almost. Almost time.' He was crying, ecstatic, head rolling from side to side.

'Almost time for *what?*' snapped Soren, getting tired of it. But if Bill heard him, he didn't show it.

'Bill …?' I said.

'Almost time,' he repeated, over and over, eyes drifting shut, tears still rolling down his face. 'Almost time … Almost …'

His head slowly rocked to a stop, and then he was gone again.

Chapter 5

'So you guys are, what, scientists or something?' said Reeve the next morning, scraping up the last of the soup Luke's mum had allocated him for breakfast.

'Something like that,' said Kara.

Reeve glanced up at Luke and me. 'And they're on our side now? Even after what they did to Tank and his mates? And to you guys?'

'It's complicated,' I said, standing to collect the empty bowls.

'Yeah,' said Reeve. 'I got that.'

We were sitting around on the beds in the boys' room. Reeve and Tank had spent the night here on the spare bunks and woke up talking as if those springy old mattresses were the best things they'd ever slept on.

'Is there more?' Tank asked.

'Yeah,' I said, taking his bowl away from him. 'At dinner.'

Ms Hunter had already given Tank and Reeve twice as much breakfast as anybody else, a decision which almost brought her and Soren to blows. Kara had broken it up, and Soren had stomped off to his room, where he was probably having a good long whinge to Mike about it.

'I'm still hungry,' Tank grumbled.

'Join the club,' I told him, taking the bowls through to the kitchen.

'What about you guys?' Luke asked. 'Where have you been all this time?'

When we'd last seen Reeve, he was running blindly into the bush, drawing a pair of armed guards away from the rest of us so we could escape from the medical centre.

'Well,' said Reeve, leaning back against the wall, 'at first it was just me. And for a good while after you kids busted me out, I spent most of my energy just surviving. Hanging around the outskirts of town, trying to get my head around what was going on. Trying to find out where my wife and my kid were. Then, about a week back, I was out at – there's a lake not far from here, and I was out there grabbing a drink, and I spotted this cave in the side of the rock face.'

'Yeah,' I said, sitting down next to Luke again. 'We've been there.'

'Course you have,' said Reeve. 'Anyway, I swam across and climbed up into the cave, and suddenly here was this kid –' He jerked a thumb at Tank. '– standing over me, ready to smash my head open with a rock.'

Tank smirked. 'Sorry.'

'It took a bit of work, but I was able to convince him that I wasn't going to hurt him. I filled him in on what was going on in town, and he explained how these overseers of his had warned him and his mates to get out.'

'They're not my overseers,' said Tank again, running a hand over his right shoulder, where Kara and Soren had branded him with a tattoo.

'No,' said Kara. 'We are not. That is why I sent you that last letter. I wanted to offer an explanation for our behaviour. I wanted to apologise.'

'No, you didn't,' said Tank bitterly. 'You never said sorry. You said you *had* to do all that to us.'

Typical Kara, I thought. She might have softened since we first met her, but some things never changed.

Kara rubbed her eyes. 'You need to believe that everything we asked of you was motivated by the best of intentions.'

'Because nothing says "best intentions" like luring innocent bystanders into a secret kidnapping cult,' I muttered, buried anger rising to the surface again. 'Who would've thought *that* would turn out –?' I broke off as Luke's fingers brushed over my hand. A gentle suggestion that rehashing this old argument might not be the greatest use of our time.

Tank's eyes widened. 'Whoa. You guys are together now? Does Pete know about this?'

I let go of Luke's hand. No, Peter didn't know about it.

'Because, you know,' said Tank, 'he's totally into you.'

'Yeah,' I said, 'I kind of picked up on that. Can we please focus?'

'We think there's a way to stop Tabitha,' said Luke, finally landing on the point I'd been wanting to get to all morning. 'Something called Tobias.'

'What?' Reeve jolted forward. 'What is it?'

'We don't know,' said Luke, voice registering the same dull thud of disappointment that had landed in my own stomach. 'We were sort of hoping you would.'

Reeve scratched at his beard again. His face was half hidden in the shadow of the bunk above his head, but I could still see the network of tiny, faint scars crisscrossing his skin, lingering reminders of his last encounter with Tabitha.

'Tobias,' said Reeve, brow furrowed. 'Where did you hear that name?'

I glanced over at Kara. 'That's complicated too.'

We'd filled the others in on the warning about Tobias, but we hadn't told anyone *how* we heard it. Not even Luke's parents. He said he didn't want to worry them. I'd told him he was being dumb, but let it drop after he pointed out that I was acting exactly the same way about my visions.

'Kara told us we had to take Tobias to the release station,' said Luke, not quite managing to keep his expression neutral. 'But she heard it from – someone else. She's got no more about Tobias than we do.'

'Brilliant.' Reeve leant forward, hands pressed together in front of his face. Then he sat up again. 'Hang on. Release station. I reckon I might know where that is. At least –' He stared into space, picturing something. 'There's a bunker, a little way out past the boundary wall. Only a few of us knew about it, and none of us ever got told what was inside, but they sent us out in the vans to do regular sweeps of the area.'

'*That's* what you were doing,' I said. 'The night we went out there. When you caught us climbing over the wall.'

'Yeah,' said Reeve. 'I had no idea what I was guarding back then, obviously. But it makes sense, doesn't it? What else would they be hiding *outside* the wall?'

Kara frowned. 'That still doesn't bring us any closer to –'

She stopped and hurried to her feet as Cathryn's voice rang out in the corridor. 'Get away from me, you little freak!'

Luke and I jumped up too, and a second later Georgia tore into the room. She crashed into me, clinging to my waist, tears streaming.

'Hey,' I said, hoisting her into my arms. 'What's up? Where's Mum?'

'Sleeping,' Georgia sniffed. 'The baby makes her sleepy.'

I carried her out into the corridor where Cathryn stood, red-faced, looking like she didn't know whether to run away or start shouting again. 'You got a problem, Cat?'

'She was going to sneak out there and give Peter some of my muesli bars,' said Georgia, pointing down the hall.

'I was not, you stupid little liar.'

'She *was*,' said Georgia, tearing up again. 'I'm not lying! She was going to steal the kitchen keys off Luke's mum. She told me!'

'Even if I was, like I'd tell you about it,' Cathryn snapped.

'Not with your mouth,' said Georgia. 'You told me in your head.'

Cathryn glared, confirming that Georgia was telling the truth, and I felt myself ratcheting up from frustration to rage. 'You *don't go down there*,' I said, closing the gap between us. 'What, you don't remember the beating he gave you last time?'

'He's sick!' said Cathryn angrily.

'And you think you can fix him? You think he beat you up because he was *hungry?*'

'She's still in love with him, that's why,' Georgia said matter-of-factly.

A second flash of sparks behind Cathryn's eyes told me Georgia was right. Cathryn turned and walked away, almost running into Mr Hunter as he came out of Kara and Soren's room.

'Sorry, Jordan,' he said wearily. 'I *was* watching her. But then I heard Soren yelling in his room and I thought I should check it out.'

'Not your fault,' I said, hugging Georgia and passing her across to him. 'Just too many children down here. What was he yelling about?'

Mr Hunter shrugged. 'The breakfast thing, I think.

He and Mike both shut up pretty quick after I got in there.' He looked down at Georgia. 'You two okay?'

'Yeah,' I said. 'I think so.'

'You're a good boy,' said Georgia, patting him on the shoulder.

'Thanks,' he smiled. 'Come on, let's go have a look at that new video camera of yours.'

Luke's dad took Georgia away and I sank back against the wall of the corridor, rubbing my eyes, listening to Cathryn muttering in the next room. She'd always been a bit emotionally volatile, but things had only got worse since she arrived down here.

The morning after we brought her and Mike in, she'd spotted her mum on the surveillance feeds and discovered something the rest of us had known for ages: Mrs Hawking was one of the original members of the Shackleton Co-operative. For days afterwards, Cathryn had just sat in the bedroom, crying on Amy's shoulder.

But as tragic as all that was, it was kind of hard to stay sympathetic when she was taking it out on a six-year-old.

I straightened up again, trying to put it out of my mind, and returned to the bedroom, where Tank had apparently latched onto the idea of Reeve being outside the wall in a van.

'Look,' said Reeve, 'there's only one exit in Phoenix, and you can't just walk up and open the door.'

'But if we *could* get through,' Tank pressed, 'we could

steal one of those vans and drive out and get the army or whatever. Come on, boss. We have to try, at least!'

Boss. The word stuck in my head. Mike had started calling Soren the same thing.

'You okay?' Luke whispered as I sat down.

I sighed. 'People keep asking me that.'

'Mate, you know I love your enthusiasm,' Reeve told Tank. 'But we wouldn't get a mile out before Shackleton blew us to pieces. If we're going to take these guys down, we'll have to do it from here.'

He turned to the rest of us. 'I don't know what to tell you about this Tobias of yours. But I've been working on some plans of my own these past few weeks. Keeping an eye on the security patrols. Intercepting them when I can. Those guys know me. A lot of them were friends, back when I was still working for Calvin. And this end-of-the-world business isn't what any of us signed up for. Some of them are still loyal to Officer Barnett, but a lot are just –'

'To Barnett?' said Luke. 'What's he got to do with it?'

Reeve raised an eyebrow. 'You kids haven't heard? Calvin went off the map about a week ago. No-one seems to know where he's disappeared to, but it looks like Barnett's in charge until he gets back.'

Calvin gone. That explained why he'd suddenly stopped interrogating my dad.

'Not exactly an improvement,' said Luke. Next to Calvin, Barnett was the most sadistic, trigger-happy maniac the Co-operative had. 'Anyway, sorry, you were saying …?'

'A coup,' I said, switching back on to what Reeve was saying and feeling a rush of excitement at the idea. 'You want to take the Co-operative down from the inside. Convince security to change sides.'

'Some of them, anyway,' Reeve said. 'I won't lie to you, though, it's slow going. Even the guys that hate Shackleton are terrified of defying him.'

'What can we do?' I asked, suddenly bursting with energy. 'How can we help?'

'Well, for a start,' said Reeve, getting to his feet, 'I'd love to get a proper look at this surveillance room of yours. I have a few sets of eyes in town, but nothing like what you guys have got.'

'Of course,' said Kara, standing too. 'Anything you need.'

'More food?' said Tank hopefully.

Kara pursed her lips. 'Don't push it.'

'Tank and I have something to take care of tonight,' said Reeve. 'We're going to need to head back up to the surface.' He looked down at Luke and me. 'You kids feel like taking a walk?'

'Absolutely,' I said.

'Where are we going?' asked Luke, like he was pretty sure he was going to regret asking.

Reeve smiled grimly. 'My tombstone,' he said. 'There's someone I'd like you to meet.'

Chapter 6

I spent most of the day putting off my promised visit
to Peter's room, convincing myself that I had other,
more important things to deal with. But after washing
up from breakfast, giving Reeve a painstakingly detailed
overview of the surveillance room, finding clean sets of
clothes for him and Tank, and convincing Luke and
his dad to help me scrub the bathroom, I had to admit
I was just stalling.

After dinner, I told myself. We weren't heading up
to the surface with Reeve until midnight. Still plenty of
time to see Peter.

We ate around the circle of tables in the surveillance
room. Luke's mum sat in the corner, hunched over a
notepad, reworking her meal schedule to accommodate
our two new arrivals. Amy had offered to help, but
Ms Hunter had shooed her away after only a couple of
minutes, saying Amy was slowing her down. In reality,
I think it was the opposite. With her accelerated brain,
Amy could run all the numbers at triple speed, leaving
Ms Hunter with nothing much to do. And I was

beginning to see that Luke was right: his mum *needed* that job. She needed there to be at least some tiny shred of her life that was still under her control.

I took my time cleaning up after dinner. Eventually, Luke came and found me. 'Hey,' he said, knocking on the open door. 'You ready to go?'

I sighed, draping a grotty tea towel over the edge of the sink. I really didn't want Luke coming down there with me, but I knew he wouldn't let me talk him out of it. 'Yeah. Come on.'

I heard Georgia's voice from the girls' room as we reached the hall. She walked out with the video camera Luke had given her. 'And here's the stinky hallway,' she said, panning around the walls, obviously over being upset about her run-in with Cathryn. 'And here's my sister and her *boyfriend*. Kiss for the camera, Jordan!'

'Not now, Georgia,' I said, brushing past her.

Georgia flipped the camera around, pointing it at herself. 'Okay, now this is a song I wrote for them: *I know a boy, his name was Luke. He kissed Jordan on – the – cheek!*' she chanted, barely getting the second line out before she doubled over in hysterics.

I stopped at the end of the hall. 'You need to stay here, okay? Go find Mum.'

Georgia ignored me. She spun the camera around again. '*I know a boy, his name was Luke. He kissed Jordan on the LIPS!*'

'Georgia,' said Mum, coming after her, a towel clutched in her hand. 'Shower. Now.'

Georgia's smile disappeared. 'I *hate* the shower,' she said. 'It's *cold*.'

The stern look on Mum's face softened a bit. 'I know it is, sweetheart. Just a quick one, and then you can go in and say goodnight to Dad.'

'Okay,' said Georgia wearily. She turned and trudged after Mum.

We mostly tried to keep Georgia out of the surveillance room during the day. No way of predicting what she might see in there. But each night before bed, Mum took Georgia in to watch Dad on the monitors for a while. It upset her a bit sometimes, but she kept going back. And it was important, I think. Georgia had as much right as any of us to know that he was okay.

'Maybe that camera wasn't such a good idea after all,' said Luke, smirking over his shoulder as we headed down to Peter's.

'I think I've seen it before,' I said, taking his hand in mine. We'd had too much insanity in the last twenty-four hours for me to dwell on it, but I'd definitely recognised Georgia's camera when Luke pulled it out of the box. 'In one of my visions. Two weeks ago, remember? I flashed – forward, it must have been – to the empty bedroom, and we couldn't figure out why. But that camera was sitting on Georgia's bed. Maybe that's the reason I was there. Maybe that camera is going to be important.'

'Important,' repeated Luke. I knew he wasn't a

hundred percent sold on the idea that there even *was* a reason for my visions.

'*Why*, though?' I wondered out loud. 'I mean, what are we supposed to do? Film what's going on in town?'

'What's the point of doing that if we can't get the video *out* to anyone?' Luke asked. 'You heard Reeve. No point trying to get out in a van. And as far as we know, the only other way to reach the outside is from the communications room in the Shackleton Building. Which, unfortunately, is *in the Shackleton Building.*'

He stopped walking, and I guess he must have seen the frustration on my face because he said, 'Sorry, I'm not – I would *love* to believe that this video camera could be some kind of solution, but ... I don't know. I just don't see it.'

'I don't see it either,' I said. 'Yet. But that doesn't mean it's not true.'

Luke put his arms around me, resting his head against my shoulder. 'The end of the world gives me a headache.'

We stood there for a minute, holding each other in the debris, and I couldn't remember the last time we'd been this quiet or still or alone.

'Are you sure you want to do this?' Luke asked finally. 'You don't *have* to go down there.'

'Yes, I do,' I said. 'I have to keep treating him like a person.'

I didn't know if there was any way to reverse the path that Peter was on. But if there was, we weren't going to do it by cutting him out of our lives. And in the meantime, I'd come up with a way to keep Luke out of the line of fire, at least for a while.

'I was thinking,' I said, as we continued down the passageway, 'Reeve and Tank are heading back after we meet this friend of theirs tonight, right? Back to the cave where they've been hiding out, so Reeve can get in touch with his people in town. I think one of us should go stay with him.'

'Why?' said Luke.

'Just, you know, to help him out. Share information.'

'Haven't we been doing that all day?' said Luke. 'Anyway, you can't just disappear with them. You have to be here for Georgia and your mum. And I'm –' Luke stopped walking again. 'Wait,' he said, bringing me around to meet him. 'Is this about me?'

'What do you mean?'

'Seriously Jordan, do you actually have a plan here, or are you just trying to get me away from Peter?'

'What's wrong with getting you away from Peter?' I said, struggling to keep the volume of my voice under control. 'Why not get you out of here while we've got the chance?'

'Right, because there's *no-one* up there who wants me dead,' said Luke. 'And, anyway, who says Peter's only interested in attacking *me?* Who says I'm the first person he comes after? All we know is what was on that video.'

'Luke –'

'I'm not leaving you down here,' he said. 'That's not how this is going to happen. We're not going to solve this by running away from it.'

I leant in again, touching my forehead to his. When had he started talking like this? When had he become the person who stared death in the face and kept walking?

'You can't die,' I said.

Luke smiled ruefully. 'I really don't want to.' He bent forward and kissed me. 'We'll work this out.'

I nodded, still staring at him, my tongue brushing over my lip. Then I realised what I was doing and started down the corridor again. 'Come on.'

We stopped just around the corner from Peter's door and I reluctantly dropped Luke's hand. He wasn't actually coming in with me. He never did anymore; no point making things more volatile than they needed to be. But he always waited outside, out of sight, just in case. I left him there and started lifting the barricades away from the door. 'Peter?'

He was at the window in a second. 'Jordan! Hey – are you okay? You look like you've –'

'I'm fine,' I said, setting the last barricade down against the wall, a dark edge slipping into my voice before I'd even made it inside.

Peter moved in to hug me as soon as the door was open. My skin crawled, but I tried not to show it. He let go and reached for my hand. I stuck it into my pocket, pretending I hadn't noticed.

We hadn't told him about the stabbing. We hadn't

told him about any of it. Neither of us was interested in having that conversation with him. Besides, what if us talking about it was what put the idea in Peter's head in the first place?

Peter returned to his bed and patted the blanket beside him. 'Come and sit.'

'Thanks,' I said, dragging the chair across and setting it down opposite the bed, trying to ignore his not-so-subtle grunt of disappointment. 'How are you feeling?'

'Better now,' he smiled, recovering quickly. He dragged his computer across and spun it around, proudly displaying a screen full of programming gibberish. 'I think I've almost figured out a way to bring down the surveillance network. Really this time.'

'That's great,' I said, although the truth was he'd been telling me the same thing for three weeks straight.

He put the laptop back down, leaning forward so that our knees were touching. 'Is Tank still here?'

'Yeah,' I said. 'He and Reeve are taking us up to the surface tonight. He wants us to meet with a contact he's made in town.'

'You and Luke,' said Peter.

I rolled back my shoulders, edging my seat backwards under the pretence of stretching, fighting down the urge to just smack him across the head and walk out. Less than two minutes in here and already I felt like I needed a shower.

'Is Tank okay?' Peter asked. 'You know, after –'

'You smashed him into a wall, Peter.'

'It was an accident!'

'Was it?' I asked, before I could stop myself.

I braced for an outburst, but instead Peter let out a kind of strangled cough and put his head in his hands.

'I didn't mean for it to go that way,' he said after a minute.

'Which way did you mean it to go?'

'I was angry. He should've – I don't know. I don't know what I wanted.' He sat up, staring at his hands, slowly clenching and unclenching his fingers. When he spoke again, his voice was strained. 'Do you think I don't get it, Jordan? Do you think I don't know what's happening to me?'

And somehow, the question pierced through everything else and I felt guilty for how I'd been writing him off. He was a million miles from the cocky, carefree kid I'd met three months ago, but he was still Peter. Somewhere under there, he was still the same person.

'Peter ...'

'What?' he snapped. 'You want to tell me to calm down? Try being locked up in this hole for a month and see how freaking calm you feel! Meanwhile, Soren's strutting around like he owns the place, my parents are trapped up there with Shackleton, and you guys won't even –'

'We're trying to help you, Peter! We're doing everything we can.'

'You don't know what it's like!' he said, jumping

up and pacing. 'You have no idea what it feels like to not even be in control of your own —'

A shout of pain burst from my throat, cutting him off. I lurched to the ground, nausea rushing up inside me like there was something trying to claw its way out.

'Jordan!' said Peter from somewhere above me. 'What's wrong?' But his voice was dim and warbled, like he was shouting underwater. I collapsed on my side, eyes squeezing shut, blocking out the blur of colour and noise as the whole world swirled around my head.

Another vision. The first in over a week. And either I'd forgotten how bad they were, or this was the most head-shattering one yet. I tried to keep breathing, riding out the shakes, waiting for it all to pass, terrified of what I was going to find when it did. Because even though I called these things 'visions', they were quickly becoming more than that. In the beginning, all I'd been doing was *seeing* things. Whatever my mind was doing, my body had stayed firmly in the present.

These days, it was a different story.

My body spasmed again, and Peter's shouting flickered out altogether, replaced by a deeper voice, still muffled but easier to make out.

'— *second iteration, approaching peak stability.*'

I rolled over, hands reaching for my head. It was throbbing violently, like it might crumble to dust under my fingers.

'*Event appears to be another Type B,*' a woman's

voice chimed in, *'magnitude four, extent … two point two four metres.'*

The pain in my head began slowly easing off, and I forced my eyes open. At first, I barely recognised it as the same room. The walls and ceiling were flat and smooth, actual walls instead of the mess of concrete and wreckage that formed them in the present. But Peter's door was still there, minus the chipping paint and smashed window.

I staggered to my feet and turned around, swaying as the world caught up. There was a whole other room behind me now, separated by a glass wall. On the other side of the glass, two people in white coats were staring out from behind a row of boxy computer monitors: a Japanese guy who was maybe in his twenties, and an older, round-faced woman with squarish glasses and dark hair pulled back into a tight bun. Neither of them had registered my sudden appearance in the room.

Because you're not here, I reminded myself. Not yet anyway.

'Diagnostic prepared,' said the man, voice muffled by the glass. *'Ready to initiate on your mark, Dr Vattel.'*

Dr Vattel.

Remi Vattel. Kara's mother. The woman who'd founded this place. Still down here, still alive. Which meant I'd come back at least twenty years.

'Soren,' she frowned at the man next to her, *'call me "doctor" one more time and I'll reconsider letting you marry my daughter.'*

He smirked, breaking the clinical veneer. *'Sorry, Remi. Old habits.'*

I glanced between the two of them, thinking I must have misheard. That wasn't Soren. Soren hadn't even been born until after the Vattel Complex was destroyed.

And then it clicked: this wasn't *our* Soren. It was his father. We knew Soren's dad had been killed in the explosion. Kara must have named their baby after him.

'Well?' said Vattel, staring over her glasses at the older Soren. *'What are you waiting for?'*

'Right. Sorry.' He glanced at his computer. *'Initiating scan.'*

Whatever they were 'scanning', I couldn't see it.

A second later, I almost jumped out of my skin as Luke appeared, centimetres from my face. He reached for me, his expression desperate. Mouth open, shouting, but I couldn't hear a word of it.

And all at once, panic came rushing at me with full force. It was happening again.

I was slipping away.

Luke wasn't here. Not really. He was back in the present, watching me disappear, trying to drag me back to reality before –

Before what?

'Luke!' I called back, grabbing at him, my fingers passing straight through him.

'Scan initiated,' said Soren's dad, apparently oblivious to all of it. *'Adjusting focus. Three. Two. One.'*

The lights cut out on my side of the glass. Nothing left to see by but the glow of the computers.

I squinted, searching for Luke in the darkness. He stepped forward again, still mouthing silently from two decades away. I stretched out my hands to meet his, but I might as well have been clutching at his shadow.

A mechanical hum rose up. *'Temperature: normal,'* Soren's dad reported behind me. *'UV: normal. EM: slightly elevated, but still within expected range …'*

Whatever was going on in here, I needed to get *out*.

I turned back to Luke, staring into his face. I tried to focus, to tune out the rest of the room, willing my body to co-operate, as though I could get back to the present by wishing it were true.

I reached for him again, swiping at the air in front of me. *Come on!*

'Anything?' Vattel asked from behind the glass.

'Not yet. All readings still report normal.'

I tried again, and again, and –

And I tripped forward, losing my balance as Luke's hands clamped down around my wrist.

'—ordan!' he shouted, suddenly audible again. 'Yes! That's it. Just focus, okay? Concentrate.'

I brought my other hand down, grabbing onto Luke's, and felt the nausea bubbling up again.

'Hold on,' said Soren's dad. *'I'm getting something,'* and at first I thought he was looking at me.

Then I saw what he was really talking about. It was glowing around me, a cloud of gas or mist or something, fluorescent blue, like white paint under a black light. A shiver ran up my spine as I pictured another empty room like this one, a Shackleton Co-operative research facility – figures contorting on the ground as Tabitha ripped them to pieces.

'Luke!' I shouted, squeezing harder on his arms as the glow grew brighter, more solid. I couldn't see where it was coming from, but –

The churning in my insides reached full force, and my legs dropped out from under me. The room started collapsing again, everything blurring together, and for a second, I could see both places – both *times* – at once. Dark and light. Solid and destroyed. Vattel staring through the glass and Peter standing over me, screaming.

And then it all melted away. For a long moment, the room disappeared completely, plunging me into blackness. Then it blinked back into existence again. Luke was there, another Luke, strapped to a steel chair. Then more darkness, invisible walls pressing in from every side. And through all of it, Luke was there, still holding on, the one solid thing in the whole world. I squeezed my eyes shut, biting down on my gag reflex, fingers digging into him until, finally, the universe stopped spinning and I crumpled to the ground.

Peter's shouts broke into my head again. '– are you *doing*? Let go of her! Give her to me!'

'No,' I groaned, as Luke's arms lowered me to the ground. 'Don't … it's okay … I'm okay.'

I gave it a minute, and then opened my eyes again. Luke was kneeling over me, looking ready to pass out. Peter was red-faced from shouting. He hadn't seen me go through this before. No-one had, except for Luke and my dad.

Peter crouched on my other side, and the two of them hoisted me to my feet.

'Thanks,' said Luke, tugging me gently away from Peter as I found my feet again. 'I've got her.'

Peter's expression blackened. I struggled to get my head back together, ready to intervene in whatever came next.

'Don't,' Luke told him, surprisingly forceful. 'Not now. Don't make this about you.'

Peter stared at him for a moment longer, then swore and dropped my arm. He grabbed his laptop and slumped down onto his bed, not even looking up again as we closed the door on him.

Chapter 7

'You know, I'd almost convinced myself it was a one-off,' I said, voice low as Luke and I crept through the bush, a few paces behind Tank and Reeve. 'The disappearing. At least, it's never been as bad as that first time, when I saw the Complex getting attacked.'

'It has now,' said Luke. 'I thought you were gone, Jordan. You *were* gone for a couple of seconds there.'

'Wherever *gone* is,' I said.

Because that was the question, wasn't it? What would happen if I faded out altogether? Would I fade *in* to the other time? Or would I just vanish completely?

I tried to push it all aside. Right now, the best thing I could do was focus on not finding out.

It was just after midnight, and we were closing in on the makeshift graveyard at the north-west corner of town. The air was bitterly cold. How had these two survived so long out here without getting hypothermia or something?

Luke shot me a nervous glance, like I might

disappear again at any moment. 'You do realise there's no way I'm leaving you on your own after this, right?'

He hadn't seen any of it. It might have looked to me like Luke was with me in the vision, but as far as he was concerned, he'd just been standing there with Peter, watching my body fade away in front of him.

I reached over and squeezed his hand.

'Right,' said Luke. 'I'm going to take that as a yes.'

It was amazing how quickly he'd become this critical part of my life. I'd known him for all of three months, but already it was a struggle to remember a time when he hadn't been there. It was as though the life I'd had before Phoenix wasn't even mine, just memories of something that had happened to some other person – netball games and family barbeques and being driven to school.

Somewhere along the line, I'd started seeing Luke's survival and my survival as pretty much the same thing. Like those two realities were tied together. And in a very real way, it was starting to look like maybe they were.

When I'd started fading out the first time around, Luke and my dad had both tried to grab hold of me, but only Luke had been able to do it. And this afternoon, Peter had apparently stood over me for almost a full minute, trying to make me come back, before Luke got him out of the way. Why was Luke the only one who'd been able to reach me? And what would happen if he wasn't around to do it next time?

Reeve and Tank came to a stop in front of us, just

short of a little clearing in the bush. We were here. Reeve whispered something to Tank, who nodded, and took off around the edge of the clearing.

'Where's he going?' asked Luke, crouching low in the grass beside Reeve.

'Just making sure we're alone.' A smile crossed Reeve's face, and something about it reminded me of Dad. 'Good kid, that one. Good head on his shoulders.'

It struck me that this was probably the first time I'd ever heard someone say a positive word about what went on in Tank's head. Even more striking, it seemed like Reeve was kind of right. Something in Tank had changed. It was like he'd finally found an identity beyond being Mike's bodyguard.

'I think you've been good for him,' I said. 'Nice for him to have someone decent to follow for a change.'

Reeve shrugged off the compliment. 'We're all following someone.'

He looked out across the clearing, fingers drumming on the butt of his rifle. I watched his gaze drift slowly from the path to the marble tombstone in front of us, marking the empty grave the Co-operative had dug for his funeral. Reminders of a time when Shackleton was still bothering to cover up the messes he made.

A few metres away, a mound of upturned soil marked another burial site. A real one. The place where Calvin had unceremoniously dumped Dr Montag's body after his murder, the night we broke into the medical centre.

If not for Reeve, we might've been down there with him.

'Thanks for that, by the way,' I whispered. 'Drawing those guards off. Letting us escape. You saved us.'

'Yeah,' Reeve shrugged again, 'you saved me too.' He reached into his jeans pocket and pulled out an old watch with half the strap missing, tilting it so its face caught the moonlight. They were late. 'I've been thinking,' he said. 'If this Tobias of yours is anywhere, it'll be in the Shackleton Building, right? Up on the restricted level, where Shackleton can keep a close watch on it.'

'Maybe,' said Luke. 'Probably. But going up there didn't work out so well for us last time.'

'Last time wasn't smart.' Reeve's focus flickered back to his tombstone. 'I should have told you that myself. Should've taken the time to do it properly. But back then, I was too caught up in keeping my family out of harm's way. For all the good that did.'

'What do you mean, *properly*?' I said. 'We did everything we could.'

'Not everything,' said Reeve. 'There's an armoury. Out in the bush, near the warehouse that holds all the town's food. I've never actually been posted out there myself, but –'

'There's another building on that road?' said Luke. 'Why didn't Bill tell us about it?'

'Maybe he didn't know,' I said.

'He went all the way out to the warehouse and then didn't bother to check what was further down the road?'

I shrugged. 'We didn't.'

'Yeah, but – we had other things on our minds at the time,' said Luke.

'Tank and I went to check it out last week,' Reeve said. 'We've been looking at getting into Shackleton's communications room, and so first we need to pick up a few supplies. The armoury's guarded, but it's not impenetrable. Not like the Shackleton Building. I'm working with my guys in town to figure out how to get in and get what we need.'

I bit my lip. 'Weapons, you mean.'

The idea of picking up a gun made me seriously uncomfortable. I tried to remind myself that Reeve wasn't a violent guy, that he wouldn't use force unless we really had to. But still, even talking about it made me feel sick.

'I don't like it either, Jordan,' said Reeve. 'But if we're going up there, we need to do everything we can to make sure it's not a repeat of last time.'

'How are you even still *here* after last time?' asked Luke, and I shivered as my mind dredged up images of Reeve handcuffed to a table, getting slashed to pieces by an early iteration of Tabitha. 'We saw what Shackleton did to you. You were ...'

'Yeah,' said Reeve. 'I can't explain it, but –' He reached down and plucked a stalk from the sharp,

spindly grass at our feet. 'Here,' he said, holding the
stalk up in front of us. 'Watch.'

He yanked the stalk across his other hand, flinching
as the sharp edges sliced into his skin. Then he held his
palm up in front of us.

A line of blood oozed up where the grass had cut
him, silvery blue in the darkness. But then, almost
immediately, the wound began to scab over. The
bleeding stopped, and the skin began to knit back
together, healing right there in front of us.

Luke leant in closer. 'Whoa.'

'Yeah,' I said. Since we'd arrived in Phoenix,
everyone here (well, everyone except Luke and his mum)
had developed a kind of accelerated healing ability.
Something to do with the fallout that had saturated this
area since the destruction of the Vattel Complex.

But this was way beyond that. If my body had got
a boost, Reeve's had been strapped to a jetpack.

'I'm not the only one, though, am I?' said Reeve.
'I mean, not *this* specifically, but all of us who were
getting tested on in the medical centre –'

He broke off. There was a rustle of leaves from
the far side of the clearing, and two men stepped
out cautiously from between the graves. Security
guards, both armed. One of them pointed at Reeve's
tombstone. He turned towards us and I got a proper
look at his face.

'Officer Miller,' I whispered.

'You know him?' said Reeve.

'He's helped us out a couple of times.'

'Yeah, he's a good bloke,' said Reeve. 'First one to jump onboard with all this.'

The two officers stopped at the tombstone. Miller let go of his gun and scratched his left elbow.

'All clear,' said Reeve, standing up. 'Let's go.'

He walked into the clearing, and Luke and I followed. There was a clatter of metal as the two guards raised their guns, saw that it was Reeve, and relaxed again.

Miller shot a curious look at Luke and me.

'Matt!' The other guard gaped at Reeve. He was an older guy, maybe my dad's age. 'You're ... You're actually here ...'

Reeve smiled and reached out to shake his hand. 'G'day, Ethan. Yeah, still kicking, whatever the chief might tell you.' He turned back to Luke and me. 'Guys, this is Officer Hamilton.'

I recognised the surname. 'You're Lauren's dad.'

Lauren was a girl from school who'd helped Luke and me out when we were hiding from the Co-operative in town. Georgia used to go over to her place sometimes to play with her little brother, back in the days when kids lived in houses.

'That's right,' Hamilton nodded, but for some reason he didn't quite meet my eye as he said it.

'Have you spoken to my dad?' I asked, advancing on him without really meaning to. 'Is he okay? Can you pass a message on to –?'

Reeve's hand came down on my shoulder. 'We might want to give Ethan a minute.'

I stopped talking, stepping back again, but the uneasy look didn't shift from Hamilton's face.

'How are you guys holding up?' Miller asked, shrugging off a backpack and handing it to Reeve.

'Surviving.' Reeve nodded at Luke and me, waving a hand at his new clothes. 'Better for having run into these two. How's life in town?'

'About the same as the last time you asked,' said Miller. 'We're all just stuck in a holding pattern. Waiting. People get restless, start fights. We move in to break it up, settle things down before they get out of hand. Only a matter of time before it all blows up.'

'Which is why we need to be ready to move when it does,' said Reeve, pulling the backpack open, revealing a jumper and a few tins of food. 'Thanks.'

'The surveillance network,' I said. 'One of you needs to shut it down. Until that happens, we're –'

'Jordan,' said Reeve, cutting me off. 'Slow down.'

'It's not that simple,' said Miller. 'Security personnel have no real access to the new network. We can monitor the feeds, but we're locked out of the network hub. Not even Barnett has clearance.'

'Oh,' I said.

'There's something else,' said Miller, returning his attention to Reeve. 'Weird rumours floating around town today. Something called Tobias.'

A chill shot up my spine, piercing through even

the cold of the graveyard. Reeve looked significantly at Luke and me. 'We've heard that name too. Any ideas what it is? Or where?'

'Hard to say,' said Miller, brow crinkling. 'I mean, obviously there's no way to tell what's real and what's just speculation, but it definitely sounds like something the Co-operative doesn't want us to know about. The most convincing theory I've heard is that it's some kind of emergency shutdown mechanism for Tabitha.'

I suppressed another sigh. That was no further than we'd got.

'Right. Well, keep an ear out. Let me know as soon as you hear anything more solid.' Reeve zipped up the backpack. 'Now,' he said, focusing on Hamilton, who was starting to look like he regretted coming. 'Let's get to business. I assume you know why you're here.'

'Yes,' said Hamilton, glancing nervously over his shoulder. 'You want to drag me into this. You want me to join your revolution.'

'Not yet,' said Reeve. 'Right now, I just want to know whose side you're on.'

Hamilton's eyes flashed around the clearing. 'Listen, Matt,' he said, suddenly defensive, 'you've got no right to drag me out here and start making demands.'

'Who's making demands?' I said. 'He just wants to know where you're planning on pointing that gun. That's not a reasonable question?'

'It's not that simple.' Hamilton's voice was shaking

now. He jabbed a finger towards Reeve. 'And you know it's not!'

Luke shot me a warning look, and part of me knew that I should probably listen to him. But we'd been dealing with blind, useless townspeople since forever, and I wasn't about to let this one go without a fight.

'You want simple?' I said. 'In less than two weeks, the Co-operative will wipe out every human being on the planet outside this town. They're going to murder seven billion people. You're either working to stop that from happening, or you're working to *make* it happen. So if you're still having trouble picking a side –'

'They have my daughter!' he shouted.

Luke flinched, glaring at him to keep quiet.

'They have my dad too. You think you're the only one who –?'

'No,' said Miller. His voice was low, but it shut down my rant in an instant. 'No Jordan, that's not the same.' His eyes dropped to the ground, like he needed a minute to gather himself. Then he looked up at Reeve. 'You haven't told them about the loyalty room?'

'The what?' Luke asked.

'The old staff cafeteria,' said Hamilton. 'In the Shackleton Building. Every security officer has a family member in there. As long as we're completely obedient to the Co-operative, they're well treated. Better than everyone else. Real beds, double food rations … But if we put *one foot* out of line, they get …'

'They get hurt,' I finished, guilt surging up.

'Shackleton came to each of us – one at a time,' said Hamilton, starting to break down now. 'He – he described *exactly* what he would do to Lauren if I ever disobeyed an order.'

My mind sparked with a thousand nightmarish images. I'd been dealing with Shackleton long enough to know that he didn't waste time on empty threats. 'I'm sorry,' I said.

Hamilton didn't even look at me. He turned away, heading towards the path into town.

'Ethan …' said Miller half-heartedly.

He kept walking. Reeve dashed forward and caught him by the arm. 'Ethan, just wait a minute.'

'No.' Hamilton whirled around, pulling free. 'No. You can't ask me to choose between saving the world and saving my daughter. You can't.'

'I don't like it any more than you do,' said Reeve. 'But Jordan's right. You're *already* choosing. We all are.'

Hamilton just shook his head, refusing to hear it. He walked away again, and this time Reeve let him go.

Chapter 8

'Sorry,' I said, finally breaking the silence as Luke and I tracked back to the Vattel Complex alone. 'I shouldn't have got fired up like that. He was twitchy enough already without me blowing up at him.'

'Do you really think it would have made any difference?' said Luke, craning his neck to watch out for security. 'I mean, yeah, maybe you could have been a bit more diplomatic or whatever, but it's not like you said anything that wasn't true.'

'Mm,' I said, still mad at myself, mad at Hamilton, mad at myself for being mad at Hamilton.

Really, it was Reeve I should have been apologising to, but he and Tank had already gone back to the cave hide-out. Reeve's whole operation was set up to run from there, and he said it would be a while before he could safely shift things down to the Complex.

I sort of wished we were going with him. He might be sleeping in the cold and struggling to recruit anyone over to our side, but at least he was *doing* something. We were going to catch up in a couple of days to compare notes and see if we were any closer to getting into the armoury, but in the meantime, I was back to watching surveillance feeds.

I'd asked Miller to get a message to my dad and Peter's parents. Let them know we were okay. The last time Dad saw me, I was being carried away from him with a pickaxe wound in my gut.

'Here's what I don't get,' said Luke. 'How can there be all these rumours suddenly floating around town about Tobias, and still no-one knows what it is? Surely someone must have seen something.'

'Not if it's up on the restricted level,' I said, grateful for the change of subject. 'That's the one place left in town that even security don't know about. Reeve's right: if we want to find Tobias, we need to find a way to ge– *EEUUGH!*'

I collapsed forward, slamming into the undergrowth like someone had shoved me over. My arms rushed to my stomach, and I swear I could *feel* it churning underneath my clothes.

'Crap,' said Luke, crouching beside me, hands resting hesitantly on my side.

Not just my imagination, I thought. I started gagging, chest heaving, as though my body was trying to shove my guts out through my mouth. This was worse. They were definitely getting worse.

'Try to – try to keep your eyes open,' said Luke, rolling me onto my side. 'Try to focus, okay? See if you can –'

He swore, ducking closer to me as light flickered in the distance. Panic signals fired inside my head, but I couldn't work out what it all meant. Luke drifted in and out of focus above me, his face stretched with panic. I had just enough time to feel him clamp a hand over my mouth before he melted into the darkness and the whole scene folded in on itself.

The hand disappeared, and the light on the other side of my eyelids changed colour.

A cockatoo squawked above my head.

I sat up gingerly in the scraggly undergrowth.

I was alone.

The sky was shot with pink and gold. Sunset. I was still surrounded by bushland. No clues at all about how far I'd shifted this time. It might have been hours or years.

Voices rose up from somewhere off to the south. Not loud, but obviously not trying all that hard to be secretive either. Whoever was speaking obviously didn't think they were in any danger out here.

I was still dizzy. Disoriented.

The voices got closer. My head began to clear, and I realised who was talking a second before he stomped in front of me. It was Mike, smiling and clean and dressed in a school uniform that looked almost new. He studied the crumpled bit of paper in his still five-fingered hands.

'*Over here!*' he called back into the bushes.

Tank and Cathryn walked into view behind him. Tank was lugging a giant cardboard box. It was stamped and labelled just like the ones Luke and I had taken from the truck.

'*This was a bad idea,*' said Cathryn, picking something out of her stocking, looking extremely unimpressed to be getting this close to nature. A thick coil of rope was weighing down one of her shoulders. '*What if someone catches us out here?*'

'*Like who?*' Tank taunted. '*Security? Come on. What are they gonna do?*'

'*Hurry up and get over here,*' said Mike. '*We need to find a tree stump.*'

'*You find a tree stump. You're the one not carrying anything.*'

'*I'm carrying the map,*' said Mike.

Despite the obvious weirdness of following a note from their overseers out into the bush, there was something impossibly *light* about their conversation. Like this was all just some exciting adventure. This was months ago, back before everything got swallowed up in darkness and the constant threat of death.

The thought dragged me back to reality and my mind rang with the sudden realisation of what I'd seen back there in the present. The light was a torch. Someone had heard us. And now Luke was stuck out there, trying to bring me back.

So where was he? What was taking him so long?

Or worse, what if I'd finally slipped out of his reach entirely?

'*Found it!*' said Mike, darting closer to me. I pressed

down into the bushes. If I really *was* here, I didn't want to take chances.

Mike shoved his hand into the tree stump he'd spotted and pulled out an envelope sealed with black wax. A message from the overseers.

'Here,' he said, handing the other paper he'd been holding to Cathryn. *'Burn this one.'*

Cathryn took a lighter from her skirt pocket and held it to the old note, while Mike tore open the new one. I pushed up from the ground again, trying to get a look at it, but then the bushland was blocked from view as a face flashed into existence, right in front of me. Luke.

'How come she gets to burn everything?' grumbled Tank.

'Because if I let you do it, you'd start a bloody bushfire,' said Mike. *'Besides, you've got a box to carry.'*

I sat up, reaching for Luke, but my hands sank straight into him like he didn't exist.

'What do the overseers need so many freaking candles for, anyway?' Tank muttered, pulling my attention away.

'How should I know?' said Mike. *'Not your job to ask questions, man. Just do what you're told.'* He looked up from the note in his hand and pointed towards the lake. *'All right. This way.'*

The cave, I realised. That was what the candles and the rope were for. We were way back at the beginning. Kara and Soren were luring these guys out to set up their creepy little cult headquarters.

Luke launched himself back into my field of vision.

Jordan! he snapped silently. *Pay attention!*

'Yeah,' I muttered, turning away from Mike and the others again. I held out my arms, trying to focus.

Luke reached for me again. Nothing.

'*What about Peter?*' Cathryn asked behind me.

'*They didn't ask for Peter,*' said Mike. '*They chose us.*'

I tried to tune them out, but part of me kept getting drawn back into the conversation, wanting to know why I was here in the first place.

'*No, I mean –*' Cathryn began, the lightness vanishing from her voice. '*Why do they keep asking us to find stuff out about Peter? They're acting like he's dangerous or something. What if – What if they're going to do something bad to him?*'

'*You saying you don't trust them?*' said Mike.

Luke grabbed at my shoulders like he was trying to shake me. Snap me out of it. His hands dropped through and he almost overbalanced.

'*No!*' said Cathryn, horrified, like she was sure they could hear her. '*No, I do! I do trust them! But –*'

'*You swore an oath, Cat! We all did. We swore that we would* die *for them if we had to!*'

Luke jolted, startled, and whirled to look over his shoulder. He turned back, face white. Whoever was out there, they were coming closer.

'*Get moving,*' Mike spat.

'*Mate, come on,*' said Tank. '*Don't be such a –*'

'*DO IT!*'

Mike set out in the direction of the cave, and the others followed.

I locked eyes with Luke, willing my hands to make contact, furious at myself for putting him in danger. If my stupid curiosity had just got us –

My hands smacked down hard into Luke's arms. I held on tight, pulling him towards me.

'That's it. That's it,' he hissed. 'Hurry!'

'Hey ...' said Tank behind me. *'What the crap is that?'*

I turned around. He was staring right at me.

And then the bile rose up in my throat again and everything collapsed.

And just like last time, the two worlds blurred together. Day and night. Warm and cold. Cathryn and Mike there and gone at the same time. And Tank looking straight through me, almost like I was actually there. I spun my head around, fighting the sick feeling in my gut, trying to take in everything at once. The moment stretched out. I hung there, suspended at both ends. Like time was standing still. Or like it didn't even exist anymore.

Then Luke's voice rang in my ear, 'Jordan, get back here!' and it all sped up again, the world flaring around me, just random snapshots, like someone was flicking through a slideshow.

I was sitting under a blazing sun, surrounded by knee-high saplings.

I was engulfed in complete darkness.

I was watching the day break over a barren wasteland.

I closed my eyes against the pounding nausea, clinging to Luke, sure it was all that was keeping me alive. And then finally, I was back in the present, mouth clamped shut to keep myself quiet, head throbbing like I'd smashed it into a wall.

'Shh …' Luke breathed, cradling me like a little kid. 'Shh … They're almost gone.'

I opened my eyes and the world swung slowly into focus. Two bright torch beams cut through the trees. I held my breath. They were pointing away from us, back towards town, but all it would take was one sound …

Slowly, the lights dimmed into the distance. By the time they were gone, I'd got my head back together enough to stand without collapsing or throwing up. Luke held onto me anyway, fingers lacing themselves around mine. I could feel him shaking.

Twice in two days.

Why? Why *now*, with everything else that was going on?

'That was – I thought we were dead,' breathed Luke. 'Seriously, if they had taken like two more steps …'

'What stopped them?' I asked, moving closer and resting my arm around him.

'I don't know. I was too busy hanging onto you.' He glanced over, like he wasn't sure how much more he wanted to say. 'It was worse this time, wasn't it?'

'Yeah,' I said. 'Wait. Why? Did you see something?'

'No. I don't know. It just scares me, Jordan. It freaks

me out that one day you might just – that I might not be able to bring you back.'

I shivered, looking up at the stars, wondering for a moment if all of it – everything I was seeing – really was just random. Just chaos. An unguided by-product of an unguided universe that was completely indifferent to everything we were going through down here.

But no, there had to be more to it than that. There had to be more than I was seeing.

All of this might not make sense now, but that didn't mean it wouldn't ever.

A minute or two later, we were stepping through the low, overgrown ruin that marked the entrance to the Vattel Complex. There was a dull rattle as someone downstairs opened the trapdoor, and I glanced around one last time to make sure there was no-one waiting to follow us in.

A thought struck me as we started down the mouldy stairs. 'What if those guards had shot you?'

'They didn't,' said Luke.

'Yeah, but what if they did? What if you'd, like, jumped up and waved your arms around and got yourself killed back there?'

'That would've been a pretty bad tactical decision.'

'You'd be dead,' I said.

'Yeah,' said Luke, sounding slightly exasperated. 'That's why I didn't do it.'

'You would have been *shot* dead,' I said, lowering

my voice as we neared the bottom of the stairs. 'Shot. Not stabbed.'

'That's not exactly an improvement.'

'I know, but you get what I'm saying, right? You could have changed it. You could have changed what we saw on that video. None of it would have happened.'

'That's not what Kara says.'

I breathed a frustrated sigh. This was not a new conversation. And as far as Kara was concerned, there was only one way this was all going to play out. The way she'd explained it, there was no *last time* and *this time*. It was all one time. All the same. What we'd seen on that video wasn't just *going* to happen, it had *already* happened. It was just as unchangeable as anything else in the past.

'Kara's not a scientist,' I said. 'She's a doctor.'

'Right,' said Luke, squinting at the sudden brightness as we walked into the corridor. 'Yeah. I hope you're right.'

Mum and Mr Hunter were both waiting up for us in the surveillance room, nursing mugs of tea. The teabags sat in a little dish on the table, ready to be dried out and reused.

Mr Hunter came over to meet us. He frowned at the expression on Luke's face. 'Everything okay?'

'Yeah,' said Luke quickly. 'Almost ran into security on the way back, but we're okay.'

Mum hoisted herself out of her chair, grunting with the effort. 'I can't believe I keep letting you do this.'

'I'm fine,' I said. 'What about you guys? Is everyone else –?'

I jumped back, startled, as I realised for the first time that Amy was in here too. She was sitting in the corner on the edge of the table, staring into space like she was hypnotised.

I walked up to her. 'Amy …?'

'Whoa. Hi,' she said. 'Sorry. I guess I kind of spaced out for a bit there, huh?' She blinked hard and got to her feet. 'I think I'm going to go to bed.'

I stared after her as she left the room.

'How long was she sitting there?' Luke asked.

'A while,' his dad said. 'We did ask if she was …' He looked up. 'Did you hear that?'

Everyone stopped. For a moment, all I could hear was whirring computers and the buzz of a fluorescent tube flickering in the next room.

Smash!

A noise like a battering ram, violent but far off. It was coming from somewhere in the research module.

'Crap,' said Luke, standing over one of the monitors. I joined him just in time to see a cloud of dust billow up into the camera lens.

'Is that …?' asked Mum, behind me.

'Yeah,' I said. 'Bill's room.'

Chapter 9

'Hey!' Peter shouted, as Luke and I sprinted past his door. 'HEY! What's going on out there?'

We ignored him. Another explosion of sound echoed up the corridor. Creaking, twisting metal.

'Are you sure we should be running *towards* him?' Luke panted.

'I don't think Bill's going to hurt us,' I said. 'He needs our help, remember?'

'He put me in the hospital!'

'Okay, yeah, but – we'll be careful.'

I could see something silhouetted in the dim light, blocking our path up ahead. I slowed as we reached it.

The metal bookcase that had sealed the entrance to Bill's room was lying on its side, bent in half like it was made of cardboard. It was wedged into the debris at a particularly narrow section of the corridor, forming a makeshift barrier to keep us out.

'Help me move it,' I said, gripping the bookcase with both hands. Luke leant in next to me. I dug in with my heels. The bookcase shifted slightly, scraping against the walls, but only seemed to get itself more tightly lodged into the surrounding bits of debris.

'You really want to be doing that?' said Mr Hunter, coming up the corridor behind us.

'No,' said Luke.

'Yes,' I said.

'Okay, fine. Yes.'

Mr Hunter shouldered his way in between Luke and me. 'Okay. Three. Two. One. *Push.*'

The bookcase buckled, angling forward, grinding against the concrete on either side. We pushed again. All at once it came loose, crashing to the ground.

I clambered over and ducked into Bill's room. The dust was clearing by now. Bill's bed had been thrown across the room, and was now lying on its side against the wall. The contents of Kara's medical kit were scattered all over the place. I scanned through the mess, snatching up a sedative pen and the penlight Kara had used to check Bill's eyes. We kept moving, deeper into the research module.

Another, smaller tunnel came up on our left and I almost stopped running again. I'd been down there only once before, into a room stained with Luke's twenty-year-old blood.

'What's wrong?' Mr Hunter asked.

'Nothing,' said Luke. 'Come on.'

More noise up ahead, like someone beating at the walls with a hammer. I flicked on the torch as we left the last of the functioning ceiling lights behind. We barely ever came down this deep. The tunnel pressed in all around us now, the remnants of the old labs almost impossible to pick out in the ocean of concrete. The hammering sound was louder now. Slow, irregular smashing.

'So what's the plan here?' asked Luke.

'I just want to talk to him,' I said.

'Yeah, but –'

'He knew about Tabitha!' I said. 'He knew about stuff that *no-one* was meant to know! Don't you think we should find out if that includes Tobias?'

The light from behind us had all but faded away, leaving us to navigate by the light of Kara's little torch. I flashed it around at the tunnel walls. Luke and I had spent a whole week mapping this place out, but it was such a labyrinth that I still got lost every time I came down here.

'Hang on a sec,' said Luke, pointing past me. 'Turn your torch off.'

I clicked the button on the penlight, plunging us into total darkness. *Almost* total darkness. A dim light slid across the wall up ahead, in and out of view, like it was coming from around a corner.

'There!' said Luke.

I edged towards the light, leaving the penlight switched off. The tunnel squeezed even tighter for a few metres, then widened out again, opening onto a room that seemed to have escaped the explosion and the concreting almost completely.

It looked like Peter's room had looked back in my vision with Soren's dad and Remi Vattel. Two separate areas, divided by a wall of glass that had long since shattered to the floor.

Bill was up the other end, standing with his back to us, waist-deep in smashed computers and upended tables and chairs, swinging a pickaxe out wide over his shoulder. He had one of Kara and Soren's excavating helmets strapped to his head, which explained the light we'd seen coming in.

Bill slammed the pickaxe down again, sending chips of concrete shooting into the darkness. He let out a wild, animal laugh, like nothing could give him more joy than tearing into that wall.

'Hey Bill,' I said, walking slowly towards him. 'It's good to see you awake again.'

He whirled around, face masked in shadow, spot-lighting us in the beam from his helmet. 'You're early.'

'Oh,' I said. 'I'm sorry. We didn't realise –'

'No, no, no, that's *enough!*' said Bill, raising a finger like a parent scolding their kid. 'Leave. You are the wrong one. I have *told* you this. You are not right, and you are all *far too early* for my – my purposes.' He dropped the pickaxe and put his hands to his head.

'Maybe we should come back later,' said Mr Hunter out of the corner of his mouth.

'You told us you needed our help,' I said gently, edging forward again, flicking my torch back on to see him properly. 'Remember? Out at the airport. You said you needed Luke and me to –'

'NO!' Bill bellowed, and I had to throw myself out of the way as a computer monitor suddenly leapt from the rubble and flew at me. The monitor smashed to pieces against the back wall, narrowly missing Luke and his dad.

I straightened up again. 'Please, Bill. Talk to me. If you explain what you're doing, maybe we can help.'

'No, I already –' Bill muttered, hunching over like he was trying to get his head around something. 'That's not how it works! I have seen this! You can't – *Argh!*'

He broke off in a rage, fists in the air, stomping the floor. The ground between us started moving.

Something was rising up off the floor. Glass. The shattered dividing wall, thousands of jagged, glimmering shards, lifting into the air to form a deadly barrier between us and Bill.

'Jordan!' said Luke urgently, running up to grab my arm. 'Let's *go.*'

'Leave!' Bill shouted, his face fractured and glinting behind the wall of glass. 'Leave me! I will come when you are needed!'

He snatched up the pickaxe. Luke yanked at my arm again, dragging me towards the corridor.

'The time is coming!' Bill raged on. 'It is coming! I will come for you!'

Mr Hunter grabbed my other hand. They hauled me into the shadows, a second before Bill fired the shards at the wall, drowning his own shouting in a furious explosion of splintering glass.

Chapter 10

'I want to go back and talk to him again,' I said quietly, ducking under a low-hanging branch.

'Jordan …' I could hear Luke switching into voice-of-reason mode. 'Do you really think you're going to get anything out of him? I mean, he's made it pretty clear he doesn't want to talk to us.'

It was early morning, two days after Bill's breakout. We were heading out past the south end of town to catch up with Reeve. It was a bit of a hike, but we'd made use of the journey to set up another fake campsite in the bush – half-buried rubbish and remnants of a makeshift shelter, just to keep the Co-operative guessing. And beyond that, I think Luke and I were both grateful for an excuse to get outside.

Luke's parents hadn't spoken to each other since last night, when Mr Hunter had tried to intervene in an argument between Ms Hunter and Kara about not hanging up laundry in the kitchen. Luke's mum had been furious at him for 'taking that impossible woman's side', and angrier still when he'd refused to keep arguing with her about it. This, apparently, was the same 'pig-headed, passive-aggressive crap' that had led her to divorce him in the first place.

Meanwhile, Cathryn had lost it with Georgia again – first for playing on her bed, and then for catching her making a grab at Ms Hunter's kitchen keys – and Mike had taken to sneaking around with his old overseer notebook, trying to eavesdrop on my conversations with Luke. I had a feeling Soren had put him up to it.

Bill was still roaming around in the depths of the Complex, smashing at walls, volatile as ever. It terrified me to think what might happen if he strayed into the living area. But all that didn't excuse us from trying to get answers out of him when there were only ten days left until the end of the world.

Kara was looking for a way to contain him. The sedative pens might have been an option if we'd had enough cartridges left to put him under and keep him there, but we were running low and had decided it was best to save them in case of an emergency.

Soren, on the other hand, wanted to deal with Bill the same way he wanted to deal with every other inconvenience in his life: by putting a bullet in him. Between him, Bill, Peter and Mike, it was a miracle no-one had gotten seriously hurt yet.

'I just want to know what Bill's *doing* down there!' I said. 'I mean, Kara said there's nothing left to dig up but exploded labs and concrete, so what does he –?'

And then a thought dropped into my head. An

explanation, not just for Bill's newfound pickaxe obsession, but for Bill himself.

'What?' said Luke.

'What if he's one of them?' I said.

'One of who?'

'Vattel's people!' I said. 'One of her researchers from twenty years ago! What if that's why he's so obsessed with finding something down there? Kara was just their doctor. She wasn't involved in their research. So, what if there was something going on that she didn't know about? Something that could help us. What if –?' I hesitated, stomach jolting. '*I need to go back.*'

Luke's brow furrowed. 'Back where?'

'No, that's what Bill said at the airport when we first met him. *I need to go back.* We thought he was talking about going home – going back to wherever he came from on the outside – but what if that *wasn't* what he was saying? What if he was talking about going back to the *Complex?*'

'Then why didn't he just *go* back to the Complex?' said Luke. 'Why drag us into it?'

'I don't know! But that's exactly why we need to *talk* –' I cut the sentence short as we came up on a wide dirt path through the bush. The road to the former airport. 'Hold on a second.'

I crept low through the undergrowth in the direction of town, ignoring Luke's hisses of protest. I stopped at the edge of the bushland, just out of view of the security cameras, and reached into my jeans pocket, pulling out the video camera Luke had given to Georgia. I flipped it open and hit record, panning slowly across the town. Rows of identical houses, all abandoned. And beyond them, the town centre.

My vision blurred with tears but I kept my hand steady, determined to capture as much as I could. I zoomed in, passing over the office complex, the hospital, the Shackleton Building, everything still, dead, eerily quiet, apart from a few security guards out keeping an eye on the emptiness. Even the fenced-off exercise area was deserted this early in the morning.

We could see all this on the security monitors whenever we wanted, but not like this. This was different. Sitting here in the bushes, actually *seeing* it all, knowing Dad was in there, knowing just how close and how far away he was …

I wiped my eyes on the back of my sleeve. We had to get in there.

'What are you *doing?*' Luke whispered, crouching.

I pocketed the camera again, getting hold of myself. 'Done. Come on, we should keep moving.'

'Jordan … what was that about?' asked Luke, as we backtracked to a safe distance.

'I don't know,' I said, rubbing my eyes. 'I'm not – I just figure, why wait around until I've got this camera thing completely figured out before I start using it? I have to believe it's meant to be more than just a toy for Georgia to play with.'

'Why?' said Luke. 'Why can't it just be a random thing you saw in a vision?'

'Because I saw it *in a vision,* Luke! My brain got *dragged through time* and saw *this* camera. You want to tell me that doesn't mean anything?'

For a second, Luke looked ready to drop it. But then he said, 'What do you want it to mean? Kara already gave us an explanation. The fallout. The same thing that's causing Amy's speed and Georgia's mind thing and Peter's – whatever. We *know* why you're having these visions. Why do you need to add –?'

'No, we *don't,*' I said. 'We don't know why I'm having visions. We know *how* I'm having them. That's not the same thing.'

'What do you think this is? Some, like, higher power controlling your mind? Making you see things?'

'I don't know!' I snapped, caught off-guard by how negative he was being. 'But how far do you think we would've got without them? Where did we figure out how to get into Shackleton's tunnels? How to find Kara and Soren? How to open that thing they had Bill trapped in? That was all just random too, was it?'

I realised I'd started speeding up, pulling away from Luke, angry without knowing exactly why, except that I *needed* him to believe me about this, even if I wasn't entirely clear on what I believed myself.

Luke ran to catch up, sidestepping in front of me. 'Jordan, look, don't – I'm not saying there isn't something to all this. I'm just saying be careful. You're not the first person in this place to start listening to powers they couldn't see.'

'You think this is –?' I clenched my fingers. 'So, because Mike was stupid enough to believe in Kara and Soren, that means no-one should believe in anything?'

'I didn't say that. But we've had a pretty solid *vision* of me getting stabbed to death sometime in the next two weeks. So if you're wondering why I'm not more willing to just jump onboard with this ...'

Luke trailed off and I felt my anger bleed away. That was what this was about. Of course it was.

'That's different,' I said. 'That wasn't one of my visions.'

'Doesn't feel much different,' said Luke.

'It's not going to happen, Luke. We'll change it. We'll find a way.'

I could see he wasn't convinced, but he nodded anyway, and we pushed on again. I held onto his hand, focusing on that connection, that physical reminder that we were both still here, keeping each other alive. Even now, with both of my feet firmly in the present, he felt like the only solid thing in the whole world.

We skirted around the south-east corner of town and deeper into the bush, eventually meeting up with one of the bike tracks. We followed it for a kilometre or so, until finally a familiar rock formation loomed in front of us. A giant boulder with a couple of smaller boulders sitting on top of it. We'd met Reeve here once before, the day we first told him about Tabitha.

Luke and I circuited the rock and found him waiting at the same outcropping we'd cowered under, all those weeks ago.

'Hey, kids,' said Reeve. 'How's this for déjà vu?'

I looked out through the bush. The sun was still rising, light streaking in between the trees. 'Least it's not raining this –'

The words died in my throat as Reeve moved out of the shadows and I took in his clothes for the first time. He was wearing the new jumper Miller had brought him from town. I realised I'd seen it before. A hundred times before. Over and over again, on the grainy old video and in the pictures that replayed in a constant loop in my mind. Reeve was wearing the same jumper that Luke had worn in Kara's tape. The jumper Luke was going to be murdered in.

One look at Luke told me he'd seen it too.

Reeve's eyes shifted between the two of us. 'Something wrong?'

'No,' said Luke.

'All right. Sure,' said Reeve, clearly not buying it. Then he smiled. 'Your dad says hi.'

My head jerked up and I felt the tears pricking my eyes again. 'Is he okay? What's –?'

'He's fine. Miller spoke to him. He sends his love to you and your mum and your sister. He – he says he knows he can count on you to keep them safe.'

I crashed into Reeve, hugging him, like for a minute Dad was right there in front of me. 'Right,' he said, patting me on the back, and I realised he was on the verge of tears too. 'I'll make sure Miller passes that on to him.'

I pulled away, smiling weakly, wiping my eyes dry again. 'Thanks. What about your family? Have you heard anything?'

'Yeah,' Reeve sniffed, determinedly pulling himself together. 'Miller keeps me posted. They're keeping their heads down. Doing as well as anyone. And Katie knows I'm alive now, so that's ... That's something.'

Luke gave us a minute to gather ourselves, and then said, 'So, what's the news? How's the revolution going?'

'Slowly,' Reeve admitted. 'The boys are all scared. Everyone's waiting for someone else to move first.'

'But you've already made the first move,' I said. 'I mean, you have *some* of the guards onboard, right?'

'We've made a start,' said Reeve. 'But it's only a start. There are seventy-eight security staff in Phoenix, not including those who are out of action.'

'And how many are on our side?' Luke asked.

'Hard to say.' Reeve laced his fingers together behind his head. 'I reckon there's only about a third of them that are actually *loyal* to the Co-operative. But, like I said before, most of the rest are like Hamilton. Too scared of crossing Shackleton to commit to anything.'

'All right,' I said, 'so where does that leave us? How many could we actually count on in a fight?'

Reeve chewed the inside of his cheek. 'Four.'

'Four?'

'Like I said, it's going slowly. Miller, Lazarro, Ford and Kirke are all solid. There are others who could go either way when the moment comes, but it's not much to mount a mission on. The guards get six hours a day to sleep, but otherwise they're on duty. Take out the guys posted to other parts of town, and you're still left with something like forty guards awake and on duty in the Shackleton Building at any given time.'

'Yeah,' I said grimly. We'd come up with a similar number from the surveillance feeds. 'So we'll just have to sneak in again, right? Just a couple of us. Get up there and find Tobias. I mean, we've only got ten days left. That's our first priority.'

'No,' said Reeve, suddenly grave. 'It can't be.'

'Reeve –'

'Think about it, Jordan. What if you succeed?'

I shook my head. 'What are you *talking* about?'

'Let's say it works,' Reeve pushed on. 'Let's say, somehow, you get in and out of there in one piece. You get Tobias to the release station. You stop Tabitha. What happens next? What do you think Shackleton's going to do with those two thousand prisoners he suddenly doesn't need anymore?'

Reeve leant against the rock, letting the answer to that question sink in. Letting my mind fill with images of security officers mowing down the crowd with their rifles, transforming the town hall from a concentration camp to a mass grave.

Luke let out a heavy breath, his expression just as bleak as ours. 'What are we supposed to do, then?'

'We need to get to the cafeteria,' I said. 'That *loyalty room* or whatever you guys call it. If we take away the danger to the guards' families, we take away their loyalty to Shackleton.'

'Exactly what we're thinking,' said Reeve, digging a hand into his pocket. 'Which brings me to the next piece of good news I have for you kids. Miller's done some digging. Managed to get his hands on this.' He pulled out a scrap of paper with five numbers scrawled on it.

'What's that?' asked Luke.

'This,' Reeve grinned, 'is our way into the armoury. What do you say we go get what we need to end this nightmare?'

Chapter 11

I rolled over in the bed, eyes shut, trying to find a position where the mattress springs didn't dig into me so much. It was late now, probably around midnight. I'd been drifting in and out for a couple of hours now, too preoccupied to rest properly.

Finally, we were getting somewhere. After weeks of just treading water, we finally had a solid direction to head in, something that could make a real difference in the fight against Shackleton. Reeve had a couple more meetings up on the surface, and then he and Tank were coming down here tomorrow afternoon to figure out a plan. An *actual* plan, with a beginning, middle and end, which was kind of new territory for us.

I pulled a scratchy blanket over my shoulder, listening to the gentle rhythm of Luke's breathing from the bed next to mine. He finally seemed to have fallen asleep.

Mike, meanwhile, still hadn't come in from the surveillance room. It wasn't like him to sit in there pining for his family. He barely even spoke about them, as though the only way he could cope was to shut them out of his mind altogether. Mostly he sat in the bedroom, drawing in his sketchbook, but even that was a frustration now with his injured hand. The floor under his bed was littered with scrunched-up paper.

I tried not to think about it. But after several minutes of turning it over in my head, I realised I was never going to get to sleep until I'd seen what he was really doing out there.

I sat up, grunting as one of the mattress springs jarred the newly-acquired bruise on my shoulder. I'd picked it up earlier tonight when I'd gone to see Bill and take him some food. Like Luke had predicted, he wasn't interested in talking.

I'd asked him about Tobias. He'd shot me a disdainful look and said that 'wasn't his concern'. I'd tried to push the issue, but all I'd got was more indecipherable shouting and another computer monitor thrown at me. Phoenix's healing powers would take care of the bruise soon enough, but right now it was just one more little hassle.

And for what? The one person down here who might give us a chance of finding Tobias, and he was too busy smashing at walls to help us.

I froze in the bedroom doorway, hesitant to let Luke out of my sight. *Let him sleep,* said the rational part of my brain. *You'll be ten metres away.*

I started towards the surveillance room, but then something made me change course and I found myself heading for the other bedroom instead. I eased the door open and peered inside. Georgia was murmuring in her sleep, curled up next to Mum. I thought of Dad, sleeping at gunpoint on a chair in the town hall. Counting on me to keep them safe.

I knew he'd only said it to be encouraging. He wasn't trying to burden me with anything. But he didn't need to. I'd already been carrying that around with me since day one.

'You too?' said a voice in the darkness.

I whirled around, heart pounding, then breathed again as I realised who'd spoken. Amy was sitting up in her bunk, staring into space again.

'Sorry,' I whispered. 'Did I wake you?'

She waved the question away. 'No. I was awake.'

Her voice was more controlled than I'd heard it in weeks, almost none of the speeding and slowing that had haunted it since the fallout took hold.

'Are you doing okay?' I asked. 'You seem like you've been a bit out of it lately.'

Amy smiled. She'd turned to look at me, but it was like she was staring straight through my head and out the other side. I shivered, bringing a hand up to my face to remind myself that I was still here.

'It's funny.' She crossed her legs under the blanket, dark hair tumbling over her shoulders. 'This thing – whatever's happening to me – you know, I was always so obsessive at school. About everything. My classes, my gymnastics, my music. Just obsessed with *achieving*.

And there was never enough time for it. I was like this constant battle, trying to be better, smarter, *faster*.'

'Faster.'

'I know. Be careful what you wish for, right? But that's the thing. It's like the fallout gave me exactly what I wanted, but now none of those things even matter anymore. And not just because the school's abandoned and the teachers have been captured by terrorists. This speed thing – you all think of it as me being fast. But to me, it's not like that. It's like the whole universe has slowed down. Like my *life* has finally slowed down enough for me to stop and pay attention to the important stuff.'

'And what's the important stuff?' I asked.

'I don't know,' said Amy, smiling again. 'Still working on that one.' She tilted her head, sending ripples through her hair. 'Anyway, don't you want to go check on her?'

'Check on who?'

'Cathryn. She left ten minutes ago. Usually she'll talk to me, but – anyway, I thought that was why you were here.'

My eyes shot to her empty bed. 'Wonderful.'

Amy started to apologise, but I was already out in the corridor.

Mike and Cathryn, both out of bed. That couldn't be good news. But they'd barely even spoken to each other for over a week, so why the sudden change?

I ducked into the surveillance room. There was

Mike, over in a corner, deep in a whispered conversation with Soren. But no Cathryn.

'What do you want?' said Soren, spotting me.

'Where's Cathryn?'

'How should we know?' said Mike.

'But – crap,' I said, realising where she must have gone. I darted back out, racing down the corridor towards Peter's room. Part of me wondered whether I should stay back to figure out what Mike and Soren were up to but, no, Cathryn and Peter were the more immediate problem right now, and unfortunately I couldn't be in two places at once. Not on purpose, anyway.

It wasn't long before I heard voices booming up the passageway. 'How many times do you need me to say it, Cat? I can't.'

'Yes you *can*,' said Cathryn. 'You can get up right now and walk out of this room. We'll go together.'

'No,' said Peter.

I slowed down, just around the corner from Peter's doorway.

'Why are you doing this? Why are you letting them treat you like an animal?' Cathryn's voice was thick with tears. 'Come on, Pete. Please. Come with me.'

'*No*. Not like this. I'm not leaving her.'

My fist clenched against the wall.

'Oh, *honestly*,' spat Cathryn, 'you think Jordan cares about you? You think she's keeping you locked up in here because she *wants* you or something?'

'As if you would have any idea what –'

'Have you *seen* her and Luke together?'

A surge of heat swelled in my stomach. I strode around the corner, breaking in before this went completely to pieces. 'Peter? What's going on?'

They were sitting together on the bed. Cathryn was a wreck. As soon as Peter saw me, he leapt away from her, holding out his hands like he was trying to fend her off. 'Get out.'

Cathryn spluttered and stood up. 'I'm sorry. I'm sorry, okay? I'm trying to help –'

'Get out of here!'

'Look at him!' she screamed, turning on me. 'Look what you're doing to him!'

'Cathryn …' I caught her arm as she pushed past, lowering my voice to a whisper. 'Not now. Please. I'll talk to you –'

'Don't bother,' she said, shoving past me.

Peter watched her go, waiting until her footsteps faded out. 'She wanted me to run away,' he said. 'She wanted me to break out, but I didn't. I stayed.'

He sat back down, and I was so tempted to just walk out and shut the door on him. So sick of these blatant attempts to score points with me. But that was always the choice, wasn't it? Stick around and validate it or walk away and risk infuriating him even more.

'Thanks,' I said, letting go of the door.

Peter stretched out a hand as I came over. 'I won't leave you, Jordan. I'll find a way to bring down the cameras again. I will. And then we'll go out there and get our parents back.'

'Yeah,' I said, ignoring the hand. 'You keep trying.' More and more, it seemed like a pointless exercise, but at least it gave him something to do. 'Anyway. I should get back to bed.'

'Wait.' Peter stood up. He took a steadying breath, like he had something important to say, then rested his hands heavily on my arms. 'I'm sorry. For all of it. All this – Whatever's happening to me. I know I keep stuffing up. I get it. But I'm *trying*, Jordan. You know that, right? You have to let me keep trying. Because if you give up on me ...' He swallowed hard, eyes boring into me. 'I *need* you, Jordan. I can't do it on my own.'

He snaked his hands around my waist. I returned the hug, just for a second, then leant back to release him. Peter leant with me, moving us around. I took a backwards step, felt the cold steel of the bed frame behind my knees, and a second later I was down on the mattress with Peter on top of me.

I twisted under him. 'Peter –!'

His mouth came down against mine.

I grabbed him by the shirt, trying to push him away, but he held on, lips working furiously, one hand rubbing up and down my arm and the other moving to my face. His body pressed against me, a writhing, paralysing weight.

Peter's eyes stayed closed, either not noticing or not wanting to notice me fighting to shove him off.

I parted my lips to yell at him again, and he took the opportunity to force his tongue into my mouth.

I hesitated just a second and then bit down hard.

Peter screamed into my mouth. He scrambled off me, spitting blood onto the concrete. '*What was that for?*'

'Don't,' I said, getting up, shaking with anger, backing out of the room as he approached me again. 'Don't touch me.'

'Wait! Jordan, no, please –'

I slammed the door on him, leaning against it while I dragged the first barricade over with my foot. I shoved it into the brackets, grabbed the second one, and stood up to find Peter's face filling the gap in the door.

'I'm sorry!' he said. 'I thought we were –'

'Go to bed, Peter.'

I smashed the barricade down across the door and walked away.

Chapter 12

'All right,' said Reeve, sticking the cap on the whiteboard marker in his hand. 'That's about it. What do you think?'

We were standing around a cracked marble table down in some old back room of the research module, listening to Reeve outline our way into the armoury. All of us except Mum and Georgia, who were up the other end of the Complex, probably reading some of the 'picture books' the two of them had been making in PowerPoint on one of the laptops.

I could tell Mum was torn about it – she wanted to be in on the planning as much as anyone – but the last thing Georgia needed to hear was more talk about guards and guns.

Reeve had been drawing on the table as he went, sketching out a diagram of the armoury. I looked it over again, taking it all in.

Two storeys. Weapons on the ground floor, vehicles on top, with a ramp running up the outside to let them in and out. Four guards on duty at any given time; two inside and two guarding the perimeter.

We were going to break in, grab what we needed, then load it into a few skids (the fire-fighting units Calvin's men used out in the bush), and make a break for it down the second-floor ramp.

'It's a good plan,' I said, looking up again. 'Good as we're going to get it, anyway.'

There were nods from around the table.

'Okay, great,' Reeve said. 'So. Numbers. We've got Kara, Jack and myself as our designated drivers, plus Amy as runner. Luke, Jordan, I'm assuming you guys are in? That gives us six.'

'I'm coming,' said Soren, speaking up for the first time since we'd started. 'And so is Michael.'

Mike's head jerked in surprise, but he didn't argue.

'Yeah,' said Tank, 'me too, boss.'

Reeve held up a hand. 'No. Too many. Sorry guys, but we can't afford to get slowed down by a crowd.'

'Screw that!' said Mike. 'If Soren wants to go, he's –'

'Oi!' Tank barked, glaring at him. 'You shut up and do what he says.'

Mike raised his crippled hand to give Tank the finger, and Tank's anger evaporated. Mike stared at his missing digits, realising what he'd done. He jerked the hand away, looking sick.

'He's coming,' I said, breaking the uncomfortable silence that followed. 'Soren's with us.'

Luke looked at me like I'd gone insane.

'Trust me,' I breathed. I didn't *want* Soren to come with us, but something told me leaving him and Mike down here together was an even worse idea. Better to split them up. 'Soren's coming. But Mike stays.'

'Fine,' said Soren, stifling the argument halfway out of Mike's mouth.

'What about me, boss?' Tank asked Reeve.

'Stay here,' I said, before Reeve could answer. I walked around to his side of the table. 'Keep an eye on my mum and my sister. And keep an eye on *them*,' I said, pointing at Mike and Cathryn. 'Make sure no-one goes in to see Peter. And if anyone comes to the entrance, if anyone figures out we're here, you *run*, down into the panic room, and you *hide my family* until we get back.'

'Boss?' Tank asked.

Reeve nodded. 'Do it.'

'OK,' said Tank. 'I can do that.'

I went back to my place at the table, rubbing my eyes with the bases of my palms. Sick of this. It should have been *simple*. Two sides: us and the Co-operative. Was that really so impossible for everyone to get?

'Right,' said Reeve. 'I reckon that should do it. We'll head out tomorrow arvo. Two o'clock. It'll be a good few hours on foot. Ideally, we'll get there around sunset: dark enough to give us some cover but not so dark we go smashing into trees on the way out.'

'Hang on,' I said. 'What should we be looking for? I mean, what are you actually hoping to find in there?'

'What do you think?' Soren sneered.

'No. This isn't –' I faltered, already regretting the

decision to let him come. 'We're not starting a militia here. You really think we're going to get Shackleton's men to switch sides by shooting at them?'

'They don't need to switch sides if you've shot them already,' said Mike.

'Mike!' said Cathryn, appalled.

'Look,' said Reeve, putting both hands down on the table. 'We've got a partial idea of what's in there, but nothing even close to a full inventory. Some of these decisions have to wait until we're in there. But, yeah, I'll be looking to pick up rifles, ammunition –'

'And then what?' I said, voice rising to cut him off. 'We shoot our way into the Shackleton Building? Murder anyone who gets between us and Tobias?'

Reeve looked me right in the eye. 'Is that really what you think of me, Jordan? I don't want this any more than you do. And I'd love to say there'll be a convenient, non-lethal way to deal with the guards we need to deal with, but I just don't know. We may not be able to get out of this without spilling some blood.'

'Exactly,' said Soren, punching the table. 'We need to make them understand that we are serious. We are at war. Collateral damage is an acceptable risk.'

Mike nodded in agreement, as though Soren had just delivered some rousing speech. Kara made a kind of disgruntled noise.

'Right,' I spat, rounding on Soren. 'Yeah, as usual, *other people's* deaths are an acceptable risk to you!'

'What's your solution?' Mike stepped in front of

Soren, like he was getting ready to stop a bullet. 'Hug it out?'

'*Enough,*' said Luke's dad, pulling the three of us apart. 'He's just told you he doesn't know what we're going to find until we get there. Let's survive that step first, okay?'

'Agreed,' said Kara. 'May I remind you that, even armed with all the weapons we could carry, we would still be hopelessly outnumbered against the Co-operative in a direct assault on the Shackleton Building. This argument remains a pointless exercise until we can deactivate the surveillance network again.'

'Fine,' I said. 'But don't think this is —'

I crashed down into the table.

'Jordan!' Luke rushed over, pushing everyone else out of the way.

I screamed as the vertigo kicked in. The room whirled around me, colours bleeding together. I dropped to my knees, losing my grip on the dusty table, stomach hurtling around inside me, matching the pace of the disintegrating room. I fell back, hearing the shouts, feeling the hands grabbing at my arms and legs, cradling my head.

And then all of it disappeared. I was gone again.

The floor flattened out under me. I lay there gasping, tears streaming from my eyes, until a nearby spluttering sound brought me around.

I wasn't the only one crying in here.

I sat up. The room was gleaming, pristine. The

cracks and chips in the marble table had vanished,
and it was now surrounded by half a dozen leather
chairs. The door was wide open, revealing a brightly
lit corridor.

There was another little sniffle, and I realised
the sound was coming from underneath the table. I
crawled over, reaching to pull one of the chairs aside,
but my hand went straight through it. I bent closer to
the ground, peering under. It was a girl, maybe five or
six years old, face in her hands, long brown hair spilling
past her shoulders and down across her lap.

I jumped as another face appeared in my peripheral
vision. Luke, here for me already. I turned to look
at him, trying to fix my mind on getting back, but
my attention kept flickering back to the girl under
the table. Even without seeing her face, there was
something familiar about her.

A shout echoed in the distance, harsh and guttural.
The girl's head snapped up, revealing dark eyes shot
with red, and again I could have sworn that I'd seen
her before. She cringed and buried her face again.
Someone out there was badly hurt.

Luke was still reaching for me. Reaching through
me. I reached back, catching fistfuls of air – and then
crashed straight through Luke's body as a furious
explosion shook the room from somewhere up the
corridor.

I sprawled across the ground, grazing my hands.
The shaking continued, more and more violent,

sending chairs toppling over and dust raining down from the ceiling, and a deafening roar rose up in the room, like a horrible dark creature sweeping up the corridor towards us. The little girl screamed, cowering in a ball. It took me a second to realise that I was screaming too.

I fought my way to my knees, grabbing desperately at Luke's arms and still not making contact. The roar intensified to an impossible, mind-crushing sound – and then the whole room was swept up in a wave of white-hot light. It spewed through the door, blinding, shattering, swallowing everything.

He was gone. *Everything* was gone but that roaring, all-consuming light.

'LUKE!' I screamed, clawing blindly at the air. 'Luke! Get me out of here! *Please!*'

Two hands came down around my wrists. I let out a terrified shudder, falling into him, fingernails digging into his skin.

The others flashed into view around me. Reeve, Mike, Soren, Amy, Mr Hunter, silhouetted against the light. Then all of it dissolved again, swirling away like someone had pulled out the plug.

Everything shifted, and I found myself drowning in darkness. It rushed through me, penetrating every part of my body. Luke pulled me towards him, arms wrapping around my back. It all changed again, and I landed back in the meeting room. Remi Vattel was alone at the desk, surrounded by paperwork. She jumped up, knocking her chair over.

And then I was back. Back in the present, still shaking, gagging, face pressed into Luke's chest. Panicked voices broke out around me, adding to the throbbing in my head.

'Get back!' said Luke, face white. 'Guys, come on, give her some space!'

Luke's dad stooped over me, and the two of them heaved me to my feet, shuffling me out of the room, tears still streaming down my face. I glanced blurrily at Kara on the way past. She frowned like she was trying to piece something together.

'What was it?' Luke asked when we were out of earshot of everyone else. 'What were you screaming at?'

'I was there,' I said, still shaking. 'I was right in the middle of it. I think I just saw this whole place come down.'

Chapter 13

'You sure you're okay with this?' I asked Amy, sneaking down the dark corridor ahead of her.

'It's fine. I – oops, sorry,' she said, accidentally speeding up and bumping into me again. 'It's fine. Good practice for tonight.'

I stopped at the first glimpse of light up ahead. 'All right. He's up there. Just around the corner.'

I turned sideways, letting her past, listening to the *shink – shink – shink* of Bill's pickaxe driving into the wall. I readjusted the rope over my shoulder.

'Okay,' said Amy, psyching herself up. 'Okay.' She raised her fists in front of her, and I could just make out the dark shapes of the sedative pens clenched in each one.

A rush of footsteps and she was gone. I waited, hoping. Bill let out a howl of rage, and suddenly Amy was right on top of me again, almost knocking me to the ground.

'Sorry, sorry,' she panted, the words speeding out of her mouth. 'Oh my goodness. That was nuts.'

'NO, NO, *NO!*' Bill shouted, charging around like an angry bear if the sporadic flashing of his helmet light was anything to go by. There was a series of loud smashing noises, like he was determined to tear the whole room apart before he went under. 'I DON'T HAVE TIME FOR THIS! This is not – This is *unacceptable* – I need … I have to …'

Bill's throat gave out and the torch on his helmet drifted to a standstill.

'Nice work,' I whispered, flicking on my own torch and heading down the corridor for a look.

Bill was on his stomach, face pressed into the concrete. He'd made a lot of progress with his excavating since I'd last been in here. There was now a hole in the back wall big enough for a person to climb through, leading into what looked like a whole other room.

I walked past Bill, tiptoeing around him despite the fact that he'd just been pumped with a double shot of sleeping drugs. The empty space on the other side of the wall turned out to be part of another old corridor, blocked up with concrete and junk in both directions. The far side was all gouged and cracked, where Bill had made a start at clearing a path.

What could possibly be down here that was so important to him? If Tobias wasn't his concern, then what was? And why didn't he just *tell* us about it?

I turned back, shrugging the coil of rope off my shoulder. I prodded Bill with my foot to make sure he was really gone, then got down by his side, dragging his arm out from under him.

'Do you, um, need a hand?' asked Amy behind me.

'No, I've got it.' I crouched over him, one foot on either side of his body, roping his wrists together behind his back, and then moving down to start on his legs. I looked up. 'You get why I have to do this, right? I mean, I know he hasn't come near us since he woke up, but you know what he was like back in town. He's not stable. I can't have him roaming around the place while Mum and Georgia are –'

'Whoa. What the –?'

I swung the torch around. It was Mike.

'I told you not to come down here,' I said.

'I heard shouting,' said Mike. 'Anyway, screw you. Since when did I start taking orders from –?'

I grabbed him by the front of the shirt, dragging him up to me until his face was an inch from mine. 'Listen Mike, don't think I haven't considered knocking you out too. But honestly, we can't afford to waste the sedatives on someone whose arse I could kick with my eyes closed. So here's the deal: you go back to Tank right now, and you don't leave his side until we get back.'

'And why would I –?'

'Because,' I said, twisting his shirt around my fist, 'if anything happens while we're gone – if anything happens to my *family* – I'm going give you to Peter. Let him decide what to do with you. You understand me?'

Mike swore at me bitterly, jerking out of my grip.

I bent back down to finish dealing with Bill. 'Good.'

The rain came out of nowhere about two hours into
our hike to the armoury, pounding through the trees
and turning the ground to mud. Reeve said it was a
good thing, that the noise of the downpour would
disguise our approach. But then, as Luke had pointed
out, it would do a pretty good job of disguising anyone
who was approaching *us* too.

We trudged on. By the fourth hour, I could barely
feel my feet and yet the rain showed no sign of easing
up. We'd moved into some particularly sparse bush. A
few scattered trees and not much else. I didn't like it.
But the sun was setting now, so hopefully the darkness
would help hide our escape on the way out.

Reeve was in front, checking our trajectory with
a compass. He stopped as we reached the road again,
meeting it for the third time that afternoon as it wound
itself around and around the town.

'Don't forget to look both ways,' he said, scanning
for any sign of movement.

We darted over the road.

'Right,' said Reeve. 'I think that was our last cross.
Shouldn't be too far now.'

I looked over at Luke, who'd been talking quietly
to his dad for the last few minutes. Mr Hunter was
carrying another one of our three rifles. Not because

he wanted it, but because it meant Soren couldn't have one. Luke patted his dad on the back and came over to me, rain sticking the shirt down against his front, outlining a body that was really starting to show the strain of being underfed for so long. A body that was going to have a knife plunged into it any day now, if history played out the way it was supposed to.

I shoved the image away as he reached me. 'What's up?'

'Sounds like Soren's not too happy with you,' said Luke, holding my hand and leaning in to be heard over the rain.

'And?' I said. 'When is Soren *ever* happy with me?'

'Mike told him you threatened him.'

I rolled my eyes. 'Only to make sure he didn't do anything stupid while we were gone. And where does Soren get off, lecturing me on being kind to others?'

I glanced over my shoulder at Soren. He was skulking along behind the rest of us, eyeing the rifle in his mum's hands. It wasn't loaded yet – we were down to Reeve's last two clips – but if things went to plan, it would be soon enough. Kara looked back and waved at Soren to hurry up.

I hadn't asked her yet about the little girl in my vision. I was still trying to work out a way to approach the subject without raising too many questions about how I even knew the girl existed.

'So what are you going to do when he wakes up?' asked Luke. 'Bill, I mean.'

'He'll still be out when we get back,' I said, hoping I was right. 'I guess we just wait and see what happens after that. We can always put him under again if we need to.'

'Not for long,' said Luke. 'How many sedative cartridges do we have left?'

'What else was I supposed to do, Luke? Just leave him down there with Mum and Georgia?'

'No, that's not –' He stared at the mud, rain dripping off the end of his nose. 'I'm not saying you did the wrong thing. We just need to think about it, that's all.'

Reeve threw out a hand, signalling us to stop. A narrow dirt road cut across in front of us. He raised his rifle and then signalled us all to cross.

After about five minutes, the bushland dropped away and an enormous grey warehouse appeared, the same one that Luke, Peter and I had broken into almost three months ago. I slowed down, pulling out Georgia's camera to do a quick pan across the clearing. The warehouse was surrounded by a towering razor-wire fence with padlocked gates at the front to let the delivery trucks in and out. A guard slumped lazily against the wall, barely even bothering to watch the entrance.

'C'mon,' said Luke, pulling me away.

'We could get back in there,' I said. 'I mean, if it comes to it.'

'Yeah,' said Luke. 'Although Mum reckons our supplies should be okay for a week or so. And by then …'

By then, one way or the other, it probably wouldn't matter.

On our last trip to the warehouse, we'd escaped through a hole in the fence and run straight back into the bush, too focused on evading security to wonder if there was anything else out here. But it turned out Reeve was right; the dirt road kept going, and about five hundred metres further up, we came to a second clearing.

The armoury was twice as big as the warehouse. Its walls were plated with a gleaming silver metal that reminded me of the tunnels under the town. Narrow, black-tinted windows dotted the building at regular intervals.

The one positive was the lack of cameras. Reeve said that was because back before the concentration camp, this place was meant to be hidden even from most of security.

The dirt road curved around to the front of the building, dead-ending at the ramp. We crouched in the undergrowth, keeping well back from the edge of the clearing. I grabbed Georgia's camera again. The rain and the trees obstructed my line of sight a bit, but I still had a pretty good view of the front of the building, and down one side. A tall, broad-shouldered security officer stood guard at a huge set of double doors. He looked much more alert than the guy at the warehouse.

I guess you took things more seriously when you were guarding explosives instead of groceries.

I glanced sideways at Amy and Reeve, who were peering out from a fallen tree a little way off. Reeve whispered something to Amy. He pointed down the side of the armoury. Amy nodded. I leant out from my hiding place, trying to see what they were looking at. A second guard had come around the corner. Officer Cook. We'd run into him before.

There was an explosion of wet leaves, and Amy was away. I caught a glimpse of her flitting through the trees, and then she was out of sight.

'All right,' said Reeve to the rest of us. 'Get ready.'

I turned my attention back to Officer Cook just in time to see Amy sprint up behind him, swinging the sedative pen above her head like a dagger. She plunged it into his neck.

Cook whirled around with his rifle and a shot exploded through the bush. Amy screamed, sprinting back into the bush, apparently unhurt. Cook moved to follow her, but the sedative was already starting to kick in. He staggered to the edge of the clearing and fired again.

There was a shout from the other end of the building as the front guard came splashing around. Officer Cook turned to yell something at him, then collapsed into the mud. The other guard slowed, nervous now. He stared out at the bush, weapon raised.

Cook tried to push himself up into a sitting position,

but his arms were giving out. He barked at the other guard to help him. The guard backed towards Cook, still not taking his eyes off the edge of the clearing. He took one hand off his weapon to help Cook to his feet.

Amy flew back out into the clearing. The other guard dropped Cook, aiming his rifle again. Too late. Amy blurred behind them, jabbing the guard in the back, and disappeared into the trees again. The guard staggered back, tripping over Officer Cook.

More crashing bushes and splashing feet and Amy was right back on top of us. 'Oh my goodness. Oh my goodness. Come on! Hurry!'

She kept moving, out to the front of the building, and the rest of us jumped up and got ready to follow.

There was a keypad next to the entrance. Amy hammered in Reeve's code. The double doors edged slowly apart, trundling away into the walls. Amy leapt back in case anyone decided to come at her from inside.

'*Go!*' said Reeve, vaulting over the fallen tree in front of him. We sprinted into the clearing.

Amy shifted from foot to foot. We must have seemed torturously slow to her. 'Hurry! Hur–!'

Another blast of gunfire ripped through the clearing, and she fell to the ground, screaming.

Chapter 14

I spun in a circle, heart hammering. Where were they shooting from?

Soren froze. 'Back! Go back!'

'*No!* Get her inside!' Reeve pointed his rifle up above our heads and any argument from Soren was silenced by another roar of weapons fire.

Then I saw it. An open window on the top level.

'Jordan!' shouted Kara, wrenching my attention away. 'Over here! Now!' She was stooped over Amy, stretching out her leg. Kara dug her fingers into an already-tattered patch of Amy's jeans and pulled, ripping them open at the thigh. Amy cried out again, a strained, accelerated sound, way past controlling the speed of her voice. Her right leg was a mess, torn open and glistening with blood. The rain spattered against the wound, trailing pale red streaks across her skin.

Kara tore the jeans down to the ankle and pulled the shredded fabric aside. 'Take that off,' said Kara, nodding at my jumper. 'Give it to me.'

I pulled it over my head as Reeve let off another spray of bullets. Amy groaned, clutching her leg.

'Calm down,' said Kara, squeezing the worst of the water out of the jumper and knotting it around Amy's leg. 'You're going to be fine. Hold still and let me stop the bleeding.' She pulled the knot tight and Amy gasped.

I glanced over my shoulder at Luke's dad, who was standing guard at the door, rifle in hand. Luke was with him, staring at Amy with wide eyes. It looked like Soren had already run inside.

'Can you stand?' I asked Amy as I hefted her up.

'I – I don't know,' she said. 'I think –' She broke off into a shrill scream and slumped down again.

'Here,' said Luke's dad, scooping her over his shoulder in a fireman's carry. He ran through the door just as Reeve came racing up behind us.

'Quick as you can, guys,' Reeve said, forcing himself to stay calm.

We followed the others inside, and I realised the firing from upstairs had stopped. 'Did you …?'

'Hurt him?' said Reeve. 'No. Just a warning. Not the best way to start a conversation, but he didn't give me a whole lot of choice.'

'Idiot,' said Soren, appearing in the doorway with a rifle he'd found inside. 'You are here to *end* a conversation, not –'

'Quiet,' said Kara tersely, and Soren shut up.

The ground floor of the armoury was one huge, open room divided up by row after row of racks and shelves and storage units. A department store for dictators. Reeve moved to the front of the group and led us down the nearest aisle. 'Stay low, everyone.'

We passed by racks of rifles like ours, followed by shelves piled with hundreds of boxes of what I assumed was ammunition. Reeve stopped. 'Somebody grab some of these.'

Luke started piling boxes into the empty bag on his dad's back, careful not to bump Amy, while Kara and Soren stopped to load their weapons. I dug my nails into my bare arms, wanting to go over there and rip the rifle right out of Soren's hands.

'Good,' said Reeve, as Luke tugged the zipper closed. 'All right, this way.'

We moved off again. Kara and Soren stayed back, still stuffing around with their weapons. I hissed at them to hurry up.

Reeve led us down the next aisle, past big stacks of boxes with labels I couldn't make any sense of. Reeve seemed to know what he was looking at though, because he shook his head and said, 'No. None of this.'

I looked around at the ceiling. According to Reeve, there were two more guards. So what were they –?

Reeve spun around, signalling us all to stop. Kara and Soren scurried to catch up. Reeve put a finger to his lips, and they stopped moving. Amy's ragged, rapid-fire breathing continued for a second longer before she bit down on her fist, holding her breath.

Silence. Almost. All except for the faint footsteps

padding on the concrete floor, maybe a couple of aisles over.

'That you, Webb?' Reeve called out.

No answer. The footsteps stopped.

'Yeah, I thought so,' said Reeve grimly. He raised his voice. 'We're not looking for a fight, mate. How about you just sit tight and let us get what we came for?'

Still nothing. Reeve nodded down the aisle and we kept walking. Soren fell back again, muttering something about Reeve giving away our position. He pointed his weapon behind us, ready to open fire on anything that moved.

Down the next aisle, still no guards in sight. Reeve brought us to a stop again alongside a cabinet filled with bricks of grey-white plasticine-looking stuff that I recognised from a hundred different action movies. C-4. Plastic explosives.

Shackleton really had planned for every contingency.

Reeve smashed the cabinet open with the butt of his rifle. 'Don't worry,' he said, catching the look on my face. 'Not going to use it on people. Stick some in my bag, will you?'

Luke eyed Reeve nervously as I piled the bricks into his backpack. 'Is that safe?'

'Should be,' said Reeve, picking up some other wires and stuff and passing them back to me. 'This stuff doesn't detonate on physical impact. You'd need –'

A volley of gunfire cut the conversation short. I looked back to see Soren clutching his rifle with jittery fingers and Officer Webb ducking for cover at the end of the aisle.

'Stay back!' Soren yelled. 'Next time, I will not miss!'

'You really want to do this, Webb?' called Reeve, shooing us all away to the other end.

'You shouldn't have come here!' said Webb. 'You know we have to defend this place.'

'She's only sixteen, Webb. The girl you shot –'

'That wasn't me! It was Reynolds!'

'And what about you, mate? Coming up behind us with a –'

'They have my *kid!*'

Soren opened fire again, knocking something loose at Webb's end of the aisle and sending a pile of boxes crashing to the floor.

'Soren!' I snapped.

He glared back at me. 'No more talking!'

'Yeah,' said Reeve. 'He's made up his mind. Come on.'

We raced to the end of the aisle. All except Soren, who stayed planted to the spot, aiming another spray of bullets down at Officer Webb.

'Soren!' I yelled again. 'Get up here!'

'Jordan,' said Reeve from around the corner.

I darted around the end. Reeve was up at the back wall, hefting what looked like a gas canister down into Luke's arms. 'I think we've found what we're looking for.'

Luke grunted under the weight. Kara had slung her rifle over her back and was lugging a second canister. Reeve brought down a third and handed it to me. 'Here.'

'What's this?' I asked.

Bits of concrete shot into the air as bullets tore up the ground only a metre or two away from us. We dived for cover, crouching low behind the shelves. I closed my eyes, forcing myself to stop shaking and breathe.

Reeve pointed his rifle towards the ceiling, searching for the source of the gunfire. He shifted around, sights landing on a figure crouched at the top of the emergency stairwell in a far corner. 'There you are.'

Reeve fired up at him. The other guard – Officer Reynolds, I assumed – stopped shooting and hid.

Luke's dad crouched beside me, still lugging Amy across his shoulders. Her eyes were shut tight, tears streaming down her face. 'Where is he?' asked Soren, appearing next to us. 'Where is the other guard?'

Reeve ignored him. 'Time to get out. Let's head up top. Lift's just a bit further along. Everyone stay low and follow my lead. Ready? *Now*.'

We sprinted along the back wall of the armoury. Somewhere in the middle of our thundering footsteps, I was sure I could hear Officer Webb off to our left, running to catch up.

We reached the lift and I hammered the button until the doors slid open. We piled inside and I turned back to see Officer Webb sprinting up the aisle towards us.

Soren fired at him through the closing doors, drowning the whole world in the sound of it, the force of the weapon knocking him backwards into me. His backpack crunched into my chest and I made a mental note to take it from him as soon as we got back.

Something exploded between us and Webb, detonated by Soren's haphazard gunfire. Flames swelled into the air. Then the doors slid shut, sealing it all away.

'You moron!' I said, as the lift trundled upwards. 'You could have –!'

'Up against the sides,' Reeve ordered, crouching low and aiming his weapon at the doors. 'We've still got Reynolds to worry about.'

We all did as we were told, except Soren, who got down next to Reeve, rifle raised. The lift slowed to a stop, and the doors edged open again. Reeve and Soren leapt out, scanning the room. But if Reynolds was there, he wasn't giving himself away just yet.

I crept after them onto another open floor, dimly lit, all laid out with neat rows of security vans, skid units, big chunky things that looked like missile launchers or something, and –

'Whoa – Jordan!' said Luke. 'Over there!'

'Yeah,' I breathed. 'Yeah. I see them.'

There were three of them, side by side in the very centre of the room.

Glimmering black helicopters.

Chapter 15

A sudden, reckless hope flared inside me, threatening to cloud out my brain altogether.

'You didn't feel it was worth telling us there were *helicopters* in this facility?' said Kara, spotting a toolkit up against the wall and shoving it between the lift doors with her foot to keep them from closing again.

'Might have mentioned them if I'd known,' Reeve whispered, eyes brightening. He started across the floor, sticking close to a row of parked trucks.

I fell into line behind him, one hand slipping from the gas canister in my arms to the little rectangular bulge in my pocket. Georgia's camera.

This was it.

This was what it was for, why I'd been gathering footage all this time. *We were getting out.*

'Look up there!' I said, mind buzzing with nervous energy. The middle third of the ceiling was different. Long, interlocking plates instead of the seamless steel on either side. 'That looks like it opens up.'

'Sure,' said Reeve, stepping out from the last truck

in the line. 'But we're not talking about driving a car here. Unless one of you has a secret pilot's licence you haven't told me about –'

He reeled back as a guard opened fire from off to our left. Glass shattered above his head, and the whole truck shifted as a bullet blew out one of the tyres. Amy gasped, and Mr Hunter ducked lower, pulling her clear of the windows.

'I can fly them,' said Kara. 'If those helicopters are open and fuelled, I can fly one of them out.'

Luke twisted around, like he thought he'd misheard. 'Really?'

'How do you think we came and went before the Co-operative arrived?' she asked.

'You're talking *out* out?' said Reeve. '*Civilisation* out?'

I could hardly take it all in. It was too big. I was dizzy, my whole body and brain charged with a kind of wild electricity.

But then another stream of bullets pelted the far side of the truck, dragging me back to earth. Mum and Georgia were waiting back at the Complex. This was no time to get stupid.

Reeve pointed to a big metal box near the choppers. 'We're going to make a run for that storage unit. I'll do what I can to keep our mate over there busy. The rest of you, don't stop until you're under cover again. Ready? Three, two, one –'

He leapt out, firing in the direction of the guard.

I bolted past, hefting the gas canister up against my chest. I looked left. The guard was out of sight again.

Luke and Kara sprinted along on either side of me. Ten metres to the storage unit. Five.

The guard fired again, his rifle flashing in the corner of my eye. Someone shouted behind me. I dived for cover, the canister crushing against my arm as Luke and Kara dropped to the ground next to me.

'Everyone okay?' panted Luke's dad, lowering Amy to the ground.

'Y-yeah,' I said, jumpy with adrenalin. 'I think we're – Wait, where's Soren?'

I glanced back to see Reeve tearing towards us, rifle firing with one hand, dragging Soren along with the other. He pulled him down behind the storage unit. 'Haven't got time for heroics, mate. If I want backup, I'll ask for it.'

'It won't be a pleasant takeoff,' said Kara grimly. 'That wind might not have seemed like much from the ground, but –'

'We can't go,' I said, holding onto one little part of me that was still capable of being pragmatic. 'Not all of us. We need to keep fighting here too.'

I peered out between the choppers to the skid units, way over on the other side of the building. Only sporadic bits of cover between here and there, and even when we reached the skids, we'd still need to figure out how to open that door at the top of the ramp.

'Right,' said Reeve, peeking out around the side

of the storage unit again, 'we've got work to do. But I don't think Kara should be heading out on her own, either. Someone else needs to go with her. Someone with firsthand –'

'Me,' said Soren.

'No,' I said. 'How about Luke?'

Luke gave me a weary look. 'Jordan, don't even – You know I can't.'

'Amy then,' said Mr Hunter. 'Get her to a hospital before –'

'No …' Amy murmured. 'Not without my mum and dad.'

'Not Amy,' said Reeve. 'Look, I hate to be cold about this, but she'll heal fine and we're going to need her. We can't afford –'

Another round of gunfire spattered the storage unit behind us. Reeve jumped up and returned fire. The concrete shook with the sound of it.

The guard fired again. Reeve cried out, lurching. He landed on top of me and I felt something warm against my arm.

'No!' Luke shouted.

Reeve rolled off me, landing on his back. Blood dribbled from his side. Kara rushed over to him, but Reeve weakly shoved her away. He winced and pulled the jumper up to reveal a ragged gash at his hip.

'Just – a graze,' he grunted, struggling to sit up.

'Reeve, don't – don't move,' I said breathlessly, eyes darting in search of the guards. 'You shouldn't be –'

I broke off. The blood flow had stopped. As I watched, the wound dried and scabbed over. In a few seconds, he was on his feet like nothing had happened.

'Reynolds is coming around the side,' he reported, as I gaped at him. 'If we're doing this, we need to do it.'

'Dad,' said Luke, pulling his eyes away from Reeve. 'I think it should be you.'

'No,' said Mr Hunter. '*No*, Luke. I'm not leaving you out here on your own again.'

'You won't be. I'm not on my own. And I don't *want* you to go, you know I don't, but –' He broke off, swearing, as someone opened fire right behind us.

Soren. He was backing away from the storage unit, shooting erratically in Officer Reynolds' direction. Reynolds fired back, but stopped instantly as Soren rolled behind one of the missile launcher things.

'Going to get himself killed,' Reeve muttered. Then, to the rest of us: 'That security van over there. Ready? Go.'

We ran, weaving between the helicopters. Reeve hung back to cover us. Gunfire exploded all around me, but I had no idea where it was coming from. It was all just noise. I didn't stop running until I was around the other side of the van.

Amy moaned again as Luke's dad slammed into the passenger door beside me.

Luke flew after them, breathing hard. 'It's – open!'

I saw where he was pointing, risked a look around the van and felt my heart skip a beat. Kara had just tried the door on one of the helicopters. And she was climbing inside.

I couldn't believe they'd left it unlocked like that. But I guess if you keep your secret helicopter inside a secret armoury protected by guards armed with semi-automatic weapons, you probably figure you've got security covered.

Kara jumped out of the chopper again. She did a frantic circuit, yanking a bunch of red plug things out from the engines and exhausts and throwing them aside.

Reeve leant out to lay down some covering fire. He swore under his breath at the sound of bullets tearing through glass. 'What in the world is Soren trying to –?'

A giant, echoing groan boomed down from the roof of the armoury. The ceiling was moving, splitting apart. Rain streamed through the gap like a waterfall.

I peered around again. Soren was way over the other side of the armoury, half-hidden in shadow. His hand hovered over a black control panel. He pressed another button and a metallic clattering sound joined the groaning of the roof. At the far end of the room, the door at the top of the ramp had just started rolling open.

'I take it back, kid,' Reeve grinned, sticking out a hand to let Soren know where we were. 'We'll make time for all the heroics you want.'

Chapter 16

Soren weaved through the vehicles, firing an occasional burst from his weapon. Then Reynolds must have caught sight of him, because he stopped running and hit the ground behind some machinery.

The rain hammered down louder and louder as the roof split further apart, drenching the concrete behind us, then the top of the van, and then pouring down on our heads. The sky outside was growing dark.

I heard a shout from one of the security guards. And then another noise, something I hadn't heard since the day I got here: the long, high drone of a helicopter powering up.

Over my head, on the far side of the van, I saw the rotor spring to life, pushing the blades in a slow circle.

I tried to steady myself, but my attention was sucked up completely by the whir of the engine and the spinning of the blades.

Reynolds switched targets, opening fire on the chopper. Reeve shot back, pinning Reynolds down behind wherever he was hiding.

'Dad, please!' Luke shouted over the noise. 'It can't just be Kara. Go. People will listen to you.'

'Come with me,' said Mr Hunter. 'They can listen to both of us.'

'I can't!'

Luke's dad stepped away from the van, Amy still hanging in his arms. 'Why? Why can't you?'

'I have work to do!' he said, voice unsteady. '*Here*. I can't just –'

Thunder cracked the sky overhead, swallowing up the sound of his voice.

'Luke …' I said.

'*I'm the only one who can bring you back!*' he shouted, and even in the pounding rain I could see that he was crying. He turned back to his dad. 'I *have* to stay. I have to.'

I shivered, wet fingers slipping on my gas canister. If he stayed here and got himself killed because of me …

Mr Hunter looked sick. He lifted his eyes to the ceiling, rain sliding down on his face. The noise from the chopper was shifting, the high-pitched whining overtaken by the *whump-whump-whump* of the blades. The downdraft swirled around us, like a blizzard to our saturated skin. 'All right,' he said, sitting Amy down against the van, then shrugging off his backpack and handing it to Luke. 'All right. But I'm coming back, okay?' He clutched Luke with both hands. 'I'm bringing help. We are *all* getting out of here.'

Luke didn't answer. He put his gas canister on the

ground and squeezed his father into the same kind of desperate, crushing hug he'd given him when he first arrived here.

I pulled Georgia's camera out one last time, panning the armoury just as Reynolds fired at Soren again. 'Here,' I said, handing the camera to Mr Hunter. 'Take this. Show them what's happening here.'

He shoved it into his pocket and turned back to his son. 'Hey. Tell your mum …'

But Luke was already bending down to get Amy, staggering under the weight of her and the weight of everything else.

Mr Hunter clapped a hand to my shoulder. 'You get him home, Jordan. Keep each other safe.'

'All right,' said Reeve, from the front of the van. 'Count of three, you run to the chopper. I'll keep Reynolds off. One. Two –'

Mr Hunter ran. Reeve leaned out around the corner and fired again. Luke hovered on the spot for a few seconds, then put Amy down again and dashed forward to see what was going on. Reeve stuck a hand out to block him. 'Don't. He's okay. He made it.'

Luke slumped back against the van, then jolted upright again at another flash of gunfire. Soren was sprinting towards us from out beyond the choppers.

'Time to go,' said Reeve, ejecting the ammunition clip from his rifle and smacking in a new one. He hoisted Amy up off the ground and handed her back to Luke. 'Gonna do all the rest in one shot. Load those skids and get down that ramp.' He picked up Luke's gas canister and tucked it under his arm. 'GO!'

Gunfire exploded behind us the second we were out from the van. Reeve fired back, but only for a second. He let go of the trigger, shouting something behind me, but my ears were still ringing from the noise of the rifle. We kept running, deafened and shivering, buffeted by the wind from the chopper, and a few metres later we were out of the rain again, back under the cover of the roof. Almost there.

I glanced over my shoulder and saw the chopper lifting up into the air. For one tiny moment, I felt my heart lift with it. And then I realised Reeve wasn't with us anymore.

He was running back to the chopper. Back to Soren, who was standing there in the rain, completely exposed. Soren turned in a circle, hands to the sky, screaming up at his mother. 'No! No! Take me with you!'

'Soren, *get over here!*' Reeve roared, crouching behind the van. 'You want to get yourself killed?'

Luke and I kept moving, closing the last ten metres to the skid units. I dumped my gas canister in the back cage of the nearest one, shifting the fire-fighting gear aside to make room, then gave Luke a hand lowering Amy in with it.

Reynolds fired his rifle and I almost dropped her. But he wasn't aiming at anyone on the ground. He was targeting the helicopter.

Someone in the helicopter fired back.

The shooting silenced Soren for only a couple of seconds before he started shouting at his mum again. Wild, desperate nonsense on an almost Crazy Bill level. He was melting down. Losing it completely.

His whole life, Soren had never been separated from his mother for more than a couple of hours. She'd been his only family, his only friend, his only *anything*. And now she was leaving him.

Reeve dropped Luke's gas canister and bolted out from the van. He grabbed Soren from behind, spun him around and smacked him across the face, yelling at him to shut up and get it together. The chopper kept rising, swaying erratically in the wind.

Reeve threw his free hand out past Soren, firing his rifle again.

And then more gunfire, much closer this time, shredding the concrete at my feet. Officer Webb was taking aim at us from the top of the stairwell. His hands were shaking on his gun, attention flitting from us to the chopper. My stomach lurched at the thought of what Shackleton would do to these guys when he learned they'd let a helicopter escape.

I ducked between our skid unit and the one next to it, crawling past the massive tyres to the driver's seat. The skids only had one seat up front, but there were platforms around the cage where other people could ride standing up.

I peered under the line of skid units and saw Webb's legs dashing across the floor. I couldn't work out whether he was coming after us or the helicopter, and I don't think he knew either.

'Quick!' I climbed into the driver's seat. 'Hop on!'

'You don't know how to drive!' hissed Luke, but he was already clambering into the cage with Amy.

The key was in the ignition, and the set-up looked pretty similar to Mum and Dad's car back home. Steering wheel. Accelerator. Brake. I could do this.

'Go!' Reeve shouted behind me. 'Go, go, go!'

He'd finally got Soren away from the helicopter and was dragging him, still screaming, to catch up with us.

I turned the key. The skid unit roared to life and started rolling forward. I stomped my foot down on one of the pedals, which turned out to be the brake, and the skid ground to a stop.

Webb fired again and Luke cried out behind me.

'Luke!' I yelled.

'No, I'm fine! I'm fine! Just go! Hurry!'

I hit the other pedal. The skid jerked forward. We hurtled straight for the back wall, and I spun the wheel just in time to avoid a collision. Too far. The skid hurtled around, heading almost directly back the way we'd come. Luke cried out and I heard the cage rattle behind me as he fought to keep Amy steady.

I caught a glimpse of Soren shoving Reeve away as he tried to pull him aboard another skid; the chopper pitching forward, almost catching on the roof; Webb lining up his next shot; Reynolds running towards us.

I turned the wheel again, gentler this time, and we veered away at a right angle.

Webb fired. I ducked, swerved, almost fell out of my seat and, miraculously, found myself staring straight down the ramp. We lurched forward, speeding through the door and into the rain. And even over the storm and the shooting and the noise of the engine, I could still hear the glorious thumping of the chopper as it floated into the air above the armoury.

We shot down the ramp. I squeezed the steering wheel with both hands, terrified I was going to drift sideways and send us rolling over the edge. But we made it. Off the ramp and onto the dirt road. I glanced back and saw two more skids shooting out of the building behind me. Soren had somehow pulled himself together enough to drive on his own.

An exultant laugh escaped my throat. We were all out. Kara and Mr Hunter were clear of the building, clear of the trees, rising into the charcoal sky.

Finally – *finally* – the world was going to know about us. We were going to be okay.

Bright light flashed in the corner of my eye from somewhere in the bush. A rumble echoed out from the source of the light, starting low but quickly getting louder, and a dark shape streaked above our heads.

I had just enough time to register that it was heading straight for the helicopter before the sky was torn apart by a blinding explosion.

Chapter 17

I slammed on the brakes and the skid spun to a stop in the mud. Luke was screaming. Raw, gut-wrenching cries. I looked back, expecting to find flaming wreckage raining down behind us, but the explosion had passed and everything was shadowy grey again.

'Keep going!' yelled Reeve.

A fourth skid unit shot out from the top of the ramp. They were coming after us. Soren zoomed past me, screaming and screaming but still streaking forward, like he'd forgotten he was in control of his skid. I hit the accelerator again.

'NO!' Luke gasped behind me. 'Go back! You have to go back!'

'For *what?*' I said desperately, heart plummeting from my chest. 'There's nothing we can –' I swerved again, narrowly avoiding a tree as we sped up the muddy track, back to the main road, right behind Reeve. 'Wait. Do you hear that?'

I strained my ears, trying to tune out the rain and the skids, making sure it wasn't my imagination. But no, I could still hear it. Fainter now, but definitely there. The helicopter was still flying.

Back in the cage, Luke let out a kind of coughing sob. He'd heard it too.

But I had no time for feeling relieved right now. I glanced down at my hands and realised there were mirrors on either side of the steering wheel, reflecting what was behind me. Officer Webb was right on my tail, leaning forward in his seat, close enough for me to see the look of terrified determination on his face. Reynolds stood on one of the platforms at the back.

I floored the accelerator, knuckles white against the steering wheel, more or less okay as long as the path was there. But sooner or later, I was going to have to pull off into the bush, and then things were really going to get interesting.

Another dark blur rocketed past above our heads, lighting up the sky as it exploded.

'He'll be okay!' I said, not needing to see Luke's face to guess at his expression. 'If they dodged one of them –'

I coughed, catching a mouthful of dirty water as Reeve's skid hit a dip in the path in front of us. I splashed through after him, wiping my eyes clear with the back of my hand.

I glanced at the mirrors again. Security were still coming. They'd gained another couple of metres on us. Officer Reynolds was leaning out the cage, hanging on with one hand, aiming his rifle with the other.

'Turn!' Luke shouted. 'Get off the road!'

It was all too fast. The trees blurred past us on both sides. There was no way I could turn off without smashing the skid into a ball. Not until the bush thinned out.

'I can't!' I said. 'Do something!'

'What am I supposed to –?'

Reynolds fired his rifle. I swerved again. There was a *crunch* and a snapping of branches as I drifted too close to the side of the road. The skid shuddered horribly, spinning its wheels, and then jolted forward again.

Another burst of brilliant light flashed overhead. I couldn't hear the chopper anymore, but that didn't mean much with everything else that was going on.

I felt the skid tip slightly as Luke started moving around in the back. 'Okay – okay – just go straight for a second.'

'That's what I've been trying to do!'

I checked the mirrors again and saw Reynolds lining up another shot.

Luke grunted, lifting something. Whatever it was clattered against the back of the cage. There was a dull, wet thud and a jangling of metal behind us and suddenly Webb and Reynolds were skidding into the bushes at the side of the road. We pulled away and I caught the reflection of a giant toolbox lying in the mud.

'Nice one,' I said, teeth chattering in the cold. The rain pelted down against my arms, turning my fingers numb. Amy moaned, and I wished we had a blanket or something to put over her.

I squinted through the spray from Reeve's tyres. The landscape had just shifted abruptly, trees falling away from the side of the road. We'd reached the other clearing. The warehouse.

A rifle erupted on the other side of the razor-wire fence and I almost dived out of the driver's seat. Reeve fired back, aiming the rifle up above head height, trying to scare the guards off without actually hurting them.

'What's he doing?' Luke panicked, clambering up behind me.

'It's okay,' I said, 'he's not –'

'No, what's *Soren* doing?'

Soren had made it to the far end of the warehouse. Despite his meltdown, he was somehow managing to keep his skid in one piece. He peeled off the road, sending his skid hurtling down the narrow gap between the fence and the edge of the clearing. Reeve's skid plunged in after him.

'Slow down!' said Luke.

'*What?*'

'When you turn, you're meant to slow –'

I spun the wheel hard to the left, foot shifting to the brake pedal. We slid across the wet grass, spraying mud, and crunched sideways into a tree. Amy gasped in pain.

'Sorry, sorry, sorry!' I said, hitting the accelerator again. We surged straight over the gap, colliding with the fence on the other side.

Luke shouted behind me. 'JORD–!'

Gunfire roared in my ears, tearing into the cage behind me. My left mirror exploded and disappeared. I pumped the accelerator. The skid shuddered, still scraping against the fence. The guard fired again. I twisted the wheel to the right and the skid finally broke free.

'You guys okay?' I called back, gunning it after Reeve, who'd slowed down at the warehouse to wait for us.

'Yeah,' said Luke. 'I think so.'

I could still hear the guard splashing through the mud on the other side of the fence. He shouted at us to stop and give ourselves up. Yeah, right.

Reeve picked up the pace again as we approached. Into the bush. I followed after him, scanning frantically for a safe path through the trees. Soren was way up ahead by now, almost out of sight.

I felt like I was getting the hang of the steering now, as long as there were no more sharp corners, anyway. The skids were definitely at home out here. Their oversized wheels tore through the undergrowth like it was nothing. I was just starting to think that I could get this thing home without any more disasters when I heard the growl of another engine.

Webb and Reynolds. Still coming.

I looked into the bush, searching for the source of the noise, taking my eyes off the path for just a second too long.

A boulder loomed out of nowhere. I heaved at the steering wheel, pulling us away to the right, but it wasn't enough. The skid's left wheel ran up over the rock, tipping us sideways. There was an awful sliding and crashing from the cage as everything – and everyone – rolled to one side.

The shifting weight was enough to bring the skid over completely. We hit the ground and I was flung out of my seat, ribs smashing against something sharp in the mud. Amy screamed in pain.

Another skid roared up in front of us. Reeve jumped out of the driver's seat and came over to pull me up. I steadied myself against the closest tree. Luke was already back on his feet. He bent down, trying to help Amy who was crying on the ground, but he couldn't lift her. It looked like he'd sprained an ankle or something.

'Get in,' said Reeve, pointing Luke towards the upright skid. 'I've got her.'

Luke left Reeve to it. I saw a gas canister lying in the mud and hobbled over to grab it, battered arms protesting as I hefted it into the air. I dumped the canister in the back of Reeve's skid and jumped in after it. Reeve lowered Amy on top of me, and then helped Luke over the side of the cage.

The guards' skid raced closer, coming at us from the side, near enough for me to see Reynolds lining us up with his rifle.

Reeve jumped into the drivers' seat as Reynolds fired.

'GO!' said Luke. 'What are you waiting –?'

Reeve whipped his weapon around and shot back.

The guards' skid shuddered, throwing Reynolds to the ground as the front tyres blasted apart.

Officer Webb hit the brakes, bringing the skid to a stop only a few metres away from us. He threw his hands into the air, the rain pasting his blonde hair to the sides of his face. 'I'm sorry! I'm sorry! Please don't –'

He shrieked and leapt from the skid as Reeve shot out the other two tyres.

'I'm not going to hurt you, mate,' said Reeve, lowering the rifle. 'We're the ones trying to *stop* the bloodshed. Might be a good idea for you to remember that.'

He pushed the accelerator, driving us away into the night.

Chapter 18

WEDNESDAY, AUGUST 5
8 DAYS

'It must have been some kind of automated defence system,' said Reeve, shifting his grip on Amy and scanning around us one last time as the entrance to the Vattel Complex rolled open at our feet. 'To take out anything that might fly over and spot us. I'm so sorry, mate. I had no idea.'

'Yeah,' Luke croaked, limping down the steps. 'Not your fault.'

We'd left the skid out in the bush at a safe distance, and made the last leg here on foot. The rain was still coming down. Not that we could get any wetter or colder at this point.

I gazed down into the tunnel, eyes barely focusing. I needed to rest. *Not yet,* I told myself. Not until I'd made sure everyone else was safe.

'We *know* they dodged the first one,' I told Luke, coming down behind him. 'They have to have dodged the rest.'

Luke made a kind of noncommittal noise.

'She's right,' Reeve grunted, struggling a bit on

the stairs under Amy's weight. 'That was one of *his* choppers. You don't think Shackleton's got a way of dealing with his own defence system?'

I couldn't tell if he honestly believed what he was saying or if he was just trying to make Luke feel better, but I was grateful for the effort either way.

Mum and Ms Hunter rushed to meet us at the bottom of the stairs. Mum gaped at Amy, at the bloodied mess of my jumper hanging from her leg. 'Are you okay? Where are the others?'

'Where's Soren?' I asked, following Reeve as he headed for the laboratory. 'He needs to patch Amy up.'

Luke's mum pursed her lips. 'He's not with you?'

'We got separated on the way out,' said Reeve. 'He was ahead of us, though. He should've beaten us back.'

We pushed through the surveillance room, past Mike and Tank, who jumped up and followed us into the lab.

'What about your dad?' Ms Hunter demanded, trailing behind us. 'And Kara? Are they with him?'

Luke turned around to face her, threatening to fall apart again. 'They're gone.'

'Gone. Luke – what are you saying?' She held him with both hands, just like his dad had done before he left.

'There were helicopters at the armoury,' I explained, helping Reeve lower Amy onto one of the beds. 'They took one of them –'

'They got out?' said Tank, lighting up.

Mum's mouth fell open. She closed it again at the look on my face. There was a long silence.

'We're not sure,' said Reeve, looking Amy over. 'They triggered some kind of automated weapons system on the way out. They survived the first shot. We didn't see what happened after that.' Amy winced as Reeve loosened the jumper around her leg. He looked back at Mum and Ms Hunter. 'Don't suppose either of you have any medical experience?'

Ms Hunter shook her head. She dragged Luke towards her, hugging him, looking like she might start crying herself.

'No,' said Mum. Her hands rested absently on her stomach, and I realised the full weight of the words. That baby was coming any day now, and we'd just lost our only doctor.

'Not much more than a scratch, anyway,' said Reeve, peeling back the fabric from the mangled flesh of Amy's thigh. 'I'll just have to sort you out myself.'

Mum came over and put an arm around me. 'My brave girl,' she said softly.

I reached up, clasping her hand in mine. 'What about you guys? Any drama while we were gone?'

'No, everyone's been behaving themselves.'

'Georgia already asleep?'

'About an hour ago,' said Mum. 'Cathryn turned in not long after.'

Luke pulled silently away from his mum and left the room, wincing at his injured ankle.

'Back in a sec,' I said, releasing Mum's hand. I went to the boys' room and found Luke dragging his towel down from the end of his bed. He turned to look at me as I came in, but didn't say anything.

'They made it out,' I said, putting my arms around him and resting my head on his shoulder.

'You don't know that.'

'No. I believe it, though.'

Luke didn't answer. He just held onto me, the warmth of his body slowly radiating through all the layers of wet clothes between us. I thought back to the nights we'd spent hiding out from the Co-operative in that abandoned house, just the two of us, taking turns watching each other sleep.

A lot had changed in that week.

Luke lifted his head. 'Even if he did get away, chances are I'll be gone by the time he gets back.'

'Don't.' I leant back, hands slipping to his hips. 'Don't even –'

But then a voice cut into the room from out in the hall.

'*No*,' Cathryn was hissing, apparently not asleep after all. 'They're back! You need to get out of here.'

'Get your bloody hands off me!' yelled a second voice, sending panic jolting through my stomach.

Peter. Out of his room.

I heard the sharp *smack* of a hand against skin and Cathryn stumbled into the doorway, clutching the side of her face. Peter appeared and shoved her out of his way. He froze in the doorway, staring at Luke and me. At Luke's hands *on* me.

And then he was charging at us like a crazed animal. He grabbed Luke's head with both hands, fingers digging into his eyes and mouth, tearing him away from me.

'Peter!' I snatched at the back of his jumper, attempting to hold him back as Luke rolled to the ground, grabbing his ankle and moaning in pain.

Peter twisted around, tearing free.

'HEY!' boomed Reeve from the doorway, Tank right behind him. Reeve's voice had such force behind it that Peter actually stopped and looked up. He eyed the rifle hanging from the strap over Reeve's shoulder.

'You should go back to your room now, Pete,' said Tank.

Peter stared down at Luke, dark fury in his eyes. 'You *stay away* from her.'

'All right, mate,' said Reeve, stepping forward, 'that'll do.' He put a hand on Peter's arm, and I flinched, half expecting Peter to throw him across the room or something.

But whatever else the fallout was doing to Peter, I guess he still had enough reason in him to feel threatened by the presence of a gun in the room. He roared, backing away, hands shaking like he didn't know what to do with them. But he didn't attack again. Reeve and Tank steered him through the door.

I bent down to help Luke to his feet.

'Sorry,' said Cathryn, back in the doorway. A tear streaked down the red mark on her face where Peter had hit her. 'I didn't – He was so *calm* before. I thought if I just let him out for a little bit –'

'Get out,' I snapped.

She sniffed and disappeared, leaving Luke and me alone on the floor.

Chapter 19

'It's about us, isn't it?' said Luke dully, hobbling
sideways to get through a particularly narrow section of
the passageway out to Bill's excavation site. 'That's why
Peter's going to do it. He comes after me because he
wants me away from you.'

I felt my fist tighten on the torch in my hand.
'That's such –' I growled in frustration. 'How does that
even make *sense*? Even to *Peter?*'

'I think we left sense behind a long time ago,' Luke
said. 'I mean, even *before* all this fallout stuff started, he
was pretty obsessed with keeping you to himself.'

'When have I *ever* given him any reason to think
that I was –?'

'You haven't. You didn't need to.' He kept his voice
steady enough but I could hear how shaken up he was.

We were down to our last week. Down to *his* last
week. And, whether Luke's dad had made it out or
not, losing him again hadn't exactly improved Luke's
outlook on life.

I took a breath. 'There has to be more to it. Surely.

You did not come all the way out here and go through all this crap just to get killed over some stupid thing about a girl!'

'Trust me, I'm totally open to suggestions on how to stop that from happening.' He sighed. 'Hopefully Cathryn's learnt her lesson about letting him out of his room, at least.'

Tank had spent all last night apologising for letting Cathryn out of his sight. But the funny thing was that the apologies weren't directed at Luke or me. They were directed at Reeve. As if Tank's biggest regret in all of this was letting *him* down.

The two of them had gone back to the surface this morning. Reeve wanted to see if he could use our newfound weapons supply to leverage some more support from security before we started planning our attack on the Shackleton Building.

Not that there *could* be an attack on the Shackleton Building as long as that surveillance network was still online. Whatever we might have achieved by going to the armoury last night, it was worthless without a way to bring down the cameras.

I lowered my torch as we got closer to the end of the passageway, listening for any sign of movement. According to our previous experience with the sedatives, Bill *should* still be unconscious on the ground, but there was every chance the usual rules didn't apply.

Everything was silent. I moved forward again,

feeling for the auto-injector pen in my pocket loaded up with Kara's last sedative cartridge. Just in case.

I would've breathed slightly easier if it was Amy wielding the pen instead of me. But given she'd already taken a bullet for us in the last twenty-four hours, it seemed like a stretch to ask her back down here.

Like Kara had said back at the armoury, Amy's injuries were nothing too serious. Reeve had put his Co-operative security first-aid training to work, stitching and bandaging her up, and we were hoping the fallout would take care of the rest. Already, she was limping around on her own. Still, she'd gone straight back to bed after breakfast this morning and hadn't gotten up again since.

Soren, meanwhile, had made it back to the Complex about half an hour after us, still a bawling mess and covered in mud from head to toe. Apparently, he'd taken a wrong turn and run off into a ditch. Not surprising, given the mental state he was in.

Mike had gone crazy with relief when Soren reappeared at the entrance, like he couldn't imagine anything worse than not having a violent psycho to run his life. He'd been delivering food and drink to Soren's room all day, and had got into another fight with Ms Hunter after she'd refused to give him Kara's share of the rations as well.

I stopped again at the end of the passageway and shone my torch cautiously around the corner. Bill was right where I'd left him, tied up on the floor with his arms and legs behind his back.

'Okay,' said Luke, limping behind me, 'what now?'

'I want to find out what he's doing down here.'

'Didn't you look already, when you knocked him out?'

'Yeah. I want to talk to him,' I said. 'While he's still tied up. It's been twenty-four hours. The sedative should be wearing off by now.'

I felt Luke's hand tense on my shoulder. 'You really think him being tied up is going to make any difference?'

'Guess we'll see,' I said, walking out and crouching in front of Bill's face.

'He broke out of a prison cell,' said Luke, exasperated. 'You don't remember that?'

'This is different. He needs us.'

'Didn't stop him throwing a computer at your head.'

I shone the torch into Bill's face. He grunted, shrinking away from the light.

'Hey,' I said gently. 'You awake, Bill?'

Bill's eyes snapped open. He rocked from side to side, trying to push himself off the ground, and I saw the anger flare up behind his eyes as he realised he was bound.

'THERE IS NO TIME!' he shouted. 'NO TIME FOR THIS! I must – I must be released!'

'I'll untie you,' I said, getting up. 'I'll let you go, but I want you to tell me –'

'No, no, no, *NO!*' An invisible force pounded my

stomach and I staggered backwards into Luke. 'I don't need you! Not yet. You are an obstruction.'

'We should go,' said Luke.

'What are you trying to do?' I straightened, not ready to back off without an answer. 'What are you looking for down here?'

'*Nngh!*' Bill groaned, his face screwed up in concentration. He rolled over onto his side, and I saw the ties begin to loosen all by themselves. 'I need to – *Nngh!* Timing is critical for the undertaking to be ... to be ...'

'What undertaking?' I asked. 'Bill, please, does this have something to do with the Co-operative?'

'I don't care about it!' Bill spat. 'Not until – not until – no. All things in sequence. Your concern is premature.'

'Not until *what?* What are you looking for?' The invisible hands shoved me again, harder this time. Luke's injured ankle rolled under him and he collapsed.

Bill dropped onto his stomach, face contorting again. All at once, the ropes came undone, slithering apart like they were alive. Bill stumbled to his feet, woozy from the sedatives. He gave his hand an angry shake and the last coil of rope fell to the floor. 'These two will take me back,' he said, switching his helmet light back on. 'That is the mandate. But first – first, I need the space. This is critical. Cyclical.' He was pacing now, hands clutching his head. 'I require the location. It must end the same. Inevitable. Inevitable. It cannot be altered.'

'Bill ...' I said slowly, wary of interrupting him. 'Anything that was down here – it all got destroyed twenty years ago.'

Bill's head snapped up, like he'd only just realised we were still here. 'NO!'

He lumbered up to the other end of the room, grabbed his pickaxe, and crawled through the hole he'd made in the back wall. I heard the *shink* of splintering concrete as Bill returned to his excavation.

FRIDAY, AUGUST 7
6 DAYS

'Freakin' stupid dumb-arse *morons*,' spat Tank. 'All of them!' He kicked his chair, sending it skittering across the surveillance room floor. 'Don't they get it? Don't they have people *outside* that they care about?'

Reeve sighed. His last round of meetings had not gone well. 'Yeah mate, I know it's frustrating,' he said, resting a hand on Tank's back, 'but you've got to see it from their point of view. Our trip to the armoury hasn't exactly improved Shackleton's mood.' He smiled at the rest of us. 'And we did pick up *one* piece of useful information while we were away. Word on the street is that we were right about where Shackleton's keeping Tobias. Miller's heard several officers talking about an emergency shutdown mechanism hidden somewhere in the Shackleton Building.'

'The restricted level,' I said. 'Has to be.'

Luke frowned. 'But security don't know about the restricted level, do they? So where's this information coming from?'

'Hard to say,' said Reeve. 'But we're hearing lots of voices all saying the same thing, and it seems to tally pretty well with what we've figured out on our own.'

'And have these voices said anything about *what* Tobias is?' Luke asked.

'No,' Reeve admitted. 'Nothing specific, anyway.' He turned to the bench behind him and grabbed the padlock on a big steel box with a red Co-operative logo on the side. A toolbox, like the one Luke had dropped into the path of the security officers. Reeve had gone back to the other skid and retrieved this one for us to use as a weapons locker.

I looked around the surveillance room, which was suddenly feeling extremely empty. Soren and Mike were holed up in Soren's room again. They'd been weirdly quiet all day, especially Mike, who'd skipped breakfast and spent most of the morning sitting alone on his bed. Luke said he'd heard him throwing up in the bathroom last night. I didn't want to think about it. The last thing we needed was some flu or whatever sweeping through this place.

Mum and Georgia were across the hall too, setting up another video camera for Georgia to replace the one I'd given to Luke's dad. Georgia hadn't been too happy with me when she'd found out it was missing.

That left six of us. Reeve, Tank, Cathryn, Amy, Luke and me.

I spaced out for a second as Reeve undid the padlock on the toolbox, distracted by a glimpse of Dad and Mr Weir lining up for lunch on one of the monitors. I knew both of them would jump at the opportunity to help us out, but what chance did they have against a pack of armed security guards?

'Here's what we've got,' said Reeve, grabbing my attention back. I got up to join the others, who had already gathered around him (all except Amy, who was staring into space again, bandaged leg propped up in front of her). 'There's the ammunition from Jack's bag, plus those few extra clips Jordan confiscated from Soren when he got back. Still only two rifles, though, since the others went up in the chopper.'

Reeve moved his hand across to the neat stacks of grey-white bricks at the other end of the box. 'Then there's the C-4. We've got enough to do a decent amount of damage, but there's a bit of fiddling around with detonators involved. If we're going to use it, we'll need to get the timing right.'

'What about that stuff?' Tank asked, pointing at the gas canister standing up behind the toolbox.

Reeve picked it up, spinning it around to reveal the words *Inhalational Anaesthetic* followed by a bunch of letters and numbers. 'Sleeping gas,' he said, 'or something like it. One of Dr Galton's concoctions.'

'Brilliant,' Luke muttered. Galton was Shackleton's

second-in-command. She was also the person we had to thank for Tabitha.

'How do you know it's one of hers?' I asked.

Reeve turned the canister over again. The words *Sparkbrook Technologies* were stencilled onto the other side, next to a logo with eight black arrows spinning out from a central point.

'Sparkbrook Tech was the company Dr Galton founded before she came to Phoenix,' Reeve explained. 'I wouldn't be surprised if the whole thing was a front for what they were planning to set up here. Back in the early days, before you kids got here, there were rumours going around that a few of the construction workers who'd helped build this place were called away to take part in some testing. We'd hear stories about – Well, I guess they were more than stories, weren't they?'

I shuddered, mind burning with slow-motion images of a young couple being torn inside out. Sleeping gas wasn't the only thing the Co-operative had been testing.

'Anyway,' said Reeve, replacing the canister behind the toolbox, 'if we want to get into Shackleton's "loyalty room" and take away security's reason to –'

'Um … guys?' a voice broke in, making me jump. It was Amy, suddenly right behind me. 'Should they be doing that?'

I followed her gaze to the row of monitors along the wall and saw movement in the feed of the tunnel entrance.

Soren and Mike had just clambered up onto the surface. Something about Mike's body language made me think he was going to be sick again. Soren twitched around like a cornered bird, checking that the coast was clear. He tugged on Mike's arm, pointing at something, and then the two of them were swallowed up by the bush.

Chapter 20

'Jordan!' Luke panted behind me as I leapt up the steps to the tunnel entrance. 'Wait, are you sure this is –?'

He gave up, saving his energy for running. His ankle still wasn't a hundred percent, but he pushed on anyway, determined to keep up.

Reeve had started to follow us too, but I'd told him to stay put. If Soren was about to do something stupid – which was almost a certainty at this point – I wanted to deal with him myself. And if he was going to bring trouble on the Complex, I wanted someone down there who I trusted to take charge.

As soon as my head was above ground level, I scanned the bush and saw Soren and Mike skulking towards the east side of town. I hurried after them, quick as I could without giving myself away.

The rain had stopped since the last time we were up here, but the sky was still a pretty menacing shade of grey. Soren spun around as he ran, weird little pirouettes, as though he was trying to see in every direction at once, far less sure of himself now without

Kara. He'd thrown a white lab coat on over his clothes, the one he used to wear when he was playing overseer. Stupid to wear something that bright out here, but I doubted he'd even done it consciously.

After a few minutes, they pulled away to the right, heading south in the direction of the airport road.

I broke into a full run, abandoning the thought of sneaking up on them. Almost instantly, I felt a stitch in my side. I kept running, ignoring the pain, but then my stomach started churning and I realised what was really going on. I let out a groan that was equal parts fear and frustration. *Seriously? Right now?*

Luke called out behind me. My vision blurred, collapsing the bushland, reducing it to liquid. My foot caught on something and I dived into the swirling undergrowth. I rolled onto my side, writhing on the ground, fighting with everything I had not to cry out, sure I was going to just disintegrate completely this time and melt away into the dirt.

But somehow, my body managed to hold itself together. The convulsions finally began to ease and slowly, slowly, the world spun back into place. I lay there, remembering how to breathe again, then opened my eyes and sat up.

The landscape had shifted completely. I was still surrounded by trees, but not the towering, ancient-looking things that filled this place in our time. I was sitting in a vast field of saplings, as though someone had swooped in here overnight and planted a whole forest. Phoenix was nowhere to be seen.

Kara had told us about this. It wasn't just people who'd been affected by the fallout. Before the destruction of the Vattel Complex, this whole area had been nothing but wasteland. The seemingly centuries-old bushland that surrounded Phoenix had all sprung up from nothing in the last two decades.

Which meant that, judging by the shoulder-high growth all around me, I'd probably landed not too long after the Complex went down.

'Why did you bring me here?' asked a girl's voice over my shoulder. *'You know I hate this place.'*

I searched for her, standing up to see over the saplings, and found a large, dome-shaped tent only a few metres behind me. An older man and a teenage girl were sitting out the front on folding chairs.

'No, you don't,' the man said patiently, pressing his fingertips together, and I felt a chill stab through me as I realised who I was looking at.

It was Shackleton. Maybe ten years younger than he was now, brown hair instead of grey, and dressed in a tan safari shirt instead of his usual jacket and tie, but there was no mistaking the calm, icy malevolence glinting in his eyes.

The girl stared up at the sky, brushing a strand of hair away from her face, and I recognised her as well. She was the girl from the Vattel Complex in my last vision. The one who'd been crying under the table when it all blew up. Older now; maybe my age.

What was she doing with Shackleton? Kara and Soren had never mentioned either of them, so why –?

Then Luke was there in front of me, derailing my train of thought. He was mouthing at me, hands hovering at my arms.

'Seriously, Noah –' the girl began, but Shackleton cut her off.

'Father,' he said, the patient tone vanishing from his voice. *'You are to call me "father".'*

I leant past Luke to look at them. Luke mouthed a word I'd never heard him use before.

'You're not my real dad,' the girl said sulkily.

'I adopted you, did I not?' said Shackleton. *'I took you into my home. That makes me your real father. The past is dead, girl. You would do well to remember that.'*

Luke sidestepped in front of me, reaching for me again, and the frustration on his face dragged me back to reality. Soren and Mike were getting away. And I was probably disappearing almost completely by now.

I reached for Luke's hands, fingers passing through his only once before he locked on and took hold of me.

Behind him, Shackleton leant forward and put a hand on the girl's knee. *'And as I have told you before, you do not hate this place. This place has made you who you are.'*

'What are you talking about?' The girl jerked her leg away, suddenly defensive.

'You are a very special girl, Victoria.'

Victoria. I stretched up to look over Luke's shoulder, taking in the girl again. Dark brown hair, piercing eyes, slim build, sharp jaw line ...

It was Dr Galton.

Luke tightened his grip on my arm, pulling me closer to him. *Come on! Get back here!*

'Wait!' I said. 'Just let me –'

But it was too late. The nausea flared up again, and the world of the present crashed into this one. And just like before, I was in both places at once, the sky simultaneously grey and clear, the bushland ancient and new. I could still see Shackleton and Galton, but they were flickering in and out with everything else. I held on, pushing down my gag reflex, trying to catch as much of their conversation as I could before they were gone.

The teenage Dr Galton was looking up at Shackleton like he'd caught her doing something shameful. *'I'm not. Why would you say that? I'm not – I'm just like everyone else.'*

'Your body is resilient beyond any normal human standard,' said Shackleton gleefully. *'I can use that.'*

Now I felt two kinds of sick. But instead of being appalled by Shackleton's blatant desire to 'use' her, Galton looked almost relieved. Like she'd been expecting him to say something else.

'The world is a mess, Victoria,' Shackleton continued. *'Humanity has lost its way. It is our job to*

rectify that. If this place can be used to change others the way it has changed you –'

Galton's eyes narrowed. *'This is about your Tabitha project.'*

I was shaking harder now, leaning into Luke for support. I dropped one of his hands to wrap an arm around my convulsing stomach.

'What are you doing, Noah?' Galton pressed. *'What's this all about?'*

'Patience,' said Shackleton. *'That is all a good many years away. For now, I just want to conduct a few –'*

My legs fell away and the campsite disintegrated, along with the rest of the universe. It all spun together, like mixing paint, and I squeezed my eyes shut, clutching Luke's arm, sure I was going to throw up all over him.

Light sparked on the other side of my eyelids and for a few seconds, I felt rain pouring down across my back. Then everything went dark and I was dry again. The light shifted a few more times, and then everything straightened out again and I felt Luke lowering me to the ground.

'Are you okay?' he asked, completely spooked. 'What was going on over there? It was like you didn't want to leave or something.'

'Sorry,' I said, letting him pull me to my feet. 'Did you see where Soren went?'

Luke pointed in the direction they'd been heading when I flashed out. I jogged off again, but slower than before, still recovering from the after-effects of my vision.

'You sure you don't want to stop for a minute?' asked Luke, racing to catch up.

'Why? I'm fine.'

'Because,' Luke caught my wrist, pulling me back, 'Jordan, you were – I don't even – even after I grabbed you this time, it was like you were still stuck back there. Or, I don't know, like you were stuck halfway or something. I could see you, and I could feel you, but – I don't know. You definitely weren't fully here. And then you – you started glowing. Well, not – like, it wasn't bright or anything. But *something* was happening to you. I – I thought I was going to lose you.'

'I'm sorry,' I said again, trying to ignore the little ripple of anxiety running through me at the idea that I had 'glowing' to add to my list of bizarre symptoms. 'I was holding on, trying to hear as much as I could. That might have been what did it.'

'Holding on?' said Luke. 'You can control it?'

'No, not like – I don't know. A little bit.' I released Luke's hand and we picked up the pace again.

'What did you see, anyway?' he asked.

'I think I just found out how Shackleton first discovered this place. It was –'

But then I spotted something white through the trees up ahead of us. Soren. I broke into a sprint again. He jerked his head around, seeing me coming, but didn't try to run away. I caught up and found him standing at the edge of the airport road, hands twitching excitedly at his sides.

'You are too late,' he said.

'For what?' I demanded. 'Where's Mike?'

Soren smiled. 'He's coming.'

I shoved Soren into a tree. 'What are you doing?'

'I am doing what is necessary,' said Soren coldly.

A low rumbling noise rose up. Something was coming down the road. I backed into the bush, taking cover behind another tree.

It was a skid unit, zig-zagging all over the road, like the guy behind the wheel had about as much driving experience as I did. Like he was just another fifteen-year-old kid.

'Crap,' Luke breathed.

The skid shot past, finally straightening out, and I saw Mike hunched over the wheel, eyes fixed on the path ahead, black hair fluttering out behind him. He'd taken a pair of scissors to the sleeves of his shirt, exposing the black spiral of his overseer tattoo for the whole world to see.

'Where's he going?' I hissed at Soren.

He said nothing.

I started sprinting after the skid.

'Jordan, no!' Luke shouted. 'You can't –'

There was a crash of bushes and I heard his footsteps come pounding up the path behind me.

Mike hit the end of the dirt path and kept driving, out onto the bike track that would take him straight into the town centre. Every second, he pulled further away from us.

I should've stopped at the end of the path. I should've just turned back to the safety of the bush and left Mike to it. But I hammered forward, hesitating for only a moment at the edge of town before sprinting out in full view of the surveillance cameras. Luke shouted another half-hearted protest, but kept following. Back into town for the first time in weeks.

The skid rocketed between two blocks of identical houses, all lifeless and empty, overgrown grass in the front yards.

'MIKE!' I yelled, pounding after him but still losing ground. At the end of the block, the bike track opened up onto the town centre. Mike slowed down just a little bit, glancing off to his right. Further up ahead, the prisoners in the fenced-off exercise area out the front of the Shackleton Building looked up. A few of them ducked for cover. Others shouted out words of encouragement.

I stopped at the end of the block, just short of the town centre, survival instincts finally kicking in. Security were already pouring out of the Shackleton Building and the security centre, spreading across the street to head us off. Mike veered away to the right.

One of the guards opened fire. I dropped to the ground. The skid kept moving, full throttle again, and the guard dived out of the way.

Mike was heading straight for the security centre.

More gunfire. The skid rattled and shook but somehow kept going, swerving erratically and then resuming its collision course, juddering up the security centre steps and smashing through the front doors.

For a long moment, everything seemed to stop.

The guards held their fire.

The prisoners fell silent, gaping out from behind the fence.

'No …' I breathed, leaping to my feet, realising what he was about to –

The whole world shook and I was thrown to the ground as the security centre blew apart in a ball of fire.

Chapter 21

'Jordan!'

The voice was muted, distant, like he was yelling underwater.

Fire fell from the sky all around me. Glass shattered as the windows of surrounding buildings gave way. There were shouts, screams, thundering footsteps, all of it muffled by the ringing in my ears and the splitting pain in the back of my head.

Luke swam into view above me and thrust out a blurry hand to drag me up. I swayed, finding my feet, eyes watering at the haze of dust and smoke.

The security centre was a shell, flames towering above what little was left of the roof, spewing inky smoke into the air. The heat was unbearable.

There was a shout from behind the fence and one of the guards fired his rifle into the air. Apparently, a couple of the prisoners had made an escape attempt.

More guards moved in to subdue the crowd, trying to herd them back inside. I craned my neck, looking for my dad, but couldn't see him.

Another wave of security officers came out from the Shackleton Building. A few of them were wearing backpack things with hoses twisting out from the sides, but the rest of the fire-fighting stuff was stored in the security centre. It had all gone up in the explosion. One of the guards turned in our direction, squinting through the smoke.

Luke tugged at my arm. 'We need to go.'

I staggered again, pressing a hand to my head, and felt the blood seeping through the mess of matted hair.

A security van screeched to a stop in the middle of the street and half a dozen officers piled into the back. The van roared away again, gunning it for the south end of town. Out to the armoury for more gear.

There was an enormous cracking noise and the guards with the hoses ran for cover as a section of the security centre wall that had somehow survived the initial explosion came toppling down above their heads. For a second, I thought I saw the charred remains of Mike's skid unit lying upside down in the middle of the flames, but then a fresh cloud of dust billowed up, swallowing it all again.

Jordan,' said Luke, putting an arm around my shoulder, steering me away.

'Yeah. OK.'

We raced back out to the cover of the bush.

We made it back to the Complex and found Soren heading into the ground just ahead of us. I sprinted

down after him, dizziness fading now, the shock of
what I'd just witnessed giving way to a cold, dark fury.

Mike was gone.

Dead.

Hysterical screaming echoed up the stairwell.
Cathryn. 'Stop! Let me *go! Let me GO!*'

'He's – *Oof!*' Tank grunted like he'd been bashed in
the stomach. 'He's gone, Cat!'

Cathryn kept screaming.

'Jordan!' cried Mum, throwing her arms around me
as soon as I reached the bottom of the stairs. We were
both knocked sideways as Ms Hunter brushed past to
meet Luke.

'I'm fine, I'm fine,' I said, disentangling myself
and going after Soren. I caught him going into the
surveillance room and slammed him against the
doorframe with my forearm across his throat. 'YOU
KILLED HIM!'

Through the crack in the door, I saw Cathryn, half-
collapsed and sobbing in Tank's arms. Reeve stood behind
them, stony-faced. He'd had friends in that building.

'No,' Soren coughed. 'I did not kill him. He chose
it. Michael gave his life to give us a chance at –'

'His life!' I shouted. 'His! Not yours! You sent *him*
out there to die because *you –*'

'*Look!*' Soren shoved me off and pushed the door
open, storming across to the surveillance computers.
'Look at what he died for and tell me it was not worth
the sacrifice!'

I stared at the circle of computers. The feeds were gone, replaced by flickering static on every screen. When the security centre was destroyed, so was the surveillance network.

'You think that changes what you did?' I said. 'You think you can justify a murder by –?'

Cathryn let loose another agonised scream and tore herself out of Tank's grip. She charged at Soren, grabbing at his hair. 'You killed him!'

Soren shrieked, pulling back, but she dug her nails in, swinging her other hand around and smashing her fist into his nose. He kicked her away and she fell to the ground, sobbing. 'You killed him … You killed him …'

Soren brought a hand up his nose, trying to stop the flow of blood. He moved in to kick her again.

'Oi!' barked Reeve, 'that's enough.' And suddenly he had a rifle trained on Soren's chest. 'Touch her again, and we are going to have a serious problem.'

'She attacked me!' said Soren, throwing his hands in the air.

Reeve twitched his rifle to the side of the room. 'Up against the wall.'

'You going to shoot him, boss?' asked Tank.

Reeve didn't answer. He gestured at the wall again and Soren leant up against it. 'Hands behind your head,' said Reeve.

'I just handed you the keys to the Shackleton Building!' Soren spat, but he did what Reeve told him.

Reeve's rifle came down between Soren's shoulder blades.

Soren's knees began to buckle. 'He was supposed to get out! He was supposed to park the vehicle and –'

'Shut up.'

'Reeve …' I said, moving to intervene. I wanted justice for this as much as anyone, but shooting Soren wasn't the solution. More bloodshed wouldn't fix anything.

Reeve turned to Luke, who was standing in the doorway behind me. 'Where can we put him?'

'In his room,' said Luke. 'We'll barricade the door.'

Reeve grabbed Soren by the back of his collar and hauled him towards the door. 'Get moving.'

Luke led them along the corridor. I left Tank with Cathryn and followed, feeling cold all over.

Mike was not a good guy. He was obsessive, ruthless, borderline psychotic. Sometimes not even borderline. We had never been anything but enemies. But he was gone now. And somehow, none of that other stuff made this feel like any less of a waste. Not to mention the guards on duty in the security centre that Mike had taken down with him.

Reeve shoved Soren into his room and held him in the corner long enough for us to drag out a couple of beds to barricade the door with. Soren gave up protesting pretty quickly and sat on his bed, sulking. Luke's mum stood in the corridor, watching, but didn't say anything.

When he was safely sealed away, we returned to the surveillance room and found Cathryn lying on the floor, head resting on Tank's lap.

For a long moment, no-one spoke. No sound except the hum of the computers and Cathryn's muffled, spluttering sobs.

Tank looked up, teary-eyed but stoic. 'What now, boss?'

Reeve pulled a chair over and slumped down with his arms on his knees. 'This changes things. What those two did was –' He breathed out, gathering himself. 'It was inexcusable. But we've just been handed an incredible opportunity.' Reeve stood up again. He looked back at the sea of static. 'I'm going to need a couple of days to meet with my people. Assuming they're still out there.'

'Reeve, we're running out of days,' I said.

'Which is exactly why we need to take the time to get this right.' Reeve pulled a few clips from the weapons locker and padlocked it shut again. 'The price on our heads just went up again. Shackleton's going to be more determined than ever to find us and snuff us out. But Mike just took the Co-operative's eyes out. I don't need to tell you kids how huge that is.' Reeve ejected the empty clip from his rifle and slapped in one of the new ones. 'Give me two days. Whatever we do next, we need to make it count.'

Chapter 22

A nauseating jolt shot through my body and I shuddered awake. It was dark. Everyone else still asleep.

Slowly, I registered the sound of my own breathing, hard and uneasy, like I'd just woken up from a nightmare. I reached up to rub my eyes. My face was slick with sweat. But whatever I'd been dreaming about, I couldn't remember it.

The lights in the bedroom were all off, but I could still make out the shape of Luke's body sprawled on the bed above me.

Wait. Above –?

I was on the floor. I sat up, groggy, feeling like I was missing something important. I hadn't fallen out of bed since I was Georgia's age.

Voices drifted in from over the hall and I got up to investigate, head spinning. I yawned, barely awake, ignoring the weird rumbling in the pit of my stomach. I stumbled through the open door to the surveillance room and gasped at the figure looking up from the circle of computer monitors.

'Kara!'

She didn't answer. She was too busy staring across the room.

Cathryn had just come in from the laboratory. The security feeds were all back online, and she was gazing at them, open-mouthed. *'This is how you watched us ...'* she said, taking a hesitant step towards Kara. *'It was just cameras.'*

And finally, it clicked. This wasn't happening. Not now. It was a vision. I must have slipped into it in my sleep.

The night we'd brought Cathryn and Mike down here for the first time, we'd dragged Mike straight into the laboratory so Kara could operate on his bullet-shredded hand. He'd passed out on the way downstairs without laying eyes on Kara or Soren. Even after the surgery was done, Cathryn had refused to leave his side, so we'd let her sleep in there on the other bed. Kara and Mr Hunter had taken turns keeping an eye on them so Luke and I could rest.

But now here I was again.

I felt a stab of panic as I finally woke up enough to realise the full danger I was in. Luke was still asleep. There was no-one to come for me.

I glanced out into the hall, thinking about going back to the bedroom, but what was the point? I could scream all I wanted but he still wouldn't hear me. I was too far gone. Too deep into the vision.

'Mike!' Cathryn called back through the door. 'Get in here!'

A shiver ran up my spine as Mike's terrified voice rang out from the next room. 'No. Not – not until she tells me I can.'

I watched Kara's face shift from resignation to something deeper. And I realised that *this* was the moment. This was when she'd finally started to take it in, to feel some of the weight of the damage she'd done to these guys. 'You may come in, Michael.'

I tried to tune them out and focus in on my own body – maybe somehow I could get back by myself – but my concentration shattered as Mike stepped out from the laboratory.

He edged slowly, hesitantly, into the room, holding his bandaged hand up against his chest, eyes to the ground like he still thought Kara might strike him down with thunder if he looked at her. His other hand was clenched into a fist, but it wasn't anger. It looked like he was trying to keep himself from shaking.

For a minute, I forgot about trying to get back to the present. I forgot about everything. He was right there. Still standing. No idea that he only had about two weeks left to live.

'Mike!' I shouted, knowing it was pointless but calling out anyway. 'Mike!'

He stepped straight through me, edging towards Kara. 'That letter,' he said, still refusing to lift his head. 'That – that was really from you?'

'*Yes,*' said Kara.

I let out a startled yelp as Luke suddenly appeared between Mike and me, bleary-eyed and frantic.

'Luke!' I said, grabbing at him. 'How –?'

'*It was a test,*' said Mike behind him, nodding like he understood. '*The letter. After what happened out at the lake – after we f-failed you – you had to test us to make sure we were still –*'

'*No, Michael.*' Kara's voice was steady, but I could see tears glinting in her eyes. '*It was not a test. It was the truth. We are not who we claimed to be.*'

Luke's hands crashed down against my sides. '– up and get back here!' he shouted.

I sneaked a quick glance over his shoulder. Mike hadn't moved. His fist was still clenched. His head hung there, face hidden in his ragged hair, and all at once it hit me that I had seriously underestimated just how deep Mike's obsession with the overseers had gone.

A tear ran down Kara's cheek. '*Please, Michael. Look at me. There's nothing to be afraid of. It's over.*'

But it wasn't over. Not as far as Mike was concerned. He just stood there, shaking his head.

'Jordan!' said Luke, shaking me. 'C'mon, *please* –'

'*Let me speak to him,*' said Soren behind me, slinking in from the corridor. He took Mike gently by the arm. Mike flinched, but didn't pull away. '*Let me explain the situation. I believe he will listen to me.*'

'NO!' I shouted, struggling under Luke's grip. 'No, you filthy piece of crap! Get away from –!'

A tidal wave of nausea slammed into me, knocking the words from my throat. The two timelines blended together again, and Mum and Georgia flickered into view, standing in the same place Kara was sitting in the past. One of them must have heard something and run in to get Luke. They hung there for a moment, horrified, and then the room was dashed to pieces, everything falling apart and me falling apart with it. My insides clenched, like my body was trying to turn itself inside out.

The pieces rushed back together and suddenly there was sunlight streaming down on top of me. I looked up and found myself standing at the bottom of an enormous square hole in the ground. Construction workers milled around me, drilling holes and laying concrete and scooping up the soil with heavy machinery. Building the Vattel Complex.

My knees buckled and I dropped to the ground, bringing Luke down with me. The scene shifted again and I found myself back in the surveillance room. But it wasn't a surveillance room now. Soren's dad and another man I didn't recognise were locked in a heated game of table tennis while more people in Vattel Complex jackets stood around, cheering them on.

They all disappeared in a swirl of colour and then the lights switched off around me. Darkness took over, surging through my body like it had done before, rushing into every part of me but somehow never filling me up. I shuddered, convulsed, nails digging into Luke's skin.

And then it was over. The darkness drained away and the surveillance room slowly took shape around me. The convulsing stopped. My muscles relaxed again. Luke was kneeling over me, chest heaving. He pulled me up into a crushing hug, breath hissing in my ear. I looked over his shoulder and saw Georgia crying behind him.

'Is she okay?' Mum asked desperately. 'Jordan, are you –?'

'Yeah,' I said, releasing Luke and getting to my feet. 'I'm fine. That's not the first time that's happened.'

Mum threw her arms around me, squinting as Luke switched the lights on. 'Your "fainting spell" out in the meeting room. Emily told me – but it was this, wasn't it? Jordan, what –?'

'Gross!' said Georgia, cutting her off. She'd come over to hug me too, but then stopped herself. 'Why are you all dirty?'

'Huh?' I backed off from Mum and looked down at myself.

'See?' said Georgia. 'Where did that come from?'

Yeah … I thought, stretching my arms out for a better look. *Good question.*

Every centimetre of my body was caked in a layer of crusty black mud.

'He believed it,' I said, hunched over the surveillance room table with my head in my hands. 'All the way to the end, even after everything he'd seen. He still believed in the overseers. He was totally devoted to Soren.'

'I guess we're all like that about something,' said Amy from her seat in the corner. Her bandage was off, leg almost completely healed.

'Yeah,' I sighed. 'Well, Mike picked the *wrong* something.' I sat up, feeling like pulling my hair out. 'But – why did I get the vision *now?* If I was going to see all that, why not show me two days ago when it might have made a difference?'

'Maybe it did make a difference,' said Mum, who was slumped back in a chair, watching Georgia drawing with some old crayons we'd found. 'Maybe you saw that to help you understand why he did what he did. To help all of us understand.'

'Yeah,' I said, head dropping down into my hands again. 'Maybe.'

But there were things I would have liked to understand even more than Mike's death wish. Like what Tobias was, and where the Co-operative was keeping it. And how in the world Luke was going to wind up dead twenty years in the past.

I'd finally explained to Mum about the visions. After last night, I didn't really have a choice. She'd been surprisingly calm about it all, under the circumstances. I guess when you've already got one daughter who can read minds, finding out that the other one sometimes dislodges herself in time is just the icing on the cake.

The door swung open and Luke backed into the room, carrying a tray crammed with bowls of rice.

We were running low again. According to Luke's mum, we had food enough for a few more days. Maybe a bit longer, now that –

I suppressed a shudder, disgusted at myself for the thought that losing some of our number at least meant more food for the rest of us.

In any case, with four days left until Tabitha was released, it wasn't food we were short on. It was time.

Luke went over to Mum, who sat forward and took down a couple of bowls.

'Careful, sweetheart,' she said, as Georgia abandoned her drawing and reached up to grab one of them, 'that's going to be hot.'

I stretched across the table and picked up one of Georgia's crayons. For all we knew, they might once have belonged to Dr Galton.

'Shackleton must have changed Galton's name after the adoption,' I said. 'Kara and Soren would've worked out who she was ages ago, otherwise.'

'Is that normal?' Luke asked, moving around to

pass a bowl to Amy. 'I mean, you said she was six or something, right? Bit late to be changing someone's name. And if he was going to change it, why not make her a Shackleton?'

I tossed the crayon back into the box. 'Something tells me it wasn't the only thing about the adoption that wasn't normal.'

I caught myself staring absently at the laptop in front of me, like I was expecting to see my dad wandering around in the static somewhere. We'd left the computers switched on, just in case anything changed, but it looked like Shackleton's surveillance network really was gone for good.

Two days had passed since Reeve went out to get in touch with his people. He'd taken Tank and Cathryn with him, which I think was good for everyone. In fact, with Soren and Peter still locked up in separate rooms and Bill at the other end of the complex, digging, the past couple of days had been surprisingly peaceful, apart from the incident last night.

'But, hang on,' said Luke, as his mum walked in with a jug of murky water and some glasses, 'what about Galton's crazy mind powers? If the Co-operative's known about her all along, then why were they so surprised when they found out about Bill? Why were they so unprepared when other people started changing? Surely they should've seen it coming.'

'Could Galton's abilities be more recent than that?'

asked Mum. 'What if they didn't appear until she came back here as an adult?'

'Maybe,' I said. 'Or she might have – I'm not sure. When I saw them talking, it almost seemed like Galton was hiding something from Shackleton. Like maybe *she* knew what she was capable of, but didn't want to tell him.'

'There's something else that doesn't make sense,' said Ms Hunter. 'If Dr Galton lived in this place as child – if she knows where it is – then why hasn't she led them to us already?'

'Galton couldn't have been any older than Georgia when she left here the first time,' I said. 'I don't know how much she'd even remember.'

'Plus, the Co-operative doesn't think this place exists anymore,' said Luke, sitting down. 'They think it was all abandoned and flooded with concrete twenty years ago. That's why they're all up there, searching the bush.'

In the last two days, it seemed like Shackleton had diverted a bunch more resources to scouring the bushland, trying to track us down. We'd seen more than a few guards near the entrance to the Complex. None of them had stopped or shown any sign of suspicion, but I still held my breath every time they crossed the path of Kara and Soren's security camera.

And in the meantime, what was I doing? Babysitting prisoners. Lying in bed, worrying that Peter was going to break out and kill Luke while I slept.

Sitting around eating rice while Reeve was out there getting things done.

It wasn't that I didn't trust Reeve. I did. But the waiting was driving me insane. It just didn't feel right. This was *my* fight. I wanted to be *doing* something.

'Tomorrow,' said Luke, like he was reading my mind. He leaned in, rubbing my arm. 'He's back tomorrow night. We'll come up with a plan. I'm sure you'll get the chance to do all the running and screaming you want.'

I shivered at his touch. *Four more days.*

The invasion of the Complex. Mum's baby. Luke's murder. Whatever Bill was digging for. And the end of the world. It was all coming. All of it at once.

Luke was right. I should be saving my strength. Enjoying the peace while it lasted.

If I was looking for a chance to risk my life for the cause, there was going to be no shortage of opportunities in the days to come.

Chapter 23

'We're going to have to bring Soren with us,' said Reeve.

'*No*,' I said instantly, almost shouting it. 'Reeve, he's completely unstable!'

We were back in the conference room. We'd spent the last hour thrashing out our plan to get into the Shackleton Building, which was actually shaping up to be three plans that had to be pulled off all at the same time.

Plan number one involved two of Reeve's guys, Miller and Ford, creating a distraction to keep security busy, and then heading up to the old staff cafeteria – Shackleton's loyalty room – with our sleeping gas. They were going to incapacitate the guards on duty and free the security staff's families – and they were going to film the whole thing.

Meanwhile, the rest of us would be sneaking in the back way: through the secret tunnel underneath the school. While Reeve's guys held the cafeteria, Reeve, Tank and Amy would run their footage down to the audio-visual control centre on the third floor, hijack the P.A. system and the big screen, and let every security officer in the building know we'd just taken away their reason to co-operate with Shackleton.

That left Luke and me with one job: head up to the top floor of the Shackleton Building, find Tobias and get it out to the release station.

It was our last shot, our *only* shot, at taking Shackleton down. It was risky, complicated, and the whole thing was completely reliant on our ability to work together.

No way in the world was I about to let a maniac like Soren come in and derail it all.

'Look,' said Reeve, 'I know it's not ideal, but –'

'No,' I said again. 'It's insane. *He's* insane! What could you possibly –?'

'We need someone to get past the security on the A/V computers and feed through that camera footage,' said Reeve. 'And they're going to need to do it in a hurry. So unless there's someone else here who knows how to do all that ...'

'Peter could do it,' said Cathryn.

'Right,' I said, 'because things went so brilliantly the last time you let him out.'

'What do you expect? You want him to be grateful or something? You keep him locked up like a circus animal for a whole freaking month and then he finally gets let out and the first thing he sees is this guy –' Cathryn jabbed a finger at Luke '– with his hands all over the girl he –'

Tank banged his fist down on the table. 'Both of you, shut up! We're not talking about Pete. We're talking about Soren.'

'Right,' said Luke. 'No way are we bringing Peter into this. I'm not ecstatic about the Soren option either, but if those are the choices we've got …'

'Jordan, all of this hinges on getting the word out to the guards about their families,' said Reeve. 'Soren will be with me the whole time. He'll be unarmed. I'll make sure it doesn't get out of hand.'

'He goes straight back to his room,' I said, admitting defeat. 'I don't care if he finds Tobias and saves the world single-handed. As soon as it's over, he goes back to his room and he stays there until it's over. We're not going to forget what he's done.'

'Sure, absolutely,' said Reeve.

'Wait a minute,' said Mum from the other end of the table. She was lower than the rest of us, sitting on a chair that Tank had brought in for her. 'What about everyone else in town? I realise we're doing everything we can to convince security to switch sides, but some of the guards will still be loyal to the Co-operative, won't they? Even without the threat to their families.'

'True,' said Reeve.

'Well, they're not just going to surrender. If we go ahead with this, won't we risk putting everyone else in town in the middle of a fire-fight?'

'I don't think so,' Reeve said. 'Both sides have a

vested interest in keeping the prisoners alive. They'll keep them out of it as much as possible.'

The room fell silent. And despite everything, despite Soren, despite the countless other ways this could fall apart, I felt the excitement rising inside me.

This might just work.

'All right,' I said. 'How soon can we leave?'

'Well, first Miller and Ford need to set up our little distraction out at the mall. That's no small job, and they'll be doing it right under Shackleton's nose. Still, Miller reckons they can get it done within forty-eight hours. We'll move out as soon as they're ready.'

'Forty-eight hours?' said Luke. 'That's the night before Tabitha is meant to be released! You don't think that's cutting it a bit close?'

'Yeah, mate. I do,' said Reeve. 'I realise we're down to the wire here but, look, this either works or it doesn't. We're not going to get another chance. This is it, folks. One way or another, this ends here.'

TUESDAY, AUGUST 11
2 DAYS

'How is she?' I asked, hanging the last pair of wet jeans over our makeshift clothesline just as Luke came in. Not that our clothes actually got *clean* anymore, but it didn't hurt to wring out the worst of the grime once in a while.

Luke crashed on the couch behind me. 'She's freaking out a bit. I mean, this isn't exactly within Mum's comfort zone. She'll be fine, though. She's gone into project-manager mode. She's got a job to do and she'll get it done if it kills her.' He smirked. 'Still can't believe she put her hand up in the first place, though.'

'Yeah,' I said, coming over, 'no offence to your mum, but I'm hoping this will all be over by then and Mum's baby can be delivered by an actual doctor.'

Luke pulled me in for a hug as I sat down next to him. 'Pretty sure that's what Mum's hoping for too.'

At some point in their lives, Reeve, Mum and Ms Hunter had all taken a trip to the delivery room, and between the three of them, they'd come up with a plan for how Luke's mum was going to deliver the baby if Mum went into labour while we were gone.

Part of the plan involved getting Cathryn to babysit Georgia. I wasn't totally comfortable with *that* arrangement either, but at least it would keep Cathryn away from Peter.

'Two days ...' said Luke, shaking his head. 'How did that happen?'

I curled my legs up on the couch, snuggling in closer. 'Do you even remember life before this?'

'It's so weird,' he said, playing with one of my hands. 'Like, four months ago, we were just – Everything was *normal*. I thought Mum and Dad getting divorced was the most traumatic thing that would ever happen to me. And now ...'

We sat there for a while, the familiar torn-apart feeling swelling in my stomach. Yet again, my mind returned to Kara's surveillance tape, replaying Luke's twenty-year-old murder in a grainy, black-and-white loop.

It's not going to happen, I told myself. *You're going to stop it. You'll find a way. Even if you have to keep Peter tied up and sealed away until all of this is over ...*

But even as my mind started running through ways of keeping Peter and Luke apart, I couldn't escape the feeling that it wasn't going to be that simple. Luke's murder wasn't just a thing in the future. It had already happened. I was fighting to save someone who had *already* died.

Forget about it. Forget what happened before. He's not dead. Not now. Deal with what's in front of you.

And there was Luke, right in front of me. He shifted on the couch, shot a furtive glance out the door, then leant forward, his lips closing softly on mine. His hand brushed my face, fingers slipping into the mess of my hair, and I closed my eyes, arms lacing around his, a tear running down my cheek and over his fingers, and for a moment, all the clutter and chaos in my mind seemed to fade a little.

When we finally broke apart, Luke's face was serious. 'Jordan ... You know I love you, right?'

I sat bolt upright. 'Why? I mean, yes. Yeah, I do. But why are you saying that? Why now, I mean?'

'Because,' said Luke, holding my hand, 'Jordan, we've got *two days*. I'm running out of time to –'

'No you're *not*,' I said. 'You're not. Don't talk about it like that.'

'Like what?'

'Like it's already over! Like you're just going to die and there's nothing we can do about it.'

Luke stared at our interlaced hands. 'And what if there *is* nothing we can do about it?'

'I could go down there right now and shoot him through the hole in his door,' I said. 'That would change everything.'

'Could you?' said Luke. 'How do you know he wouldn't throw you across the room with his brain again? Plus, we both know you *wouldn't* do something like that.'

'No, I know, but –'

'And what if we *can* change it? If I *don't* go back? Then what? The only reason we even know to look for Tobias is because I went back and told Kara about it. If I don't go back – I mean, if the future changes, won't that mean the past changes too? Won't that mean we never get the warning about Tobias in the first place?'

'I don't know!' I said. 'I don't know how it works. None of us do. But I'm not going to let you roll over and die just because some surveillance tape says you have to.'

'Listen,' said Luke, 'I am *more* than happy to avoid the dying part. But I can't just act like that tape doesn't exist. And anyway, you're the one who keeps saying there's a reason for all of this.' He took my hand again, his grip almost painful. 'What if you're right? If I really am here for some kind of bigger purpose or whatever … then what if this is it? What if this is what I have to do?'

Chapter 24

I couldn't sleep.

I sat alone in the surveillance room, everything dark except for the grainy glow of static from the monitors. Everyone else had gone to bed hours ago.

I should have been excited. After all this time, we were finally confronting the Co-operative head-on. But all of that was crowded by the screaming dread that churned through my insides every time I thought about –

I stood up, finally coming to a decision. I couldn't do this anymore. I wasn't just going to sit around, waiting for Peter to snap. I had to confront him. Make him understand what was going on here.

He's still a person, I told myself, turning to the bank of old computers along the wall to see what Peter was doing before I went charging in. *He's still in there somewhere. There has to be a way to get through to him.*

He was awake, standing in the middle of his room, staring out through the gap in his door.

A face stared back from the other side. Bill.

I raced back to the bedroom, grabbed the sedative pen I'd been holding onto since Kara left, and then ran all the way to Peter's room.

Bill was gone.

'Peter …?' I said hesitantly, approaching the door. The barricades were in place. He should still be –

'Jordan!' Peter's face appeared in the window and my heart skipped a beat. 'Hey, listen, I am *so* sorry about before. You know, when we were –' He dragged his hands through his hair. 'I shouldn't have – I don't want to do anything you're not comfortable with. I just thought –'

'Peter,' I said, biting down on a rush of revulsion. 'Why was Bill here? What was he saying to you?'

Peter cocked his head, like he couldn't understand why I was changing the subject. 'He was – It didn't really make sense. Like, first it was about a room or something. Something he was looking for –'

'The room he's digging to out there.'

'Digging?' said Peter, looking slightly confused. 'Yeah, okay. Yeah. He didn't tell me anything about it, though. He was just really set on making sure I knew where it was. And then the rest was like he was trying to warn me about something. "Get back faster." That's what he kept saying. "Get back faster." But then he totally veered off again, like he was arguing with himself. Just, "inevitable, inevitable," over and over again.'

Inevitable. He'd said it to us as well. That was the last word I wanted to hear right now.

He's insane, I reminded myself. *He's worse than Peter. Don't read into it.*

'Anything else?' I asked.

Peter frowned. 'No, that's it. He bolted when he heard you coming.'

I stuck Kara's sedative pen into my pocket, hoping Peter hadn't had a chance to spot it.

'Peter –' I paused, steadying myself, realising I was shaking. 'There's something I need to talk to you about. If I come in, will you promise me –?'

'Yeah,' he said eagerly. 'Of course. We don't have to do anything you don't want to do.'

I pulled the barricades away from the door and eased it open. Peter reached out to grab me, then thought better of it and sat down on the bed, looking up expectantly. I brought his chair over and sat on it.

'What did you want to talk about?' he asked, leaning forward to touch my leg.

'You care about me, don't you, Peter?' I said, gently taking his hand and lifting it away again. 'You wouldn't do anything you thought was going to hurt me.'

Peter's mouth fell open. 'No, of course I – How can you even ask that?'

I took another deep breath, forcing my voice to stay even. 'A few weeks ago, the day after we broke into the medical centre, Kara and Soren came to Luke and me with an old surveillance video from the day this place was destroyed. We don't know how, but you – you were in that video. You and Luke.'

'What do you mean?' said Peter, putting his hand on me again. 'They, like, edited us in or something?'

'No. You were *there*, Peter. This thing opened up. Some kind of – I don't know – like a portal, I guess. Luke appeared out of it. And then you came through after him, and you –' I stopped, seeing it all over again. I could feel the tears coming, but I held them off long enough to finish. 'You *killed* him, Peter.'

Peter didn't respond. If anything I'd said had reached his brain, it didn't register on his face.

'Did you hear me?' I shouted. 'I said you killed him! You stabbed Luke through the chest and you left him back there to bleed to death!'

I buried my face in my hands, breath coming in gasps, suddenly overwhelmed with the weight of it all. In a few seconds, I was sobbing openly.

And still, Peter kept silent.

'Please,' I said, looking up again, hardly getting the words out. '*Please*, Peter. Don't do it. Don't hurt him. If you really care about me – If you really –'

'Why him?' he asked, voice low.

'What?'

'Why Luke and not me?'

I brushed the tears out of my eyes. 'Peter ...'

'It's not like you didn't know how I felt,' he said coldly. 'Admit it. I had you first. And then Luke came and –'

'That's not how it works!' I said, standing up. 'You don't get to call shotgun and then act like you own me!'

'Like it was all me!' Peter jumped up too, eyes flaring. 'You think I didn't see how cut you got when you saw Cathryn kissing me, back at school? You think I missed all of your –?'

'All of my *what?* Peter, in case you've forgotten, Cathryn was trying to kidnap you!'

Peter balled up his fists, growling in frustration. The chair I'd been sitting on bounced up and smashed into the wall behind me. *'He's not even supposed to be here!'*

'Stop!' I said, backing off. 'Please, just listen to me. Hurting Luke is not going to fix anything!'

'He took you,' said Peter, advancing on me. 'We were *fine* without him, but he –!'

'No, he didn't!' I shouted. 'None of this is his fault! If you want to blame someone, blame me. But if you do anything to him, you can forget about me ever even speaking to you again. Understand me? I will *never* –'

'You will!' Peter grabbed hold of my arms, fingers digging into me. 'I won't let you leave me!'

He started shoving me towards the bed. I jerked one arm free and ripped the sedative pen out of my pocket. Peter thrust his hand out to grab me again but I knocked it aside, lunging forward and jamming the sedative into his leg.

Peter reeled away, howling, and I got shakily back to my feet, tears still flooding down my face.

'YOU CAN'T DO THIS!' he screamed, coming after me again, unsteadier now as the sedative kicked in. 'You can't just walk away like nothing ever –'

I sidestepped him and he fell down against the bed. He barked out a string of obscenities and wheeled around again, diving at me, grabbing my leg. I kicked him off and he collapsed on the ground, cursing some more. He rolled, trying to get up again, but his body wouldn't co-operate.

I stood there, watching Peter until his body gave out completely, reeling at the realisation that I'd just made everything much, much worse.

The door creaked behind me and I whirled around.

Bill was standing just outside, staring down at Peter's unconscious form. His eyes drifted up to meet mine.

'You're too late,' he said, with a hideous smile. 'Both of you. It has already happened. All of it. It will happen again. All of this – All of this is inevitable.'

Chapter 25

Mum groaned, gripping the sides of the mattress, eyes squeezing shut. The sound echoed off the laboratory walls. It was happening. Right now. Right as we were leaving.

My mind kept circling around my vision from a few weeks ago of security storming into the Complex, but what was I supposed to do about it? There was no way Mum was giving birth down in the panic room.

Georgia was in my arms, clinging to me, staring at Mum with a look of terror on her face. I hugged her back, not much calmer than she was.

Mum looked over from the bed as the contraction passed, obviously struggling to keep us in focus. 'It's okay, sweetheart. Mummy's fine.' She took a couple of heavy breaths, and her eyes fluttered shut.

I felt a jolt of panic. 'Mum?'

'That's normal,' said Reeve, coming in from the surveillance room, rifle hanging from his shoulder. 'The drowsiness. My wife did the same thing when she was in labour with Lachlan.'

'She's three months pregnant with a full-term baby!' I said. 'Like we have any idea what "normal" is!'

Georgia whimpered, fingers clawing my back.

'Sorry,' I whispered. 'I didn't mean to yell. Mum's fine. She's fine.'

'You're scared too,' said Georgia accusingly.

'Yeah,' I said. 'Yeah, I am. We're all a bit scared. But everything's going to be okay.'

Luke and his mum bustled into the room, lugging the old bathtub we used for laundry, splashing hot water onto the floor. They set it down beside the bed.

'Okay,' said Luke's mum frantically, smoothing down her hair. 'Okay, I think that's everything.'

Luke put an arm around her. 'Breathe, Mum. You're doing –'

But then her head snapped up. 'Towels!' She ran out of the room, almost bowling Cathryn over as she and Tank arrived from the hall.

Tank had the other rifle slung over his shoulder. It made me kind of uncomfortable, but I trusted him not to do anything Reeve didn't order him to do. Better Tank than Soren.

Cathryn came over and held out her hands to take Georgia from me.

'All right, Georgia,' I said, trying to ease her off me, 'Cathryn's going to look after you while I go up to –'

Mum jerked in the bed, wide awake again as the next contraction hit. She let out another groan and Georgia seized hold of me again. 'No, you're not going!'

'Georgia –'

'Hey,' said Luke, coming up behind me and brushing a hand over Georgia's hair. 'It's all right. I'll look after Jordan for you. I'll make sure she's okay. Hey, have you got any paper left for your crayons?'

Georgia looked up. 'It's on my bed.'

'Well, how about you and Cathryn go and draw a picture for the new baby?' he said. 'You can show it to Jordan and me when we get back.'

Georgia thought about it for a minute, then nodded and relaxed her grip on me. I gave her one last hug and passed her over to Cathryn.

'Thanks,' I said, turning back to Luke.

He shrugged and went to say goodbye to his mum as she raced back in with a stack of almost-clean towels.

'Where's Amy?' asked Reeve.

Cathryn glanced over her shoulder. 'Bathroom.'

'Is she peeing or throwing up?' asked Tank.

'You're disgusting,' said Cathryn, pulling a face. But then she put her free arm around him and stretched up to kiss his cheek. 'Be safe, okay?'

'Yeah,' he said, patting her on the back.

Cathryn took Georgia out of the room, and I went across to Mum's bed. She had her head on the pillow now, catching her breath between contractions. I bent down and kissed her cheek. 'See you soon.'

Mum wrapped her arms around me. 'Love you, Jordan. *Please* look after each other out there.'

'We will,' I said. 'I love you too.'

I grabbed Ms Hunter as she bustled past again. 'Remember, first sign of movement outside –'

'Panic room,' she finished, glancing uneasily at Mum. 'But, Jordan, how exactly –?'

'Just make it happen,' I said. 'Please.' I crossed to the bed again, just as Amy appeared in the doorway.

'Sorry,' she said, wiping her mouth. 'Ready.'

Reeve did a quick head count. We just had to pick Soren up on the way through and we'd be ready to go. Reeve's fingers snaked around the grips of his rifle.

'Right,' he said. 'Let's go save the world.'

Chapter 26

'I am not going back,' Soren muttered as we climbed in over the back fence of the school. 'After tonight, you are all going to owe me your lives. You are not making me a prisoner again.'

'Shut up,' said Tank, shoving him. Soren went sprawling to the grass on the other side of the fence. His hands shot to his lower back, like he'd landed on something hard, but I couldn't see what it was in the darkness.

It was almost 10.30 p.m. Only a few minutes until Miller and Ford pulled the pin on their diversion in town.

This was it. The end. By this time tomorrow, it would all be over – either for the Co-operative or for everyone else. And here we were, fighting each other in the school playground.

'Get up,' I said, nudging Soren roughly with my foot. He stood up and rounded on Tank and me, looking like he'd really love to start something with him, but then Reeve stepped in between them and Soren backed off.

We crept out towards the front office, sticking close to the shadows of the buildings. The security lighting was still on all over the school, shooting spotlights through the cold drizzle drifting down from the sky.

It was so bizarre. Like visiting an old house you used to live in as a kid.

The last time we'd been here, the whole place was packed with students. Normal teenagers grinding through normal school days, blindly going about their lives like the biggest hassle in this town was a curfew or a blood test. We'd spent weeks wishing everyone would wake up and realise what was really going on.

This wasn't exactly what we'd had in mind.

Reeve slipped out from the end of the English block and swept his rifle around through shadows. He waved at us to follow and we darted across the quad to the admin building. Amy flitted in circles around us, burning off nervous energy.

'Well, this is familiar,' I whispered, peering through the glass door into the front office. It felt like almost an exact replay of our last trip up to the Shackleton Building, right down to the weather.

There was a second set of glass doors on the far side of the room. I could see all the way out to the main street. The mall was directly opposite us, completely intact – at least for the moment.

Luke came up next to me and squeezed my hand.

It was cold and slick with the rain. I breathed out, fogging the glass in front of me.

Any second now …

My thoughts went back to Mum. Her contractions had started just after lunch today and for a while, I'd been holding out hope it would all be over before we had to leave, but apparently these things take longer in real life than they do in the movies.

At least Peter wasn't going to be a problem. I'd gone back this morning while he was still unconscious and tied him facedown to his bed. Then I'd got Luke to help me lug a big chunk of concrete in front of his door. Even if Cathryn was stupid enough to come looking for him again, there was no way she'd be able to –

BOOM!

The sliding doors of the mall blasted apart, sending bits of glass and metal raining down over the street. Distant shouts rang out from the Shackleton Building.

Time to go.

'Out of the way, kids,' said Reeve, bringing his rifle up over his shoulder. He drove the butt of the weapon into the door, smashing through the panel at the bottom and stepping through. I ducked in after him and dashed to the front doors, eyes landing on the big glass dome of the food court.

That first detonation was just a warning. A chance for anyone in the exercise area to run for cover before –

'Jordan, get back!' Reeve shouted.

BOOM!

The noise was incredible, even bigger than the security centre. An enormous ball of flame erupted inside the dome, lighting up the whole street. The glass shattered, exploding outward in all directions, and then it was swallowed up in roiling black smoke.

Everything shook. I staggered back, momentarily blinded. Loud *thunks* split the air as debris hammered down on the office roof.

Amy raced up, screaming. *'Jordan!'*

Reeve dragged us to the ground as a big hunk of something smashed in through the front door. Half a food court table. It bounced off the back wall, flames licking up the sides, curling the plastic veneer. Any second now, that fire was going to spread to the carpet.

'Go!' shrieked Soren. 'Run!'

'No, wait, they haven't –'

BOOM!

Light flashed in my peripheral vision as a third and final explosion shook the hallway off to our left, much smaller but deafeningly close. Smoke billowed in the hall and a heavy *thud* signalled that the door to the principal's office had just been successfully removed from its hinges.

Outside, the rumble of skid engines rose up over the shouting and snapping of flames.

'C'mon!' I said, staggering up the hallway, feet crunching on broken glass. Through the smoke and plaster dust I saw more wreckage burning at the far end of the hall, flames splaying out across the ceiling.

I stopped outside Pryor's office, glancing back to make sure we were all still here, and almost tripped over the heavy steel door at my feet.

'Hurry!' said Reeve, clambering after me. 'In a few minutes, this whole place is going to be burning too.'

We piled into the room. Reeve heaved the door aside. As soon as it was out of the way, Luke crouched and started rolling Pryor's ornate antique rug back from the floor, while I darted behind her desk to the giant tapestry that hung on the back wall. I pushed the tapestry aside and flicked the two switches on the power outlet underneath. A hiss of compressed air cut through the room as a metre-squared section of Pryor's floor slipped away into the ground.

'This was here the whole time?' said Amy, staring at the shining silver stairs leading down into the ground.

'Thieves,' said Soren under his breath.

'Okay,' I said, pushing past him and leading the way into the tunnels, 'this is where it really gets interesting.'

Chapter 27

The trapdoor hissed shut above our heads, sealing us off from the chaos outside.

The six of us were squished into a tiny, silver-walled room, maybe half as big as Pryor's office. Reeve moved up to the far end and opened the door on a narrow, brightly-lit tunnel. He turned to Tank. 'You mind watching our backs?'

Tank hung at the rear while Reeve went ahead. I shivered, remembering the way our last trip down here had ended: Reeve 'dead' and the rest of us stabbed with tracking devices.

The tunnel was a direct line to a big underground bunker at the base of the Shackleton Building. It was the only way to access the lift to the top level, short of strolling in through the front doors.

'Those things are all off, right?' said Amy after a minute, glancing at the security cameras that peered down from the ceiling every few metres.

'Should be,' I said. 'I assume they were hooked up to the same network as the ones outside.'

'You *assume?*' said Amy.

'Shh!' said Luke. 'Almost there.'

Reeve slowed as we approached the foot-thick metal door at the end of the tunnel. The last time we'd come down here, it had opened automatically. But I guess the Co-operative were feeling a bit more cautious these days. The door stayed closed. No handle. No anything.

'Crap,' said Luke.

Fire behind us. A locked door in front of us.

We were not off to a good start.

'Everyone quiet,' said Reeve. He stepped up and pounded the door with his fist.

There was a moment's silence, then: 'Yes? Who's there?'

I recognised the voice. It was Aaron Ketterley, Phoenix's 'residential liaison', the man who'd shown my family and me around town when we first arrived. He might have been a really nice guy if he wasn't trying to help exterminate humanity.

'Sir,' said Reeve, deepening his voice slightly. 'Officer Tracey here. We've had some hostile activity up above ground, and –'

'We're aware of that, Mr Tracey,' said a second voice I couldn't place.

'Yes, sir,' said Reeve. 'The chief sent me to make sure everything's okay down here.'

'We're fine,' said Ketterley. 'Thank you.'

'Sir, the chief's orders are for me to get a visual on the two of you to confirm that you aren't being –'

A booming, clattering sound filled the tunnel as the door in front of us slowly shuddered open. 'Mr Tracey,' grumbled the second man, 'you can thank Officer Barnett for his diligence, however –' He stopped short. It was Benjamin More, Shackleton's vice president.

'Down on the ground,' Reeve ordered.

More edged backwards. 'You.'

'Yeah,' said Reeve. 'Down on the ground.'

'Officer Reeve,' said Ketterley bracingly, 'I understand that these past few months have been traumatic for you, but you need to realise that hurting us is only going to –' His moustache twitched and he threw his hands in front of him. 'Who's that? What is he –?'

Soren shoved his way forward, knocking me into the wall. He reached under his jumper, pulling something from the back of his jeans, and –

BLAM! BLAM! BLAM! BLAM!

Ketterley and More dropped to the ground, blood trickling from the holes in their heads.

I stumbled back, mouth open, air disappearing from my lungs. Luke caught me and hoisted me to my feet.

'Oh my goodness …' Amy shuddered behind me.

Soren stood frozen in the doorway, arm straight out in front of him, pistol clenched in his fist. He must have taken it from the armoury and hidden it in his room somewhere.

'Give it to me,' I said, recovering myself, grabbing at Soren's arm.

He whirled around, pointing the gun back at the rest of us. 'No.'

'Soren –!'

BLAM!

I ducked to the ground as he fired again. Luke cried out behind me. I whirled around, but he was still standing. The shot had been fired at the ceiling above our heads.

'*What are you DOING?*' I roared, heart thundering.

Soren's hands shook. He brought the gun back down. 'Step back! I will not be –'

Reeve launched himself forward, throwing a fist into Soren's jaw. He grabbed Soren's arm and slammed him into the wall, pinning his face against the gleaming metal.

'Get to the lift,' he told the rest of us, wrenching the pistol from Soren's fingers. 'We're not the only ones who heard all that.'

Soren cursed furiously, but didn't try to take the weapon back.

We ran through the bunker, stepping around the bodies on the floor.

More death.

More stupid, senseless murder.

He might've just taken care of two our greatest enemies, but still, I couldn't muster anything but disgust for what Soren had done.

The bunker was one big round room, stocked with everything Shackleton and his underlings needed to stay alive and unharmed in case of an emergency. And

I guess the current situation qualified, because most of the beds off to our right were unmade and surrounded by bags of clothes and supplies.

'Oi! What are you doing?' said Tank.

I looked over my shoulder and saw Luke stooped over Ketterley, reaching a hand into his pocket, a nauseated look on his face. He pulled something out and tossed it to me. It was Ketterley's phone.

Luke took More's phone too and gave it to Reeve, who was already waiting at the lift. 'Here. In case we need to talk to each other.'

The words were barely out of his mouth when More's phone started vibrating in Reeve's hand. His eyes widened. He held up the phone, showing us the caller ID. *Bruce Calvin.* Wherever the chief had disappeared to these past few weeks, apparently he was back.

'What the crap?' said Tank, mesmerised by the phone. 'Those things actually work?'

'They can only call each other,' I said. 'The only way they can reach the outside is if ...'

'What?' said Tank.

'External Communications,' Luke said. 'The room up on the top level.'

The lift doors slid open.

'Right,' said Reeve, stepping inside. 'Bit late for a rescue party now, though.' He stopped halfway through the doors, catching himself. 'Besides Kara and your dad, I mean. I'm sure they're still –'

'Yeah,' said Luke.

Reeve was right. Tobias was still our best hope at saving the world.

There were two lifts in the Shackleton Building: one that moved between the five floors that the public was allowed to know about, and this one, a direct line from the basement to the executive offices and the secret top floor above them.

We squeezed in after Reeve, and Luke hit a button on the wall, sending the lift trundling upwards.

'Here,' said Reeve, handing Soren's pistol over to Luke.

Luke cringed. 'I don't –'

'Just in case.'

Soren scowled at him.

The lift came to a stop at the pretend-top floor of this place, and the doors opened onto an empty room, even smaller than the lift itself.

'This is us,' said Reeve, stepping out and pulling open a steel door like the one at Pryor's office.

There was a guard standing on the other side.

He wheeled around at the sound of the door opening, hoisting his weapon up in front of him. 'Whoa, whoa, whoa –' He broke off. It was Officer Hamilton, the guy from back at the graveyard. 'Matt?'

'Ethan,' said Reeve, raising his own rifle. 'Listen, Miller and Ford are downstairs right now, taking control of the loyalty room. In about five minutes, you're going to have a fight on your hands. You need to choose a side. Now.'

Hamilton hesitated.

'Come on, Ethan,' said Reeve. 'I know you want to do the right thing.'

Hamilton held out for a moment longer, then lowered his weapon. Reeve patted him on the arm. 'Good on you, mate.' He turned to the others. 'This way, kids.' He led them away down the hall, leaving Luke and me alone in the lift.

Luke hit another button and we started rising again. He looked at the pistol in his hands. His eyes flickered around the floor of the lift, like he was looking for somewhere to get rid of it, but in the end he stuck it into the back of his pants the same way Soren had done.

'Remember,' he said, as the lift slowed again, 'no dying.'

'Neither of us is dying,' I said. 'Not tonight.'

The doors slid open and we walked out into the darkness on the other side.

Chapter 28

As soon as we stepped clear of the lift, a series of loud *clunks* beat down from the ceiling as the automated lights came on.

Luke tensed for a second, then relaxed again. 'Forgot about that.'

'It's good,' I said. 'Means we're alone.'

But it surely wouldn't be more than a few minutes before security realised we were up here.

On first glance, Shackleton's secret top floor could have been just another ordinary office building. A big open-plan central workspace – computers, desks, filing cabinets – with five doors leading away to other, smaller rooms. Nothing here that looked like it could stop the end of humanity.

Orange light flickered in the sky outside. I crossed to the edge of the room, where giant windows ran from floor to ceiling. One-way glass, like the rest of the building.

The mall was still blazing. Bits of the food court were scattered across the street, smouldering like campfires. A big slab of concrete had torn through the fence at the foot of the Shackleton Building, obliterating the fountain, but if any of the prisoners had escaped, they were long gone. I twisted around, pressing my face up against the glass. It was hard to get a good look at the school from this angle, but I was pretty sure the admin building was burning too.

A dozen or so security officers swarmed around the town centre, but it would be a while before they had the fire under control. In the meantime, that was a dozen fewer guards keeping an eye on things in the Shackleton Building.

'We should split up,' I said, turning around again. 'You take the main office, I'll –'

I froze. Luke was gone.

I jumped at the sound of a door opening, and he emerged from one of the side rooms.

'It's empty,' he said in a hollow voice.

He'd gone straight to the *External Communications* room. I went over to join him. The whole place had been gutted. Nothing left but a little hole in the wall with a cable hanging out where the computer used to be hooked up.

I guessed the Co-operative had moved the equipment somewhere else after we discovered it the first time. That or they were just past needing it. If all went to plan, by this time tomorrow there'd be no-one left to answer the phone.

'Reeve's right,' I said, turning away. 'If help's coming, it's already on its way. Come on, let's – hey. That's new.'

A monitor had been mounted to the wall across from us, back over near the entrance to the lift. The monitor showed two digital clocks counting down in unison:

Final Lockdown Procedures
00:00:06:24
Tabitha Release
00:18:06:24

'Final lockdown procedures?' said Luke. 'What's more locked down than a concentration camp?'

But it was the second countdown that had my attention. 'Eighteen hours,' I murmured. We'd been doing that countdown in our heads for months now, but there was something about seeing it up there on the screen in stark white numbers that made it seem so much more imminent.

This was all really happening.

'Five o'clock tomorrow afternoon,' said Luke. 'A hundred days after Mum and I landed.'

'Better get to work, then,' I said, tearing my eyes away, annoyed at being so easily distracted. 'I'm gonna check some of these rooms we didn't get to last time.'

Luke nodded and sat down at the nearest computer.

I moved to the next door over: *Research Centre*.

More lights clunked on as I went into a short corridor that had three gleaming silver doors spaced out along the opposite wall. Alongside each door was a bank of monitors, all switched off. The whole setup made me feel vaguely uneasy. *Get a grip,* I told myself, pushing the first door open. *It's probably just –*

I recoiled, almost falling over.

It was Dr Galton's testing room. The one from the DVD Bill had slipped us, way back in the beginning. The place where those two unsuspecting construction workers (and who knew how many others) had spent their last terrified moments before Tabitha tore them apart.

I forced myself to stay long enough to check the other two rooms – exact copies of the first – then backed out of the corridor and slammed the door, skin crawling like I'd been infected with something.

'What's up?' asked Luke, glancing up.

'Nothing,' I said, cold shivers shooting up my spine. 'Find anything?'

He sighed, typing something else into the computer. 'Not yet.'

I kept going, shaking off the rush of nerves. This was no time for a breakdown.

In the corner of the room was a door marked *Roof Access.* I tried the handle, but the door wouldn't budge. Funny that *that* was the one they bothered locking.

Not like they'll be keeping Tobias up on the roof, anyway.

But how did I know? What was I expecting? A shiny little box with *Tobias* stamped on the front?

You'll know it when you see it, I thought, pushing

on. *You didn't come all this way just to end the night empty-handed.*

The next door was the conference room Shackleton and Calvin had dragged us into when they caught us up here last time. Nothing useful.

I pulled the door closed again. Luke had given up on the computer and was flipping through a filing cabinet next to one of the desks.

His head jerked up as a burst of gunfire rang out from somewhere downstairs. It sounded like things weren't going to plan for Reeve and the others either.

Luke slammed the filing cabinet shut. He started circling the desks, more and more frantic, not even looking properly, just scattering stuff across the floor.

'Luke,' I said, 'slow down. You're going to –'

'What if it's not even up here?' he snapped. 'I mean, what are we basing this on anyway? *Rumours* from security. How do we even know they're –?'

'Stop. It's here, okay? It's got to be. Just keep looking.'

Luke grabbed the back of a chair, fighting to calm himself. 'Yeah. Sorry.'

But *where* was it? As much as I didn't want to admit it, we were running out of places and time to look.

I left Luke rattling through a row of cupboards and went into the last unexplored side room. *Medical Analysis.*

More sensor lights flashed on, but not just from the ceiling this time. The walls flickered to life as well, revealing a sprawling grid of grey and white transparencies.

X-rays.

My feet echoed on the tiled floor as I took in the glowing images of arms and legs and heads, all labelled and grouped together by name.

Watson, Thomas, Reeve, Park, Lewis, Kennedy, Burke, Burke, Anderson, and a set labelled *Unidentified,* which I assumed belonged to Bill. Everyone who'd been dragged down under the medical centre by the Co-operative.

Mum and Amy had told us as much as they could about their time down there, but the reality was that they'd spent most of it locked up in their communal sleeping area or knocked out in the labs. Who knew what Montag and Galton were doing with them while they were unconscious?

After all the X-rays came some brain scans. There were only two sets, and my breath caught in my throat when I read the names.

Georgia Burke and *Bruce Calvin.* Side by side, like they'd been trying to compare their brains.

I turned away, revolted, and a monitor in the centre of the room caught my eye. It seemed to be running some kind of scan.

J_Thomas_Tissue_Modification_Treatment_4-3-1 Analysis: 51% Complete

'J. Thomas' was Jeremy, a Year 7 kid from school. Out of all the weird abilities that had resulted from the fallout, Jeremy's habit of imprinting his skin tone onto anyone he touched was probably the most useless. But it was enough to have him hauled off to the medical centre along with all the others. As far as we knew, he was still down there.

I stared at my right hand, at the place where he'd marked me with his fingertips back at school. The discolouration had faded by now, but –

Enough, I ordered myself, starting back towards the door. *This isn't what you're here for.* The best thing I could do for Jeremy and the others now was to hurry up and find –

I stopped moving, taking in a set of pictures across the room that I hadn't noticed before.

Ultrasound images. Pictures of Mum's baby lined up in neat rows, dated from the time Dr Montag first discovered the pregnancy right up until the day before we'd freed Mum.

I stepped closer to the wall, tracing a hand over the timeline of this tiny life. 'We're going to get you out,' I whispered, tears stinging my eyes. 'You are *not* getting dragged into this –'

'Jordan!' Luke shouted from outside. 'Get out here.'

'What? What is it?' I asked, snapping out of it and sprinting back into the main office. 'Did you find –?'

I grabbed the doorframe to bring myself to a stop. The lift doors had just slid open again.

Mr Shackleton stood on the threshold.

'Ah,' he smiled, like he couldn't be happier to see us. 'I was wondering when the two of you might pay me another visit.'

Chapter 29

'Stop!' said Luke, pulling Soren's pistol from the back of his jeans and levelling it at Shackleton. 'Stay there. Stay where you are.'

Shackleton raised his hands into the air, opening his mouth in a caricature of fear, then smiled again and lowered them to his sides. 'Come now, Luke. Do you really think yourself capable of that?'

'Where is it?' I demanded, charging over. 'Where's Tobias?'

Shackleton eyed me curiously. 'Tobias who?'

I slammed him into the wall, smashing his head into the countdown monitor behind him. 'Listen,' I said, shaking. 'It's over, okay? We've got the cafeteria. And any minute now, every guard in the building is going to know it. So either you tell us where you're keeping Tobias, or –'

I stopped as another round of gunfire echoed up through the floor. Was that our guys protecting the cafeteria? Had they even got that far?

Shackleton raised an eyebrow.

How much did he know? Clearly he hadn't come looking for us, or he would have brought security.

Shackleton reached up and touched the back of his head. It came back glistening with blood. 'I assure you, there is no Tobias here – as you seem well on your way to discovering,' he added dryly, casting an eye over the mess Luke had made. 'However, if you would like to discuss the matter further, the conference room might be a more suitable place to –'

'No,' I said, a desperate plan forming in my head. 'Luke, see if you can find some rope or something.'

'How is your mother?' Shackleton asked as Luke took off, like we were just catching up over lunch. 'The poor dear. It can't be easy, out there on the run in her condition. It really would have been much kinder to –'

I punched him in the stomach. 'Shut up.'

Shackleton coughed, a tear trickling from one eye. He smelled like old man's cologne.

'And your sister?' he said, recovering. A smile crossed his face. 'Precocious little monster. She gave Dr Galton quite a time until I suggested –'

More noise from outside cut him short. Not gunfire this time. These were deep whirring and clunking sounds, like heavy machinery warming up. The sound was coming from above us.

On the screen behind Shackleton, *Final Lockdown Procedures* had ticked down to zero.

'What's going on out there?' asked Luke, rushing back to us. He tossed me an extension cord.

'Well?' I said, giving Shackleton another shove.

His smile spread wider, exposing perfect teeth.

'Fine,' I said, spinning him around and mashing that stupid smile into the wall. 'You can tell us when we get outside.'

'Wait – what?' said Luke.

Luke held Shackleton's arms in place while I tied them together with the extension cord. 'Jordan, what are we doing?' Luke asked warily, as if he knew he wouldn't like the answer.

'We're taking him with us,' I said.

Luke shook his head wearily. 'Of course we are.'

'We can't stay here. And I'm not leaving him. Either he tells us where Tobias is or we use him as bait so that someone else will.' I shoved Shackleton's watch up his arm and pulled hard on the ends of the cord. 'Done. Let's go.'

Luke brought Soren's pistol out again, although I think it was pretty clear that we weren't going to use it. Shackleton didn't struggle at all as I dragged him back from the wall and shoved him inside the lift. His confidence unsettled me a bit, but I guess that was the point.

I hit the button to take us down to the bunker. The doors slid closed.

'You're remembering the fire, right?' said Luke.

'Plenty of other tunnels,' I said, mind ticking over the options. 'We can get out through Ketterley's office. Nice and close to the bush.'

'Your attention, please,' said a voice over the P.A. My heart leapt as I realised who it was. *'Repeat: Your attention please, all security staff. This is Matthew Reeve speaking. If you turn your attention to the video screen in the town hall, you will see footage, captured only a few minutes ago, recording the liberation of the Shackleton Building's cafeteria.'*

Shackleton's face registered only the slightest flicker of concern before returning to its normal wide-eyed amusement.

'The threat to your loved ones has been neutralised,' Reeve continued. *'I invite you to join us in taking up arms against the leadership of this town.'*

Reeve kept going, giving more instructions to anyone who wanted to join him and pleading with the rest of the town to stay calm and keep out of the fighting, but something else shoved its way to the front of my mind, distracting me from his speech.

Our lift wasn't moving.

I punched the button again. Nothing happened.

Shackleton frowned. 'Perhaps your escape won't be as easy as you'd hoped.'

I shoved him again and hit the other button, the one leading down to what everyone else thought was the top floor of this place.

The lift slid downwards. In a few seconds, we came to a stop again, doors opening on the tiny room Reeve and the others had left through before. The entryway to the main office complex. The fire-fight downstairs now seemed a whole lot louder.

'Now what?' said Luke. 'We can't exactly –'

'I know,' I said. 'Looks like we'll just have to take him out the front door.'

Chapter 30

I pushed Shackleton through the little room and out into a corridor lined with offices, heading for the other lift, the one that would take us down to the ground floor. Abstract artworks hung along the walls on either side. Shackleton sighed wistfully at them as we passed. 'I hardly ever seem to have time for my painting anymore.'

We reached the far end of the corridor. Luke hit the button on the wall and we waited for the lift to arrive. Shackleton started humming to himself.

Luke glared at him. 'Stop that.'

The lift finally arrived, and we got inside. Reeve's speech over the intercom had ended, but the machinery or whatever it was on the roof was still clunking away above our heads.

As we started moving again I realised the button for the floor below ours was lit up too. I glanced at Luke. 'Was that you?'

Luke shook his head. He raised Soren's pistol again. I dragged Shackleton around. They wouldn't shoot if he was —

The lift stopped and the doors slid open on another office level. Gunfire blazed just out of sight. There was a rush of movement, and the first thing my eyes landed on was another weapon.

'Whoa, hey, stop!' said Luke. 'Stop! It's us!'

I got a second look and realised who they were. Amy blurred into the lift, followed by Soren, who'd somehow managed to get his hands on another rifle.

'Close it! Close it!' shouted Amy, spinning in a circle.

A guard appeared at the far end of the room, spotting us just as the doors began to slide shut. He opened fire, and I dived sideways, dragging Shackleton with me. Bullets pelted the other side of the lift.

And then we were moving again. On our way to the ground floor.

Soren raised his rifle at Shackleton's chest. Shackleton flinched, backing into me, seeing straight away that Soren wasn't playing by the same rules as the rest of us.

'Wait – no!' I said. 'We need him!'

'Where's Tobias?' Amy asked us.

'Not up there,' said Luke. 'At least –'

'That's why we've got Shackleton!' I said, eyes still on Soren. 'We need to get him out so we can question him.'

Soren relaxed his grip on the trigger but kept the weapon right where it was.

Shackleton straightened, the veneer of calm back up. He nodded at Soren, tugging slightly against my grip. 'I don't believe we've been introduced.'

Soren sneered.

The lift stopped again and we peered out across the enormous Shackleton Building foyer. As far as I could see, it was completely empty. Abandoned in a hurry when the explosions started going off outside. Food sitting uneaten on tables. Toilet doors hanging open. Water still running in one of the portable showers.

I balled up the end of Shackleton's tie and shoved it into his mouth. 'Keep quiet.'

'Where are the others?' Luke whispered.

'Busy,' said Soren.

'Doing what?'

'Tank went back to help defend the cafeteria,' said Amy, still jittering. 'Reeve is – somewhere. We got separated, getting out of the A/V place.'

The sound of weapons fire was almost constant now, but it looked like the fighting was contained to the floors above us for the time being. The entrances to the town hall were all closed, and I could hear shouting coming from inside, but no guns. At least, not yet. We moved out past the doors and I slowed to the back of the group. Dad was in there somewhere. He'd be able to help us if –

'No,' said Luke, pulling on my arm. 'We can't. We have to get out of here.'

I gave it up.

I pointed through the front doors at the exercise area. A hunk of wreckage from the mall had punched a hole through the razor-wire fence. 'There's our way out. Straight through there, and then follow me.'

Surprisingly, Soren didn't argue about the following part. I peered out and then sprinted at the automatic doors, dragging Shackleton with me. I half expected the doors to be locked, but they sprang open and a gust of scorching air blew in from the street. Luke grabbed Shackleton's other side, and we dragged him down the front steps of the Shackleton Building. Out into the heat and the haze and the rubble.

We veered towards the gap in the fence, dodging the debris underfoot. Security were still way across the street and I was hoping they'd all be too caught up in fighting the fire to notice us slipping out.

I squeezed through the hole and then turned to pull Shackleton through. He winced as a bit of the fence dug into his back.

'This way,' I hissed when we were all out, and we darted up the bike path between the Shackleton Building and what was left of the security centre.

I glanced back. It didn't look like anyone had followed us. And between the fire and the mutiny, I doubted there'd be any guards left on patrol out here.

Shackleton spat the tie out of his mouth. 'I believe you were wondering about the source of that noise earlier?'

I followed his gaze to the top of the Shackleton Building. A thick black pillar was slowly stretching up from the centre of the roof, ten metres tall and still growing. An antenna or something. It made the whole building look like a giant walkie-talkie.

'What is it?' I asked.

Shackleton smiled. 'Just a bit of extra protection. It would be a terrible shame if all our efforts came to nothing at this late stage.'

'Yeah, wouldn't that be a hassle?' I said, shoving him forward again. Whatever that antenna thing was for, I knew we'd find out about it soon enough.

We continued up the street, between the rows of abandoned houses, keeping to the shadows. My mind was racing, trying to work out what to do next. Taking Shackleton back to the Complex would be a mistake.

'In here,' I said, opening the front gate of one of the houses.

We ran up the verandah steps. Soren smashed his rifle through the frosted glass of the front door. He reached through to the other side, unlocked the door and let us in.

I'd never set foot in this house before. I had no idea who it had even belonged to. But it could just as easily have been mine, or Luke's, or Peter's, or any other house in Phoenix, and all of those memories rushed at me as I stepped through the door. My parents sitting me down and telling me Mum was pregnant, Peter tackling a guard down the stairs, Luke sleeping up on the landing, Mum and Georgia getting dragged away at gunpoint … It was like the whole of the last hundred days was converging into this single moment.

I brought Shackleton through to the lounge room and threw him down on a couch. Soren stood over him, rifle trained on his chest, while Amy zoomed across to the window to keep watch. Luke closed the front door behind us, then came in and sat on the other couch. 'What now?'

I folded my arms, staring down at Shackleton, the ultimate cause of all the suffering we'd been through, tied up at gunpoint on the couch in front of me. 'Now we get some answers.'

Chapter 31

'You're the one behind the attack on my security centre,' said Shackleton, fixing Soren with a penetrating stare. 'Aren't you?'

Soren's eyes shifted from me to Luke, like one of us must have told him.

'I must say, that whole business was quite a mystery to me. I knew none of your fellow insurgents had such violence in them.' The smile returned to Shackleton's lips. 'But *you* ...'

I pushed between them, grabbing Shackleton by the front of his jacket. 'Enough!' I snapped. 'What's Tobias and how do we get it to the release station?'

'Now, that's interesting,' said Shackleton, still infuriatingly calm. 'What has led you to believe that you need to take something out to the release station?'

I threw him back down against the couch. 'Answer the question! What's Tobias?'

Shackleton furrowed his brow, a look of genuine curiosity on his face. Then his eyes lit up and he burst out laughing.

'*Answer her!*' Soren demanded, pushing past and poking the end of his rifle into Shackleton's chest. 'Answer her or I will kill you!'

'He will,' said Luke, looking uneasy.

'I am sorry.' Shackleton shook his head, regaining his composure but clearly still amused by something. 'I don't know how you came by the name Tobias, but this is all terribly ironic.'

'What is?' I demanded. 'What are you talking about?'

'Shh!' said Luke, glancing to Amy at the window. 'Jordan, someone's going to hear you.'

'If this "Tobias" of yours really did hold the key to unravelling the work we are doing in this town,' said Shackleton, serious again, 'do you honestly think I would share that information with you, even in exchange for my own life?'

'Why don't we find out?' said Soren, jabbing his rifle into Shackleton again.

'No, *wait*,' I said, pushing the weapon aside. 'Just –' I crouched, eye to eye with Shackleton, a last, desperate hope springing up in my chest. 'What if it was *her* out there? Your daughter. What if *she* was one of the people on the outside, about to get massacred?'

Another tiny glimmer of surprise registered on Shackleton's face. He wiped it away again. 'I have no daughter.'

'Dr Galton,' I pressed. '*Victoria*. What if –?'

'Do not think you can sway me with sentimentalism,

Jordan.' Shackleton looked more engaged than he had all night. 'I am well beyond the point of entertaining such trivialities. The new humanity being created in this town is of far greater importance than any *feelings* one might have about those who are to be jettisoned in the transition.'

He smiled coldly over at Luke. According to the Co-operative, Luke and his mum were here by accident. A glitch in the system. Which meant they weren't immune to Tabitha like the rest of us apparently were.

'*Jettisoned*,' repeated Luke.

Shackleton shrugged. 'Or *killed*, if you prefer. The semantics are quite beside the point.'

Soren barged forward again, smacking Shackleton across the face with his rifle. 'If you *have* a point, *get* to it!'

Shackleton writhed on the couch, twisting his bound arms around to push himself back into a sitting position. His tongue ran over his teeth, smearing them with blood. When he spoke again, there was an edge of impatience to his voice. 'The point, children, is that humanity is rapidly plummeting towards a depth of depravity and self-destruction so severe that we will soon be powerless to extract ourselves again.'

'I think we might already be there,' said Amy softly, speaking up for the first time since we stopped here.

'The human race is critically ill,' Shackleton continued. 'A cancerous wreck, sacrificing at the altar of its own vapid self-interest. For all our talk of progress and enlightenment, we are no less barbaric than when we were tossing spears and dressing in animal skins.'

'Look around you, Shackleton!' I shouted. 'You're not exactly helping the situation!'

'But that's exactly what we *are* doing,' Shackleton said. 'There comes a point at which the only viable means of saving something is by wiping the slate clean and starting afresh. You may question the cost involved, but Phoenix represents humanity's best hope of –'

'You don't get to decide that!' I shouted, shaking him. 'What right do you have to choose who lives and who dies?'

A little trickle of blood spilled from the corner of Shackleton's mouth. 'Everyone dies, Jordan.'

'You're disgusting,' I said.

'Come now, Jordan.' Shackleton leant forward. 'We have spoken about this before. Your great weakness is your insistence on viewing "good" and "evil" in such inflexible terms. Such ideas are merely human constructs. We invented those definitions, and we are free to adjust them as we see fit.'

'That's *crap!*' I spat. 'You can't just *change* right and wrong to suit yourself.'

'Give it a year,' said Shackleton. 'Two, maybe. Give the people of Phoenix time to experience the new world that I will lead them into. Then ask them if they still think my actions were unjustified.'

'It doesn't matter! None of that –' I balled up my fists, resisting the urge to throttle him. 'It's still evil! Even if every person on Earth turned around and said you were right all along, you'd still be the same filthy monster you are now!'

Shackleton smiled again, teeth pink with blood. 'Who says?'

'Enough!' barked Soren, pushing forward again. 'I did not come here to argue philosophy!' He kicked Shackleton in the ribs, knocking him over onto his side, and jammed the gun under his chin. 'You will tell us what we want to know, or –' Soren faltered, staring down at him. 'What is that?'

Something was blinking behind Shackleton. A tiny blue light, flashing against the back of the couch. I pulled Shackleton over onto his stomach. 'It's his watch.'

'Yes,' said Shackleton, dragging his mouth away from the couch cushion. 'I'm afraid you're out of time.'

There was a gasp from the window, and a half-second later, Amy was across the room, squeezing my arm with both hands. 'They're coming!'

Chapter 32

Luke leapt out of his seat. 'How many of them?'

'I think three,' said Amy, the words spewing out at triple speed. 'Officer Barnett and two more behind him. I couldn't really see. I don't know. I don't know. We have to get out!'

'It's a tracking device,' I said, tearing off Shackleton's watch and throwing it on the ground. 'Like the suppressors you put in us.'

'Something like that,' said Shackleton.

I dragged him up from the couch and started hauling him from the room.

'What are you doing?' said Soren.

'Back door,' I said. 'We'll jump the fence and –'

'He is not coming.' Soren pointed at the carpet with his rifle. 'Put him on the ground.'

'Come on!' said Amy, already in the hall. 'Hurry!'

I pulled Shackleton towards the door, but Soren grabbed the front of his suit.

'Just leave him!' said Luke. 'Jordan, we don't have ...'

He trailed off as a tinny burst of music suddenly

d the room, something classical I vaguely recognised. My pocket started buzzing.

Ketterley's phone. I'd completely forgotten about it. I pulled it out and checked the caller ID.

Andrew Barnett.

'Don't answer it,' said Soren, but I was already sliding the phone open. Something told me it wasn't Ketterley he was calling for.

'What?' I snapped, holding it to my ear.

'Jordan,' said the cold voice on the other end. 'Why don't you have a look out the front window?'

'We have Noah Shackleton!' said Soren, listening in. 'Leave, or I will blast his face apart!'

'Charming,' said Shackleton.

'That would be a mistake,' said Barnett. 'Come to the window, Jordan.'

I got down low and edged my way to the front of the room, trying to keep out of sight. There was every chance he was just calling me out so he could get a clear shot.

'Jordan, come on,' said Luke, 'let's just go.'

I peered up over the windowsill and almost dropped the phone. Officer Barnett was standing out in the middle of the street, lit up by one of the streetlamps. Officer Cook was next to him, holding a gun to the head of a sobbing 12-year-old girl.

It was Lauren. Hamilton's daughter. The Year 7 kid who'd helped us out with food and clothes while we were on the run from the Co-operative in town.

'You sick bastard,' I breathed.

Barnett chuckled on the other end. 'Let me speak to Shackleton.'

I backed off from the window and lowered the mobile from my ear, hand shaking. I hit the speakerphone button. 'He can hear you.'

'Andrew,' Shackleton leant towards the phone, 'how nice of you to come for me.'

'You okay, sir?'

'Oh yes, we're having a fine time,' said Shackleton. 'Although I do think I should head back to attend to our little disturbance in town.'

'Yes, sir,' said Barnett. 'You still there, Jordan?'

'Let her go,' I demanded.

'That's not how this works, Jordan. Either you release Shackleton to us or the girl takes a bullet. And let me tell you, we have plenty more where she came from.'

'Do it then,' said Soren.

'No!' said Luke and I together.

'Listen to me.' Soren ripped the phone out of my hand. 'I have already killed two of your superiors tonight. I will not hesitate to kill a third. If the girl dies, Shackleton dies with her.'

'Stop!' said Luke, face white. 'Everyone, just – just *stop* for a second.'

The room fell silent. I could hear Lauren whimpering on the other end of the phone.

'Yes?' said Barnett.

'We'll swap you,' said Luke. 'Lauren for Shackleton.'

Shackleton stretched towards the phone again. 'Do it, Andrew. We've lost enough candidates already tonight.'

I took the phone back from Soren. 'You hear that, Barnett?'

'All right,' said Barnett, clearly not happy with the situation. 'Get out here.'

'No,' I said. 'You guys need to back off first. Into the yard across the street.'

'Fine.'

'There are four of them in here,' said Shackleton quickly. 'Burke, Hunter, Amy Park, and our trigger-happy friend to whom I've not yet been –'

Soren punched him in the face and he stopped talking.

I shut the phone. 'All right. Let's do this.' I turned to Amy. 'Do you think you can carry her?'

'What? Oh.' She zipped to the window and back again. 'Yeah. Yeah, I think so.'

'Good,' I said, heading into the hall. 'As soon as they give us Lauren, you pick her up and run her out of here, okay? Soren, I want your rifle trained on Shackleton the whole –'

'I am not a fool, Jordan,' Soren snarled.

There were so many ways I could have responded to that statement, but this really wasn't the time.

Luke crawled up to the hole Soren had smashed

through the glass on our way in. 'Okay, they're back against the other house.'

He opened the door and I jostled Shackleton out onto the verandah. Soren rushed out after me, sweeping his gun around while I got Shackleton down the steps.

'Looks like it's just the three of them,' said Luke, surveying the street. He pulled the pistol out of his jeans again.

The air outside was hazy with smoke. I could still hear the distant crackle of the fire and the shouts of the guards. Lauren let out a terrified moan as we approached, and I felt another surge of rage at Barnett for dragging her into this.

We marched Shackleton through the gate, stopping when we reached the footpath. We were maybe twenty metres apart from them.

'All right,' said Barnett. 'Let him go.'

'On three,' I called back. 'One – two –'

I released Shackleton, raising my hands above my head to prove that he was really free. Officer Cook shoved Lauren away and she ran towards us, tears streaming down her face. She screamed as Amy raced out to grab her, hoisting her awkwardly off the ground and running her up the street towards the bush.

The air splintered as Soren fired his rifle.

Barnett cried out, shuddering violently as the bullets tore through him. He dropped to the ground.

BLAM! BLAM! BLAM!

I dived behind the garden fence as Officer Cook returned fire.

'*C'mon!*' said Luke, heading towards the house.

I scrambled after him, sticking low to the ground. Amy and Lauren were already disappearing into the darkness at the top of the hill. I couldn't see Shackleton anywhere. He'd just –

BLAM! BLAM!

Soren shrieked and collapsed to the ground. Cook crossed the street, holstering his pistol and reaching for his rifle instead.

'Jordan, *run!*' Luke yanked me backwards.

Soren let out another horrible, agonised screech, clutching his arm. Impossible to tell in the darkness how bad it was, but he wasn't getting up. I hesitated. But what were we supposed to do?

Cook raised his rifle, aiming at us this time. Luke jerked at my hand again, and we sprinted away down the side of the house.

Chapter 33

We stumbled through the bush, returning to the Vattel Complex on autopilot, not even stopping to think whether going back there was a good idea.

I dropped to my knees at the entrance, overwhelmed by the sudden urge to vomit. Luke knelt beside me, breathing hard, probably thinking I was about to start slipping away again. But this wasn't a vision. It was just my guts finally registering the insane horror of everything we'd been through tonight.

Soren's cries had followed us for only a few seconds before abruptly cutting out. He was gone. I had no idea how I was supposed to feel about that.

I braced myself against the low, crumbling ruin that ran past the entrance, and heaved my dinner into the dirt. Luke stayed with me, rubbing my back and trying to keep my hair out of my face.

'We should get inside,' he said, when I was finished.

'Yeah,' I coughed, wiping my mouth.

Luke pulled a paperclip from his pocket and started feeling along the ruin for the broken power socket that would pop open the trapdoor. I stared around at the bush, still dizzy from the vomiting. Amy and Lauren were nowhere in sight. Soren was dead or getting there. Reeve and Tank might not be any better off. And for all of that, we were still no closer to finding Tobias.

This isn't how it was meant to happen! I raged inside my head. *Where is it? Where's Tobias? If it's not even up there, then what's the point? What's the point of any of it? Why drag me into this and fill my head with visions and put me through all this misery if we were just going to fail at the finish line anyway?*

There was a whoosh of compressed air as Luke got the trapdoor open. Screams echoed up from the bottom of the stairs.

Mum. The baby was still coming.

I hurried down the steps, Luke right behind me. Mum's violent panting and groaning rang out into the empty corridor. I could hear Ms Hunter too, yelling at her to keep pushing. It sounded like she was crying.

I ducked into the girls' bedroom on the way past. Georgia was crashed out in her bed, somehow sleeping through it all. Paper and crayons littered the floor around her. No sign of Cathryn.

Then I spotted the picture Georgia had drawn before she fell asleep. I breathed in sharply, suddenly cold, bending to pick it up.

Almost the whole page was taken up by a huge man, dressed in black. A security officer. Somehow, I was sure it was Officer Calvin. The man stood in the middle of some scribbly trees with an enormous red smile on his face. He was holding the baby.

'That's not – it's just a drawing, right?' said Luke over my shoulder. 'I mean, she can hear thoughts or whatever, but she can't see the future.'

I tore my eyes away from the picture, almost ready to wake Georgia up and ask her about it. But then Mum cried out again from the lab and I decided it could wait. Georgia didn't need to hear that.

I spun around, looking to the doorway as footsteps came pounding up the corridor towards us.

Cathryn, I thought bitterly, striding out to meet her. *If you've –*

But it wasn't Cathryn.

It was Bill.

He reached out to Luke and me with filthy hands, his eyes wide and glistening with tears. Bill's mouth worked soundlessly for a moment, slowly opening and closing, before the words finally escaped his throat in a wild, breathless whisper. 'It's time.'

Chapter 34

Bill leapt forward. He latched onto Luke and me, fingers closing around my arm with shocking strength. 'Quickly! You must come with me. You have a role. You must fulfil your function.'

'What –?' I jerked back my shoulder. 'Bill, what do you need us to do?'

'I need you to hurry!' said Bill, face contorted in a kind of wild, desperate glee. He dragged us into the corridor.

Ms Hunter's barely-contained panic was still streaming out from the lab. 'Okay, it's – oh. Oh my –' She swore loudly. 'Here it comes. Just – just –'

Mum screamed again, long and gut-wrenching, like she was being torn apart. I started for the lab door, but Bill yanked me roughly away. Finally, the screaming stopped. Mum shuddered for breath, and a tiny, strangled cry rose up in her place. Bill kept hauling us away out of earshot, forcing us down into the bowels of the complex.

'Let me go!' I said, almost skewering my head on

a bit of pipe as I fought to get free of him. 'I need to make sure my mum's okay.'

'She's fine,' Bill grumbled.

'You don't know that! Look, please, just give me five minutes to –'

'WE DON'T HAVE FIVE MINUTES!'

He pressed on, faster now, shoving me in front and dragging Luke along behind him.

We reached the open area outside Peter's room, and it wasn't until Bill crashed into me that I realised I'd stopped walking.

'Oh, crap,' said Luke behind me, sounding sick.

The concrete slab we'd used to block the door was now lying in two pieces across the old couch on the other side. Peter's door was open a crack, the barricades scattered on the floor. I could hear him murmuring inside.

'*You*,' I said, stumbling forward as Bill forced us on again. 'You did this! Bill, stop, we have to close it again. If Peter gets out –'

'Inevitable,' said Bill. 'It has already happened.'

'No, it's *not* inevitable! Not if you –'

Bill twisted my arm behind my back, heaving me deeper into the research module. 'There is no time! No time! The ends are connecting. The timing – this is critical. Critical.' He kept going, muttering to himself, more agitated with every step.

I kept struggling, but it was pointless. He was too strong.

I tensed up as we approached the tunnel Soren had dug into the side of the wall. The place where Luke was supposed to die.

'*Go!*' said Bill, pushing me straight past it.

'Can you at least explain what you're planning here?' said Luke. 'I mean, how are we supposed to help you if we don't even –?'

'Redundant!' said Bill, stumbling into me as he tripped on something. 'You will know. When it begins, you will know what is required of you. Now turn on my light.'

'Huh?'

'You mean this?' I said, turning on his helmet lamp. It blinked on, blindingly bright against my face.

'Good,' said Bill, bumping into me again. 'Good.'

We reached the room where Bill had first started his excavation. He brought Luke and me through the mess of smashed furniture and computer parts, and shoved us through the gap he'd made in the wall.

We stumbled into the blocked-up corridor I'd visited when I came to tie him up. The section of the opposite wall he'd been attacking back then was now a second gaping hole, big enough to crawl through. I clambered inside before Bill pushed me again.

Bill's helmet flashed around the room as he climbed in after us. Mouldy concrete spilled down two of the walls, but apart from that, it was completely empty. I glanced around, searching for another hole in the wall or whatever that was going to lead us on to the place

Bill was so desperate to show us. But apparently this was all there was.

Bill reached back through the gap in the wall and picked up a faded yellow camping lantern. He switched it on, gave it a whack, and it flickered to life. The battery seemed to be almost dead, but it lit up the room more brightly than his little helmet torch – enough to prove that there really *was* nothing in here.

Bill straightened up, rubbing his hands together, staring expectantly at Luke and me. Like either of us had any idea what was going on.

'Well?' I said.

Bill kept staring, eyes tearing up again, chest heaving under the filthy hospital gown he'd been wearing since we brought him down here. 'Here I come. Here I come, Jordan. Get ready.'

'For what? What are you expecting me to ...?'

I swayed sideways, crashing into Luke, head swimming with an all-too-familiar nausea. But worse. Even worse than before. The ground warped under my feet, concrete reverting back to sludge, the whole room running together into a dull grey nothingness.

'No ...' I murmured, eyes rolling back into my head, chest and throat heaving. Not now. Not with Bill right there, threatening to lose it if we didn't do what he wanted.

I tried to will myself out of it, to swallow it down and get back to reality, but since when had that ever worked? Luke held me for as long as he could, but I slipped away from him and crumbled to the ground.

And then Bill began to laugh. Wild, breathless, out-of-his-mind laughter, like he might explode from the excitement of it all.

'YES!' he cried. 'Oh – Oh, yes! At last! Here I – here I come! Oh, Jordan – Jordan, I'm –!'

His voice cut out and the room fell silent. I shuddered on the floor, cradling my head to keep it from smashing against the concrete, until the world finally straightened itself back out and my body settled down again.

Someone was crying. *Sobbing.*

I opened my eyes. Luke and Bill were gone. Cracks had appeared in the walls around me, and there were bits of concrete strewn across the floor, but everything else looked pretty much the same. I got up, spinning around to locate the source of the tears.

It was *me*. Some future version of myself, collapsed on the floor, half-hidden in the shadows in the corner. Mouth open. Nose running. Face twisted up in desperate, uncontrolled misery.

'*Luke* …' she moaned, sucking in a spluttering breath. '*Luke* …'

My insides went cold. I felt my hands rise to my face, knowing what this meant.

It had happened. Not just in a grainy image on some old surveillance tape. It had actually happened.

Here, in the real world – or future, or whatever. He was gone.

I staggered back from the other Jordan, distancing myself, wanting to run screaming from the room.

The light from Bill's lamp caught me in the face. It was still there, still glowing. How long did the batteries last in those things? Surely I couldn't have jumped ahead more than a few hours.

I gasped as Luke burst into view in front of me, arms already outstretched to bring me back, but we passed straight through each other. He reached for me again, glancing sideways at the hole in the wall. Whatever Bill was doing back there, Luke didn't like it. I reached out my hands, getting ready to head back.

Surprisingly quickly, Luke and I made contact again, and I felt myself being drawn back to the present. The gagging started up again and Luke wrapped his arms around me, holding me steady as my body was wracked with shakes.

Everything spun out of focus for a second, and then the two timeframes collided. I could still see the other Jordan, but I could see Bill again too. He was even more worked up than before. Laughing, bouncing from foot to foot, eyes streaming.

Why? Did he even understand what was going on? Had someone told him about my visions?

It almost seemed like he'd *known* this was going to happen. But how was that possible? There was no way to predict my visions until they happened.

The other Jordan sat up. She stared straight at me, like she knew I was there. Which I guess she did, given that she *was* me only a few hours ago. She wiped her eyes, breathing deeply, like she was trying to get herself together enough to speak.

But she was already evaporating, growing fainter as I was sucked back into the present. I clamped down on Luke's arms, swallowing hard, trying to hold on, to calm the shakes, to stay connected to the vision long enough to hear what the other Jordan had to say.

Luke jolted back from me, staring into my eyes like something horrible was happening. I remembered what he'd said before about me *glowing* or whatever.

Fine. Let me glow. Just as long as I got to hear whatever Future Jordan was trying to tell me.

I looked back. Her face was in her hands again. *Come on!* I thought. *If you've got something to say, then –*

Luke whirled around, letting go of me with one hand. A dark silhouette had appeared through the hole in the wall.

Peter.

He skulked through the shadows, and for a moment I couldn't work out what timeframe he was in. But, no, of course, if Luke could see him, then he must be in the present. He must have –

Peter leapt through the hole, sights locked on Luke. His hands were flecked with blood.

Luke panicked, letting go of me completely and

drawing the pistol that was still stuffed down the back of his jeans. He thrust the weapon out at Peter.

I grabbed my stomach with one hand as the nausea soared to new heights. I opened my mouth to yell at Peter, but I couldn't get the words out. Everything was blurring. But not like before. Not like the room was collapsing. This time, *I* was collapsing.

Luke took a shaky step forward, waving the pistol, and Peter backed off, shouting something I couldn't hear. I glanced back at the other Jordan. She was down on the ground again.

The room was getting even hazier now, like I was staring at it through a thick fog. A wall of sound rose up against my ears, like rushing wind, blocking out everything else. I squeezed my eyes shut against it all, trying to pull myself together.

When I opened them again, Bill was striding towards me. He'd stopped laughing, but the crazed, ecstatic look was still etched across his face. He kept coming until we were face to face. Hesitated for a moment, taking a breath.

And then he dived. Straight into me. Straight *through* me.

I whirled around to where he should have landed, but he wasn't there. He'd just *disappeared*. I stared down at my chest, as if I was expecting to find him hiding inside me or something. But, no, he was definitely gone. I turned around again. Past Luke, trying to focus on me and fend Peter off at the same time. There had to be something I'd missed. Something –

And then Bill was back, soaring through the air like there'd been no interruption to his dive. He crashed to the ground next to Future Jordan.

She looked up. Her expression turned dark. She scrambled to her feet, backing up against the wall. She could *see* him.

Bill advanced on her, weeping openly, reaching out to Future Jordan like she was his long-lost child or something. She opened her mouth, but whatever she said to him was drowned out by the roar of noise in my ears.

The fog around me was so thick that I could barely see anything now. Just glimpses. Jordan slamming a fist into the side of Bill's face. Bill waving his arms, trying to say something. Jordan lashing out, screaming.

I blinked hard, swaying on legs that were barely there anymore. The fog swirled around my head. The wind howled. I was falling to pieces.

Somewhere through it all, I saw Bill looking back at me, a horrified expression on his face. He glanced at the Future Jordan, mouth open, hands clutching his head. Then he ran at me again – whatever was left of me – diving through my body and disappearing again and finally coming out the other side. Luke gasped, reeling back.

And then all of it collapsed and I blacked out.

When I came around, the fog and the noise were gone and I was on the ground, convulsing as if my whole body was trying to turn itself inside out. Everything was shaking. There was a loud cracking sound as chunks of concrete rained down around the room, and then I must have blacked out again because suddenly Luke was kneeling under me, stroking my face, begging me to wake up.

I opened my eyes. Luke shuddered with relief and bent down to kiss me on the forehead. I took hold of his arm and he helped me sit up.

'Where's Peter?' I asked, looking around, still struggling to focus on anything.

'Gone,' said Luke. 'He ran when he saw the gun. But, Jordan, what just happened? Bill was right there, and then he was gone, and then –'

'I don't know,' I said. 'In my vision, I was – it must have been tomorrow. I saw myself. A future version of myself. I think she was trying to tell me something. You started to bring me back to the present, but I held on again. Tried to hold onto both timeframes at once. You know, like I did out in the bush.'

'Yeah, you were – you were doing the glowing thing again. But so much – so much worse this time. When Peter ran, I looked back and – you were getting all, like, sucked up into this mist stuff. Like you were fading out, but also kind of – I don't know. I don't even know how to describe it. But it looked like …' He trailed off, pale and shell-shocked. 'Well, it *looked* like …'

'Like the thing you appeared through in the video,' I finished, feeling suddenly hollow. 'Right before you got stabbed.'

That was how it was going to happen.

That was how Luke and Peter would wind up rocketing back through time.

It was me.

'I'm so sorry …' said Bill. 'I'm so, so sorry …'

My head snapped up. I'd forgotten he was even here.

Bill was over in the corner where I'd seen the other Jordan. Slumped on the ground, crying, just like she had been. There was something different about him. Something about the way he moved, the sound of his voice, the way he put the words together. Somehow, he didn't seem quite so out of his mind anymore.

Bill's teeth clenched. He held his head in both hands, fingers clawing into his scalp. 'I'm so sorry …'

I stood up, completely thrown by his sudden mood shift. 'It's – it's okay. Just –'

'No it's not!' he choked. 'It's not. Not after what I did.' He stared up at the ceiling, mouth open in a silent wail.

'Bill,' I tried again. 'Tell me what –'

'I'm not Bill.'

I shook my head. 'What do you mean?'

'My name's not Bill,' he said. 'It's Peter.'

Chapter 35

'Peter,' said Luke. 'You have the same name as –?'

'No,' said Bill. He got up, wiping his face on the sleeve of his gown. 'No, mate, I *am* Peter.' He leant against the wall with one arm, head down, gathering himself. And again, I noticed the change in him. He was still a total emotional wreck, but he was *here* in a way he hadn't been before.

My brain was about ready to explode. 'Bill, you're not – what are you saying?'

'Look,' he said, 'Kara and Soren showed you the video, right? They showed you what I did.'

'The surveillance tape?' said Luke. 'Peter appearing through that portal thing and killing me?'

'That was me. Twenty years ago. I was …' Bill reached out for Luke, and he flinched away. 'I'm sorry.'

'That doesn't even make sense!' I said, struggling to understand, let alone figure out if I believed him. 'Peter came back. We saw him go back through the portal again, right after he stabbed Luke.'

Bill shook his head. 'No. I *tried* to go back, but

I never made it. The whole thing – the portal or whatever you want to call it – collapsed around me before I could get through. You must have broken the connection. It exploded – this massive bright light all around me – and I got spat back out again, into the past. And then this whole place started caving in, and –' He shrugged, pulling an uncannily Peter-like face. 'I must've got knocked out, I guess, because the next thing I knew, I was waking up in hospital.'

I sat down again, the hollow feeling intensifying, as if someone was scooping out my insides like a jack-o'-lantern.

'It was me,' I said eventually. 'All of it. If I was the one who sent you back there – if that portal thing we saw in the video was me – that means the explosion was me too. I was the one who destroyed the Vattel Complex.'

It was insane. Unbelievable. All those people dead …

'Jordan, listen,' said Bill, 'you're not the one who –'

'Wait,' I said, realising something. 'That portal – that was one of the "events" Kara was studying. That was why they built the Complex in the first place! To figure out what those things were! If that last one was me … Then all the others were me too, right?'

I glanced between Luke and Bill, desperate for one of them to contradict me. 'Right? Something to do with my visions. When I went back to their time, it must have left some kind of a trace or something.

Something Kara's people could measure with all their lab equipment. That's what they were studying. Me.'

Luke came over and joined me on the floor. 'Jordan ... even if that's true – none of this is your fault. This isn't something you did. It's something that happened *to* you.'

'He's right,' said Bill. 'Nothing you could've done. This was already set in motion way before you guys got here. This is my fault. No-one else's.' He heaved a heavy sigh and went on with his story. 'When the Vattel Complex collapsed, they flew emergency crews in to rescue the survivors, and I guess they picked me up along with them. No-one knew who I was, though. I mean, I hadn't even been born yet. They questioned me in the hospital, but what could I tell them? Besides, you know what I was like. What your Peter is like now. They couldn't have got a straight answer out of me even if they tried.'

'So then what?' I asked. 'What have you been *doing* for the last twenty years? You didn't try to find your family?'

'I didn't *have* a family. My parents hadn't even met yet. And, anyway,' Bill sniffed loudly, tears coming back again, 'the only thing I cared about – the *only* thing – was getting back to Jordan. That's why I killed Luke. To get rid of him. All I had to do was find a way back to Jordan and there'd be nothing to stop us from being together.' He screwed up his face, disgusted with himself. 'I know. I know. It was insane. Monstrous. But that was where my head was at.'

I hugged myself, suddenly overcome with shivers. Luke leant in and put his arms around me.

Bill looked down at us, expecting some kind of response. But what was there to say?

'So, yeah,' he went on, 'when I woke up in the hospital a few weeks later, the doctors said it was a miracle I was alive. I'd lost so much blood, and I had burns pretty much everywhere, and – I mean, look at me.' He held out his scarred, mangled hands. 'Not surprising you guys never realised who I was. Anyway, as soon as I could, I broke out of the hospital.'

'Where were you?' asked Luke. 'What hospital?'

'I don't know,' said Bill, looking up again. 'Somewhere in Sydney, but I didn't care where I was. All I cared about was getting back to Phoenix. Which was stupid. Phoenix hadn't even been built yet. But I wasn't thinking like that. I mean, my brain was totally screwed. It was all ...' He closed his eyes again, clenching his fists in front of his face. 'Mate, you have to understand, this is the first time I've actually thought about any of this. When I went through Jordan just then – I don't know what happened, but it was like waking up. Like I've just got my brain back for the first time in twenty years.'

He broke down again, shaking with tears. Part of me wanted to get up and leave. I needed to check on Mum. Make sure *our* Peter wasn't doing anything stupid. But I couldn't just walk out. Not yet.

Bill took a couple of spluttering breaths. 'I had nothing,' he said. 'No money. I didn't even *exist*. Plus, I had no idea where Phoenix even was. All I knew was that I had to get back here.' He waved a hand at the room around us. 'Back *here,* to this moment. I remembered coming in here and seeing Bill disappear. I needed to make that happen again. I needed to get the two of you back together in the same place and open another portal and get back to my own time.

'So I waited. For nearly twenty years, that was *all* I did. I was totally obsessed. All I had to do was wait it out, and then I could be with her again. When the time got closer, I tracked down Shackleton's old office in Sydney. I stole a computer and hacked into the Co-operative's candidates register. I had to make sure you were both on the list, that you were both coming.' Bill turned to Luke. 'You weren't there. You or your mum. I deleted two of the other names and added you guys in their place.'

'That's why we're here,' Luke breathed. 'Even though we're not candidates. It was you.'

'But *why?*' I said, finally finding my voice again. 'Why did you have to make all of this happen again? Why go out of your way to *bring* Luke to Phoenix if he was your whole problem in the first place? And why put *me* through all of this? All the clues and messages and dragging us out to the airport – if you were that obsessed with me, why not just break into my house?'

'Because I wasn't looking for *you*,' said Bill. 'I was looking for *her*. My Jordan. The one I'd left behind when I went through to the past.'

'We're the same person!'

'I know!' Bill choked. 'I know that! I mean, now I do. But that wasn't – I told you, my mind was – I had a *plan*. Get Luke out of the way, and get back through the portal to my own time. Get back to the Jordan I'd left behind. Right from the beginning, I knew that was what I had to do. And even after I got stuck, I couldn't look past my perfect freaking plan. Nothing else mattered. When I got back here and saw you – You might as well have been a completely different person. I mean, I knew who you were, but by that point you weren't even people to me. You were just tools I could use to get what I wanted.'

Bill's eyes dropped to the concrete. He laced his hands around behind his neck. 'I sneaked into Phoenix in a cargo plane, and started gathering information, waiting for you to get here. As soon as Luke landed, I put those memory sticks into your rooms and used the threat of Tabitha to bring you together.'

'But, hang on,' said Luke, 'when you got us to come and meet you that first time, why did you choose the airport? Why not just bring us straight here if that's where you wanted us to be?'

'I didn't know where here *was*,' said Bill. 'I was

unconscious when Mike and the others brought me down here. And the only other time I'd been up to the surface since then, you guys had stuck me with a sedative. But I knew we'd all get down here eventually because I'd seen it happen the first time.' He shrugged his shoulders. 'The airport was a mistake. I'd already seen Calvin and his guys show up and drag Bill away last time. I thought maybe I could change it. Speed things up. But I couldn't. I can't. All of it was fixed, because it had already happened before. That whole night turned out exactly the same way as it had the first time around. But I'd left myself a backup plan. I'd left clues for Peter – the other Peter – to find.'

'The map out to the wall,' said Luke. 'And those pictures. And the Tabitha DVD.'

'Why didn't you just tell us who you were?' I asked. 'Or why didn't you warn *Peter* what was going to happen?'

'*I don't know!*' Bill shouted, getting to his feet. 'I couldn't – I wasn't thinking like that. He was just like you. Just a tool. A piece of the puzzle. I didn't even think of … of …'

He cried out, tearing at his gown, and I backed off. He might be thinking straighter, but for all I knew he could still throw me across the room if he wanted to.

'It's happening again! Just like before. Just like –' Bill's hands shot to his head. 'I have to stop it. I – I have to stop it.'

He turned in a circle and bolted from the room.

Chapter 36

We ran, grazing against the walls, sprinting to keep up with the light that danced from Bill's helmet as he raced through the passageway ahead of us. He didn't look back, didn't seem to care whether we were following him or not.

I felt like I was going to burst into tears any second. It was all too big, too weird, too overwhelming. I couldn't even begin to wrap my mind around it all. But I could run. I surged forward, pushing through the darkness, blocking out everything else and concentrating on putting one foot in front of the other.

We tore past the scene of Luke's death and kept running, through the minefield of wreckage and back into the entryway to Peter's room. A figure staggered through the door and I dug my heels in, ready to fight him off with my bare hands if I had to.

But it wasn't Peter. It was Cathryn. Bleeding from deep scratch marks in her arms and face. Terrified beyond anything I'd ever seen in her before.

'He almost k-killed me,' she shuddered, hands

shaking over her blood-smeared cheeks. 'Pete – he almost … He almost …'

'Where did he go?' I demanded. 'Which way?'

Cathryn's eyes flickered towards the living area. 'Out there. But I don't know what he was –'

I took off again, Luke right behind me.

'Wait!' Cathryn begged, stumbling after us.

Bill hadn't stopped. He was way ahead now, already out of sight.

In a minute, we were bursting into the undestroyed corridor that led up to the entrance. The laboratory door was open. I veered inside and found Mum sitting up in her bed, holding a tiny, wrinkled baby wrapped up in a towel. Georgia was curled up next to her, still half-asleep, gently stroking the baby's cheek.

Luke's mum was resting against a bench, looking completely shattered. She jumped up as we arrived, brushing Luke's arm on the way past and then rushing over to help Cathryn.

'You're back already?' asked Mum sleepily. 'What happened? Where are the others?'

'Where's Bill?' said Luke. 'Did he come through here?'

Ms Hunter looked up. 'No. We heard footsteps, but –'

'What about Peter? Have you seen –?'

'No, we haven't seen anyone since you left. Luke, what's –?'

Luke ignored her, racing through to the surveillance room.

I crossed to Mum's bed and gazed down at the baby and for one tiny moment, everything else faded into the background. Despite everything – the weirdness of the pregnancy, the less-than-ideal birth – the baby looked completely healthy. Completely normal.

I clutched onto the head of the bed, forcing myself not to cry, knowing I probably wouldn't be able to stop.

'She's amazing,' I murmured.

'He,' said Mum. 'It's a boy. Abraham. We always said that if we ever had a son, we'd name it after –'

Georgia looked up, brow furrowed. 'That's not his name.'

Mum smiled. 'That's what we've picked, sweetheart. He's going to have the same name as Daddy.'

'No,' said Georgia firmly, shaking her head. 'That's wrong. He already told me his name. He's called Tobias.'

Chapter 37

I let go of the bed frame. 'Georgia, no – You might
have heard us talking about that name, but –'

'No, that's not why,' said Georgia. 'He knew his
name already, even when he was in Mummy's tummy.
He *told* me.'

Mum stared at me, the colour draining out of her
face. 'Is that – is that possible?'

'I don't know,' I said, reeling away from the bed.
'Georgia, are you *sure?* Are you sure it was the baby
who told you that?'

'*Yes,*' said Georgia emphatically. 'I'm not lying. He
said it in my head just before he got born.'

'What about that drawing you did?' I asked, trying
to keep my voice even. 'That picture of the security
man holding the baby.'

'That's Mr Calvin,' said Georgia. 'Luke said, "Draw
a picture for the baby." That's what the baby wanted a
picture of.' Her eyes narrowed. 'Why arc you angry?'

'We're not angry, sweetheart,' said Mum faintly.
'We're just trying to understand.'

'Jordan!' said Luke, rushing into the lab again. 'He's upstairs. He just ran out into the … What? What happened?'

'It's the baby,' I said. '*Tobias*. Georgia just – She can communicate with him, or read his mind or something.'

'He told me,' said Georgia. 'That was always his name, ever since he got into Mum's tummy.'

Luke walked across to the bed. 'Did he tell you anything else?'

'No,' Georgia shrugged. 'That's all. He only started talking today.'

I glanced at Luke, then out into the corridor. If we were going to catch up with Bill, we had to do it now. I turned back to Mum. 'Wait here. But get ready to – Do you think you can walk?'

'I think so,' she said. 'But, Jordan, I don't think –'

'Okay. Stay here. But get ready to run if you have to.'

'Run *where?*' asked Luke's mum.

'I don't know,' I said. 'Just get ready.'

We shot back into the hall. Up the stairs. I hammered the trapdoor button and we leapt out onto the surface, pacing in a circle, searching the darkness.

No Bill. No Peter.

'Where would he go?' Luke panted. 'Where would either of them –? Surely they haven't gone back into town?'

But who knew *what* was going through Peter's head right now? He could be anywhere.

Luke rested an arm around my waist. My head pounded. I could smell the vomit from before, and I thought I might throw up all over again. I closed my eyes for a minute, focusing on my breathing, leaning my head against Luke's shoulder.

'I believe her,' I said. 'Georgia. She's telling the truth about the baby. About Tobias.'

Luke blew out a lungful of air. 'Yeah.'

All our searching, and he'd been right here with us all along. But what now? What hope did that tiny little baby have against a Co-operative super-weapon?

'Hang on,' said Luke. 'What about all the rumours in town? If *he's* Tobias, then –?' He stepped away from me as something flashed in the sky behind us. 'Whoa. Was that lightning?'

There was a loud crackle, and a sound like one of the rocket things that had launched at Kara and Mr Hunter's helicopter. A line of sparks lanced through the air, far above our heads, shooting towards town from somewhere out in the bush.

'Not lightning,' I said.

There were more of them. Dozens. Tearing through the night in every direction, all converging on the town centre.

'Missiles?' said Luke, voice brightening. 'Maybe Dad got the army or something. Maybe –'

'I don't think so.' I started jogging through the bush, gazing upwards. A dark line cut across the sky overhead, marking out a path behind one of the projectiles. Some kind of big, thick cord.

There was a rapid series of *thunks* as the cords converged above the town centre.

'That antenna thing on top of the Shackleton Building,' I said. 'I bet that's where they've –'

An explosive crackle of electricity filled up the sky, impossibly loud, like lighting smashing into the ground right next to me. Sparks rained down on us, and for a moment the bush was bright orange as all the cords above our heads lit up at once.

Luke gaped up between the trees. I could see his lips moving, but couldn't hear a thing over the noise. The cords had laced themselves together into a massive, electrified grid. A dome, stretching out as far as I could see in every direction.

All the way out to the wall, I thought, mind dredging up an ancient memory from the night we scaled the giant barrier surrounding the town. Peter had spotted this deep metal groove in the top of the wall, running the length of it. None of us had ever been able to work out what it was for. It looked like we might have our answer.

'Final lockdown procedures,' Luke murmured, as the light and the sound faded away again. The grid still crackled and spat, but not so ferociously now. I guessed maybe that had just been while it was powering up.

Whatever the case, it looked like our trip out to the

release station had just ratcheted up from 'dangerous' to 'impossible'.

Luke hit the backlight on his watch and I glanced down. The time had just ticked over to midnight.

'Doomsday,' he said.

Seventeen hours until the end.

I could still hear the distant echoes of gunfire from the centre of town. How much of Phoenix was even going to be left by the time this was all over?

And then another sound. Heavy breathing and pounding feet, and then the dark shape of a person exploded from the bushes in front of me. The figure pitched forward, face illuminated for a fraction of a second as the grid sparked above us.

Soren, bruised and bleeding. He collapsed at our feet.

'Soren? You're alive!' I said. 'How did you –?'

Soren shook his head wildly, scrambling to get up. His legs gave out and he stumbled to the ground again.

'Help!' he shrieked. 'Help me! We have to get away from here!'

'Why? Soren, what's –?'

'Calvin!' Soren gasped. 'He's back! They know where we are! They're coming!'

book 6

doomsday

Chapter 1

LUKE

THURSDAY, AUGUST 13, 12.02 A.M.
16 HOURS, 58 MINUTES

We ran.

Torches swept through the bush behind us, closer every second. Soren wailed in pain as Jordan and I dragged him through the mud.

'Quiet!' hissed Jordan, steering us back towards the entrance to the Vattel Complex, but Soren kept right on shrieking. He writhed under my grip, swollen, bruised, slick with the blood from his interrogation.

A torch beam sliced past us and I caught a flash of Jordan's face, stretched tight with anger. She shot a dark look at Soren, like she was half-tempted to throw him to the guards and be done with it.

'No!' Soren gasped, losing his footing. 'Please – I did not mean to –!'

He broke off into another wail as Jordan jostled him again. 'You didn't *mean* to?'

We'd thought Soren was dead. We'd *seen* him get gunned down, back in town. But apparently he hadn't been gunned down enough to keep him from selling the rest of us out to Shackleton.

I looked back, stomach churning. At least five guards were crashing through the undergrowth behind us, and there was no mistaking the towering silhouette of the guy up front. Calvin. Back on duty after weeks out of action, just in time to ring in the end of the world.

The sky above our heads crackled with electricity. Moments before Soren's arrival, Shackleton had unleashed the final part of his plan to keep Phoenix locked off from the outside world: a domed network of electrified cables, stretching out over the town like an enormous spiderweb. I couldn't see it anymore – after one brilliant flash as it powered up, the shield grid had faded into the darkness – but I could still hear it. I could still *feel* it pressing down on us.

Smoke billowed up from the south, blotting out the stars as the fire in town continued to blaze. Reeve and the others were still back there, fighting for control of the Shackleton Building. But they couldn't be doing much better than us if Shackleton had security guys to spare for a search party.

We reached the entrance to the Complex and some-one inside opened the trapdoor to let us in.

'Stop! *Stop!*' Soren demanded, digging his heels into the dirt, like he'd only just realised where we were taking him. 'We have to get *away* from here!'

I ignored him, hitting the stairs as soon as the

gap was wide enough, my feet sliding on the mouldy concrete. I wasn't about to just abandon Mum and the others.

'Run!' he railed on. '*Leave* them! There is no time!'

'You want to stay out here?' Jordan snapped, releasing her grip on him. 'Fine. *Stay.*'

Soren swayed, almost collapsing, and latched onto Jordan again.

There was a shout from the bush, way too close, and I swore as another torch beam caught me in the face. I turned and hammered down the stairs, bracing for an explosion of gunfire, but it never came, and a few steps later I heard the entrance rolling shut above our heads.

'We need to get the others into the panic room,' said Jordan. 'Barricade the corridor. Hold Calvin off.'

My head swam. 'Jordan, how are we meant to –?'

'You've killed us!' Soren wailed. 'You've killed us! There is no way out!'

Jordan didn't want to hear it. She tore down the stairs, three at a time, hauling Soren behind her.

I staggered down after them, feet heavier with every step. It wouldn't take Calvin five minutes to get through that trapdoor. And in the meantime, I knew the Co-operative weren't the only ones who wanted me dead.

He was down here somewhere. Peter. Out of his room and hours away from putting a knife in my chest.

Earlier tonight, Crazy Bill had dragged Jordan and me down into the depths of this place, to the half-buried lab he'd finally finished excavating out of the concrete. He'd cornered us, watching with wild excitement as Jordan's body began fading out of existence, into one of her 'visions' of another time.

Almost like he'd known it was coming.

As always, I'd grabbed onto Jordan, fighting to stabilise her, to drag her out of the vision and back into the present before she disappeared completely. But this time, things had spun even further out of control than usual.

For a moment before she returned, Jordan had somehow got caught between the two timelines; one foot in the present and the other in wherever she'd been fading away to. She'd become a kind of gateway between our time and the other one. And in that moment, Bill had run at her – run *through* her – and disappeared. Into the other time.

A minute later, he'd returned. And suddenly, Crazy Bill wasn't so crazy anymore. Somehow, his trip through Jordan, through *time*, had cleared his head enough for him to tell us the truth about who he really was.

Bill was Peter. A twenty-years-older Peter who'd spent the last two decades trapped in the past. Because this wasn't the first time he'd used Jordan as a time machine.

Sometime in the next seventeen hours – in Bill's past, and our future – Jordan was going to fade out again. And when she did, she'd become a gateway between our time and another: a day twenty years ago. One we'd seen replayed over and over again on Kara and Soren's old surveillance video.

The day of my murder.

I was going to go back in time, armed with a message that just might help us save the world. And Peter – our Peter – was going to follow me back. He was going to kill me. And then he was going to dive back through the gateway, back to the present.

But he was going to be too slow. The gateway was going to collapse, spitting him out, stranding him in the past with no way back to the present except to wait out the next two decades until it all happened again. And the next time Peter showed his face in Phoenix, it would be as a mentally unstable homeless man who seemed to know a bit too much about what the Shackleton Co-operative was up to. Which was all very tragic and whatever, but given the part of the story where he stabbed me to death, I wasn't shedding any tears for him.

And I *was* going to die. I got that now. If there'd been any hope left that I could escape all this alive, it had disappeared the moment that trapdoor had closed over our heads.

Bill was right: there was no undoing the past. This wasn't just *going* to happen. It had *already* happened. More than that, it *had* to happen. The only reason we had any clue how to stop Tabitha eating humanity alive from the inside out was this: I'd gone back to the past the first time round and delivered our message to Kara.

Take Tobias to the release station.

That was it. Everything we had. A one-sentence save-the-world plan based on –

Based on *what?*

I stumbled down the last few stairs. Sick. Emptied out. It would have been the easiest thing in the world to just let it all go. Curl up into a ball right here on the stairs and wait for the end to come. But some stubborn corner of my mind kept me stumbling forward. If I had to die, I was going to make it count for something.

It was chaos in the corridor. Mum raced to meet us at the bottom of the stairs, an appalled look on her face at the sight of Soren's mangled body. Cathryn stood behind her, sobbing violently, still bleeding from the gashes Peter had scratched into her face on the way out of his cell. Jordan's mum was leaning against the doorway to the surveillance room – on her feet, which was something – with a screaming Georgia clinging to one leg and a minutes-old baby cradled in her arms.

Tobias.

The annihilation of the human race was scheduled for five o'clock this afternoon, and the weight of the world was resting on someone who couldn't even support the weight of his own head.

Mum opened her mouth to speak, but Jordan immediately shouted her down. 'RUN!'

'What's happening?' Georgia wailed, burying her face in her mum's leg.

'They're coming! They're already at the entrance! All of you, get down into the panic room!' Jordan dragged Soren over to Cathryn, dumping him in her arms. 'Take him.'

Cathryn shook her head. 'I don't –'

'Take him!'

'Where's Peter?' I asked, grabbing hold of Mum.

'I don't know. We heard noise in the kitchen, but –'

'GO!' Jordan screamed. 'GO, GO, GO! *NOW!*'

They got moving, Soren limping against Cathryn, Mrs Burke dragging Georgia along with one hand, clutching Tobias in the other. I waited for Mum to fall in behind them, then moved to follow.

I'd only taken two steps before I realised Jordan wasn't with us. She'd run off into the surveillance room. I doubled back, stomach sinking even lower.

'No!' said Mum, shooting out a hand to grab me. 'Luke, you're not –'

'Right behind you,' I said. I reached into the back of my jeans and pulled out the pistol I'd picked up on our trip to the Shackleton Building earlier that night. 'Here.'

Her eyes went wide. 'Luke, no, I wouldn't even know what to –!'

She twisted around at a sudden moan and a splattering sound behind her. Cathryn let out a nauseated shriek. Soren had just thrown up all over the ground.

'*Please*,' I said, pressing the gun into Mum's hand. 'They need you.'

She sucked in a shuddering breath and took the pistol, holding it away from her like she was afraid it might spontaneously combust. 'All – all right. But …'

She pulled me into a hug, then ran off to get the others moving again.

I raced to the surveillance room. Static spat from the circle of laptops that had once fed us footage from the cameras in town, back before Mike blew up the security centre. I glanced around the room, half-expecting Peter to come bursting out from under one of the desks.

Jordan was across the room, staring at our one remaining eye on the outside: the camera feed from the entrance above our heads. Then she dashed past me, taking hold of a desk near the door.

'He's up there,' she said, voice hard, eyes red with tears. 'Calvin. They're all around the entrance. But I can't –'

Smash!

Jordan lifted up the desk, upending it, knocking a pair of laptops to the floor. '– I can't see what they're doing. Too dark.' She ran the desk out into the corridor.

I followed her out. 'Jordan, what are we –?'

There was another echoing crash as she threw the desk to the ground, ramming it between the walls of the corridor.

'Come on,' she grunted, almost knocking me over as she ran to grab another desk.

A barricade. Or at least, an attempted barricade.

Pointless. No way was this going to stop them, or even hold them up for more than a minute or two.

But there was a glint in Jordan's eye that told me this was not a good time to argue. Her family was in danger. We were way past reason now.

I ducked back into the surveillance room, upending another desk, hands barely keeping their grip on it. Maybe Peter wasn't going to finish me off after all. Maybe it wouldn't even get that far.

A few more desks, and we'd made a heap that stretched to the ceiling. But it would take just one solid push to send the whole thing crashing to the ground.

Jordan stayed at the barricade, trying to wedge the desks more tightly together, while I sprinted back to the surveillance room for some chairs to shove into the gaps. I returned just in time to see Jordan lose her grip on the desk at the top of the pile, sending it clattering to the ground on the other side. She screamed in frustration, pounding her fist against the wall.

I tried again. 'Jordan –'

'Pass me that chair,' she snapped, wrenching it out of my hands. She jammed it between two of the desks, and the whole pile shifted, almost collapsing.

'Jordan, listen, I don't think this is –'

She wheeled around, face twisted in desperation. 'They're not getting in here, Luke!'

'Yes they *are!*' I said. 'You know they are! You've *seen* it! You want to help your family, we need to get down to the panic room and keep Calvin out of *there!*'

She twisted away from me, sprinting down the corridor. I ran to catch up, relieved that she was actually listening to me. But then –

'Beds,' she said frantically, veering through another doorway. 'They'll be harder to move.'

'Jordan, *stop,* they won't even –'

I froze at the door, catching sight of the mess spilling out from the kitchen at the end of the bedroom. It had been completely ransacked. Drawers yanked open, cupboard doors ripped from their hinges, ground littered with the smashed remains of mugs and bowls and –

And cutlery.

Knives.

This was Peter's work. He'd found his murder weapon.

I shivered, creeping into the kitchen to investigate, and almost jumped out of my skin at a loud scraping behind me. Jordan, shoving a bed at the door. There was a clatter of rusty metal as it slammed into the doorway and got stuck. She dragged the end around, throwing her weight against it. The bed shifted a few centimetres and got lodged again. She cried out, rattling the bed with both hands, panic threatening to swallow her completely.

I came up behind her, resting my hands on her shoulders. 'Look –'

'Would you help me with this?'

'*Look,*' I said again, pointing at the mess in the kitchen.

Jordan's eyes dropped to the floor, taking it all in for the first time. I felt her shoulders slump, and some of the manic energy seemed to drain out of her.

'Please,' I said. 'Please, can we just get out of here?'

Jordan turned around, cheeks still glistening with tears, an agonised look on her face.

'C'mon,' I said, moving to drag the bed back out of our way.

My hands had barely hit the bed frame when an explosion rang out above our heads, echoing down the stairs. Then a distant shout and the sound of thundering footsteps.

They were here.

Chapter 2

JORDAN

'Crap!' Luke heaved at the bed, but it was stuck fast. He gave up, vaulting over, nearly slipping as his foot skidded in the puddle of vomit on the ground.

I leapt out behind him, finally dragging my head back into the game, hurling silent abuse at myself for letting the panic take over like that.

What was I thinking? What was I *thinking*, wasting time on that joke of a barricade when I could have been getting Mum and Georgia to safety?

And Tobias.

Tobias.

My baby brother, who hadn't even been alive long enough to see a sunrise, but who was somehow meant to be the answer to all of this.

If we could even get him out of here alive.

We pounded down the corridor. I could hear voices approaching from the other side of the barricade. They were already –

Crash!

The barricade collapsed, my misguided attempt at protecting my family exploding in a pitiful avalanche of furniture. I ducked, screaming, as someone opened fire on us.

BLAM! BLAM!

A fluorescent tube fell from the ceiling, shattering on the floor at our feet.

'Freeze!' Calvin boomed.

But I'd already stopped running. Calvin didn't miss that shot. Not from ten metres away in an empty corridor. It had been a warning. That was the only reason we were still alive.

'Turn around,' he ordered.

I turned, heart hammering, but keeping my head up, forcing myself to look at him.

Calvin waded through the mess of upended furniture, flanked by four guards, all armed with Shackleton's standard-issue assault rifles. Whatever had been keeping him out of action these past few weeks, he'd clearly gotten over it.

Luke slid a hand into mine. He was shaking like crazy, and I felt a throb of guilt for keeping him up here when he could have been finding a place to hide.

One of the guards let out a snicker.

Something flashed behind Calvin's eyes. Just one tiny, fleeting moment, and then gone again. He kicked aside the last chair in his path and paused a few metres short of us, sneering at our filthy nest of a hideout, probably wondering how on earth we'd kept it a secret all this time.

He raised a red-gloved hand, aiming his pistol again. 'Where is it?'

Neither of us spoke.

I clenched my teeth, blinking the tears out of my eyes, stomach roiling. It couldn't end like this. It couldn't. What was the point of finally figuring out Tobias if we were going to die before it even had a chance to matter?

Calvin's men stood poised behind him, waiting for an order. I'd run into all of them before at one time or another. Seasoned officers who Calvin could trust to stay loyal and get the job done.

At the back of the pack stood a guard I'd seen down here once before, in a vision of this place, destroyed and abandoned. A vision of today.

'The baby,' Calvin growled. 'Where is it?'

I swallowed, remembering the picture Georgia had drawn earlier tonight – Calvin standing out in the bush, Tobias in one hand, a gun in the other – and the ominous words that had come with it: *that's what the baby wanted a picture of.*

The silence stretched out.

I squeezed Luke's hand, my mind whirring frantically and coming up with nothing. But if Calvin thought I was going to spend my dying breath selling out my family –

'Answer him!' snapped one of the guards, losing patience. It was Officer Cook, hands still caked with Soren's blood.

Calvin held up a hand, signalling Cook to lower his weapon. 'Last chance, Jordan. We will find that child one way or another. The only decision you are making here is whether or not you'll live long enough to see it happen.'

'You sick freak!' I said, dropping Luke's hand and striding forward, rage boiling over. 'How can even *you* be okay with –?'

Calvin rushed up, meeting me halfway. He shot out an arm, grabbing me by the throat and shoving me into the wall. '*Listen,*' he snarled in my ear. 'Believe me when I tell you, this is not a fight you can –'

WHAM!

Calvin was flung into the ceiling – two metres, straight up – crunching with shocking force into one of the light fixtures. I ducked out of the way just in time to avoid getting crushed as he plummeted to the ground again.

Before he'd even landed, the corridor filled with panicked shouts as all four of Calvin's men were thrown off their feet, tumbling backwards through the air like they were caught in a hurricane. They crashed to the floor at the end of the corridor in a heap of desks and chairs and limbs.

Another startled cry and Luke rocketed past me, sliding across the floor. He reached out a hand, somehow managing to catch hold of the bed still lodged partway out of the bedroom door. He dragged himself to a stop and a wild, inhuman scream rang out behind me.

Peter. Red-faced and rabid, fist clenched with white knuckles around the handle of a knife. *The* knife.

For a second, it was like the whole universe had stopped in its tracks.

Then the guards began to stir.

Luke scrambled to his feet.

Calvin felt around for his pistol.

'LEAVE!' roared Peter, charging. 'LEAVE HER!'

Luke dragged me sideways into the surveillance room just as one of the guards opened fire with his rifle. Peter screamed again, and a sick thought flashed through my mind: *he can't kill Luke if they kill him first.*

We raced across the surveillance room, stumbling through the pile of smashed laptops to the door on the other side. But we were only stalling. This was all just a circuit. The surveillance room led through to Kara's laboratory, which opened into the corridor again through a second door. Nowhere to run but back into the fray.

We burst through to the lab and I slammed the door behind us. Luke ran to grab one of Kara's old operating beds and shoved it up against the doorway.

He took a breath. 'Now what?'

Rifle fire split the air in the next room. One of the officers started shouting, but it was swallowed up in a scream and a smash and dull thud.

'We need to keep going,' I said, lunging across the lab. 'Find the others.'

Luke cringed. 'Yeah, but …'

'We can't stay here,' I said. 'And we'll come out right

up the other end of the corridor from where we started. We might be able to sneak –'

SMASH!

A massive crack appeared in the door we'd just blocked off as something – or someone – heavy was hurled into it. The bed Luke had shoved back there rattled away across the floor.

'GET OUT!' cried Peter, voice breaking. 'YOU DON'T GO NEAR HER!'

'Quick,' I said, already at the second door, peering into the corridor.

I could only see one guy out there. Only one still on his feet, anyway. Officer Blake or something, the one from my vision. He was staring into the surveillance room, weapon halfway raised, like he knew what he was supposed to be doing but didn't want to risk catching Peter's attention.

I heard Peter scream, and Blake reeled away in fright. I looked across the lab just in time to see the first door splinter apart and the limp form of a security guard come sailing through the air towards us. The body thudded to the ground and rolled to a stop against the wall.

Luke shoved me into the corridor.

Officer Blake twitched around, spotting us. He raised his rifle and fired. Too late. Mouldy plaster exploded from the wall behind us, but we were already through the door at the end of the corridor and out into the dark, debris-strewn passageway that wound through the bowels of the Vattel Complex.

After only a couple of seconds, I heard pounding footsteps, and a pair of torches tore up the corridor behind us. But here, at least, we had the home-ground advantage. We sprinted along on autopilot, ducking and weaving instinctively to avoid the countless bits of jagged, rusting shrapnel spiking out from the walls and ceiling – the familiar hazards of a place that had been blown up and concreted over and dug back out of the rubble again. I heard one of the guards cry out, swearing bitterly as he collided with something sharp.

Ahead of us, I spotted the place where the passageway widened out, leading off to the room where we'd been holding Peter. Still no sign of Mum or Georgia. Good.

I pushed forward, and almost tripped over a small, dark shape in the middle of our path. I leapt over it, glancing back at Luke. 'Watch out –'

'Argh!' Luke stumbled, kicking the thing over. It toppled onto its side and I realised it was some kind of gas canister. There was a bit of string tied to it, leading off down the passageway.

We kept moving and the string changed course, running in under the door to Peter's room. Suspicion flared inside of me and I shoved the door open, ignoring Luke's moan of protest.

Inside, Soren was crouched behind Peter's broken bed, holding an old lighter to the end of the string.

'*Come on!*' he barked at us, bloodied fingers twitching on the lighter. '*Come on! Come on! Come on!*'

There was a spitting, crackling sound, and a spark

ignited at the end of the string. It shot along the fuse, way faster than I'd expected, across the floor and out into the passageway.

'Close the door!' Soren shouted. 'Close it!'

I heaved the door shut and dived behind the bed, dragging Luke –

BOOM!

The whole world flashed bright orange and I rushed to shield my head as the bed was blown back into us. A cloud of dust and smoke rushed into the room, swirling into my nose and mouth, and I curled up on the concrete, coughing violently.

Everything was black, the lights above our heads destroyed by the explosion. Finally I could breathe again, and I sat up.

Luke's hand came down on my arm, groping in the darkness. 'You okay?'

'Yeah.' I dragged myself to my feet. 'Soren?'

A torch flashed on beside me and I saw Soren's battered face suspended in a haze of grey dust. He stood, grunting, and stepped over the bed. I helped Luke up and we followed him back into the passageway.

Soren swung the torch back the way we'd come. But instead of lighting up the empty corridor, the beam shot straight into a sprawling heap of concrete boulders. An entire wall of rubble that hadn't been there two minutes ago.

He let out another grunt. '*There* is your barricade.'

Chapter 3

LUKE

'I hope they kill each other,' Soren growled, wincing in pain as I half-supported, half-dragged him up the passageway. 'Peter and Calvin. Solve both our problems.'

'Hurry up,' I said, shoving him along. Jordan was pulling ahead of us, flashing Soren's torch around at the walls. The passageway was starting to smooth out again by now, the debris clearing as we moved further away from the centre of the explosion that had ripped through the place two decades ago.

A shadow slid across the wall and I flinched.

Just the torch.

Surely there was no way Peter could have made it through before the cave-in. But that didn't stop me seeing him around every corner. Didn't stop my mind skittering between hair-trigger panic at the thought of him leaping out at me and a cold, creeping dread at what would happen when he finally did.

Jordan stopped at a row of lockers along the right-hand wall. She pulled open the door of the last locker in line, and a scream exploded from inside. Two hands shot out, clutching a pistol.

Jordan leapt back. 'Whoa! No! It's okay! It's us!'

The hands hovered in the air, still pointed straight at Jordan's chest, then finally dropped down again. My mum stepped shakily out of the locker. 'Sorry. Sorry, I was …'

'It's fine,' said Jordan. 'Quick, get back inside.'

Mum ducked back in and we followed after her. Straight through the locker and out the back, into the room hidden on the other side.

Jordan and I had set this up weeks ago. The lockers had originally been inside the room, but we'd dragged them out into the hall and punched the back out of this one. We had food in here for a day or two, and a couple of blankets to shield us against the worst of the cold. Not exactly Narnia, but it would keep us alive until the end of the world, at least.

'Where are they?' Mum asked, returning to her guard duty. There was something so horrible about the sight of her holding a gun that I wished I'd never given it to her.

'Back up near Peter's room,' I said. 'Soren rigged up an explosion and caved in the passageway.'

'So we're trapped,' said Cathryn, stepping out of the shadows.

'You were already trapped,' said Soren, limping in behind us.

Jordan spun her torch around the little room and practically dived on top of her mum, who was over in the corner feeding the baby. Georgia was curled up next to her, sniffling. I looked away, not exactly clear on the breastfeeding privacy rules.

'So what do we do now?' Mum asked.

'Um,' I said, still a little thrown by this bizarre new world where Mum turned to *me* for instructions. 'Let's just sit tight for a while. Keep hidden. I mean, with everything going on in town, they might eventually decide to just give up on us.'

Mum pursed her lips, seeing straight through me. But what else was I meant to tell her? She didn't know about Peter. Not the part about him stabbing me to death, anyway. And there wasn't much point dumping that on her now.

'How is he?' whispered Jordan, drawing my attention back to the family reunion on the floor. She brushed a gentle finger over Tobias's head.

Mrs Burke shrugged. 'He seems fine so far. Normal. I mean, he's feeding like a super baby, but so did you and Georgia.'

Jordan shot me a sideways glance. End of the world or not, it's never okay for your mum to start discussing your 'feeding' habits in public.

Her eyes drifted back to Tobias, and mine followed, the same question running through both our heads: how in the world was this tiny kid supposed to stop a killer virus from exterminating seven billion people?

Somehow, that seemed even more impossible than the rest of Phoenix's cavalcade of insanity.

And what if it really *was* impossible? What if Tobias wasn't the saviour we all thought he was?

The only reason any of us believed Tobias was special was that *I'd* said he was, twenty years ago. But what did I know? What if this was all just some stupid endless loop of me fooling myself into believing something that had never been true in the first place?

Stop, I thought fiercely. *Stop it. You're not getting out of it that way.*

This wasn't about my doubts and I knew it.

This was about fear.

I knew what the right thing was. I knew I couldn't just ignore humanity's best chance for survival. And with a day left until the end, I knew I was dead whether I confronted Peter or not.

Which was all good and rational, but there's a pretty massive difference between *knowing* what's right and actually having the guts to do it.

All these weeks, I'd been wishing for a clear way forward. A tangible answer that I could pick up and run with. Now I had it. Or as close as I'd ever get, anyway.

And all I wanted to do was run the other way.

I sat on the ground, back against the cold wall. Stalling.

We'd been down here for what felt like days now, but was probably more like half an hour. Somewhere in that time, Jordan had remembered the phone in her pocket, the one I'd pulled from Ketterley's body earlier tonight. We'd crowded around as she tried to call Reeve, but we were way too deep underground to get reception, even on Shackleton's secret supervillains' network.

Jordan had pocketed the phone again and no-one had spoken since. Cathryn was sobbing in one corner, Soren sitting silently in another, picking at a scab. Mrs Burke was doing her best to keep Georgia from freaking out, but even a normal six-year-old wouldn't have missed the despair in the room, let alone a kid who could see inside other people's minds.

Mum hadn't left her place at the door for a moment. Not even when the rest of us were fixated on the phone.

And through it all, Tobias just lay there, sleeping. No sign in the world that he was anything other than an ordinary newborn.

But he had to be. He was all we had left.

Which meant I had a job to do.

I stared down at Tobias, so impossibly tiny and frail. Just a *baby*.

You'd better be worth it.

Jordan was circling the room, pacing like a caged animal. I reached for her leg as she passed. She dropped down next to me, knees bent up against her chest.

'Hey,' I whispered. I put an arm around her and the dull ache in my stomach intensified. Not that we'd ever had great odds of surviving this place and living happily ever after, but it's one thing to see something coming a mile away, and another thing to be there when it arrives.

Jordan leant into me. 'This is stupid,' she breathed. 'We need to *do* something.'

'Yeah,' I said.

But for a minute, I couldn't get the words out. I just sat there, feeling her next to me, knowing it was probably the last time we were ever going to be together like this.

'We have to go back,' I said finally, keeping my voice low enough that only she could hear. '*I* have to go back. I need to deliver that message to Kara.'

Jordan straightened up.

'Don't,' I said. 'Please. Don't argue about it. It's hard enough –'

'So, what, I'm supposed to just stand back and watch you die?' she hissed.

'We need to know, Jordan! If Tobias is the answer to all of this, then we need to make sure we know about it. And if he's not – Well, I'm dead anyway, aren't I? As soon as Tabitha gets out, I'm gone. And in the meantime,' I said, with way more courage than I felt, getting up before either of us had the chance to talk me out of it, 'I can't just sit here. And I'm pretty sure you can't either.'

Jordan got up after me, and Mrs Burke jolted. 'What's going on? Did you hear something?'

'No, it's okay,' I said. 'We're just going to duck

outside for a sec. See how far along they are, clearing through the rubble.'

'I don't think that's a good idea,' said Mrs Burke tersely.

Jordan glared at me, and there was an uncomfortable silence as she decided whether or not to play along.

'We'll be careful,' she said finally, bending down to hug her mum. 'Whatever happens, stay quiet and don't give yourselves away.'

Jordan scooped Soren's torch up off the ground. Georgia buried her face in her mum's side.

'Back soon,' I lied, heading for the door.

And suddenly, I guess my survival instinct kicked in or something, because every step became a massive effort, an order I had to force my body to carry out against its will.

After weeks of turning this moment over and over in my head, I was finally stepping out to meet it. It wasn't just an idea anymore – some weird, unexplainable thing we'd seen on an old video tape. It was actually going to *happen*.

Mum turned as I reached her, face barely visible in the darkness. She held out the pistol. 'Take this.'

I shook my head. 'We'll be fine. You need to protect the others.'

Mum hesitated, then lowered the gun. She put her arms around me and I almost lost it.

I'd walked into the jaws of death before, but not

like this. Not with the outcome already decided and played out and caught on camera before I'd even started. Not *knowing* that I wasn't coming back.

I kept hold of Mum, a crushing hollowness flooding through my chest, like I was being pushed apart from the inside. I let the moment drag out as long as I could, knowing that this was it, that letting go meant *letting go*.

Mum made a noise in my ear. The sound was so unfamiliar, so out-of-character for her, that it took me a second to realise she was crying.

'I'm sorry,' she said, voice cracking. 'I'm sorry I brought you here. I'm sorry I dragged you into all this. If I'd just looked up from my work for a half a second and stopped to think what you might be –'

'Mum, stop,' I said, taking a breath to keep back my own tears. '*No-one* knew what this place was! That was the whole point. And, listen, whatever happens to me – whatever happens to any of us –'

'Luke …'

'No, *listen*,' I said, determined to get it out while I still could. 'You need to know I don't blame you, okay? Whatever happens to me, I need you to know that none of this is your fault.'

Mum held me out at arm's length. 'Luke, why are you –?'

'Because it's the end of the world, Mum.' I took another steadying breath, thankful she wouldn't be able to make out my face in the darkness.

She pulled me to her again. 'Be safe out there, okay?'

'Yeah,' I said, wrenching myself away from her.

She moved back into position at the door, and we slipped past her, out into the gloom of the passageway.

Chapter 4

LUKE

THURSDAY, AUGUST 13, 1.22 A.M.
15 HOURS, 38 MINUTES

The nausea hit me as soon as I stepped outside. I pushed up the corridor, stumbling, everything fuzzy with tears, breaking into a run before I even knew what I was doing.

'Wait!' called Jordan, as soon as we were out of earshot of the panic room.

I kept running, like my dread was a monster bearing down on me, and all it would take was a moment's hesitation, one false move, and it would overtake me completely and –

'Luke!' Jordan caught hold of my wrist. 'Luke, *stop*.'

I wiped my eyes clear with the back of my hand and realised that she was crying too.

'*Talk* to me,' she said. 'What are we doing here?'

'You know what we're doing,' I said, walking again, but keeping hold of her hand. 'You're going to send me back twenty years, and I'm going to tell us all about Tobias.'

Jordan made an exasperated noise, but it got caught

DOOMSDAY – 315

in her throat and came out more like a sob. 'I can't just *send you back*, Luke. That's not how it works.'

'No, I know, but –'

'And even if I could, that still wouldn't get us past Calvin. What's the point of knowing about Tobias if we can't even get back up to the surface?'

'I don't know, okay? I don't *know* anything, but – Seriously Jordan, what choice have we got? What else can we do but go back to the room from the video and see what happens? Maybe it doesn't have to go the way it did last time. If we go now, maybe you can send me back and I can deliver the message before Peter even knows we're there.'

'You don't believe that,' Jordan croaked. 'You're the one who keeps saying that there *is* no "last time" and "this time". That it's all just some big, unstoppable loop.'

'And you're the one who says it's all happening for a reason,' I said, more aggressively than I'd meant to. 'You've been telling me since forever that there's some unseen purpose to all this. Do you actually believe that, or is it only true when it suits you?'

Jordan didn't answer, and on top of everything else, I felt a swell of guilt. 'Sorry,' I said. 'That wasn't –'

But before I could even get the words out, Jordan pulled me to a stop again, stepping in front of me, eyes red and shining with tears. Her hand slipped up through my hair and she brought my head closer and kissed me.

I let out a sob, torn up and exhausted, sighing into

her mouth, the impulse to run vanishing in an instant. My hands laced around behind her back, pulling her to me, and I could so easily have just stayed there like that until they broke through and came for us.

But eventually, Jordan split apart from me. Her hands slipped down my arms and she stared at the ground between us. For a long time, she was silent. I stood, holding onto her, knowing we should push on but not able to bring myself to do it.

'It's not fair,' she whispered.

Which, even though it was the kind of complaint a four-year-old would make, was actually a pretty perfect way to sum it up.

We kept moving, neither of us speaking until we reached a little side-tunnel that had been clumsily cut out of the concrete; the pathway out to the last room I was ever going to see.

Jordan went straight past the mouth of the tunnel and kept walking.

'What are you doing?' I asked as she let go of my hand.

'Checking on Calvin,' she said. 'Wait here.'

I ignored her, trailing behind as she slipped up the passageway. Before long, we heard noise up ahead, muffled sounds of concrete on concrete. Jordan flicked off the torch and we continued on by touch.

After another minute or two, we rounded a corner and I flinched as a tiny shaft of light pierced through the blackness up ahead of us, twitching erratically and then flickering out again. Another torch, shining in through a tiny gap in the wall of rubble. They were quickly getting through.

I tightened my grip on Jordan as the noise continued. The shifting of debris, and frantic, breathless grunting.

There was an explosive *smash*, like a boulder getting hurled into a wall, and one of the guards shouted, 'Hey! Watch –'

A roar rose up from the other side of the cave-in, silencing the guard.

'Leave him!' said Calvin, sounding unusually strained. 'Let him work.'

The noise dropped away, a momentary stand-off on the other side of the wall, and then the grunting and smashing started up again.

'He's clearing the rubble,' said Jordan, sounding sick. 'He's coming after us.'

Another beam of torchlight shot through the rubble, bigger this time. We had a few minutes, maybe less. Jordan pulled on my hand and we doubled back, running, putting as much space between us and Peter as we could.

I think we both knew it wouldn't be enough.

We weren't going to change it.

I was already dead. I had been for twenty years. All that was left was to take back the message about Tobias and hope that my death made some kind of difference after I was gone.

In what felt like seconds, we got back to the low

tunnel out to my murder room. Jordan made a half-hearted attempt to keep us moving past it, but I pulled away from her and crouched at the tunnel's mouth.

Jordan made a kind of gasping noise, like she'd started to say something and then given up. I closed my eyes, head spinning, fighting down the urge to vomit, knowing that once I started down that tunnel, I wasn't coming out again.

Move, I told myself, with as much resolve as I still had left. *Go. Either* you *die or everyone else does.*

I forced myself inside, not knowing if that was even true, not knowing anything anymore, my mind capable of nothing except pushing me through the tunnel, and hardly even capable of that. My whole body shook like it was coming apart, teeth chattering uncontrollably, arms barely holding me up off the ground.

Light flashed up the tunnel as Jordan crawled in behind me, torch clutched in one hand. I squeezed my eyes shut again, trying and failing to steady myself, half-expecting her to grab my leg and try to drag me back out of there. But she just moved silently up the tunnel behind me.

I almost rolled over the edge as the tunnel came to a sudden end. Thanks to Soren's dodgy excavation work, there was a metre drop down to the ground on this side. I stretched out my arms and crawled to the concrete below.

Jordan dropped in behind me and flicked off the torch, but not before I caught a glimpse of the dull brown stain smeared out across the floor. My two-decade-old blood, due to be spilled from my body any minute now.

I shivered in the dark, reaching out to Jordan, pulling her into a hug. Her breath was ragged in my ear, and I felt the moisture seep through the fabric of my shirt as she started crying again.

I steadied myself against her, soaking up the warmth of her body and the feeling of her arms around me, waiting for the telltale lurch that would signal the arrival of her next vision. Time stretched out.

And nothing.

No vision. No anything.

'You have to go,' I said shakily after a minute. 'When this is done. When I'm – You have to get out of here and go kick Shackleton's arse. Get your family out. And my mum. Make sure she's –'

Jordan loosened her grip, finding my face in the dark. She kissed me, missing my mouth. 'Stop it! This isn't finished! Don't you dare just lie down and stop fighting!'

'I'm *not*. But Jordan, you know this is –'

We sprung apart as an enormous clattering and crashing of concrete echoed along the passageway outside, followed by a triumphant shout from one of Calvin's men.

The celebration was cut short almost immediately as a louder, wilder shout rang out over the top of it. There was a split-second roar of gunfire, quickly replaced by a scream from whichever of the guards had been stupid enough to get in Peter's way.

Silence fell for just a few moments before it was broken again by the sound of footsteps hammering up the corridor outside.

Chapter 5

JORDAN

'JORDAN! JORDAN!'

Peter's voice raged up the passageway, sucking the air out of my lungs.

'Wait here,' I said, reluctantly letting go of Luke. 'No – *wait*,' I insisted, as he moved to follow. 'Stay here. Let me check it out.'

I shoved the torch – still off – into my back pocket and clambered into the tunnel again, blinking the tears out of my eyes, scrambling towards the sound of Peter's voice.

I'd told him.

Two days ago, I'd gone to see Peter in his cell and I'd told him all about what we'd seen in the video.

What if I was the one who'd put all this in his head in the first place?

'JORDAN!'

A torch flashed on up ahead and I froze at the mouth of the tunnel, thinking he'd seen me. But no, not yet. He was still further up the passageway. I shuffled back a bit, pressing myself low against the base of the tunnel, and waited, grateful that I'd at least had the sense not to tell him *where* Luke was going to be when he murdered him.

The torchlight grew brighter, bouncing along in time with Peter's footsteps, and suddenly he was right in front of me. From this angle I could only see up to his chest, which I hoped meant he wouldn't be able to spot me without bending down. He slowed, catching his breath, torch in one hand, knife in the other, both arms covered in blood and bruises. He turned in a circle, crying out again. 'JORDAN!'

Peter's torch beam flickered right over the top of me, and I was suddenly struck by the stupidity of what I was doing. If Peter found me, it was going to lead him straight back to Luke.

But the torch kept moving, flashing back the way he'd come. Peter muttered something to himself, then turned around again, still bellowing my name.

The sound of his voice faded away. I inched forward again, craning my neck out of the tunnel to see along the passageway. Then someone somewhere stifled a gasp of pain, and I jerked my head back before realising they were a little way off – a guard back up the corridor who'd just collided with something in the dark.

They were still coming. Hanging back, torches off, keeping their distance from Peter. But Calvin had come here for Tobias, and he wasn't going to leave without him, which meant –

A sudden jolt of energy shot through my body, and I leapt out of the tunnel, a wild, reckless idea bursting to life inside my head. I was back on my feet and sprinting after Peter almost before I knew what I was doing.

I flicked my torch on, no time for caution, ignoring the corner of my brain that kept insisting this wasn't going to work, that I'd never been able to change the past before and this time would be no different.

Almost immediately, I saw the light of Peter's torch dancing up ahead. He wheeled around as I approached, face contorted with fury. But then he saw who I was and his expression melted into one of freakish, single-minded joy.

'Jordan!'

He threw his arms around me, mashing his lips against mine, tongue everywhere, like he was trying to swallow my whole face. I squirmed, acid rising in my throat, but he just dragged me closer, and I felt the cold handle of his knife pressing into my back.

'Pete –!' I pulled back, coughing. 'Peter, not now! They're coming!'

Peter's eyes narrowed. 'Where's Luke?'

'Not here,' I said, determinedly keeping my voice even. 'Peter, please – I need your help.'

Suddenly, I had his full attention. 'What is it?' he asked, still not letting go of me. 'What do you need?'

'They're coming,' I said again. 'Calvin and his men. They want –'

'I'm not scared of them.'

'No, I know, that's –' I glanced over my shoulder, thinking I'd heard something. 'That's why I need you to protect my family.'

Peter may have been a murderous lunatic, but he was also the only one down here who could protect my family from Shackleton's security. And he'd do it, too. If he thought it would help prove his undying love for me, he'd do pretty much anything. And if I could keep him busy enough with that …

Then maybe Luke didn't have to die. Maybe we could get the word out about Tobias and get Luke out of here before Peter even knew what was happening.

Peter took a step back from me. He stared down at the knife in his hand.

I gritted my teeth, fighting the urge to scream at him. 'Peter –'

'Yeah,' he said, nodding emphatically. He put his hands on me again. 'Yeah, of course. Of course I will.'

I broke away from him and took off down the passageway. 'This way.'

The panic room wasn't far off. I sprinted along the last stretch of half-destroyed laboratories, into the more-intact section of the Complex on the other side, with Peter right behind me, panting in my ear like a wild dog.

I told myself I was doing the right thing, that this

was the best way to protect my family and keep Luke alive. But who knew what Peter would actually do when the time came?

A few metres short of the row of lockers that hid my family, I reached out my hand, bringing Peter to a stop.

'Okay, they're just down there,' I said, already bringing up my mental map of the Complex, trying to work out how I was going to get back to Luke without getting caught. 'Whatever you do, don't let the guards – *Peter!* What –? No, *stop!* Let go of me!'

Peter's hands clamped down around my arms, terrifyingly strong. He hauled me down the corridor to the lockers, throwing a door open at random. I twisted under his grip, kicking at him, but it got me nowhere. 'What are you *doing?* Get –!'

'Quiet!' he snapped, shoving me in with one hand and finally letting go. I tried to jump out again, but I couldn't do it. I couldn't move myself forward. Peter was still holding me there, telekinetically pinning me to the back of the locker with his fallout-addled brain. He ripped the torch out of my hand, switched it off and slammed the locker shut again.

There was a *clank* of metal on the outside of the doors as Peter jammed something through the handles, locking me inside.

I stared out through a little grate in one of the doors. 'Please,' I whispered, as Peter dropped out of sight. 'You need to let me out of here. I have to –'

'No,' he panted. 'I'm keeping you with me.'

His torch clicked off, plunging the corridor into complete darkness.

I slumped down, losing my balance as Peter released his telekinetic hold on my body. I pushed against the doors, but they wouldn't budge, and I was too scared of attracting the attention of security to try anything that would make more noise.

'Shh!' Peter breathed through the grate. 'Shut up. I'm looking after you.'

For a second, I thought I heard Georgia's voice from the panic room. I strained my ears, trying to work out what was going on in there, but the sound had already disappeared. I put my face in my hands, barely keeping hold of myself. This was a disaster.

'How are you even going to see them coming?' I asked. 'They could be right –'

'I said *shut up*,' Peter snapped.

I heard his feet twist on the dirty ground as a tiny creak of metal sounded behind him. The door to the panic room cracking open.

'Jordan …?' whispered Luke's mum uncertainly.

Peter let out a growl. 'Where's Luke?'

'Not here,' said Ms Hunter, even more nervous now. 'He's with –'

'Shut the door!' I hissed.

'Jordan?'

'Do it!'

The door clanked shut, and I heard more shuffling of feet on concrete as Peter started after her.

'No, wait!' I said. 'He's not –'

But the plea was silenced almost immediately by a furious spray of weapons fire. A rifle flashed from somewhere off to my left and Peter cried out, thudding to the ground.

My heart jolted into my throat. *Did he just –?*

'Lights!' Calvin demanded, and a pair of torches cut through the darkness of the corridor. I squinted away, blinded.

There was a fierce scraping of metal: the locker next to mine pulling away from its place against the wall. I opened my eyes just in time to see it go blurring past me, up the corridor in the direction of the guards. The air was filled with an ear-splitting clatter as the locker was hammered with bullets.

Peter gasped like he'd been holding his breath, and I heard the remains of the locker crumple to the ground. In the shifting light of the torches, I saw him stumble to his feet in front of my grate, exhausted but apparently unharmed. Then he disappeared again.

'Sir?' said one of the guards, spooked but still waiting for an order.

Before Calvin could respond, Peter let out a breathless shout and I heard the locker scrape up off the ground again. The guards cried out and the corridor fell back into shadow as their weapons clattered to the ground.

'Peter!' Calvin called. 'Enough of this!'

'STAY BACK!' shrieked Peter, and the locker on

my other side started scraping away from its place on the wall.

Calvin pushed on, raising his voice over the sound. 'Do you want to end this? Do you want to protect your friends? Hand over the baby and we will spare the rest. I give you my word they will not be –'

'NO!' With an enormous crunch, the locker shot across the corridor and slammed into the opposite wall.

'Get back, get back!' said one of the guards as Peter, still out of sight, lifted the locker into the air again, angling it around to get a clear shot.

'Fire!' Calvin ordered. 'Take him –'

'WAIT!' shrieked a new voice from the direction of the panic room, and I felt my heart crash down into my stomach.

Peter's locker dropped out of the air, filling the corridor with a deep, echoing clatter.

One of the guards found their weapon again, shining their torch in the direction of the voice, and a trembling figure stepped out in front of me, hands above her head. Cathryn.

No, no, no, no, I screamed inside my head, fists balled up in front of my mouth to keep myself from crying out. *No, no, no, what are you DOING?*

'You c-can't do this!' Cathryn said, taking a shaky step forward. 'I'm Louisa Hawking's daughter!'

You IDIOT! I pressed my face up to the grate, panic washing over me, wave after wave. *You stupid, brainless coward! You think that's going to make any difference?*

Calvin laughed. 'Your mother's wishes do not concern me, Cathryn.'

'If you kill me, she'll –'

'She will do the same as the rest of us,' said Calvin. 'She will do what she is told.'

Cathryn opened her mouth, but no sound came out. She looked back at the panic room, despair on her face. Her one bargaining chip had failed – of *course* it had – and now she had –

One of the guards let out a shout, and a dark blur spun across my grate. A rifle. Cathryn shrieked as it hurtled past.

I heard a grunt and a click as Peter caught the weapon, and then gunfire filled up the corridor again. The sound ricocheted inside my locker, pounding my head from all sides.

'EVERYBODY BACK!' yelled Peter, charging up behind Cathryn who was still on her feet, paralysed with fear. 'EVERYBODY –!'

One of the guards returned fire, drowning him out, and a scream rose up in the corridor. Cathryn collapsed, clanging noisily against one of the fallen lockers. Peter glanced down at her, focus slipping for just a second.

And suddenly Calvin was leaping into my field of vision, through the mess of battered, bullet-strewn metal, rifle swinging out over his shoulder like a baseball bat. He cracked the weapon down across Peter's head. Peter staggered, swaying on his feet, but didn't fall. Calvin pounded the weapon into his head again, and he finally dropped to the ground.

I slumped against the locker doors, my knees threatening to give way. The doors *thunked* into whatever Peter had jammed through the handles, but the sound was covered up by another wail from Cathryn.

Calvin glanced down at her for only a moment before turning back to his men, hand outstretched towards the panic room. 'In there. Bring Tobias to me.'

It took everything I had not to start pounding on the doors in an attempt to break out.

They rushed past me. Still four of them, even after the carnage back up near the entrance. Calvin must have roped in a couple of others after the corridor caved in.

'Do not harm the others,' Calvin called after them. 'Shackleton wants them alive.'

One of the guards spoke up. It sounded like Officer Cook. 'Sir? Barnett's orders were to –'

'Officer Barnett is no longer in command,' Calvin said coldly.

An uncomfortable pause, then: 'Yes, sir.'

Screams flew from the panic room as the doors were flung open. Ms Hunter started to yell, but there was a clatter of metal on concrete as her pistol was tossed aside. I heard Georgia wailing, Mum begging the guards to leave her children alone. Then one of the guards fired their weapon and my heart almost burst out of my chest.

The screaming stopped.

My insides went cold.

I slumped down inside the locker.

No, no, no, no …

'On your feet!' Cook boomed. 'Now! All of you! Next person to speak gets a bullet.'

Georgia sobbed again, and I felt the light flicker back on inside me. Just a warning shot. They were all still alive.

Footsteps shuffled into the corridor. A guard stepped into view in front of me, waving the others through. Mum came out after him, Georgia shuddering in her arms and the barrel of another guard's rifle poking into her back.

I pressed my face up against the grate, clenching my fists, telling myself over and over again that my best hope of helping them now was to stay hidden and wait until I actually had a shot at doing something constructive. It was excruciating, every second an eternity.

They paraded the others out, over the unconscious heap of Peter's body, with Cook at the back, cradling a silent Tobias.

Cathryn whimpered as Calvin dragged her to her feet. Cook came up to hand Tobias over. He looked Cathryn up and down, then rolled his eyes. She was completely uninjured.

Calvin shoved her roughly across to Cook, and then reached to snatch up Tobias. A smile broke across his face, eerily reminiscent of the one in Georgia's drawing.

'Everybody out,' Calvin ordered, nodding at the entrance. 'We've got work to do.'

The guards filed past him, hauling my family away. I choked down a shudder, fingers clawing the walls of the locker, only barely managing to stay quiet.

'What about the others?' asked Cook in an undertone, hanging back to speak with Calvin in private. 'Hunter and Burke?'

Calvin glanced back down at Tobias. I couldn't read his expression in the darkness, but the next words out of his mouth were clear enough. 'We've got what we came for. If you find them, kill them.'

Chapter 6

JORDAN

I held out for as long as I could, waiting for the guards
to get some distance on me, hands wrapped around
myself to keep from breaking down before they got out
of earshot, head filled with so many blood-spattered
images of Mum and Georgia and the baby that I barely
even knew where I was anymore.

Finally, my resolve gave out and I started hammering on the doors of my locker, trying to shake loose
whatever was holding the handles shut. The doors
rattled but didn't budge. I felt the tears pricking my
eyes again, panic threatening to boil over completely
and send me into meltdown.

'Come on!' I pleaded, pounding the metal. *'Come on,
come on, come on, COME ON!'*

I threw myself, screaming, at the doors. An
explosive *bang* shot up and down the corridor and the
locker rocked, almost toppling over. I backed off, panic

shooting up my spine. The locker tipped into place again, and I crashed into the back wall, shaking.

I straightened up, trying to steady my breathing. *Think, you idiot! Get it together before you kill yourself.*

I stared through the grate at Peter, still unconscious among the bullet-riddled lockers, face lit up by the torch on his rifle. I swallowed hard, trying to work out if waking him up would put me in more trouble or less, and then a burst of clarity flashed just bright enough for me to see another way out. I couldn't tip myself forwards without crushing Peter's legs and trapping myself even worse in the process. But Peter had thrown aside the locker next to mine.

If I could knock this thing over sideways …

I spread my feet, digging them into the foot of the wall on each side of me, heart still threatening to punch its way out of my chest. With another furious shout, I threw my weight hard to the left. The locker rocked slightly, but clunked back down again.

I swung to the other side, building momentum, then heaved left again. Another swing and a miss but I kept moving, back to the right, and then back to the left, and then right, left, right, left –

And then suddenly I was in free-fall. I twisted around, trying to brace myself, barely even getting my hands down under me before –

CRASH!

My arms cushioned some of the blow, but not enough to stop my head thumping down into the ground. I groaned, head spinning, maybe even blacking out for a bit. As soon as I'd got my breath back, I rolled over and kicked at the door in front of me. There was a thump as whatever had been blocking the handles came loose, and the door fell open, crashing to the ground.

I jolted backwards. Peter was right there in front of me, face lit up like he was about to tell me a ghost story. Eyes closed, but still breathing.

I crawled out, doing my best not to touch him, skin crawling as my mind flashed back to the night he'd cornered me in his bedroom. My foot caught on the strap of his rifle and I almost face-planted into the ground. Peter stirred, mumbling something under his breath. I wrenched myself away, half-expecting to get thrown into a wall, but he settled into unconsciousness again.

My torch lay on the ground in front of him. I picked it up and pushed myself back to my feet, still woozy from the fall.

What now? I thought, leaning against the wall.

The panic inside me had settled for a moment as I'd escaped the locker, but it was already surging to the surface again. I took a deep breath, forcing myself to focus.

Calvin would have them all out of the Complex by now. Off to be interrogated by Shackleton. He'd keep them alive for a while at least.

Or would he? How did I know that? How did I know Shackleton didn't just want to slaughter them in person? And what about Tobias? Would he even make it to Shackleton, or would Calvin just wring his neck out in the bush somewhere? If Tobias died, so did everyone on the outside. So did –

Luke.

I had to find Luke.

I took off, but made it only a few steps up the corridor before skidding to a stop and running back to Peter. I crouched down again, tearing his rifle away from him. I ran my hands over the ground, searching for his knife, but it was like it had just disappeared.

No time! I screamed inside my head. *Just go!*

The panic took hold again and I abandoned the search, reaching down and rolling Peter over, into the locker I'd just escaped from. I slammed the locker shut and ran around behind it, pushing it over onto its front, sealing him inside.

Even dizzy with fear, I wasn't stupid enough to think that would hold him for long. But it might give us a few minutes, and maybe that would count for something.

I started running again, through the mould and the dirt and the decay, straight for the epicentre of the explosion that had started all of this. The explosion *I'd* caused, twenty years ago, on the night of Luke's murder.

My head was a dead weight, throbbing with the pain of my fall and still reeling from the revelation that everything we'd been through in the last hundred days had only been possible because of *me.*

I'd caused the fallout, which had caused my powers, which had caused the fallout.

What would happen if we changed it? What if Luke

never went back in time? What if I didn't let him? If there was no trip back through time, then there was no explosion to bring down the Complex, no fallout to attract Shackleton here in the first place, no *any* of it.

We could stop all of this before it even started.

So why hadn't I?

Surely I'd known all of this the last time around. But I'd still made the way for Luke to go back. I'd still let it all happen.

Why?

I kept moving until finally my torch lit up the entrance to the tunnel. Instantly, the impossible, circuitous time travel questions flew from my mind and things became a whole lot simpler: I needed to get inside, get Luke out of here, and go after my family.

I crawled into the tunnel, head still pounding, but with a clear goal to latch onto now, at least. My torch flashed into the room at the far end, slipping over the grimy walls.

'Luke!' I hissed. No answer.

I scurried forward, faster now, a fresh burst of dread shooting through my stomach. 'Luke!'

I reached the end of the tunnel and dropped to the floor, spinning my torch in a frantic circle. He was gone.

I shone the light into every corner, as if I could have missed him the first time in this tiny, empty room, then dropped back against the wall, raising a hand to my injured head.

Calvin had found him. Luke must have left to come

after me and got caught by security on their way back from –

I snapped upright at the sound of heavy breathing in the darkness, fingers playing over the torch as I debated whether or not to turn it back on again. The breathing grew louder. I couldn't take it anymore. I switched on the torch and thrust it back in the direction of the tunnel. It was Luke.

My heart lifted for just a fraction of a second before plummeting back to earth as I realised what he'd done.

He'd been back out to the living area. He'd changed his clothes.

Luke crawled out of the tunnel, dressed in a mud-stained tracksuit with the hood pulled up over his head. His murder clothes. The same ones he'd been wearing in Kara's surveillance video.

He wasn't just *letting* things happen the way they had before. He was *making* them happen, making sure everything played out the way it was supposed to.

'No!' I said, backing off from him. 'Luke, please – *please* – you're not doing this. You can't …'

Luke stepped towards me, eyes bloodshot and streaming. He opened his mouth to say something, but all that came out was a sob.

My arm was still frozen in place, lighting him up with the torch. Luke pushed it gently aside, closing the gap between us. He wrapped one hand around my waist and brought the other up to my cheek. His lips closed around mine, soft and slow, and the tears that had been needling my eyes since I crawled in here spilled over and ran down my face.

Luke's hand traced across my back, rubbing slow circles between my shoulder blades. His thumb moved over my cheek, brushing away the tears, and I tightened my hold on him, overwhelmed with the deep, dark *wrongness* of it all – that this brave, beautiful boy should lose his life while a murderer lived to see another day and a sick old man built an empire on the back of –

What are you DOING?

I pulled away from him, overwhelmed with my own stupidity. Luke shows up in his murder room in his murder clothes on his murder day and I just stand there and *kiss* him? I dived at the tunnel entrance, ignoring his gasp of confusion, desperate to get out before history had a chance to repeat itself.

But I didn't get two steps before the nausea erupted in my stomach. I collapsed mid-stride, a breathless groan tearing its way out of my throat.

Luke was by my side in an instant.

'*No*,' I pleaded, shoving him weakly away. 'Run! Leave me! I won't let you –!'

The protest died in my mouth and I curled into a ball, wracked by another bout of uncontrollable gagging. The room hurtled in circles around me, the torchlight fracturing into a thousand tiny shards, and still Luke would not leave me. He cradled my head, both of us trembling out of control.

'Please …' I choked, not even sure I was saying it out loud.

I could hear Luke speaking to me, trying to comfort me, but his voice was all warbled.

'I'm sorry …' I murmured as he swam in and out of view above me. 'I'm so, so sorry …'

And then I was gone, falling to pieces in a hurricane of swirling blackness. I squeezed my eyes shut, blocking it out.

But slowly the pain died down, the universe straightened out, and harsh, white light blasted through my eyelids. I lay on my back, forgetting where I was for a moment. Forgetting everything. Then it all came flooding back and I opened my eyes and dragged myself up from the floor.

I was sitting in a stark, white laboratory. Completely empty. And spotless, unstained by Luke's blood. In front of me was a second room, sealed off from mine by a wall of glass. I'd been in a place like this before. Vattel and her people used these rooms to investigate the mysterious 'events' at the centre of their research. Events that, as it turned out, were me.

I wiped my eyes, dragging in shallow, shuddering breaths.

On the other side of the glass were desks covered in boxy computer equipment, which had been designed to pick up the trace or residue or whatever that I left behind whenever I popped in from the future. Previously, I'd seen Vattel Complex scientists working the computers, running scans to try to figure out what I was. Today though, the room was unoccupied.

I stood up, arms out to balance myself. This was it. The day from the video. The day of Luke's –

No. Not this time.

I turned, searching for Luke, waiting for him to appear like he did every time I faded out, the only one who could drag me back to the present.

A door clunked open behind me. I leapt back, some stupid part of my brain freaking out that it was Peter.

A head poked through the door, just below the handle. A little girl, Georgia's age or maybe a bit younger, with long brown hair and deep, penetrating eyes. A young Dr Galton, back before Shackleton secretly adopted her. She peered furtively around the room, like she was looking for a place to hide. Her eyes swept straight through me without any hesitation. As far as she could see, the room was still completely empty.

Galton froze as a voice called along the corridor outside. *'Ashley!'*

She ducked back out of the room. The door swung wide and I saw her scamper away.

Any other time, I would probably have gone chasing after her, fascinated to find out what was going on out there. Not now. I didn't care about any of it. There was no room in my mind for anything but Luke.

'Ashley! What will your mother say when she finds out you've been sneaking off again?' The voice up the hall raced closer. Kara, two decades younger and gentler, but

still unmistakeable. She waddled past the open doorway and I caught a glimpse of a flowing white nightgown and an extraordinarily pregnant belly before –

Jordan! Luke mouthed, flashing into view, centimetres away from my face. I reeled back, startled, then reached out, grasping for his arms. My hands passed straight through him and I lurched, almost tripping over. He tried again, nose running, tears streaking his face with mud. But again, we failed to make contact.

Luke looked away for a second, like he'd heard something behind him, and I felt my chest turn to ice.

Peter.

'Run!' I screamed, trying pointlessly to shove him away. '*Go!* Get out of there!'

But where was he supposed to go? There was no other way out. If Peter was coming up the tunnel, then –

'– BACK!' Luke gasped, suddenly audible again, hands collapsing at my sides. His voice was all stretched and distorted, like a Skype call on a bad connection.

Out behind the wall of glass, the computers whirred to life – an automated process to track the 'events' when there was no-one here to do it in person.

Luke's gaze flickered back out behind him again and I could see the pale, sick dread rising in his eyes. 'Please – please – you have to let me –'

He flinched, almost losing his grip on me as I jerked backwards, convulsing. I clung onto him, nails digging in through his jumper. All around me, the room began to decompose, swirling away into a sludgy blur.

And then suddenly, it all sprang back into place, but now I could see the world of the present as well, one time superimposed over the top of the other. The room was pristine and destroyed, immaculate and filthy, gleaming white and dim and dark, all of it fusing together into a flickering, mind-bending mess.

Luke's hands trembled against me. I could still see the doorway behind his back, but now the ragged outline of the tunnel's mouth had reappeared alongside it. And there, barely visible in the glow of my abandoned torch, was the dark silhouette of someone moving.

'Hurry!' Luke cried, attention flitting back and forth between me and the tunnel. 'Please! Whatever you – You have to let me in!'

The shadow in the tunnel scuttled closer. Light glimmered as the blade of Peter's knife caught the torch beam. I couldn't breathe. My chest felt like it was closing in on itself. The world began to break down again, my grip on the past slipping away, and all at once I understood what I had to do.

Luke was dead. If he was still in the present when Peter arrived, he'd be gutted right there where he stood. But if I could get him into the past, if I could give him somewhere to run …

Maybe this time it would be different.

Please! I begged, some deep, primal part of me crying out for help. *Please, don't let him die.*

The bile rose up in my throat and I felt the ground start to give way underneath me, but I held on, focusing whatever strength I had left on keeping up the connection between the two timelines.

A furious wind rose up, rushing into my ears and under my skin. I felt myself splinter apart, my vision blurring as my body lost cohesion. Over Luke's shoulder, I saw Peter shuffling closer, his dark form filling the tunnel now. Luke whirled around, letting go of me. He turned back, face drained of colour, wrapping me up in a frantic, desperate kiss.

I love you, he mouthed over the tornado spinning through my head. I tried to respond, but I was too far gone, pulled open and stretched apart.

Peter twisted around and dropped to the floor.

Luke cast a terrified glance over his shoulder.

Peter raised the knife high over his head, screaming something at Luke. Luke spun back to me, and I had to force myself to keep watching, keep the connection alive.

Don't let him die. Please.

Luke ran straight at me, and I jumped back – or would have if my body was still capable of moving like that. I looked down at my stomach, caught a fleeting glimpse of him blurring into me, and then he was gone. Somewhere in transit between the blood-stained ruin and the gleaming laboratory.

But he wasn't there yet. I couldn't let go. Not until –

Peter cried out in fury, loud enough for me to hear even over everything else. He rolled back his shoulders, knuckles white on the handle of his knife, glaring into me with bulging, inhuman eyes.

'*NO!* I screamed, throwing my hands out as if that was going to do anything. The whole world shuddered and roared around me, like it knew what was coming next.

Peter looked into me, looked *through* me, a hideous grin spreading across his face.

He lowered his head and charged.

Chapter 7

PETER

He was getting away. Straight through her and gone, just like Crazy Bill before.

Coward. Filthy cheating coward bastard!

I felt my fingers drumming on the knife. I knew what I had to do.

Straight through her and gone and kill the dirty bastard and then finally – *finally* – Jordan would be mine again.

She swirled, glowing and brilliant and hardly even Jordan anymore but still beautiful, still mine. I smiled at that. The thief was trying to escape, but she was holding the way open for me to go in there and kill him.

Kill the bastard and get back what's yours.

I ran, straight in, straight through, into her body that was not her body, light everywhere, spinning all around me. I grabbed hard on my knife, rocketing through the big, bright silence.

And then there was a room again, still bright, but

walls and floor and solid. I landed wrong, almost falling but not.

And I saw him.

DIRTY UGLY THIEF!

Everything else was gone. Everything but the rage, rage, rage, filling me up and showing me what I had to do.

RUN!

He tried to shake his head, to open his mouth and scream, but he was too slow. Stupid and ugly and slow. I swung my arm, up in the air and down in his chest. The knife was blunt but I was strong and *now* the scream came out, all wet and pathetic.

BLOODY COWARD! BLOODY WEAK STUPID TRAITOR!

I took back my knife, sticky and oozing. Back into his chest again, hitting the bone underneath, and again, breaking something open, and the blood poured out faster and faster. He coughed and fell down, taking my knife with him, still *taking,* even now.

I looked back at Jordan, still there, a shimmering perfect haze, ready to welcome me back to her. My chest swelled up with the thought of it. Time to go home.

The bastard screamed again. I crouched down, getting my knife back, cursing him as he kept trying to breathe. Shallow, slippery gasps, like a fish. I stood, disgusted with him, and then froze, my eyes flickering to the ceiling.

There was a camera up there. It had been watching me the whole time.

I looked away. Not important. *Nothing* was important except that he was *gone* and the world was right again. It was done. Finally, it was done.

I ran back into her, into the glorious, consuming light. Anger gone now. No sight, no sound. Nothing but surging, soaring joy. So furiously bright, so all-consuming, tearing me up and hurtling me along and tossing me over and over myself, over and over and –

Something was wrong.

Where was she? Where was the filthy room with the stains on the floor? The first trip had been nothing. Seconds. This was too long.

The brightness dimmed. Sound rose up in my ears. Transcendent light covered over by grey, roaring mess.

No. This was wrong. This was *wrong*.

Turbulence rattled through me, pummelling muscle and bone. I was screaming. Burning. Not fire, but something, curling around me, licking up my body and into my mouth and nose, consuming everything.

Then *smack* into the solid ground, everything bright again. I was back. Back in the shining laboratory, in a pool of the traitor's blood. Still shaking.

The light was everywhere, cracking walls and shattering windows with a sound like an erupting volcano. Concrete and glass and dirt rained down from the ceiling. The whole world caving in on me.

And then it was gone.

Chapter 8

JORDAN

THURSDAY, AUGUST 13, 2.21 A.M.
14 HOURS, 39 MINUTES

I saw it all.

I saw Peter charge out after Luke.

I saw his knife come down again and again.

I saw Luke cry out and fall to the ground, the life gurgling out of him.

I saw him drag himself across the room, streaking his own blood across the floor, out into the next room where he would spend his last breaths warning Kara about the end of the world.

I saw the whole thing play out exactly the way I'd seen it a thousand times over on Kara's surveillance tape.

And then the whole world blacked out and I didn't see anything.

I woke up, concrete hard against my back, and for one treacherous moment I was disoriented enough to blur the pain a little.

Then I opened my eyes and saw the dull brown

stains spread out underneath me, lit up by the glow of my abandoned torch, and reality set back in like a battering ram. I felt my chest cave in, my lungs collapsing, my whole body giving way under an avalanche of crushing, nauseating grief.

A groan burst out of me, long and low and guttural. My arms wrapped around my stomach, shivers rattling through me, tossing me against the dirty ground. His blood was everywhere. Smeared out around me, soaking into the concrete.

I had to get out.

I was on my feet before I even knew it, desperate to be *out* of there. My legs failed me and I hit the wall, hands crashing into the tunnel.

I started gagging. Not a vision. Just my body's pointless attempt to purge itself. I rode it out, head down between my arms, and then half-climbed, half-fell into the tunnel.

And then finally, the dam burst and the tears came flooding out. I crawled through the darkness, stopping and starting, overcome with ugly, unrestrained, shuddering sobs.

Some subconscious part of my mind registered a change in the way my cries echoed off the walls. I was back out in the corridor. I got up, only now realising that I'd left my torch behind. I staggered aimlessly through the black until I collided with some spongy wood sticking out from the wall. I held onto it, keeping myself standing.

But why? Why even bother? Why not just curl up and die and be done with it?

Nothing had changed.

It was all over, and nothing had changed.

I'd held out for as long as I could, longer than I'd ever done before, watching him struggle and bleed and crawl out of the room, hoping against hope that something would step in and save him. But nothing. *Nothing.* Blow for blow, scream for scream, it had all happened exactly the way it was supposed to.

WHY?

Why let him get murdered? Why couldn't he have just delivered the message and come back? Why did he have to *die* for it?

For months, I'd been hurtling along on the strength of my stupid visions, convincing myself that they were somehow helping us along, guiding us through these hundred impossible days, that somehow we were *meant* to overcome the Co-operative and make it out alive. And now this.

I spun away from the wall, rage blazing up and bursting out. 'YOU WERE SUPPOSED TO HELP! YOU WERE SUPPOSED TO SAVE HIM!'

After that, it wasn't even words. I screamed my throat raw, crying out into the endless darkness, until finally my lungs gave out and I stood, chest heaving, waiting for something, anything, that would justify what had happened here tonight.

But of course, there was no response.

Nothing but deep, deafening silence.

I started running. It was all instinct – some innate reflex kicking in below my conscious mind. I just needed to get away. I fumbled in the dark, somehow finding a path among the laboratories.

Light glowed faintly up ahead. The dying flicker of an old camping lantern. It was coming from Bill's excavation room. *Peter's* room. The place he'd spent two weeks obsessively digging up out of the rock. All in some deluded attempt to return to the Jordan he'd left behind twenty years ago. To return to me.

I pushed on, shakier with every step. Through the old laboratory with the floor covered in broken glass, through the remains of another decrepit corridor, into the room with the lantern that Bill had dragged us into, only hours before.

I stopped at the back wall, almost slamming into my own shadow, and sank to the ground again, dizzy and out of breath. Crying again. It seemed impossible that I *could* still cry. I felt so emptied-out already. But the tears kept coming, dredging themselves up from the depths of me and running together into deep, wracking sobs that left me gasping for breath.

He was gone.

Gone.

I realised now that I'd never actually believed it was going to happen. Not really. Even in my most desperate moments, I'd never let go of the stupid, stubborn hope that *somehow* this would all get turned around. And now it was finished and he was gone, and I realised I had no idea what to do next because every single one of the plans in my head had Luke in it.

I was paralysed, the grief and the emptiness drowning out everything around me until there was nothing left in the whole world but to lie here in the dirt and weep.

'Luke …' I choked. 'Luke …'

I winced, the sound of my voice driving daggers into my own injured head, but I kept crying out, as if I could call him back from the dead. 'Luke …'

My eyes snapped open.

I gazed over at Bill's old camping lantern, my mind alight with a sudden realisation. As I watched, the lantern seemed to shimmer slightly, waving out of shape, as though there was heat rising up from the ground in front of it. At first, it could have been just tears obscuring my vision, but the distortion quickly expanded and spread, growing brighter, more visible, like mist or steam or something.

Like *me*.

Another portal was opening up. The one from a few hours ago. The one I'd inadvertently created – inadvertently *become* – when Bill brought Luke and me out here to force his way into the future. This was the other end of it.

I sat up, staring into the brightening cloud. I'd seen all this before, from the other side. Which meant the other Jordan, the one from the past, could see *me*.

'JORDAN!' I yelled. 'TAKE HIM! TAKE HIM AND GO! HE'S –'

My voice became a splutter and then gave out completely. What was the point? She couldn't hear me. Of course she couldn't. That had been *me* a few hours ago and I hadn't heard a thing. Nothing had changed, and nothing was going to. Despite his misguided attempts to avert events, Bill had been right all along.

It was inevitable. All of it.

I slumped back down again, blocking it all out, trying to ignore the roiling pool of liquid light burning on the other side of my eyelids.

It wasn't until a fierce *thud* struck the ground in front of me that I remembered I still had one more ordeal to survive before this was all finally over.

I sat up. Crazy Bill from a few hours ago had just flown out of the portal, filthy and stinking, barely covered up by the tattered remains of his medical gown. He'd landed awkwardly, sprawled on his back between me and the portal, the torch in his helmet shining a spotlight onto the ceiling.

I slid away until my back hit the wall. Bill rolled over and stood. He sobbed loudly, lifting his hands to reach out to me, face taut with a kind of awestruck joy.

'I'm back,' he said breathlessly, like he almost didn't believe it. 'I'm back, Jordan. I'm here.'

I pressed into the wall, cold fury spreading through my chest.

It was him. Peter.

He advanced on me, hands trembling, spreading apart to embrace me. 'Jor–'

'MURDERER!' I yelled, lunging at him. 'You *stupid – pathetic –*!'

He lurched away, shocked, like he couldn't fathom why I wasn't pleased to see him. He gathered himself and stepped forward, trying again.

Then he stopped.

His eyes locked onto mine, slowly pulling themselves into focus as though he was just now figuring out how to use them. The smile slipped from his face. His mouth drifted open in dawning, horrified comprehension, like he'd suddenly realised where he was and what he was doing. Like he was waking up.

I slammed my fist into the side of his face, all pain and rage and adrenaline. 'YOU KILLED HIM!'

He recoiled again, waving his arms, trying to speak.

'*NO!* I cried, punching him in the stomach, in the ribs, in the mouth, fists pounding at whatever they could reach, beating and beating, sick, choking, blind with tears, screaming myself hoarse. He staggered under the blows but didn't cry out, didn't fight back. I kept going, hammering into him, head throbbing and spinning, arms aching from the effort, until finally my body said *no more,* and I collapsed at his feet, gasping for breath.

He stared down at me, an agonised moan slipping out between his rotting teeth, then wheeled around to look into the portal still swirling in the air. He steadied himself, head clutched in his hands, and took off at a lumbering run. Back through the shimmering cloud. Back into the past.

Almost as soon as he'd disappeared, the portal began to break down. The light grew brighter still, spreading out and filling the room, and the walls shook with the familiar sound of rushing wind. And I guess there was some part of me that still cared about preserving my life, because I shrank into a corner, shielding my head as cracks snaked through the concrete and bits of the ceiling broke loose and fell away.

Everything turned white as the portal erupted in an explosion of light. And then it was gone.

The darkness returned, and I lay on my back, dust raining down on my face. My chest rose and fell, gradually regaining its natural rhythm, and I waited as my eyes remembered how to see again in the dim light of Bill's lantern. By the time they did, I seemed to have got some small part of my mind back as well.

I was still here. Still alive. The gaping, invisible hole in my chest hadn't gone anywhere, but I was starting to feel like maybe I could split my attention just enough to let some other thoughts creep in around the edges.

My family was still out there.

The *world* was still out there, however temporarily.

Luke had given up his life to warn the rest of us about Tobias. Was I really going to just lie here and waste that?

There would be time to grieve later. To do it

properly. But right now I had to get out there and *do* something, or else I was going to have a lot more to grieve over.

One more day, I told myself, slowly rising to my feet. *You can do that much. Keep it together for one more day, and then you can fall apart all you want.*

But even as I moved to leave the excavation room, I caught myself glancing over my shoulder, checking out of habit to make sure Luke was with me, and my insides gave another sharp twist.

Focus, I ordered myself. *Keep it together. Think. What's next?*

My first job was getting outside. I bent down to grab Bill's lantern, carrying it with me as I climbed back through the caved-in corridor and into the lab on the other side. The light was all but dead now. Still, it was better than nothing.

I jolted as my foot struck something heavy lying on the ground, and then swung the lantern down to see what it was.

Bill's pickaxe. The one he'd been using to hack this place apart. I shivered, remembering the night Dr Galton had flung an almost identical pickaxe into my side, cutting me open on our way out of the medical centre. Luke had carried me to safety. He'd saved my life. And now –

Enough.

I took a breath, hoisting the pickaxe up off the ground with my free hand. I wouldn't use the pointy ends. I didn't want to kill anybody. But one solid whack with the broad side would be enough to take care of any unsuspecting guards who were still –

I jumped again, backing up and hurriedly switching off the lantern.

Footfalls on gritty concrete. One of Calvin's men, still down here. Left behind to take care of Luke and me. Or maybe he'd just been too injured to leave with the others.

Silently, I lowered the lantern to the floor and wrapped both hands around the pickaxe. I edged across the lab until my shoulder nudged the wall, then felt along to the doorway out of here.

He was just around the corner. Hard to tell how close he was in the darkness. But close.

I brought the pickaxe out in front of me, feeling the weight of it in my hands. One chance. Either I got him on the first swing, or I got shot full of holes.

I held my breath, straining to hear him coming, and almost shouted as a torch beam shot out from back up the passageway, lighting up the wall opposite me. The circle of light grew steadily smaller as the guard crept closer.

I shifted my grip on the pickaxe, preparing to swing.

Three ...

Two ...

A rifle poked out from around the corner and I swung, throwing all my weight behind the weapon in my hands. It sailed out in a wide arc, almost pulling out of my hands, momentum carrying me out across the doorway. The guard yelped, leaping back, and a shudder ripped through my arms as the pickaxe swung past him and struck heavily into the wall. I squeezed down on the pickaxe, desperate to get out of the line of fire before –

'Whoa whoa whoa! Jordan!'

The voice cut through everything and I froze up. The pickaxe slipped from my hands, clanking noisily to the floor.

The man lowered his weapon, spinning it around to light up the space between us. And there, in the glow of a stolen rifle, dirty but completely uninjured, completely *alive* ...

'Luke?'

2½ HOURS EARLIER ...

Chapter 9

BILL

For the first time in twenty years, I had no idea what was supposed to happen next.

I limped along the dark road, eyes on the town centre, my lungs rattling. Pain roared from feral gums, seeping cuts, and even worse going wrong on the inside. It was my same old screwed-up body, but somehow getting my head back together had turned up the dials on all of it.

I gasped for breath and it tasted like smoke.

Phoenix was burning.

Gunfire echoed in the streets, flames surged through the school and the mall, the whole town glowed orange in the light of the fire and the crackle of the shield grid strung out across the sky, and none of it even came close to the chaos raging inside my head.

I tried to block it all out. Focus. But I couldn't block out the sound of Jordan's voice. My head was full of it. The same word, over and over again, dark and poisonous and so unbearably freaking *true*.

MURDERER.

I was a murderer.

And now, finally, I could see it. I could *feel* it. Two full decades as a professional crazy person, and all that blood and death and guilt had finally come crashing down on top of me in one massive, soul-destroying heap.

And to top it off, it had all blown up just as I'd succeeded. Just as I'd *won*. Twenty years stuck in the past, twenty years waiting and scheming to get back to the girl I'd murdered for, and I'd finally *done it*. I'd got the portal to the future back open and made it home to my own time, just a few moments after I'd left it. And there was Jordan, all alone and crying on the ground, with no Luke to distract her from falling all over me.

All hail Peter, the romantic freaking mastermind.

And not only had my spectacular display of murder and craziness failed to impress Jordan, but somehow this second trip through time, this trip that was meant to be my big shiny victory, had ripped away the decades of insanity and brought me face to face with the sickening reality of who I really was.

MURDERER.

It was gone now. The haze of fallout clawing at my brain. Rewiring my thoughts. Twisting me around. In an instant, it had all been blown away. My sanity had been given back to me.

Crazy Bill was gone. I was Peter again.

Right. Like it's that simple.

Like I could just write the last two decades off as my Crazy Years and let myself off the hook. Like it wasn't me, right there, making every single one of those decisions. I might've been messed up by the fallout, but my mind was still there. It was still *my* mind.

What a twisted bloody nightmare to see yourself for who you really are.

I made it to the park at the end of the main street and crouched in the overgrown grass, knees cracking. Shouts rang through the shadows up ahead. Guards-turned-firefighters, swarming around what was left of the mall, spread too thin to do anything much. Whatever was going on inside the Shackleton Building, it had the Co-operative even more worried than what was happening out here.

I clenched my filthy hands around the key card I'd dug up from one of my old hiding places in the bush – the one I'd stolen all those weeks ago to sneak in and spy on Shackleton and Calvin.

Fear churned through me. Not the familiar, always-there crazy person panic. This was sane man's fear. Survival fear.

Deal with it, Murderer. Move.

I stood, pain creaking up through my legs again, and lumbered out across the park, my grotty old hospital gown rippling out behind me. I yanked it up around my waist, and broke into the closest thing to a run I could manage.

And suddenly, there it was. Sliding into view from behind the mall, lit up by the fire but still in one piece. The building that'd been my prison for more than half of the last hundred days: Phoenix's medical centre.

I forced myself forward, chest heaving, dodging the guards and the minefield of debris buried in the grass. My mind reeled with the long-lost terror of not knowing what was up ahead, the future suddenly wide open in front of me again.

It was bloody disorienting. For so long now, I'd been living my whole life according to the same pre-written plan, working obsessively to make sure history repeated itself exactly the way it was supposed to. And somewhere along the line, I'd convinced myself that all of it was inevitable. That my future was fixed, because I'd already seen it happen.

And maybe that was right. Maybe I *couldn't* change anything. Maybe it really was all locked in from the beginning and even now I was just playing into the same endless loop. But I was getting pretty bloody sick of second-guessing myself.

Screw time travel. All I knew was that right here, right now, I was making a choice.

I knew I could never unbreak it all. Even if this worked, I couldn't cancel out all the evil I'd done just by stacking some good on top of it now. But back in the medical centre, somewhere in the blur of my imprisonment, I'd seen something. Something that might actually make a bit of difference. Not for me, but for her.

I crashed out from the grass at the edge of the park and staggered across the street to the medical centre, firelight crackling over me. A firefighter shot past without even noticing I was there.

Up the side of the building to the main street. It was a war zone. Wreckage from the mall littered the street. This was more than just fire damage. Someone had tried to blow it up. A big hunk of concrete had punched through the razor-wire around the front of the Shackleton Building, twisting it out of shape and demolishing the fountain on the other side. The security centre had been destroyed days ago now, but no-one had even bothered to rope it off.

Now and then, I saw movement in the darkness. Escaped prisoners, but not many of them. It seemed like most of the fighting was still going on inside the –

I lurched back, crouching in the shadow of a parked delivery truck as the Shackleton Building doors slid open. Two figures raced out into the light of the fire. I felt a little pull in my chest as I realised who they were: Mr Larson, my old English teacher, getting dragged along by his wife.

Another guy ran out after them, dressed in black and armed with a rifle. He shouted at the Larsons to get back inside, and I felt another jolt of recognition, this time laced with icy hatred. Mr Hanger, our bastard of a history teacher. Trust him to sign up for Calvin's death brigade. He was never happy unless he was making someone else miserable, so this had to be pretty much the perfect –

I caught myself, disgust washing over me as a memory floated to the surface of my mind. My fists around Mr Hanger's throat, smashing his face into the floor of the school gym while he begged me to stop.

If he was a bastard, then what was I?

I shook my head, pushing it all away. No time for this.

Larson darted in front of his wife as Hanger charged over to meet them, still shouting but apparently unwilling to actually *use* the weapon in his hands.

I dragged my eyes away from them and kept moving, up the little wheelchair ramp behind me to the entrance.

My bare feet crunched on crumbled bits of safety glass. The front doors of the medical centre had already been smashed open. I jumped across the threshold, thudding down on all fours on the other side.

I grunted, picking myself up. The lights were all off, had been for weeks, but an orange glow flickered in from the street, just enough to see by. I scratched at my beard, trying to remember. I hadn't been in through the front in years. Which way was I meant to –?

An arm shot out from behind me, wrapping around my throat and dragging me back into the shadows. A twisted bit of metal hovered in my peripheral vision: the broken leg of a food court chair. 'Easy, mate. We don't want any –'

I shifted around, yanking free, my mind lashing out to shove him away, send him flying into a wall.

Nothing happened. The guy stayed right where he was. Someone screamed behind him.

I tried again, channelling all my adrenaline out into his chest.

Nothing.

I froze up, feeling suddenly defenceless, realising for the first time that it had been a package deal. My trip through the portal hadn't just stripped me of my insanity. It had taken my sci-fi mind powers away from me too.

'All right, mate. Just – just stay back.' The man stepped shakily out of the shadows, clutching his chair leg like a caveman holding a spear. His voice registered in my head and I swayed under a sudden weight, realising who he was a second before his face caught the light.

Dad.

Chapter 10

BILL

Dad's eyes narrowed at the sudden change in my expression. Mum came up behind him, freaked out but alive. Unhurt. Tears stung my eyes, and I stumbled to touch her, seeing both of them clearly for the first time in forever. She cringed away, terrified, and with an ache in my chest, I realised how I looked to them.

'HEY!' Dad stuck out his chair leg to ward me off. 'Hey. That's close enough.'

He might as well have run the thing straight through me. But what was I expecting? I wasn't their son. Not anymore.

'Listen,' said Dad. 'I'm sorry. I shouldn't have attacked you. We're only trying to –'

'How did you get out?' I asked, shocked at how weirdly unfamiliar my own voice sounded in my ears. Dad didn't answer. 'Look, I swear I'm not going to hurt you. I just …'

Dad cocked his head, like he was trying to work

out how Crazy Bill was suddenly capable of coming out with a complete sentence.

'We were in the showers when the food court blew up,' said Mum, and for the first time I took in her wet hair and the nurses' uniforms she and Dad had found to cover themselves. 'They move us through in shifts during the night. We ran. Crawled through that hole in the fence.'

Dad lowered his weapon and glanced into the shadows behind them. 'I think we're all right, Alyssa.'

A girl stepped out. Green eyes, caramel-coloured skin, dirty Phoenix High uniform. Couldn't have been older than thirteen. She had a guard's utility belt hanging over her shoulder like a beauty pageant sash.

Alyssa looked up at me, nervous but standing her ground. She glanced sideways at my mum. 'Are we bringing him with us?'

'Bringing me where?' I asked.

Dad frowned, sussing out how far to trust me. I looked away from him, pushing back another surge of tears. It was too much. Too familiar. How many times had I been on the receiving end of that look, back when the worst I'd been guilty of was skipping class?

'Vattel Complex,' he said finally. 'An old place under the town. It's where we were hiding out, back before –' He hesitated. 'Hang on. Is that where –? Have you been down there with them?'

My gut turned in on itself. 'Yeah. I have, but –'

'Are they okay?' Dad's hand hovered in midair, like

he'd been about to touch me but then thought better of it. 'Peter. My son. Is he …?'

'He's – alive,' I said. 'He's still down there.'

Mum let out a little shudder of relief. She wrapped a hand around Dad's arm and swallowed hard. What was it going to do to her when she found out the truth?

I glanced around the reception area. I couldn't do this. I had maybe an hour left before Luke's murder.

'Hey, where are you going?' Dad called after me as I started towards a doorway across the room.

I ignored him, pushing through to the corridor on the other side.

'The tunnels?' he guessed, trailing after me, Mum and the girl right behind him. 'Yeah, I thought of that too. But how are you going to get in without a –?' His eyes dropped to the card in my hand. 'Oh.'

I limped around a corner. Now what? I couldn't bring them with me. Not back to the Complex. Not now. But I wasn't about to just abandon my parents.

Keep moving, Murderer. Work it out later.

There was a *click* and a flash of light as the girl found a torch on her belt. She handed it to my dad.

I watched my shadow lumber along the walls in front of us, all huge and ragged, and that sickening sane man's fear flooded over me again. I was naked. Unarmed. Powerless except for my bare, blistered fists. A lifetime of hurling my problems across the room with my brain, and now –

'Shh!' Dad hissed, and the torch cut out behind

me. Everyone fell silent. I strained my ears. Nothing but the muffled sound of the chaos outside. Dad flicked the torch back on again, shaking his head. 'Never mind. Thought I heard something.'

I hurried down the next corridor, even more on edge now. What was I meant to do if someone *did* come?

Dad's torch flashed off again.

I skidded to a stop, just short of the next bend in the corridor, clamping my mouth shut, suddenly aware of how loud and rasping my breathing was.

A round of gunfire echoed in from somewhere on the street.

'C'mon,' Alyssa whispered. 'There's nothing –'

The whisper turned into a squeak as a door clunked open, just out of sight. There was a burst of light and a cold, venomous voice spilled out from inside.

'– honestly think him foolish enough to leave that option open to you? The countdown is *locked*, Louisa. Not even Shackleton can override it now.'

I stepped back, crashing into my dad.

It was Dr Galton. Shackleton's second-in-command, last seen as a hazy nightmare swimming past my prison cell. I stumbled to the nearest door and wrenched at the handle. It didn't budge. Mum yanked on Dad's arm, urging him to *run*.

Galton strode closer, footsteps splitting the air like gunshots. And in between, a buzzing sound. Another voice, coming through a phone. Whatever it was saying, Galton didn't like it.

'To protect himself!' she snarled. 'To protect the *world* from invertebrate cowards who would have us turn tail at the first sign –'

Her torch flashed around the corner, lighting us up. Ending the conversation.

Mum screamed. Dad dragged her back, waving his chair leg. Alyssa turned to run, but –

SMASH!

Before she'd even made it one step, she shot into the air and through the nearest window, tangling in the blinds. *How –?*

Galton. Steely concentration in her eyes. She was like me.

I charged, diving before she had time to react. Her phone and torch flew from her hands. Pain sparked through every joint I had as we dropped to the ground. She thrashed around but couldn't shake me. Her powers really were like mine: useless at point blank range.

They worked fine on Dad, though. I heard frantic footsteps behind me as he rushed in, then a breathless shout as Galton threw him back up the corridor.

I got to my knees, still pinning Galton down, one hand mashed into her face. I felt the force of her mind against me, shoving me back, but I held on, bringing my other hand around to catch a fistful of her hair. Galton cried out, eyes squeezing shut. A massive over-reaction.

Too slow, I realised what she was up to. Her hand

flashed around, all silky precision, aiming the pistol she'd just whipped out from her hip.

BLAM!

But the one upside to twenty years in the wild was that it kept your survival reflexes pretty sharp. I jerked sideways, deafened by the noise. Plaster raining down from the roof as the shot went wide. I grabbed Galton's wrist and smashed it hard against the floor, sending the weapon skittering away.

Galton snarled at me. She kicked and clawed, drawing blood. Her nails jabbed at one of my nastier wounds and a howl of pain burst from my throat. I dragged her head up off the floor, appalled all over again as I flashed back to the scene with Hanger in the gym.

Do it.

I smashed her back down again.

She cried out, whole body shuddering, and I flinched. A half-second of pity. Galton took it, rolling under me, knocking me to the ground. I rolled to catch her. Grabbed at her hair again. Missed. I threw out my other hand and caught Galton by the arm, just in time to feel her tense up and shriek as a spraycan hissed into her eyes. Galton crumpled, face red and streaming.

I twisted around. The kid. Alyssa. Back out in the corridor, armed with the capsicum spray from her guard's belt. She pumped another blast into Galton's face and I squinted away, catching the edge of it.

'Grab her!' Alyssa shrieked.

I heaved in a breath, half-blind but keeping hold

of Galton's arm. I got back to my knees, hauling her towards me, then flipped her over and pinned her down again, my hands shifting uneasily back to her head. One solid thump and it lolled to the side.

The corridor went quiet again. I backed off from Galton, pushing down the sick feeling in my stomach, and turned to Alyssa, who was checking herself over for injuries. 'Thanks.'

She nodded weakly, pulling a set of handcuffs from her belt. I took them from her, locking Galton's arms behind her back, then flinched at a light and low buzzing behind me. Galton's phone, vibrating across the floor. I crawled over and read the name blinking up from the screen. *Louisa Hawking*. Cat's mum, calling Galton back.

I snatched up the phone and ended the call. Memories flooded back from a lifetime ago. Memories of countless afternoons at Cat's place, when I had no idea that Louisa was anything more than a kind-of-highly-strung mum. Memories of Cat, of a relationship requiring zero murders that might have actually gone somewhere if I hadn't been so bloody –

A rush of footsteps pounded the thoughts away. Mum and Dad, barrelling towards me. More torches coming behind them.

I snatched up the key card and ran. Around the corner, down a little flight of stairs and there, finally, was the big steel door that led down into Shackleton's tunnel network.

'Stop! Stop right there!'

A furious, too-familiar voice. Mr Hanger. *Officer* Hanger. Either Cat's mum had realised what was up and called for help, or this was just the latest in a long history of him magically showing up to bust me. Either way, I was pretty sure he wouldn't actually *fire* that gun until –

Gunshots shattered the air above my head. Alyssa screamed.

'Bloody Ranga!' I shouted, diving for the metal door with the key card in hand. The door clunked open and I hurried inside, tripping on my gown and almost getting trampled as the others rushed in behind me.

Hanger fired again. The bullets battered into the door as Dad heaved it shut after us, while Mum raced across the tiny, empty room to activate the trapdoor in the floor.

'He's – supposed to be – a teacher!' Alyssa panted. She jumped aside as the section of grey tiles she was standing on sank down into the floor, revealing a glimmering silver staircase. 'Whoa. What *is* that?'

I ignored her, plodding down the stairs as soon as there was space, out into the light of a wide, narrow corridor. The Co-operative's secret medical research facility, AKA Victoria Galton's House of Imprisonment and Torture. My mind flashed with groggy half-memories of drips and needles and 'tests'.

Dad looked at me out of the corner of his eye, pretty uneasy himself. He was the engineer who'd designed the containment machine that kept me trapped down here.

'Sorry,' he said warily. 'For – for my part in all this. I had no idea who I was really working for. Truly. I had no clue about any of it. All I knew was that you were – They told me you were a dangerous monster.'

'Yeah,' I said, heading for a door to my right. 'They weren't wrong.'

A shout echoed behind the double doors at the end of the corridor.

'There's someone in there!' shrieked Alyssa, searching her belt for a weapon. The doors shook like someone was pounding them with their fists.

'The prisoners,' said Mum. 'The ones who didn't make it out last time.'

'We need to get those doors open.' Dad looked back at me, expectant.

'I – I can't,' I said. 'Something –'

Mum broke off from the rest of us, striding towards the doors. Dad ran after her, realising what she had in her hands. Galton's pistol. She must have grabbed it on our way down.

I left them to it. Went through a door to my right, into a dark room filled with petri dishes and medical fridges. In the middle was a bed, empty and neatly made. More unwelcome memories. During my stay here, the bed had belonged to whichever of us the Co-operative were running their latest mad-scientist experiment on, which most of the time seemed to be a pasty-skinned kid named Jeremy.

I ripped open the nearest fridge, scanning through

the labels on the vials inside. Four shelves, arranged by name and then by number: *Anderson, Burke, Burke, Kennedy.* Not what I was looking for. I slammed the door shut, then raced along the line of fridges and opened one near the end.

Bingo. Jeremy had a whole fridge to himself. I crouched at the bottom shelf and ran my finger along to the last vial in line: *J_Thomas_Tissue_Modification_ Treatment_4-3-0*

This was it. Or at least, as close as they'd come to 'it'. I pulled the vial loose and almost dropped it as I heard a gunshot outside, followed by voices and footsteps pouring into the corridor.

I straightened, heart pounding, and crossed to a store cupboard. I tore the doors open, scattering equipment to the floor until my hands finally landed on the instrument I'd seen Galton using on one of her 'assistants'.

The *infuser.*

It reminded me of the syringe/gun thing Dr Montag had used to inject me with a suppressor, all those years ago. One of the last nights of clear memory before the fallout swallowed me up. The thing was shaped kind of like a pistol, with an empty vial in the chamber and a syringe in place of the barrel. I ejected the vial, replaced it with my amber-coloured sample of *J_Thomas,* and raced for the door.

In the hall, Mum, Dad and Alyssa had been joined by five scraggly prisoners in hospital gowns. My old neighbours. Alyssa had one of them, Jeremy, wrapped up in a hug.

'Right,' said Dad, walking over to meet me. 'Where to now?'

I ran a hand down over my beard, stress bubbling up again as I looked at this terrified rabble who had all apparently decided that *Crazy Freaking Bill* was the one to lead them to safety.

I had to lose them. I ran through the tunnel exits in my head: security centre destroyed, Shackleton Building impossible, school on fire, mall –

There was a shriek behind me. Alyssa had just released Jeremy from their hug. She was staring, horrified, at her arms. Everywhere she'd come into direct contact with Jeremy, her golden-brown skin was bleached pinkish-white. Stained with Jeremy's own pale skin tone.

'It's okay!' said Jeremy weakly. 'It's – I swear it'll go away!'

Alyssa didn't seem to hear. She was clawing at her arms now, trying to scratch the discolouration off.

'Stop it!' I snapped. 'You're fine. It won't hurt you. It'll go away.'

Alyssa flinched and shut up. She stopped scratching, but still wouldn't meet Jeremy's eye when he looked at her.

'This way,' I said, making my mind up. It was risky, but so was everything. I led them all back the way we'd come, into the little room under the trapdoor.

'You guys go that way,' I said, pointing at a door leading up to Phoenix's main office building. 'You'll come out up the other end of the main street. Then run for the east end of town and circle around to the Vattel Complex.'

'What about you?' Dad asked.

'I'm – not coming,' I said.

I needed to get back to the Complex, and I needed to do it *now*. The direct route. Through the hub under the Shackleton Building and out the trapdoor in Aaron Ketterley's office at the north end of town.

The Complex would be crawling with security by now. Peter – the other Peter – would be rabidly dismantling the cave-in made by Soren's explosion. But by the time these guys took the long way back, it would all be over and the whole place would be empty. All except for Jordan and, if by some miracle this all worked out, an unstabbed, still-alive Luke.

Dad looked at me, uncertain. 'All right, well – thanks, mate. Thanks for everything.'

I couldn't help it. I threw my arms around him, eyes going from zero to bawling in about two seconds. Dad tensed, probably thinking I was about to stab him with the thing in my hand, then relaxed enough to slap me awkwardly on the back.

I released him, turning to Mum. She glanced nervously at Dad, and then reluctantly allowed me to hug her. It was all tense muscles and more awkward patting.

But I knew it was my only chance so I squeezed her tight, closing my eyes, taking what I could get.

You did this, Murderer.

Don't act like you don't deserve it.

Mum pulled away, deciding my time was up. I wiped my eyes, but the tears kept coming.

'Listen,' I sobbed, barely getting the words out. 'Both – both of you, listen. When you find out – When this is over and they tell you about me … You *can't* blame yourselves, okay? Promise me. This wasn't you. None of this was you.'

'Sure, mate,' said Dad, reverting to his talking-to-crazy-people voice. He moved closer to Mum, just in case I decided to freak out right here at the finish. 'Yeah. We'll keep that in mind.'

I watched as Dad led the others out of the room. Knowing I could never get my parents back, but hoping that somehow the next hour would make the days ahead a little bit easier for them to handle.

Assuming there *were* days ahead.

I stared down at the infuser, at the sticky orange liquid sloshing around inside the vial, everything blurry with tears.

Last chance, Murderer. See if you can do some good before your time runs out.

I shoved open the door and ran.

Chapter 11

BILL

Run, Murderer. Run.

Through the tunnels, over the road and into the bush, running and then walking and then limping, chest caving in, everything aching and soaked with sweat.

The shield grid snapped and snarled overhead, like some vicious animal, hungry for blood. I tuned it out, trying to work out where I was going, squinting through the darkness in search of a familiar landmark.

My foot caught on a tree root and I staggered, the infuser slipping out of my hands.

No!

I dived to the dirt. My hands shot out, knocking the thing up into the air and then catching it again, centimetres from disaster. I got up, head spinning, holding the vial up in the moonlight to make sure it was still in one piece. Then a scream split the night and I almost dropped it again.

Georgia. Breathless and hysterical. A guard boomed

at her to shut up, but she paid no attention. They were behind me, coming up out of the Complex. I'd walked straight past the entrance without even seeing it.

I was halfway back to them before I remembered my powers were gone. Guts churning, I crouched in the bushes, trying to quiet my wheezing breath.

Now what?

Torches swept between the trees, most of them pointing away from me, back towards the town. I dropped lower, joints cracking again, and scanned the huddle of faces. Georgia, Mrs Burke, Cathryn, Soren, Luke's mum, and guards to keep them in line.

No Jordan or Luke. No me.

Georgia wailed again, clinging to her mum. A guard whose name I'd long forgotten stepped up to them, grabbing Mrs Burke by the hair. 'You shut her up right now or I'll –'

'Saunders!' growled a voice from down in the ground, and the guard shut up. Officer Calvin came up through the trapdoor in the grass, a tiny baby in one arm and a rifle in the other. For a second in the low light, I thought his hands were covered in blood, but it was just the red gloves he was wearing.

Calvin turned to the guard holding Cat. 'Get them down to the bunker. Find Hawking, she'll let you in.'

Cat let out a sob at the mention of her mum's name.

The guard's brow furrowed. 'Chief –'

'Once inside,' Calvin steamrolled on, 'you are to put all the entrances under manual lockdown. Remain with the prisoners until I return. Keep them alive and unharmed at all costs.'

'What about you, sir?' said another officer, knees buckling slightly under the weight of a half-conscious Soren.

'I'll be back to interrogate the prisoners,' said Calvin. He stared down at the baby. 'But first, I have this one to deal with.'

'NO!' cried Mrs Burke, breaking her silence for the first time since I'd got here. 'Calvin, please! He's just a baby!'

Calvin shot her a look I couldn't read. 'I think we both know that's not true.'

The guard who'd been arguing with Calvin started back towards town. The others fell into line behind him, leaving Calvin standing at the tunnel entrance.

'Tobias!' Georgia shrieked. 'No! Give me back my brother!'

Tobias.

The name exploded in my head like a flare. It had been irrelevant to me for so long, just another part of the white noise, pushed aside in my obsession with getting back to Jordan. But now, finally, the pieces started slotting together.

This was what they'd been looking for. First Kara and Soren, and then all of them. The cure for Tabitha. The only way to bring down the Co-operative.

Take Tobias to the release station.

Tobias. Jordan's baby brother.

Seriously?

Georgia's tear-choked screams didn't let up. Calvin stood motionless, watching his men fade away into the night, waiting to make sure they were actually following orders. He muttered something under his breath. Then he turned, striding away through the bush.

Striding straight towards me. No idea I was there, but he'd work it out quickly enough when he trod on me.

I nestled the infuser in the grass and waited until he was two steps away, then heaved to my feet, screaming. Calvin lurched backwards, crying out in shock.

The baby's eyes snapped open.

Calvin swung his rifle around. Too slow. I grabbed his head with both hands, slamming it sideways into a tree. He let out a grunt, eyes fluttering shut, and I swooped down to grab Tobias before he slipped out of Calvin's grip.

Calvin collapsed against the tree, then dropped heavily to the ground.

I slung the strap of his rifle over my shoulder, switching the torch on to give myself some light, then scrounged for the infuser.

Still intact.

I raced to the entrance, carrying Tobias with me, but the trapdoor had already rolled shut. I stared down at the low, ragged lines of mouldy concrete that ran around the entrance – all that was left of some long-gone building. I traced my free hand around the edges of the ruin. Shackleton's trapdoors all opened by flipping the switches on a fake power outlet. Maybe –

There.

Two little holes, side by side in the concrete. I leant closer, carefully poking the syringe end of the infuser into one of the holes. There was a tiny hiss and the door trundled open.

I hurried down the winding stairs into an inky black corridor littered with upturned tables and chairs. I clambered through, frustrated that I couldn't just blast it all away, stopping again as I reached a bed sticking halfway out of one of the doorways.

The whole time, Tobias stayed silent, gazing up at me with his giant baby eyes. I held him against me, no idea what I was doing. I'd always just seen babies as weird attachments to their mothers, little wriggling things that got hurried across the street at the first sight of me.

I climbed over the bed, into the room on the other side, looking for somewhere safe to ditch him. I took in the kitchen at the far end, ransacked and ripped apart, and the air disappeared from my lungs as I caught a vision of myself, as Peter, tearing those drawers open, scattering their contents, searching for something powerful enough to tear through flesh and bone –

I turned away, dizzy.

There was an old couch in the corner. I laid Tobias on it, tucking him in tightly with cushions to keep him there. His mouth stretched open in a tiny yawn. Even if they got him out to the release station, what exactly was this kid supposed to –?

Not your problem, Murderer. You'll be long gone by then.

I tightened my grip on the infuser, ready to run again. But before I had time to leave, the bed in the doorway started rattling with the weight of someone else coming in from outside. Luke. White-faced and panting.

Both of us stopped moving. My hand shook on the infuser, sweat running cold against my skin.

Luke sprung up from the bed, seeming to remember why he was here. 'Where are they? Did you see Calvin? And the others? Did they …?'

'Y-yeah. They're gone. The guards are taking them to that bunker under the Shackleton Building. Calvin's ordered them to put the whole place under manual lockdown.'

I tried to subtly pull the infuser around behind my back, but what was the point? He'd already seen it. Plus, I had a freaking rifle hanging over my shoulder, so who was I kidding?

'What about Jordan?' asked Luke urgently.

'She's – fine,' I said. 'Still down here. Or not up there with the others, anyway.'

Do it, Murderer.

I moved towards him. Slow.

'I'm sorry,' I said. 'For – for the murder. All of it. I was –'

'Yeah,' said Luke, hardly paying attention, like every

second he spent talking to me was more wasted time. 'Not your fault.'

'Yes it *was!*' I said, suddenly desperate for him to understand me. 'Even with the fallout, I was still – Luke! *Look at me!*'

Luke's eyes snapped back from the doorway. He stared at me, scared.

I kept going. 'It was *me,* okay? *I* spent my whole life obsessing over her! *I* attacked all those people! *I* put the knife in your chest! Me. I was nuts, but I was still me.'

I breathed in. A shudder, wet with tears.

Luke stood there, frozen. Seconds ticked by.

His expression shifted, just the tiniest bit. Not pity or understanding or anything as strong as that, but it did feel like maybe, just for a moment, he was considering the idea that I was still a person.

'Okay,' he said, finally. 'Okay, well –'

I lunged, latching onto his arm, and his face went right back to petrified.

'No, wait! Bill – Pete – what are you –?'

I hauled him around and threw him onto the nearest bed.

'Let me go!' he demanded, kicking at me. 'Peter's still out – *oof!*'

I sat on his stomach, knocking the wind out of him. 'Quiet, then. You want to lead him straight to us?'

I reached over our heads, grabbing hold of the make-shift clothesline stretched across the bunks, and tore it down, lashing Luke's arms together against the bed frame. The rifle on my shoulder pressed against his chest as I leant over him, and he decided to stop struggling.

That decision lasted about ten seconds.

I picked the infuser up from the mattress, checking the vial one last time, and Luke started writhing again, heaving against his restraints. 'No! Get that –! I thought you said you were *sorry!*'

'I am,' I said, free hand clenching around his face to hold him steady. A tear leaked out of my eye and splashed down onto his cheek. 'I really am.'

I jammed the infuser down into his arm and pulled the trigger.

Luke gaped down in horror as the serum drained into him, glinting gold in the shadowy half-light of the rifle's torch, and then gone, swallowed up by his arm.

'What –?' Luke shook under me but didn't pull away. 'Bill, what *is* that?'

I ignored him, counting down in my head.

Four … Three … Two …

'Bill – *Peter*, come on – What are you doing to me?'

One.

I pulled the trigger again and he gasped, eyes squeezing shut as vial began to refill. Blood. Slightly too thick and slightly off-colour, infused with *J_ Thomas_Tissue_Modification_Treatment_4-3-0.*

I withdrew the syringe and stood up, leaving Luke thrashing on the bed. He'd given up trying to interrogate me, attention split between writhing free of his restraints and watching to see what I was going to do next.

My hands were shaking again, fingers slippery on the infuser. I sat down on the bed opposite Luke's, begging myself to pull it together.

Deep breaths, Murderer. Don't screw it up now.

Something glinted down on the floor. A grimy shaving mirror, sitting in a shoebox of shower stuff. I picked it up and held it in front of me, recoiling slightly at the sight of my own face. I shook it off, stilling my arms the best I could.

And I turned the infuser on myself.

The syringe touched on the soft flesh between my nose and my right eye and I winced, nearly dropping it.

I closed my eyes.

Okay.

Okay, here we go.

I pushed. My skin gave way surprisingly easily and I guided the needle in, dropping the mirror and steadying myself with both hands.

I pulled the trigger and screamed. The infuser pumped the horrible concoction of blood and serum out into my face. I clenched my teeth, forcing my finger to keep squeezing the trigger until the vial emptied out.

I dragged the syringe back out of my face.

And then my face started to move.

I hadn't seen much in my blur of imprisonment down beneath the medical centre, but I'd seen enough to know it was a miracle Jeremy Thomas still had any blood left in him. Ever since the Co-operative had first caught wind of his fallout power – the ability to imprint his own skin tone onto someone else's body – Dr Galton had been hard at work, looking for a way to harness it. Turn it into a weapon.

She'd almost sucked him dry to fuel her research, refining and enhancing Jeremy's 'natural' ability, dragging it out of his body and into the Co-operative's arsenal. And now here it was: crude, imperfect, but hopefully, down here in the dark, enough to get the job done.

I cried out, head between my knees as muscles writhed and realigned, teeth jutted through gums, bones shifted under rippling skin. The pain was incredible.

Luke was shouting something – or maybe just shouting. Either way, I couldn't take it in. I was too fixated on the nightmare staring out at me from the shaving mirror lying cracked at my feet. My whole face bubbling up and melting, like I was being boiled alive from the inside.

And then, out of the shapeless sludge, my features began to reassert themselves. Only they weren't my features. Disfiguring scars had given way to smooth fifteen-year-old skin. Brown eyes had turned liquid blue. Even my swollen gums and broken teeth had made some effort to repair themselves.

I gazed down into the broken mirror.

And Luke gazed back.

The real Luke had stopped screaming now. He lay there on his back, chest rising and falling rapidly, a look of dawning comprehension spreading over his face.

Tobias, meanwhile, was staring contentedly at the ceiling, completely oblivious to the crime against nature that had just been committed right across the room.

I stood up, tore off the shredded remnant of my medical gown, and scanned the mess of clothes around the room. I needed something to wear. Something to hide the rest of me, still as mangled and scarred as ever. My eyes landed on a mud-stained tracksuit, and a pair of shoes strewn on the ground. I pulled them on and slung the rifle back over my shoulder.

Luke was still watching me, eyes welling up again. 'Peter ...' he began, but then couldn't work out how to continue.

I reached down the back of my pants, the closest thing I had to a pocket, pulled out Galton's phone and her key card, and dropped them on Luke's stomach.

'Get her home,' I said, in a voice that was not quite mine, but not quite his either. 'You take those bastards down and you get her home.'

I jumped the bed in the doorway and stumbled away down the corridor.

Chapter 12

BILL

Minutes later, I was deep inside the Complex, sprinting towards the room of Luke's murder. My insides burned but I didn't stop moving, didn't slow down, because every second I wasn't hurtling forward was a second I might lose my nerve altogether.

The rifle bounced against my chest, splashing light across the walls of the passageway, all of it glinting and blurry through the tears.

Just shoot him, pleaded the part of me still screaming for an escape. *Just put a bullet through his head and –*

And what?

Shooting Peter meant shooting *me*. How exactly was that supposed to work?

Forget it, Murderer. Keep moving.

For once in your life, be something other than a coward.

I shrugged off the rifle and tossed it aside, then pulled the hood of the tracksuit up over my head.

A few more metres through the dark, and I was

there. I crouched at the mouth of Soren's tunnel and felt the dread overwhelm me again. Tears poured from eyes that weren't my eyes, down cheeks that weren't my cheeks. My breath caught in Luke's throat and I swayed on the spot, paralysed.

Do it, Murderer. Move.

I crawled into the tunnel.

I was about halfway through when a bright light flashed into my face. Jordan, flicking on a torch. I squinted, pushing forward, over the edge and down into the blood-stained half-room on the other side.

And there she was. Awesome and beautiful and shaking like crazy.

'No!' she said, and for a second I thought she'd somehow seen through my disguise. 'Luke, please – *please* – you're not doing this. You can't ...'

I kept walking, opening my mouth to speak and coming out with nothing except a wet sob. In a few steps I was close enough to touch her, to breathe in her smell, and for a second, everything else flew straight out of my mind. I met her in the centre of the room, hands slipping to her face and her waist, and she didn't flinch, didn't shrink away from it. I pulled her closer, electricity firing through me as our mouths found each other in the dark.

Jordan returned the kiss, all love and desperation, and I knew it was wrong, knew it wasn't meant for me, but it was tender and real, and I drank it all in anyway. She tightened her grip on me, her whole body trembling now.

And then suddenly she was wrenching away from me, throwing herself at the mouth of the tunnel. Trying to get away. Trying to stop it all.

I grabbed at her, but she dropped out of my grip, collapsing to the floor with a groan. It was starting.

I crouched beside her, my body straining with the effort, ignoring her attempts to bat me away.

'*No!* Run! Leave me! I won't let you –!' She twisted into the foetal position, gagging her lungs up. I slipped a hand under her head, trying to calm my own shaking enough to help with hers.

'Please …' she choked.

'It's okay,' I said, spluttering up the words. 'Just – just try to –'

Her eyes glazed over. 'I'm sorry …' she murmured. 'I'm so, so sorry …'

Her head slipped through my hands – straight *through* them – and thumped into the concrete.

'No! No, get back! Get back here!' I threw my hands out, but couldn't make contact. Couldn't do anything but watch as she squirmed in agony on the floor.

I kept trying. Trying and failing, again and again until, at last, the seizure passed and she sat up, eyes fluttering open.

'Jordan …?' I croaked.

No response. Jordan stared vacantly across the

room, and then slowly got up. I followed, reaching out, only to watch her slip through my fingers again.

And then, as if that wasn't already a perfect enough metaphor for the last twenty years, Jordan started to disappear, fading away in front of my eyes, like all this time she'd been just a hologram and now someone was turning down the power.

She turned on the spot, looking for me. *Looking for Luke.*

'Jordan!' I yelled. 'JORDAN!'

Her head jerked around, but not to me. She was staring into the wall. Her eyes dropped downwards, but I couldn't tell what she was looking at.

I grabbed at her shoulders, trying to jerk her around again. 'Jordan, *come on!*'

Nothing. Fistfuls of air. I shifted around to face her, getting between her and the wall. She stared blankly through me. What if I couldn't do it? What if I couldn't even bring her back?

'Please!' I cried, breaking down again. 'Please – *please* – you have to –' I jumped as she reeled back, finally seeing me. *'Jordan!'*

She reached out, tripped, reached again. Still nothing.

And then a noise behind me. Heavy breathing, shuffling hands and knees, and the *chink, chink, chink* of a knife blade bumping against the concrete.

He was here.

Jordan was still fading, almost invisible now. Her

eyes pierced into me, mouth wide, screaming and screaming with no sound coming out.

Chink. Chink. Chink.

Peter crept closer. Taking his time, knowing he had me cornered. Savouring it.

I made another pointless grab at Jordan, barely breathing now. If he killed me here, before she could get me into the past, then all of it would be for nothing.

'Jordan!' I gasped, still reaching and reaching. 'Jordan, come on, you need to get me out of here! I have to go –' My hands crashed into her. '– BACK!'

She was real again. Blurry, semi-transparent, but real.

And I knew it wasn't me. I knew it was Luke that was bringing her back, that the only reason she could reach me again was that she thought I was him. And I was okay with that. Face to face with Jordan's furious love for Luke, the love that had driven me to madness …

And I was okay.

Chink. Chink. Chink.

I glanced behind me again, and then wished I hadn't. Minutes, now. Minutes left to live.

'Please –' I begged, sick with tears. 'Please – you have to let me –'

I almost lost her as she lurched backwards, convulsing again. Her body was getting clearer now, more solid, just enough for me to see her eyes lose focus as she started retching.

Chink. Chink. Chink.

'Hurry!' I begged, catching a flash of Peter's knife

blade in the torchlight. 'Please! Whatever you – You have to let me in!'

Instantly, like she was responding to my orders, Jordan started flickering in front of me. Not fading away this time; it was almost the opposite. Like she was filling up with light.

We clung to each other, her terrified eyes boring into me. She grew brighter, brighter, unable to keep it in anymore, her whole body drifting apart, melting into the air.

Chink. Chink. Chink.

I spun around, letting her go.

He was right there. Right behind me.

I turned back, taking Jordan's face in both hands, kissing her again. 'I love you,' I told her, and it was the truest thing I'd ever said.

There was a *thump* behind me, two sneakers hitting the floor.

Peter Weir. Red-faced and shuddering, dripping sweat. He raised his knife, screaming his throat raw, all of his vitriol and spite finally pointing in the right direction.

You're dead, Murderer.

And I was. But not for nothing.

Peter hunched forward, preparing to charge.

I looked him square in the eye. Turned my back on him. And ran.

Into the blinding, blazing light.

Chapter 13

LUKE

We wasted maybe a bit too much time reuniting against the wall of Bill's excavation room.

Everything else pulled back into the shadows, like the whole world had slowed to wait for us. Nothing to do but soak up the impossible wonder of being alive. Eventually, though, the tiny form of Tobias pressed between our bodies was enough to remind us that the day wasn't over yet, and we crept back up the deserted passageway, Jordan's hand locked tight in mine.

I tried to think, tried to focus on everything we had to do, but my mind refused to co-operate. I felt my feet pushing against the stairs and my fingers dragging along the mouldy concrete and my skin prickling at the cold and the memory of Jordan on my lips, all of it so vibrant and real and alive, and in that moment, all of the horror up ahead of us felt frail and small next to the awesome privilege of being able to feel anything at all.

'So did he change it or not?' said Jordan, releasing

my hand to steady herself against the wall. I watched her move up the stairs ahead of me, just a shadow in the darkness but enough to make my heart feel like it was bursting out of my chest. 'I mean, it was still all just a loop, right? Everything happened exactly how we saw it in the video.'

'Jordan …'

'But that doesn't – We still chose it all, too. It didn't happen because it *had* to. It happened because – Like, Peter still *chose* to go back there in your place. But then, was it ever even you he was saving, or was he always –?'

'Jordan,' I said again.

She broke off, losing track of where she was going. 'What?'

'I'm *alive*.'

'No, I know, I'm just –'

She smirked, shaking her head. 'Right.'

I smiled back at her. An actual smile, for the first time in forever. 'I mean, please, go ahead, give yourself that headache if you want, but …'

'Yeah,' she said, reaching out to squeeze my hand. 'Maybe later.'

I felt light. Dizzy.

Peter was gone. Both of them, burned up into the past. One trying to kill me, one trying to save my life, both of them somehow the same person. It was totally confusing and impossible and tragic, but the thing was …

I was alive.

Alive.

Through the night I'd been running from for so long and out the other side.

The world was still ending and Mum had been kidnapped and my dad was missing on the outside and I was meant to be dead *again* by five o'clock tonight, and yeah, normally I was the king of thinking everything was hopeless. But turns out it's pretty hard to feel hopeless when your life's just been handed back to you.

What was the point of a second chance if I wasn't going to pick it up and run with it?

At the top of the stairs, I killed the torch on my rifle and opened the trapdoor. Cool air and the smell of smoke wafted in as I stepped out into the bush.

Jordan slipped an arm around me, holding tight to my hip. I looked down at Tobias, huddled against her chest. He was sleeping again.

The shield grid hummed above our heads, nearly invisible but still oppressive. Smoke hung in the sky but, here and there, the stars were coming out again. It looked like security were starting to get the fire under control, which was bad news for our guys in town.

I stared around at the darkness, pulsing with a kind of wild energy, a need to run out there and *do things.* 'Bill said the others have all been taken to the Shackleton Building. To the bomb shelter place underneath.'

'We need to get them out,' said Jordan. 'The longer they're down there –'

'Yeah, but – *How?* He said Calvin's got the whole place under manual lockdown, which means we can't use the key card he gave me. Plus, what about Tobias? We can't drag him into a firefight.'

'So, what, we just take him out to the release station and forget about everyone else?'

'No, that's not –' I closed my eyes, head spinning with the weight of it all. 'But what else *can* we do? We can't split up. What if you have another vision? – and if we get caught, then –'

'We don't even know where the release station *is*,' said Jordan, voice straining. 'I mean, it's out there somewhere, but –' Her head snapped up and she broke away from me. 'Reeve!'

A white glow shone out from her hand. Ketterley's phone. Reeve had a matching one, taken from another of Shackleton's newly deceased top guys. I shuddered at the memory of pulling the phones from the dead men's pockets.

Jordan hit the call button. She waited, phone in one hand, baby Tobias in the other. A muffled voice buzzed out of the speaker at her ear.

'Reeve!' she said, and I felt a rush of relief. He was alive. 'Where are you? Are you okay?'

The voice buzzed again.

'Yeah,' said Jordan. 'I'm still – Yeah. We're at the Complex. Luke's here. But listen –'

She broke off as Reeve spoke over the top of her.

'Yeah, we did. We found him. It's the baby.'

Incredulous buzzing from Reeve's end.

'Yeah, I know. But it's – Yeah, we're sure. Long story, but – Reeve, listen, Calvin's been here. He took everyone.'

Jordan blinked hard, getting hold of herself as Reeve responded.

'The bunker under the Shackleton Building,' she told him. 'They're – No, we've got Tobias with us. He's – No, I know. I know, but –'

She sighed, struggling to stay calm. Reeve kept talking. Jordan opened her mouth a couple of times, almost cutting him off. I put a hand on her shoulder –

And then sprung away, whirling around at a crash of bushes behind us.

Jordan crammed the phone into her pocket.

I fumbled with my rifle, flicking the torch on and jabbing it out in the direction of the noise.

There was a scream from the bushes and two figures tumbled out, hands above their heads. Amy, our friend with the triple-speed body, and Lauren, the freckle-faced Year 7 we'd rescued earlier tonight.

'Don't shoot!' Amy cried.

I lowered the rifle, heart smashing against my ribs.

Lauren fell back against a tree, shuddering, obviously still traumatised from the gunfight back in town.

'Hey – it's okay,' said Jordan, hand outstretched.

'Okay?' Lauren leapt up. '*Okay?* I almost died tonight! It's a *war* out there, and you can't even tell whose side anyone's on! The town is on fire, my family are trapped, my boyfriend is *gone*, and also I'm pretty sure the *world* is ending! *What part of that is okay?*' She slumped back into the tree again, drained by her outburst.

'Yeah, all right. Point taken.' I scanned the shadows again nervously as she slumped back into the tree, checking that no-one had heard us. 'We did kind of save your life, though.'

Lauren sighed. 'Right. Thanks for that.' She smiled sheepishly at Jordan. 'Sorry. Kind of a rough night.'

'We should get moving,' I said, all too aware of the noise we were making.

'Where to?' Jordan asked.

'I don't know. Away.' I stepped over a ruined wall of the old Vattel Complex building and we started out into the bush, walking parallel to the town.

'Wait. Where's everyone else?' said Amy.

'Gone,' said Jordan darkly. 'Taken into town.' Then, before Amy had time for any follow-up questions, 'Where are have you guys been? It's been hours.'

'We ran into more security on the way here,' said Lauren. 'Had to hide out at my old house for a bit. And then when we went to leave, Amy –' She cut herself short, looking to Amy for permission.

Amy stopped walking.

She slowly turned to face us.

Slowly.

I hadn't noticed it at first – probably because Amy's *slowly* was everyone else's normal – but as she opened her mouth to speak, the realisation slammed into me like a truck.

'Your speed,' I said. 'Your fallout thing. It's ...'

Amy closed her eyes. 'I don't know what happened. I was running upstairs to check the street before we left, and then all of a sudden it was like –' Her brow crinkled as she searched for the words. 'Like I was treading through water instead of air. Like everything inside me was groaning to a stop. I don't know how, but ...' She spread out her arms. 'I think – I think this is me now. I think I'm cured.' She didn't sound happy about it.

'When?' Jordan asked, suddenly urgent. 'When did this happen?'

Amy took a step back. 'I don't know! Sometime –'

'An hour ago,' said Lauren quickly. 'Like, twenty past two or something. I remember checking the clock on our way out.'

'Why?' said Amy. 'What's going on? Do you know what happened to me?'

Silence. All except for the hum of the shield grid and the distant sounds of the battle. Everyone stared at Jordan, who shot me a wary look.

I felt my stomach turn over.

Jordan took a breath. 'What if it was us?' she said finally. 'I mean, we know I started the fallout in the first place, so what if –?'

'Hang on,' Amy interrupted. 'What?'

'Long story,' I said. 'Not her fault.'

'The fallout was released when the portal collapsed,' Jordan pushed on. 'Right? The one that sent you and

Peter – *Bill* and Peter – back in time. Twenty years ago, when it brought down the Complex – That's when it all started. So what if – If the fallout *started* at that end of the portal, what if it *finished* at our end? An hour ago, when that same portal collapsed in the present … What if that was the end of it? What if the fallout started and finished with us?'

Lauren squinted like Jordan was speaking another language.

'So … wait,' I said slowly, and it was like a massive weight was creaking up off my shoulders. 'If that's true, then it's not just Amy who's been –' I hesitated. 'It's not just her who's been "cured", is it? It's everyone. It's *you.*'

Which would mean no more visions. No more portals. No more spending every waking moment wondering if today would be the day she finally faded out completely.

But then, if the fallout really was gone …

'What about Tobias?' said Jordan, speaking the thought out loud just as it dropped into my head. 'If we've all lost our powers, then …'

I felt the weight come slamming back down. If there was no more fallout, then what did that mean for our one hope of saving the world?

Jordan held the baby closer against her.

'We need to get to Shackleton,' I said, that dizzy, *how-am-I-even-still-alive?* energy crashing through the fear again before I had time to think the better of it.

'Get him to actually talk this time. If Tobias can't stop Tabitha anymore, then we need to find a way to make Shackleton do it.'

Jordan's eyes widened, not at the idea but at *me* suggesting it.

'What's going on in town?' I pressed. 'What did Reeve say?'

'He told us to stay away,' said Jordan, in a tone that said this advice would have zero influence on her decision. 'Leave the town to them and focus on getting Tobias to the release station.'

'What about our families? Did he –?'

'No, that was the first he'd heard about it.' She gazed out towards town again, torn.

Tobias stirred. I watched, imagining him sitting up in Jordan's arms and laying out his plan to save everyone. But he just yawned, his little face screwing up, and settled back down to sleep again.

Jordan turned. She stared into me, gathering herself, like she was still talking herself into whatever she was about to say next. 'We should split up,' she said quietly. 'Now that we can. Now that the fallout's gone and we don't have to worry about me fading out again. One of us should go out to the release station, and one back into town.'

'We don't *know* the fallout's gone,' I said.

'No, I know, but it makes sense, doesn't it? How else do you explain –?' Jordan faltered, looking sideways at Amy. 'Anyway, we've got, what, fourteen hours left? We're not going to win this thing by playing it safe.'

'Sure, but –'

Jordan ploughed on. 'Think about it: we finally make it out of the Complex – which is kind of a miracle all by itself – and we're stuck because we can't split up, and then out of nowhere, here comes Amy, all ready to tell us that whatever the fallout did to her has suddenly come undone. What if that's not a coincidence? What if the reason we ran into these guys is so that we *could* split up without freaking out about me randomly slipping off into another time or –?'

'Whoa,' said Amy, holding out a hand to silence her. 'Whoa. Do you guys …?'

Lauren shot her a puzzled look, covered almost immediately by a wide, disbelieving grin.

I heard it too. The growl of an engine from somewhere in the distance. Somewhere above us. I looked up, through the haze of smoke and the reverberating cords of the shield grid, and saw a pair of blinking lights drifting across the sky.

'No way,' Lauren whispered, and I felt a cold shiver cut my spine down the middle.

It was a plane.

Chapter 14

JORDAN

THURSDAY, AUGUST 13, 3.28 A.M.
13 HOURS, 32 MINUTES

'They're coming!' said Lauren breathlessly. 'They're finally coming.'

'Who do you think it is?' Amy asked.

'Who *cares* who it is?'

I tuned them out, hugging Tobias against me, feeling a rush of false hope before the truth came in and tore it all down again.

What were they *doing?*

Luke's eyes were fixed to the sky, his face etched with an expression that said he was thinking exactly the same thing I was. If this was help arriving, if Luke's dad and Kara had actually gotten out alive and convinced the military or whoever to come and rescue us, then why in the world were they trying to get back in here by air? Even before the shield grid went up, there was still –

The plane swooped lower and my stomach went with it. Luke swore.

It was small. Definitely military. Or, at least,

definitely not commercial. It roared above our heads, straight over the town centre, then sailed around in a wide arc, coming back for another pass.

'Get out!' Luke hissed at the plane. 'Get *out*, you idiot. You're going to get –'

'What's it doing?' asked Lauren, somehow oblivious to our panic. 'Like, surveillance or –?'

Bright light flashed from somewhere out in the bush, silencing them both, and a low rumble streaked across the sky, almost inaudible over the noise of the jet. Phoenix's automated defences, kicking into action as soon as the jet was in range.

The jet banked left. The missile swerved with it.

I had just enough time to wonder what kind of insane defensive system involved blowing a target to pieces right over the place you were trying to defend, before the missile hit home and the jet exploded in a brilliant ball of flame.

Exploded, but kept on streaking across the sky.

The missile had struck just as the jet cleared the town centre, but something – the momentum of the jet or the force of the explosion, maybe – kept the wreck hurtling forward, tearing itself to pieces out over the bushland. Right over our heads.

Lauren screamed, darting into the shadows as the jet soared overhead, spilling its guts out behind it. Amy followed, whimpering, sprinting away at what was now her top speed.

Bits of flaming aircraft plummeted towards us.

'RUN!' I yelled, yanking Luke into action. A strangled moan broke out from his mouth. I weaved through the trees, pulling him along behind me until I was sure he'd keep moving on his own, knowing what was holding him back, knowing the question that was flooding his mind.

Had his dad had been on that plane?

I released Luke's hand, holding Tobias in both arms now, racing for the edge of the storm of debris, seeing already that I wouldn't get clear before it hit.

The bushland blazed and twitched as the fire rained down to meet it. Shadows on shadows. I was running blind. My foot collided with the flickering ground and I went sprawling, automatically throwing down my shoulder to shield Tobias from the impact. I landed roughly on my back and leapt up again, ignoring the pain, frantically checking Tobias over. He was okay. *Too* okay. The fall had jolted him awake, but it hadn't hurt him, hadn't even *bothered* him. He stared up at me, wide eyes dancing with reflected light.

The light of a giant chunk of flaming fuselage plummeting to the ground, right on top of us. It screamed in like a bird of prey, burning up the night, no hope of escape or even rolling aside before –

CRACK-CRACK-CRACK-CRACK-CRACK!

The sky exploded with a new kind of brightness – harsh, sparking, electrical – as the debris from the jet crashed down into the shield grid. The noise was unbelievable. And it was everywhere. All across the sky, the shield grid sprung into action. Snapping tendrils of electricity shot between the crisscrossed cords of the grid, catching the wreckage, blasting it into oblivion. One moment, flaming debris was tumbling through the air, the next it was melting away like ice on a hot plate.

A little chunk of jet, about the size of my fist, slipped through the fingers of the grid and dropped to the ground at my feet, charred and melted beyond recognition.

And then, a few hundred metres away, with a final, deafening cacophony of sparks, the fiery shell of the jet's cockpit slammed into the grid.

I shuddered for whoever had been onboard. Even if they'd somehow survived the missile, there would be no surviving the grid.

Not Luke's dad, I told myself. They wouldn't have put a civilian on a flight like that. Surely.

In seconds, it was over. With the jet destroyed, the grid went dark again, returning to its usual ominous hum, and the world below lapsed into an eerie quiet.

It wouldn't last. Whatever might be going on in town, Shackleton couldn't ignore this. Security would be here in minutes, whoever he could spare.

I looked out through the trees, breathing hard, still half-blind from the light of the grid.

Luke was gone. They all were.

Tobias made a little sighing noise, nose wrinkling. Still not crying, despite the chaos around him. I bounced him gently, unsure whether to feel relieved or worried.

I pulled Ketterley's phone out of my pocket and found Galton's number. *Luke's* number.

He answered almost immediately. 'Where are you? Are you okay? I'm so sorry! I didn't even realise you were –'

'I'm fine,' I said, smiling. 'Tobias too. Are you with the others?'

'Just Lauren,' said Luke. I could hear her in the background. She sounded kind of hysterical. Luke hissed at her to shut up.

'Do you want me to come and find you?' I asked.

'No,' he said. 'I mean, yeah, I do, but if we're just going to split up again …'

Luke's voice was strained, his mind obviously on that plane. On his dad. But there was something else as well. A kind of fierceness, like he was ready to go charging into a burning building or something.

'So that's definitely the plan?' I said.

'Isn't it? You're the one who –' He stopped himself. 'Look, I don't like it, but it makes sense. You take the skid from the armoury. Get Tobias out to the release station and – and figure out what he's supposed to do. I'll go find Reeve. Work out the rest from there.'

I looked back towards town, aching to go after my family, sick at the thought of separating from Luke again after I'd just gotten him back, but there was no way I'd let anyone else take Tobias out to the release station. It had to be me. But then, what if Tobias couldn't even help us anymore? What if we were both better off using the time we had left to find Shackleton and rescue our families?

Do you actually believe that, or are you just looking for excuses?

Hadn't I just been saying we were *meant* to split up?

Peter would've said it was crazy. The old Peter, back when he could still tell the difference. He would've said it was insane to go driving off into the bush, pinning our hopes on a baby, when our families were in danger back in town.

But Peter was gone now. And as it turned out, he was the one who'd died to tell us about Tobias in the first place.

'Yeah,' I said heavily. 'Yeah, okay, let's do it.'

'Right,' he said. Then, with a very un-Luke-like confidence: 'We'll get them back, Jordan. I know Reeve said it's a mess in there, but we've got to have at least some of the security guys on our side now, right? We'll find Shackleton and get our families out of there. Just – Listen, no dying, okay?'

'Yeah,' I said. 'You too.'

I started walking, but kept the phone to my ear, not wanting the conversation to be over.

Luke didn't hang up either. 'Weird that this is the first time I've ever talked to you on the phone,' he said, breaking the silence.

'Yeah,' I said. 'You hang up first.'

And for the first time in days, he actually laughed. 'Love you, Jordan. Be safe.'

'You too.'

I stuck the phone in my pocket, glancing up at the smoke drifting out from the town to get my bearings. If Phoenix was over there, then the Complex was back that way, which meant –

'Jordan!' puffed a voice up ahead of me, and Amy came staggering out from between the trees. She held her side, fighting for breath. 'Oh my goodness. That was – I was so *slow!*' She stared down at herself like she'd just been transplanted into some stranger's body. 'Where are the others?'

'Heading back into town. You can probably catch them if you –'

'No,' said Amy, cutting me off again. 'I'll come with you. If that's okay, I mean. You shouldn't go out there on your own.'

'You don't –' I began, then realised how much I really *didn't* want to go out there alone. 'Thanks.'

I took off in the direction of the firefighting skid we'd stolen from the armoury last week, re-energised by having a concrete goal to run toward. Tobias lay quiet and still against me, miraculously and terrifyingly unfazed by having been taken from his mother, dragged out into the bush, and almost flattened by a crashing plane.

'I think you're right,' said Amy, crunching through the grass behind me, every step concentrated and deliberate. 'What you said before about us being meant to find each other.'

'Yeah?' I frowned, still working out how much I believed it myself.

'Down in the Complex,' said Amy, 'back when – When everything was slower – When I was faster, I mean – I had a lot of extra time on my hands. Like, literally, I had three times as much as the rest of you. All that time to slow down and pay attention. To listen.'

'Yeah, I remember you saying.' I reached up, shoving a branch out of my path. 'Hear anything good?'

Amy was quiet for a minute. I reminded myself that even thinking took more time than she was used to.

'This thing is bigger than us,' she said at last. 'I don't think –' She paused again, finding the words. 'Whatever that *bigger* part is, I don't think it's neutral on how this all plays out. I mean, I'm not saying you should read into every little coincidence, but – I don't know. When stuff feels like it's more than just random, I think maybe that's worth paying attention to.'

I opened my mouth to respond, but Tobias beat me to it. He finally let out a heartbreaking cry, his whole body tensing with the effort. The sound carried through the night, so much noise from such a tiny body.

'Shh …' I said, bouncing him as I walked, projecting a calm that was the complete opposite of what I actually felt. 'Shh-shh-shh … What's wrong? Do you –?'

Bright light smashed me in the face.

Tobias stopped crying, snapping out of it like

nothing had ever been wrong. I stepped back, almost tripping. Headlights. We'd reached the skid, but someone else had reached it first.

'Jordan,' said the figure hunched behind the wheel, and I felt the life drain out of me.

It was Calvin. He jabbed a thumb at the cage behind him. 'I need you and the baby to get into the –'

'Run!' I shouted, whirling around.

'No!' Calvin leapt down from the driver's seat, ready to give chase. 'Stop! Please.'

My feet slid to a standstill. *Please?*

Officer Calvin stepped out into the glow of the headlights. He moved slowly, like he was trying not to startle us, arms spread wide in a gesture of non-violence that didn't square too well with the pistol holstered at his hip. Or the fact that he was just about the most bloodthirsty psycho in this whole town.

'Please,' he said again. 'Don't leave. I realise this will be hard to swallow, but – I'm here to help you.'

Chapter 15

LUKE

THURSDAY, AUGUST 13, 3.47 A.M.
13 HOURS, 13 MINUTES

'So, you still haven't told me your plan,' said Lauren, jogging along beside me. 'How are we going to stop Shackleton? How are we even going to get *in* there? I mean, do you even know how to shoot that gun?' She paused, eyes narrowing. 'You do *have* a plan, right?'

I took a deep breath, glad she couldn't see me gritting my teeth in the darkness. 'We need to find Reeve.'

'Yeah, but how?'

'I don't know,' I admitted.

'I mean, if he's not answering his phone –'

'Yeah,' I said tightly. 'I get it.'

She shrank back.

I'd tried to call Reeve a few minutes ago, but he hadn't picked up. Maybe because he was too busy getting shot at, or maybe just because he believed the caller ID when it told him I was Dr Galton. Texting was a dead end too. If these phones had ever been able to do it, Shackleton had locked the function out.

'Sorry,' said Lauren. 'It's just – Dad's stuck on security duty and Mum was down in the main prison place. I haven't seen them in weeks. I don't even know if they're …' She couldn't bring herself to finish the sentence.

I pushed through a tangle of undergrowth and something clicked inside my head. 'We saw him,' I said. 'Your dad. Ethan, right? Ethan Hamilton? We saw him a few hours ago, up in the Shackleton Building.'

Lauren lit up. 'Was he …?'

'Yeah, he was okay,' I said. 'Still on duty for Shackleton, but he switched sides when the coup started.'

Like most of Shackleton's guys, Hamilton was more scared than devoted – strong-armed into submission by the 'loyalty room', the cafeteria-turned-high-security-prison where Shackleton held a bunch of their relatives to make sure everyone kept following orders.

The last we'd seen, Hamilton had gone off with Reeve and Tank to help liberate the loyalty room and undermine the Co-operative's hold on its men.

'I knew it!' said Lauren. 'I knew he'd stand up to Shackleton. He was just waiting for the right –' She stifled a shriek as I dragged her behind a tree. 'What? What's happening?'

I put a finger to my lips and pointed through a gap in the trees.

Movement in the bush up ahead. Not security. Too loud and disorganised. Laboured breathing and crunching undergrowth. The sounds of people not used to treading softly through the bush.

I thought about just letting them pass us by. If these were townspeople who'd escaped the fighting, then good for them. They were a lot safer out here than where we were going.

But something about the figure up at the front of the pack made me reconsider. I released my grip on Lauren and got slowly to my feet, flashing on my light. 'Hey. Who's there?'

The huddle froze, and I felt a jolt of recognition. It was Peter's parents, both dressed in nurses' uniforms. And five others, all wearing thin hospital gowns.

Mr Weir was holding a heavy bit of tree branch, wielding it like a club. He turned on me.

'Whoa. Hey!' I said, shifting the light so it shone up into my face. 'It's me!'

Mr Weir let out a heavy sigh, lowering the branch. 'Luke. Good to see you, mate.'

I stepped out to meet them, stomach already tensing at the conversation I knew was coming, then felt myself get shoved aside as Lauren exploded past me. She launched herself at Jeremy, a pasty kid at the back of the group, throwing her arms around his neck, kissing him roughly (and noisily) on the mouth.

She kept it up for a good few seconds before a girl with a guard's belt over her shoulder – Alyssa, I think – came up and tapped her on the back. 'Uh … guys?

I know it's the end of the world, but seriously, get a room.'

Lauren broke it off and dragged Alyssa into a hug, leaving Jeremy staring self-consciously at the ground.

'What's happening?' Mr Weir asked me. 'We were coming back to find you lot.'

'Where's Peter?' asked Mrs Weir. 'Is he okay? Is he still …?'

She trailed off, afraid of the answer. The last time either of them had seen Peter was weeks ago, back before Kara had shown us the murder video, back when Peter was still fairly newly crazy.

I swallowed, trying to work out where to start. But before I had time to even string a sentence together, Lauren and Alyssa broke into our conversation again.

'Luke! Come here!' Lauren held out her arms and I flashed the torch at her. She looked herself over, like she was checking for injuries or something, then turned to Jeremy, a huge grin on her face. 'See? Nothing!'

Jeremy stared at his hands, and I realised what Lauren was talking about. Jeremy's skin thing. His not-so-fun habit of imprinting himself onto anyone he touched. Lauren had had her hands all over him and nothing had happened.

'You're cured!' she beamed.

'You still got me,' frowned Alyssa, holding her blotchy arms up to the light.

But Jeremy was still fixated on his hands. *'How?'*

Someone moved behind them and I shifted my

torch around. Mrs Lewis, the old school librarian, had reached up to the face of a skinny bald guy. Her brow crinkled. 'I think mine's gone too.'

There were murmurs from the others. More support for Jordan's fallout theory.

Mrs Weir put a hand on my shoulder. I stiffened, feeling the tension in it.

I turned to face her again. Searching for the right words. Knowing those words didn't exist. And despite everything, I felt tears spiking at the back of my eyes.

Mrs Weir let out a sob, seeing the answer before I opened my mouth. Mr Weir pulled her into his arms.

'He got better,' I said finally. 'Before he – Before the end. He didn't die sick. He got his mind back. It took a while, but …'

Everyone was quiet now. Listening in. Mr and Mrs Weir tightened their hold on each other, but their eyes stayed unwaveringly fixed on me.

'We – we know how to stop Tabitha,' I said, and realised that I actually still believed it. 'We have a plan. As close as we're going to get, anyway. And that's because of Peter. He died to make sure we got that information. If we win this – if we stop them – it's because of him.'

It was true. Not the whole truth, not even close, but true as far as it went. Peter's parents deserved the whole story, and they'd get it. But not now. The rest could wait.

Mrs Weir stepped out and hugged me. I could feel her shaking. 'I'm really sorry,' I said. Which was the dumbest thing in the world to say, but also kind of the only thing.

'Thanks, mate.' Mr Weir patted me on the back. 'Thanks for looking out for him. I'm sure you did all you could.'

Someone grunted next to us, and Mrs Weir released me. One of the other guys from the medical centre was holding a blood-stained shirt up to his arm. He looked awkwardly at the three of us. 'Sorry guys, but can we …?'

'Yeah, sorry mate.' Mr Weir's face shifted as he forced himself back into action. He bent down, grabbing his branch and pointing it back in the direction of the Vattel Complex. 'This way.'

'Wait,' I said. 'Security know about the Complex now. They came for us a couple of hours ago. Took everyone back into town.'

'But you guys are meant to be the ones stopping all this!' said Alyssa, like they'd got themselves abducted on purpose. 'You said you had a plan!'

'Jordan got out too,' I said, ignoring her. 'She and her baby brother. Tobias. She's taking him out to the release station, this place outside the boundary wall. He's meant to be special. Like, special enough to stop Tabitha. At least, that's – that's the information Peter got for us.'

Mrs Weir pursed her lips, swelling with a kind of miserable pride, imagining Peter as the tragic hero.

'A baby?' said Skinny Bald Guy, looking around like he'd missed the first half of a joke. '*That's* the grand plan?'

'Yeah,' I said. 'I know it sounds crazy –'

'It *is* crazy.'

The others stared at each other, letting it all sink in. Alyssa sighed. 'We are so screwed.'

'Not yet, we're not,' said Mr Weir, with a very forced-sounding optimism. He set off again, back towards the Complex. Then, sensing my unease: 'We won't stay long. But Daniel needs patching up, and we need to pick up some tools.'

'Tools?' I asked, raising an eyebrow.

Mr Weir glanced at Mrs Weir, who handed him something I hadn't even realised she was holding. A dark, amorphous shape, about the size of my shoe.

'Look,' he said, 'I didn't want to get anyone's hopes up. It's probably not even fixable, but …'

He stopped walking. 'We were right under that jet when it came down. Right under the cockpit. The smaller bits of wreckage all got vaporised by the grid, but the big stuff …' He shrugged. 'A chunk of it dropped down right over Jess and me. Looked like half a storage compartment or something. This was inside. Like I said, probably a lost cause. But I guess those are about the only causes we've got left now, huh?'

I flashed my torch at the thing in his hands. Charred black, antenna gone, screen shattered, buttons half melted off. But immediately, I realised what it was. And immediately, Mr Weir's warning about not getting my hopes up shot straight out the window.

It was the jet's transceiver.

'What do you reckon?' said Mr Weir, in a voice that said I wasn't the only one ignoring his advice. 'Anyone feel like giving the outside world a call?'

Chapter 16

JORDAN

THURSDAY, AUGUST 13, 3.53 A.M.
13 HOURS, 7 MINUTES

'You're lying,' I said, barely keeping my hands steady on Tobias.

'Jordan, please –'

'What are you even saying? That the last hundred days have been just a big misunderstanding?'

My body begged me to run. But some other instinct kicked in, some subconscious *need* to confront him, and I stayed fixed to the spot.

'I know,' said Calvin, switching the skid's headlights back off. 'I know. It's absurd. And after all I've done, you have every right to just walk away from this. But for the sake of your family –'

'For the sake of my *family?* My family, who you just sent away to be tortured?'

'I sent them away for their protection!' said Calvin, a familiar growl slipping into his voice. 'Those officers will follow my orders. They will safeguard your mother and sister until we return.' He pressed a red-gloved hand to his injured head. 'Or would you prefer them to have been executed, down there in your hideout?'

'You led those guards down there in the first place!' I said. 'If you didn't want to hurt us –'

'What alternative was there?' said Calvin. 'Once your friend gave away your location, do you really think there was any stopping Shackleton dispatching a security team? All I had left was to lead them in myself and attempt to contain the damage.'

'Yeah, well, brilliant job there,' I spat.

Calvin bristled. He gestured at Tobias. 'You still have your brother. I believe you know how significant that is.'

I pulled Tobias closer against me. 'Do you think I'm *stupid?* The only reason I've still got my brother is that Bill took him from you!'

Lies. All of it. The Co-operative knew what a big deal Tobias was. Shackleton had figured it out before we had. That's why he'd burst out laughing last night, back when we were still scrambling to figure out what Tobias even was.

Somehow, in the time since we'd rescued Mum and Georgia from the medical centre, Shackleton and Galton must have discovered something in Tobias that they believed posed a threat to their work.

But if that was true, then why were we even having this conversation? You could always count on Shackleton for a self-indulgent pre-murder chat, but

Calvin was much more straightforward. He just pulled the trigger and moved on. So why –?

Like he'd read my mind, Calvin's hand suddenly blurred to his waist, snatching his pistol from its holster. Amy screamed. I twisted around to shield Tobias, eyes shut, legs shaking.

But instead of a gunshot, I heard a muffled *thump* and turned back to see the dark shape of the weapon lying on the ground at my feet.

Amy dropped to the grass and snatched it up. She stood, pointing the pistol shakily at Calvin.

Calvin nodded. 'God knows I'd deserve it. But you'd be destroying your best chance at saving the people you care about.' He spread his arms wide again. 'And trust me when I say you don't want a murder on your conscience. Not even mine.'

'Right,' I said, 'please, tell us all about having a conscience.'

But after a moment's hesitation, Amy slowly lowered the weapon.

The shield grid sparked above our heads. Tobias screwed up his face, squinting away from the flash of light. I shifted him around so he was facing my shoulder.

Calvin glanced almost wistfully at the baby. My skin crawled and I clutched Tobias closer to me. Calvin reached to his waist again, unbuckling his utility belt, throwing that to the ground as well. Disarming himself completely.

'Tell me,' he said softly, 'that day at the airport,

weeks ago, when I apprehended you and Luke in an attempt to discover where you were hiding your friend Peter ... How did you manage to escape?'

The memory leapt to the front of my mind. Calvin had caught us outside the medical centre, where Peter had just been kidnapped by Tank, Cathryn and Mike. Calvin thought we'd done it, so he'd dragged us out of town to the airport, where he'd be free to interrogate and murder us without interference. But just as Calvin had been about to pull the trigger on Luke, I'd dived at him. Somewhere in the scuffle, my thumb had ended up slipping into Calvin's mouth, and then ...

Calvin smiled grimly, spotting the gleam of recognition in my eyes. 'That was the first time I felt it. Empathy, as I'm sure you've realised, has never been a strong suit of mine. But in that moment – I felt it all. Everything you felt. Your fear for Luke, for Peter, for your own life. Your worry for your family. Your darkest nightmares about the end of humanity. Your rage at the Co-operative. Your rage at *me*. I felt all of your pain and frustration and hurt as though the feelings were my own, and it ... it was ...' His voice cracked with the memory.

Almost as soon as he'd bitten me, Calvin had stopped struggling. He'd scrambled away from me and fled the airport, sobbing like a child.

'At first, I thought it was something *you'd* done,' continued Calvin. 'But then the symptoms began to recur.'

Another memory. Two weeks later. Calvin and his men had stormed my old house back in town to abduct

Mum and Georgia. Luke had thrown himself at Calvin, and Calvin had recoiled in spontaneous, irrational fear. *Luke's* fear.

So what? I thought fiercely, pushing against the doubt creeping in around the corners of my mind. *A couple of random freak-outs. What does that prove? They wore off, and he went straight back to being evil.*

'Soon it was everyone I touched.' Calvin held up his hands, indicating the gloves. 'My condition was so severe that Shackleton pulled me from duty. He felt he couldn't trust me to carry out my orders. He questioned my loyalty to the ideals of the Co-operative.' Calvin's arms slumped back to his sides. 'He was right to question.'

Amy raised the pistol again. 'It's a trick,' she said skittishly. 'Jordan, you know it is.'

I wanted to agree with her. I *did* agree with her, mostly. But the harder I tried to just shake Calvin's story off, the more it needled at me. I'd never known Calvin to be an actor or a con-man. He wore his depravity on his sleeve. Point and shoot. Simple. Even if this was all some elaborate deception, it was still a side of Calvin I'd never seen before.

But why bother? Unless there was something I was missing. Some reason he needed me alive and on-side.

'Even if it's true,' said Amy, and even in the dark, I could see the gun shaking in her hands. 'The part about him feeling your emotions or whatever. Even if that's true, the fallout's *gone* now.'

Calvin glanced at me for confirmation, clearly thrown by this news. 'No,' he said, voice not quite steady. 'I am not – There's no going back. The fall-out may be gone, but my guilt isn't.' His eyes pierced through me, shining in the moonlight. 'I am not claiming to be a new man. And I am certainly not expecting you to forgive me. But, at least in some small way, I know how you feel. I've *felt* it. I can't just ignore that. Not even if I wanted to.'

I knew what Luke would tell me: that this was no time to be putting our trust in a man who'd only ever tried to kill us. That we should hold out for a plan that didn't involve acting like naive hitchhikers in a bad horror movie.

But he'd still come with me.

Tobias stared up at me, like he was waiting for me to make a decision. Again, Georgia's drawing popped into my mind. Calvin and Tobias and that huge, haunting smile.

That's what the baby wanted a picture of.

All right, kid, I thought, crouching to pick up Calvin's belt with my free hand. *I hope you know what you're doing.*

I started towards the skid. Immediately, Amy rushed in to block me. 'Jordan, no! You can't be – It's a trick! You can't trust him!'

'I know I can't, but we need to get out there and right now, he's our best shot. Remember how well it turned out the last time I tried driving one of these things?' I said, handing Amy the baby so I could climb into the open-topped storage cage at the back of the skid. I shot a warning look at Calvin, who kept his distance. Then I swung inside the cage and took Tobias back. 'I'm not asking you to –'

'I'm coming,' she said, gun trained on Calvin again as he returned to the driver's seat. 'You think I'm leaving you alone with him?'

On either side of the storage cage were little platforms with non-slip treads where passengers could ride standing up. Amy jumped up onto one of them, holding the cage with one hand and keeping the pistol determinedly fixed on Calvin with the other.

'You can put that down,' said Calvin without turning around. 'I give you my –'

'Just drive,' said Amy.

Calvin started the ignition and the skid rattled to life underneath me. Tobias let out a gleeful little squeak. I stared down at him, trying not to read anything into it, and crouched in the cage, wishing there was some safer way to strap him in.

We rumbled slowly through the bush, headlights off. I looked up, watching the dark cords of the shield grid slip past above our heads, trying to visualise the quickest route to the edge of the bush.

'How are we even supposed to get over the wall without that shield thing burning us to bits?' Amy asked, jolting as the skid rolled through a bush.

'We can't,' said Calvin. 'Shackleton has already

locked down the controls, and any attempt to penetrate the grid by force would be pointless. There may be another way, but it will require a detour to the armoury.'

'For what?' I asked, my suspicion ratcheting back up again. 'If you try to hurt anybody –'

'I hope it won't come to that,' he said, in that unnerving new introspective tone of his.

'Then *what?*' said Amy impatiently. 'If we can't get over the wall by force –'

'We're not going over the wall,' said Calvin, veering through a gap between two enormous trees. 'We're going *through* it.'

Chapter 17

LUKE

THURSDAY, AUGUST 13, 4.22 A.M.
12 HOURS, 38 MINUTES

'You're *WHAT?*'

'Shh!' said Jeremy. He and Lauren glared at me from their lookout at the bedroom window. I looked back apologetically, then slipped out onto the landing.

'Jordan, this is –'

'I know,' her voice crackled in my ear. 'I know what it sounds like.'

'It sounds like you've got a death wish!'

'I know, but –'

'Is he making you say this?' I asked, fingers tensing on the phone. 'Does he have a gun to your head or –?'

'No. Actually, we've got one to his,' she said, with enough confidence for me to believe that at least *she* thought she was safe. 'Did you get onto Reeve?'

'Jordan –' I began, not ready to change the subject.

'I'm *fine*, Luke. Really. It's under control. Now did you get onto Reeve or not?'

'Not yet,' I said, pacing over to a window. 'That's

DOOMSDAY – 435

kind of why I called. We've made it into town. We're
hiding out in a house for a bit, but –' I paused, my
attention snatched away by a gunshot from somewhere
out on the street. 'Listen, it's pretty crazy out there.
Wherever Reeve is – I mean, we can't just walk out
there and look for him.'

I stared out the window. We were right up against
the centre of town now, but it was still pretty hard to get
any real sense of the fight – except that we were losing it.

It didn't seem like there was any kind of organised
attack going on at all; just pockets of resistance from
the few people who'd made it out onto the streets.
Now and then, we'd hear an explosion of gunfire or see
someone scuttling through the shadows, but it looked as
though the majority were still trapped in the Shackleton
Building.

Instead of the glorious overthrow of the Co-operative
we'd been dreaming of last night, it seemed like our
coup attempt had just littered the streets with a bunch
of scared civilians with guns. And now we only had a
couple of hours left until the sun came up. If we hadn't
found Reeve by then, we could pretty much give up on
finding him at all.

'Let me try him,' said Jordan.

'Yeah,' I said, tracing a finger along the windowsill,
thick with dust after all these weeks of abandonment.
'That's what I was thinking. Reeve knows you've got
Ketterley's phone. He might answer for you.'

'Right. Let me know if you get anywhere with –

with the thing,' she said, avoiding the word *transceiver* in Calvin's hearing.

'I will,' I said. 'And look, just be careful, okay? You know who you're dealing with. If you can get him to do what you want, then great. But make sure you can get away when you need to. Don't –'

'Don't die,' she said. 'Got it.'

'Don't *trust* him.'

'That too. Okay, I'm calling Reeve. Be safe.'

She hung up and I headed downstairs.

I passed the front door and felt the insane impulse to just walk straight out.

We were wasting time. Hours left until the end and we were sitting around like we were waiting for someone to come in and tell us what to do. If I was going to find Shackleton and free Mum and the others, it wasn't going to be with this lot.

Fifteen minutes, I told myself, glancing up at the clock on the wall. If Reeve hadn't called back by then, I'd push on without him.

I walked into the lounge room, feeling like I'd just drunk ten cans of Red Bull, still jittery with the shock of being alive. Mr Weir was hunched over the coffee table, tinkering with the broken transceiver. The others crowded around. Alyssa had a torch pointed down at the table, shielded by her hand to keep the light from reaching the windows.

Mrs Weir stood at the other end of the room, looking out onto the empty street. Theoretically, she was keeping watch, but one look at her face told me she was somewhere else altogether. I caught Mrs Lewis's eye, and she went to take over.

'Anything?' I asked, taking her place in the circle.

Mr Weir held the transceiver right up to the light, pulling a screwdriver from his mouth and levering off a half-melted bit of casing to reveal the circuitry underneath. His eyes grew very slightly wider, and I felt a flicker of hope. But before he had a chance to speak, a buzz in my pocket pulled me away again.

'Luke!' said Reeve as soon as I picked up. He sounded a bit out of breath. 'Sorry mate, didn't realise it was you. Where are you? Jordan said you'd made it into town.'

'Yeah, we're behind the security centre. Where are you?'

'On the move,' he said. 'We're back out of the Shackleton Building, but – Hold on a sec.' I heard another voice at his end of the line, and then Reeve said, 'Yeah, okay, but check round the back first.' He turned his attention back to me. 'Sorry. Bit of a situation. Can you get down to the south end of town? I'll send someone out to meet you.'

'Um ... yeah, probably,' I said. 'We're –'

'No, still coming. Maybe a block behind,' said Reeve to whoever was with him. Then to me: 'Get down to the bike tracks. We'll – Hang on, mate. I think –'

He broke off, and I heard a frantic shuffle of footsteps. Someone shouted. Then a burst of gunfire

echoed through the speaker in my ear and the line
went dead.

JORDAN

'Okay,' I said, hanging up on Reeve, my voice raised
over the rush of air as we tore along the road out of
Phoenix. 'Start talking, Calvin. What happens when we
get out there? What does he actually have to do?'

Visions were spiralling through my head of the
moment when Tobias and Tabitha finally collided.
Visions of defeat, Tobias hanging limp in my arms,
failed by the fallout. Visions of victory with Tobias
dead anyway, the price of saving the rest of us.

Stop it, I ordered myself. *You know that's not how this
ends. Whatever the plan is, it has to be better than that.*

I stomped it all down and focused on interrogating
Calvin, thinking wistfully that I could really have used
an *actual* vision right about now.

The trees flew past the skid, a blur of shadows.
Tobias took it all in with gleaming eyes, eerily unfazed
by the cold or the crackling sky or the jolting of the skid.

He still hadn't cried for a feed. That wasn't right.
Not *normal,* anyway. But then, we were talking about
a baby who'd reached full term after only three months

in the womb. Abnormal had been written into his life from the very beginning.

And isn't that what you're counting on? Don't you need *him to be abnormal?*

'You going to answer me?' I pressed.

Calvin kept driving, like he hadn't even heard me speak. I grabbed him from behind. 'Hey! *Listen –*'

The skid swerved, throwing me sideways against the cage. Tobias murmured but still didn't cry out.

'Enough!' Calvin growled, steering us back on track again. 'Unless you believe running us all off the road is a productive use of your –'

'TELL ME WHAT HE HAS TO DO!'

'Pull over,' said Amy, black hair fluttering behind her as she clung to the side of the cage. The words didn't have much force behind them, but she made up for it by raising Calvin's pistol again. 'We're not going any further until you tell Jordan what she wants to know.'

The skid slowed just enough to soften the roar of the wind in my ears.

'It's better if you don't know what's coming,' said Calvin, not turning around.

I sneered at the back of his head. 'How about you let me decide what's –?'

'Better for humanity,' said Calvin, 'even if not for you.'

'You know what, Calvin?' I said, almost laughing. 'I'm not sure you're actually the most qualified person to make that call.'

'Perhaps not. But I am the one who knows what is coming, and I cannot risk losing your co-operation at this late stage.'

'You don't think you might be risking that *now*?' I said, shoving aside my apprehension at his words.

'No,' said Calvin. 'I don't. I know you, Jordan.'

'You don't –'

'I know enough. I know that with half a day left until the extermination of humanity, you are not simply going to abandon your one hope of putting things right.'

I straightened angrily, the cold wire of the cage digging into my back. I wanted to argue with him, to bite back, put him in his place. To jump out of the moving skid and prove I couldn't be so easily manipulated.

Instead, I just slumped back down to the floor of the cage. He was right. I couldn't leave without knowing. Which meant that as long as Calvin kept me in the dark, he was pretty much guaranteeing my co-operation. Amy glanced back at me, her right hand still stretched out towards Calvin's head.

'Mm,' said Calvin approvingly, taking my silence for agreement. 'You are a person of incredible moral integrity, Jordan. It is only recently that I've come to appreciate what a great strength that is.'

'Yeah, well, thanks for the compliment, Chief,' I said, gritting my teeth. 'That means a lot, coming from you.'

The skid roared up to full speed again. The wind swirled around my head, throwing my ratty dreadlocks up against my face. Tobias gazed up at me with something oddly like a searching look. Like he'd heard what Calvin had said and was trying to work out if he agreed with him. He yawned, closing his eyes, and I shoved the idea aside.

'I won't let you hurt him,' I said after a minute.

Calvin kept driving.

'Is that what this is?' I asked. 'Is he going to have to, like, go in there and get injected or something? Because I won't … I won't let you …'

I trailed off, the confidence I'd just been preaching to myself getting shaky again. My baby brother, going up against a virus powerful enough to exterminate humanity; surely that wasn't going to happen without a cost.

And still Calvin refused to speak.

'Calvin!' Amy snapped.

'It won't kill him,' said Calvin finally. 'It shouldn't –' He glanced back, frowning like he'd heard something, then turned his eyes back out onto the road.

'Jordan, I have no doubt that you will try to do what is right,' he went on. 'But if there's one thing that might persuade you to compromise that cast-iron conscience of yours, it's your family. Which is exactly why –'

Light exploded behind us.

Calvin barked in shock, and the skid swerved, throwing me to the floor on my back. I rolled over, looking back through the cage, and saw headlights bearing down on us.

BLAM! BLAM!

Calvin jolted in his seat, and the skid unit spun out of control. I wrapped both arms around Tobias, curling into a ball to shield him from the impact. Amy shrieked, lost her grip, and disappeared, thrown to the ground. The skid kept spinning, stars and shield grid blurring together above my head, so eerily like slipping to one of my visions that I almost believed I'd been wrong about the fallout being over. Then, with a nauseating jolt and a spray of gravel and dirt, we dropped into the ditch at the edge of road.

The skid lifted onto two wheels, sending me sliding across the bed of the cage, and then crashed down onto its side, scraping along through the bush, before finally hammering to a stop against an enormous eucalypt. Somewhere through the dizziness, I took in a glimpse of fading lights and the noise of an engine rumbling off into the distance.

I stumbled out of the cage, beat up and dizzy but otherwise okay. I held Tobias to the moonlight, heart in my throat, checking him for injuries. He was fine. Conscious. Nothing broken.

'Oh my goodness.' Amy came limping in through the bush, holding her side, the pistol still clutched in her other hand. 'Oh my goodness. What was *that*?'

'A delivery truck,' grunted Calvin, peeling himself off the seat of the skid. 'Probably headed for the same place we are.'

He rose to his feet, apparently uninjured, and scowled at the skid's front tyres, torn apart by the gunshots. My heart sank. No way was that getting back on the road again.

'Who were they?' Amy asked. 'Were they Shackleton's or –?'

'It doesn't matter who they were,' said Calvin. He reached into the back of the upended skid and grabbed his utility belt. 'They're gone, and so is any prospect of reaching the armoury before sunrise.'

I watched him fasten the belt around his waist, suspicion trickling through my mind again. Had this been his plan the whole time? To strand us out here in the middle of nowhere? To lure us off to some secret Co-operative facility where he could torture us in peace?

Get a grip, I told myself. *You're starting to sound like Luke.*

In a place like Phoenix, though, Luke's paranoid hunches had an unfortunate habit of being right.

Calvin pulled a compass from his belt. He threw our ruined skid one last resentful glance, and then jogged away through the trees. 'This way.'

'Now what?' Amy breathed, coming up behind me.

I wavered for just a moment longer, then sighed, setting out after him. 'Now we run.'

Chapter 18

LUKE

I snapped the phone shut, resisting the urge to shout in frustration. Still no answer.

'Give it a rest for a bit,' said Mr Weir, crouching next to me. 'That battery won't last forever.'

I stuck the phone in my pocket. I hadn't heard from Jordan in almost an hour. I'd tried her ten times since, and every time, the phone just rang and rang. I'd even tried calling Calvin's number, but he wasn't picking up either.

I shifted in the undergrowth, working out a cramp in my leg. In the end, only the Weirs and I had come to meet Reeve. Everyone else had lost their nerve when I'd told them the part about my phone call ending in gunfire. Apparently, creeping through a warzone to meet with a guy who might have just been killed was not their idea of a good time. And the longer we waited out here in the cold and the dark, the harder it was to blame them.

The transceiver still wasn't working, but Mr Weir seemed confident. Seemed *determined* anyway. While Mrs Weir had shrunk down inside her grief, Mr Weir seemed to be channelling his outward, like he'd forged some connection in his mind between fixing this thing and honouring the death of his son.

I gazed up through the shield grid at the stars.

What did it mean? A hundred days without even a hint of rescue, and now suddenly we had a jet getting shot down right on top of us.

Surely this had something to do with Dad. He had to have got out. He *had* to. And surely, I told myself with as much conviction as I could, *surely* Dad couldn't have been onboard that jet. If the military were mounting some kind of rescue mission, they wouldn't send a civilian in on their first –

I shook my head, fighting to get a grip on myself. This was pointless. Assuming Dad *was* still alive, the best I could do to keep him that way was to focus on getting hold of Shackleton.

I gazed out through the trees at the town. Where would he be?

Please not in the bunker.

Please nowhere near Mum and the others.

No, I thought firmly. Surely he had more important things to worry about. He must have realised by now that the fallout was gone. And surely he had to be at least as freaked out by that as we were.

So, what then? The medical centre? Would he

risk moving out from the Shackleton Building? *Could he risk it even if he wanted to?* If the bunker was still locked down, maybe he was just –

Wait.

My hand shot to my pocket, a dangerous idea flaring to life inside my head.

'Luke,' Peter's dad said wearily, as I pulled the phone out again.

'I'm not calling Jordan,' I said, scrolling shakily through the list of names, a shiver flashing through me as I found the one I was looking for.

Noah Shackleton.

I hit *call* and brought the phone up to my ear, a weird out-of-body feeling rippling over me.

I flinched as the ringing cut out, replaced by a howling, agonised scream. I heard hurried footsteps, and then a door slammed shut, muffling the poor man's cries.

'Who is this?' hissed Shackleton. There was a fire in his voice that I'd never heard before.

I took a breath. 'It's me.'

A moment's pause. I shuddered as another muted scream echoed in through the closed door.

'I'll kill you,' Shackleton spat. He was breathing hard. 'I don't know *how* you've managed this, you miserable ulcer, but whatever else results from your actions, I *promise* to repay you with an excruciating end.'

I dropped a hand to the ground, steadying myself. Not that I'd been expecting Shackleton to be thrilled to hear from me, but usually he kept all that buried under layers of calm, grinning menace.

'Come on, then,' I said, surprising myself by getting the words out the first time. 'Where are you? Tell me where to –'

The guy through the door screamed again, louder still, freezing the words in my throat. The noise intensified, raw and guttural, grinding through my insides. Finally, it choked itself out. Silence fell on the other end of the line.

I heard a door clunk open again. *'Well?'* Shackleton demanded of whoever had just come out.

A woman's voice. Dr Galton? 'He's dead. Negligible resistance to the pathogen.'

'Get another one,' Shackleton seethed.

'Noah, we've already lost –'

'Get another one! A woman. Get downstairs and …'

Shackleton kept talking, but I'd zoned out for a second. *Downstairs.* He was back in the Shackleton Building. Probably somewhere up on the top floor.

Mr and Mrs Weir were both staring at me now, frozen in place. How much could they hear?

'… you can inform Melinda that if she does not have the bunker back open by the time I return, it will be *her* on the table.'

'Of course,' said Galton stiffly.

The door banged shut, and I felt a glimmer of relief. Whoever they were mutilating up there, it wasn't any of our guys from the Complex. Not yet, at least.

There was a scuffling sound as Shackleton pulled the phone back to his ear. 'You will not die with the others,' he spat. 'I will not afford you the dignity of succumbing to Tabitha. Before this day is over, I give you my word, I will spill the life from you myself.'

The line went dead. I pulled the phone away from my ear and stared at the display until the light flashed off, my heart pounding like I'd just run a lap of the town.

Shackleton couldn't possibly *know* that Jordan and I were the ones who'd killed the fallout – we barely even knew it ourselves – but clearly that wouldn't keep him from pinning it on us anyway. And whatever sick experiments he and Galton were doing up there, it didn't seem like they were filling him with confidence.

What did it mean?

What would happen if the clock ran down to zero now? Would *anyone* survive? And what would Shackleton do if he found out the answer was *no*?

'Well?' whispered Mr Weir. 'You gonna tell us what he –?'

I jolted as a boot crunched in the dirt nearby. Mr Weir's hands rushed to the rifle I'd given him – then froze as the muzzle of another weapon came down between our heads.

'Nope,' grumbled the weapon's owner. 'Not a smart idea.'

Mr Weir slowly lowered the weapon and lifted his hands to his head.

'Better,' said the man, taking a step closer.

I glanced down at a muddy boot and the black leg of a security officer's uniform. The guard flashed on his torch, throwing my shadow out in front of me.

'Luke Hunter,' he said gruffly, coming around to face us.

I squinted into the light. The guy was tall (or seemed like it from down here, anyway), with massive shoulders, a shining bald head and a scar running down from his eye to his chin.

'Listen,' said Mrs Weir, 'we're not –'

But the guard was already lowering his weapon. 'Lazarro,' he said, stretching out a hand to pull me up. 'Reeve sent me.'

Mr Weir's hands shot towards the rifle.

'No, wait!' I said, the guard's name clanging in my head. Lazarro had been working behind the scenes on Reeve's coup. 'He's okay! He's on our side!' I lowered my voice. 'You *are* on our side, right?'

'You're still alive, aren't you?' said Lazarro, ignoring Mr Weir's distrustful glare. 'You guys coming or not?' He flicked off his torch and trudged away through the bush.

'Is Reeve okay?' I asked, striding to catch up. 'What happened?'

'He's fine,' said Lazarro. 'Just a little run-in with an escaped civilian with a gun. Lucky for us, he didn't have much clue how to fire it.' He frowned at the darkness ahead of us. 'Now, how about we cut the conversation until we get where we're going?'

Peter's mum and dad fell tentatively into line behind us, and we crept out around the southwest corner of town. Somewhere along the way, it started raining. The shield grid sparked and spat with it, but most of the water still seemed to make it through. Not heavy, but enough to feel it through my clothes.

After jogging down several blocks, Lazarro took us behind a row of blacked-out houses and waded through the knee-high grass of a backyard, up to someone's back door.

He crouched down, pulling a bit of paper from his pocket and slipping it under the door. There was a tiny rustle as someone on the other side picked the paper up, then the handle turned and the door clunked open.

Reeve stood in the doorway, grinning broadly. 'Hey, guys. Good to see you.' He ushered us inside. 'Sorry I never returned that call. Battery was already on the way out when we spoke the first time.'

We padded down the hall, into a lounge room identical to the one we'd left behind an hour ago. Three men sat hunched around the coffee table, weapons resting at their sides.

'Wilson, Hamilton, Chew,' said Reeve, and the officers all nodded or waved half-heartedly.

The one called Wilson had a pile of chopped-up T-shirts sitting on the table in front of him. He stood up, bringing over a handful of what looked like bracelets or something: strips of blue, red and black fabric, braided together.

'Here,' he said, handing one to each of us.

'What's this?' I asked.

'Friendship bracelet,' smirked Chew from back on the couch. 'I think he likes you.'

'Rebel ID,' said Wilson, flipping a casual middle finger over his shoulder at Chew, reminding me forcibly of Peter. 'So we know who's one of us.' He patted his own arm, tied with a woven band up near the shoulder.

'Wilson loves his braiding,' said Chew, still grinning. 'He wants to be a hairdresser when he grows up.'

'Nice to know at least one of you has plans to grow up,' said Lazarro dryly. 'Get rid of them. Stupid idea. Might as well sew a target to our chests.'

'So, what's going on?' I asked, handing the band back to Wilson, who stared down at it, dejected. 'How come you guys are back out of the Shackleton Building?'

Reeve's expression darkened. 'Shackleton Building's not such a fun place to be right now. We lost the loyalty room not long after we took it. Got a few of the prisoners out, but not many. Not enough. And now they're out on the streets, and Shackleton's locking the town centre down again. He's setting up a perimeter around the Shackleton Building to deal with anyone who tries to get back in.'

'Where's Tank?' I asked, dreading the answer. I turned around, like I might have missed him the first time. 'And Officer Miller. Are they …?'

'Still inside,' said Reeve. 'There's a few of them still in there. Laying low, or posing as Shackleton's men again.'

'Or *actually* Shackleton's men again,' said Lazarro gruffly.

'Or dead,' said Chew.

'Better dead than back in Shackleton's pocket,' said Lazarro, shooting Chew a penetrating look.

Chew shrank back in his chair a bit. Lazarro had been working with Reeve for weeks now, but the rest of these guys had only switched sides a few hours ago. It looked like the trust was still pretty shaky.

'Chew, why don't you head upstairs and take over the watch?' said Reeve, moving to break things up before they had a chance to escalate.

Chew rolled his eyes and stood up.

'I spoke to Shackleton,' I said, as he disappeared upstairs. Mouths dropped open around the room. I pulled out my phone and they all relaxed a bit. 'We need to get back into the Shackleton Building. He's up there with Galton, running some kind of –'

Reeve held up a hand. 'You'll get no argument from us, mate. But we're not getting in there with a handful of rifles – which is why we've got four guys out at the armoury, picking up some supplies. When they get back, we'll figure out what we've got to work with.'

'*If* they get back,' Lazarro muttered.

'They will,' said Reeve. 'Kirke and Ford are solid, and this place is in more than enough chaos for the guys on duty out there to believe Shackleton's sent them in as reinforcements.'

'It's not Kirke and Ford I'm worried about,' said Lazarro.

'Look,' said Reeve, 'I know the other two are inexperienced, but we don't have a whole lot of –'

'Yeah,' said Lazarro, far from convinced. 'Best we can do.'

'It'll work,' said Reeve.

Lazarro slumped down into a couch, face twisting up like he had a bad taste in his mouth. 'Just as long as no-one tries anything stupid.'

Chapter 19

JORDAN

'Stupid,' spat Calvin, squatting beside me in the mud. I twitched as he thrust an arm at me, but he was just handing over his binoculars. I took them from him, casting him an uneasy look before peering through the dripping undergrowth at the scene unfolding at the armoury.

I knelt in the wet grass, one hand on the binoculars and one cradling Tobias as I focused on the entrance. There was a truck parked outside – the one that had shot our tyres out. It was open at the back, with a ramp to the ground and boxes piled up inside. Guns and ammunition and who knew what else. And in front of it all, strapped down just inside the roller-door, another skid unit.

It looked like the guys guarding the armoury had been helping load it all up. Not anymore.

As I watched, a guard dragged a scraggly-haired officer out of the armoury at gunpoint and threw him to the ground next to a pair of others.

'The one with the hair is Ford,' said Calvin. 'The two with him are Kirke and Green.'

My ears pricked up. Ford and Kirke were two of Reeve's guys.

'And I take it at least one of those two morons lying unconscious on the ground is yours as well,' Calvin continued.

'Huh?'

'Inside,' he said.

The sun was rising by now, a faint glow creeping in through the blanket of grey clouds. I peered back through the gaping doors of the armoury and spotted two figures sprawled out on the concrete. A metal canister lay on its side between them. Sleeping gas, like the stuff we'd used last night at the Shackleton Building.

They had them fooled, I thought, passing the binoculars along to Amy and squinting out at Reeve's three remaining men, kneeling in the dirt while Shackleton's guys paced around them, shaking their rifles. *Reeve's people told the guards they were here to pick up supplies for Calvin or Shackleton or whoever. And they bought it. But then some idiot decided to try knocking them out with the sleeping gas.*

Amy gasped next to me and I jolted. 'What is it?'

She pointed at the ramp leading up to the armoury's second level. The roller-door at the top was clattering shut, and another security officer was swaggering down, rifle in hand.

'It's him,' she said.

Officer Reynolds. The last time we'd come out here, he'd put a bullet in Amy's leg.

I watched as he made his way casually down the ramp. For whatever reason, the rest of Shackleton's guys seemed hesitant to pull the trigger on their old colleagues, but I had a feeling Reynolds might not be quite so discerning.

'Do something!' said Amy, suddenly panicked. 'If you really are here to help us –'

'Stay here,' hissed Calvin. He strode out into the clearing, eyes on the ramp. 'Reynolds!' he barked.

Reynolds froze. The other two guards turned, raising their weapons, then saw who it was and dropped them again.

Calvin waved Reynolds down, and they converged on the spot where Reeve's men were lined up in the mud. Calvin glanced down at them, then turned to the officers standing guard. He started speaking, but I couldn't hear a word of it over the rain.

I hoisted Tobias up off my lap, holding him against me, ready to move at a moment's notice.

Amy flinched next to me as the guards abruptly stood back from the men on the ground. But then Reynolds thrust a hand at the scraggly-haired guy, Ford. He stepped back, helping him to his feet. The others followed suit, and in ten seconds, all three of Reeve's guys were walking off towards the truck, looking over their shoulders like they couldn't figure out what was going on.

A minute later, they'd retrieved their unconscious friend from the entrance, piled back into the truck, and peeled out onto the narrow dirt road back to town.

'Huh,' said Amy, like it was about the only word she could manage.

I nodded vaguely. 'Yeah …'

Calvin watched until the truck was out of sight, then started towards the armoury. His men fell into line behind him, and they disappeared inside the enormous, gleaming building. The heavy double doors trundled shut, sealing them in.

Tobias gurgled happily.

'What do you think?' I asked.

Amy lowered the binoculars, raised them, and lowered them again, still experimenting with the new speed of her body. She turned to look at me, long hair clinging to her face and shoulders in the rain. 'I don't know. I mean, up until right now, I would have said we should get out of here as fast as we could, but …' She shrugged. 'I don't know.'

I wished Luke was here. My hand was halfway to my pocket to call him before I remembered it was pointless. Twenty minutes into our walk here from the wrecked skid, I'd felt around for my phone and discovered that it was missing. Left behind in the crash.

I'd asked Calvin for his, but he'd refused. Said he didn't want to waste the battery unless it was something important.

I got to my feet. The rain was getting heavier now,

pasting my jumper down to my arms and back. I leant over Tobias, doing my best to keep him out of it.

We waited.

Eventually, Amy got up from the bushes and stood beside me. She opened her mouth, then bit her lip, like she'd decided not to say whatever was on her mind after all.

'What?' I prodded.

She sighed heavily, almost shuddering. 'I hate him,' she said at last. 'I mean – I *hate* him. He abducted me. He took away everything – everything I ever –' She sighed again. 'I haven't seen my family in *months*. I don't even know if they're *alive*, and now …'

She faltered, tears filling her eyes. I waited, giving her a chance to finish. Amy had hardly ever spoken about her family, these past few weeks.

'And now *this*,' she said bitterly.

'You don't trust him,' I said.

'No, that's –' Amy twisted in frustration. 'That's the thing. I don't *want* to trust him. I want to keep hating him, because that's what he deserves. But then he goes off and does all this –' she waved a hand at the armoury, '– and I just don't know what I'm supposed to *do* with that. How am I supposed to feel when the guy who's always been the bane of my life turns around and does something that might *save* my life?'

I stared back at the armoury, thinking of Peter: crazy, violent, abusive. Murderous. A killer who'd died to save Luke from a murder of his own creation.

Emotion surged in me. Everything, all at once. I held it back, pushing it down the way I'd been doing all morning. No time for it. Not now.

But now here was Calvin, Murderer in Chief, pulling the same change-of-heart trick, and this time it wasn't just one life at stake. It was everyone's.

'I don't want to trust him either,' I said in an undertone. 'You're right, it's like betraying everything we've ever fought for. But if he really is trying to help us, if the fallout really did change him, then we can't just turn our backs on that. And listen, if you're right about – If this really *is* all headed somewhere, if there's a purpose to it … What if that purpose is big enough to include even him?'

Amy frowned. 'I was afraid you were going to say something like that.'

'Look, I'm not saying you have to *like* –' I began, but then a faint clatter from the armoury put an end to the conversation. I looked up to the top of the ramp and saw the door rolling open again. A shiny new skid unit rumbled out, the cage at the back piled high with wooden crates.

'He's alone,' said Amy, handing me the binoculars.

Calvin was at the wheel, guiding the skid carefully down the ramp, a new rifle slung over his shoulder. The roller-door closed behind him as soon as he was clear.

Calvin steered onto the dirt road, idling just out of sight of the armoury.

As we splashed through the wet bush to meet him,

my eyes hovered over the crates stacked up in the cage. Before long, I was close enough to read the black writing stamped across the sides. They were all the same. Explosives.

My mind shook with stark, bright images of another skid, rigged up with C-4, tearing through Phoenix, veering into the security centre, swallowing it up in a ball smoke and flame. Mike, blindly sacrificing his life out of misguided allegiance to a deranged monster who cared about nothing but self-preservation.

And as I clambered up over the side of the cage and found a seat in between the boxes of explosives, for all my talk of meaning and purpose, a part of me couldn't help wondering if I was being just as blind as he was.

Chapter 20

LUKE

THURSDAY, AUGUST 13, 7.23 A.M.
9 HOURS, 37 MINUTES

'I saw them,' said Reeve, fiddling absently with an old tennis ball he'd found in one of the bedrooms. 'Katie. And Lachlan, my kid. They're alive in the Shackleton Building.'

I swallowed the last of a stale biscuit from a packet we'd found in the kitchen. 'They see you?'

We were down at the back of the house, sitting on opposite sides of the floor in the hallway, still waiting for Reeve's guys to return from the armoury. Chew had gone out to the edge of town to meet them and bring them back. Assuming they were coming back, which seemed more doubtful all the time.

Reeve shook his head. 'It was just a glimpse. Just as we were leaving. Back of their heads.' He bounced the ball off the wall and caught it again. 'I just hope –'

He jerked upright as a creak of wood signalled the arrival of someone outside.

I got up, holding my breath, and a wet bit of paper

462 — DOOMSDAY

appeared under the door, words scrawled across it in half-dead pen:

I showed it to Reeve. He rolled his eyes and pulled open the door. 'That's *not* the password,' he said wearily, as Chew stepped through the door, followed by two more guys in guards' uniforms.

'I like mine better,' Chew grinned, and Reeve looked too relieved at their arrival to push it.

'Kirke and Saunders are waiting back at the truck,' said one of the new guys. He had wild hair and a look of complete bemusement on his face.

'Everything okay?' Reeve asked.

'Mate,' the guard smirked, slapping Reeve on the back and moving up the hallway, 'have I got a story to tell you.'

But before he could even get started, a head popped out of the lounge room. Mrs Weir, looking more alive than I'd seen her all day. 'It's working!'

We raced into the kitchen, where Mr Weir had been working on the transceiver. One of the newcomers dumped a backpack on the floor. The others were already crowded around, except Wilson, who looked longingly over from his watch at the window, and Lazarro who was somewhere upstairs.

'It *should* be working,' Mr Weir corrected, holding up the transceiver, a Frankenstein's monster of looping wires and spare parts he'd scavenged from stuff around the house. 'Won't know until we turn it on.'

He was holding the thing just a little bit too tightly,

and again, I got the sense that this project was all that was keeping him from melting down over Peter.

'So what are you waiting for?' asked Chew, pushing to the front.

Mr Weir flicked a switch. Two lights, one green, one red, started blinking at the top of the transceiver, and the cracked screen flashed to life.

'That's good, right?' said one of the new arrivals.

'Bloody miracle is what that is,' Mr Weir beamed, tapping something on the screen. 'Now, I've left it at the frequency it was transmitting on when the jet crashed, so with any luck, we should still …'

He tapped at the screen again. Static crackled out of a speaker, and I felt my breath catch in my throat.

Mr Weir held the speaker tentatively up to his face. 'Hello?'

Static.

Mr Weir tried again. 'Hello? Is anyone there?'

More static. And then –

'Who is this?' a gruff voice demanded. 'Identify yourself.'

The kitchen hummed with stifled noise. Everyone grinning and staring at each other, fighting to contain their excitement.

'This is Brian Weir,' said Mr Weir. His hands were shaking. 'I'm a prisoner of the Shackleton Co-operative.'

The voice at the other end was silent for just long enough to make me think we'd lost the signal, then: 'This is a restricted frequency. How did you –?'

'We found your transceiver,' said Mr Weir in a rush. 'When your jet came down. I pulled it from the wreckage. It was damaged, but I –'

'Shh!' I hissed, grabbing Mr Weir's arm, pulling the transceiver closer to me.

I'd heard something. Another voice. Muffled, distant, as though the speaker was across the room from whatever they were transmitting with.

'*Stop*,' the voice demanded. 'Let me go. You're being –' He broke off, regaining his composure, and I almost lost mine completely as I realised who it was. 'Listen. *Listen* to me, I know you have your protocols, but this is –' He grunted again, still struggling. 'I'm telling you, I know that man. He's a *friend*.'

And finally, I found my voice. '*Dad!*'

'Luke!' he called back, closer this time, or maybe just louder. 'Luke, are you all right? What's happening out there? Where's –?' He growled at whoever was holding him. 'Enough! Please, I just want to –'

'Oh, for goodness sake,' snapped a third voice, sharp and impatient. 'It's his *son*, you jackass. He's fifteen. How much harm could he possibly be?'

It was Kara.

Alive. Both of them. They'd made it out.

There was what sounded like a scuffle for control of the transmitter, and then Dad's voice cut through the static again, louder and clearer. 'Luke! Are you okay?'

And without warning, all the trauma and the exhaustion finally caught up with me and I disintegrated into tears. Mr Weir handed over the transceiver and I held it up to my face, unable to speak, staggering over to lean on the sink for support.

'Luke ...' said Dad, his own voice breaking. 'Talk to me, mate.'

I took a breath, pulling myself together enough to get words out, painfully aware of the huddle of security officers standing over me. 'It's – it's a mess, Dad. Jordan's on her way out to the release station now, but –'

'You've found Tobias?' said Kara, cutting in.

'Y-yeah, but I don't even know if –'

'Where are you?' asked Chew from behind me, losing patience. 'Who are those people you're with?'

Through the static, I heard Dad sigh. Whatever was coming next, I had a feeling I wasn't going to like it.

'We're with the military, in a temporary facility outside of Alice Springs. They're mounting a rescue effort, but there's been some ... difference of opinion,' Dad said carefully, 'about how to go about it. About how much of what we've told them is actually reliable.'

'What – what do you mean?' I said. 'What about all that video Jordan took?'

'They've watched it,' said Dad, his voice crackling with static. 'And obviously they can't deny that there's some kind of hostage situation going on in there. What they aren't so sold on is Tabitha. Their surveillance hasn't shown any sign of –'

'Enough!' barked the military officer. 'That information is –'

'Their *surveillance* just got blown out of the sky!' I said. 'Tell them I *saw* it! Tell them if this isn't fixed by five o'clock –'

'I know,' said Dad bracingly. 'I know. And I'd love to tell you they'll be quicker to trust us on Tabitha than they were on Shackleton's defences, but I hon–'

His voice cut out, and the static went with it.

'No …' I breathed. At first, I thought the connection had been cut at his end. But then I held the transceiver away from my face. Lights, screen, everything dead.

Mr Weir pulled the transceiver out of my hands.

'What happened?' the scraggly-haired guard asked. 'What did he do?'

Mr Weir didn't answer. He was too busy poring over the transceiver.

I spun away, pushing out of the circle.

'Mate, I didn't mean …' the scraggly-haired guard began, but Reeve held up a hand and said, 'Leave him.'

I stumbled back into the hall and slumped on the carpet, grabbing for my phone, needing to talk to Jordan, not even to tell her about Dad, just to know she was still out there, but again, the phone just rang and rang. I tried Calvin's number, expecting nothing and getting it, and by the time the call rang out, my tears had evaporated into stony anger at the guards in the other room.

I could hear their hushed tones, probably griping about all the time I'd wasted crying to Daddy when we should have been exchanging information. Like any of them could lecture me on not having my priorities straight. Like they hadn't wasted *months* fighting on the wrong side of this war.

Not helpful, whispered the rational part of my brain. I got to my feet. No point dwelling on dead ends.

We had to get out of here, out to wherever they had this truck and –

'Back from the windows!' hissed Lazarro, thundering into view down the stairs. 'Everybody down!'

'Where are they?' asked Reeve, appearing in the doorway, already armed. 'How many –?'

He dragged me down just as a spray of gunfire tore into the house, splintering the front door off its hinges.

'Don't want to alarm anyone,' said Lazarro from the stairs, taking aim at the half-destroyed doorway, 'but I think they might have found us.'

JORDAN

THURSDAY, AUGUST 13, 7.26 A.M.
9 HOURS, 34 MINUTES

'It is *not* moronic,' Calvin insisted as we roared along the road. 'It is the most extraordinarily sophisticated surface-to-air defence system on the entire planet.'

'Sure,' I shouted over the wind in my ears, 'except for the part where it gunned down that jet over the place it was meant to be defending.'

Calvin's shoulders arched up a bit. 'That was your fault, not ours.'

'*Our* fault?'

'We have protocols in place to ensure that our automated systems are not disrupted by the movement of our own aircraft,' said Calvin, wiping the rain out of the goggles he'd pulled from under the driver's seat. 'Protocols which were disregarded completely last week when your people commandeered one of our helicopters.'

I rolled my eyes, sinking into the wall of boxes at my back. 'How thoughtless of us.'

Amy was hanging on to the side of the cage again, shivering in the wet and the wind. Silent since we'd left the armoury. She still glared disparagingly at Calvin, but she'd given up pointing the pistol at him.

'The system *should* have been manually recalibrated as soon as Officer Barnett was notified of your escape,' Calvin continued. 'Yet another duty he mismanaged in my absence, it seems.'

'Why didn't you just shut the whole thing down while you were in the armoury, then?' I asked.

'The controls aren't in the armoury,' said Calvin. He slowed the skid down, eyes drifting to the right side of the road. 'Now that the security centre has been destroyed, they can only be accessed from Shackleton's office, and my removal from active duty has made sneaking in there somewhat more difficult than it might once have been.'

'Of course it has,' I grumbled, shifting Tobias as my arm started to cramp. He lay there, all bundled up, shivering occasionally but still never complaining, never crying out.

Which would have been unnerving enough without the eyes. I watched them swivel in their sockets, tracking my face with an intensity that no baby should have been capable of, and tried to convince myself I was just imagining things.

What could possibly be going on inside that tiny head of his?

My mind burned with a swirl of sickening visions of what might be waiting for him outside the wall. I shook them off, readjusting Tobias's covers again. Calvin had found Tobias a waterproof blanket in the armoury to replace the grotty towel he'd been wrapped in before. What was that? An actual gesture of humanity, or just Calvin protecting his interests? Clearly, he needed Tobias alive for *something*, but –

The skid slowed as Calvin turned off onto a faint dirt trail leading off into the bush. I realised I'd seen this area before, way back in the beginning, when Luke, Peter and I had come trekking out to the wall, following a map scrawled in a library book by Crazy Bill.

We'd known *nothing* back then. No idea who we were really following, or where he was taking us.

And now, after everything, after all we'd learned, here I was, riding out to the wall again. Just as lost and confused as ever.

The skid splashed down into the wet bush, onto what was not even a proper path. Just a winding trail worn into the grass and the mud. We'd known since our first trip out here that there must be a way through the wall – how else had Reeve brought us back from the outside in a van? – but we'd never actually been out here to see it.

Calvin's hand slipped from the wheel. His head tilted down in the direction of his pocket.

I sat up. 'Who is it?'

Calvin's eyes shot back out to the road.

'*Calvin*,' I snapped. 'Who's calling you?'

'No-one,' said Calvin. His hand returned to the wheel. 'I was checking the time.'

'He's lying,' said Amy, drawing her pistol. 'I saw the caller ID. *Victoria Galton.*'

'That's Luke,' I said. 'Give me the phone.'

'We do not have time for distractions,' said Calvin, swerving to avoid a fallen tree.

'Give it to me,' I said. 'It could be important.'

'More important than saving the world?' Calvin asked. 'Worth running down the last of my battery? He has been calling for hours, Jordan. And he is *still* calling, which means that whatever's happening to him, it isn't –'

Amy leant over, pressing the pistol into the back of Calvin's head. 'Give it to her.'

'Put it away,' said Calvin.

'*Give it to her!*'

'I think we've established by now that you're not going to –'

BLAM!

The skid screeched to a halt, spraying muddy water, almost smashing into a clump of trees. I grunted in pain as a box of explosives thumped into the back of my head.

'Oh my goodness,' said Amy shakily. 'Oh – Oh my goodness.'

I clambered to my feet, shoving the dislodged boxes back into place.

Amy was frozen, clinging one-handed to the side of the cage like it was the only thing keeping her standing. The pistol was pointed straight up into the air above her head.

Calvin stared back at her, face twisted with fury. He thrust out a hand. 'Give me that!'

Amy shakily lowered the weapon and pointed it at Calvin. 'The phone,' she said. 'First, give Jordan the phone.'

Chapter 21

LUKE

THURSDAY, AUGUST 13, 7.37 A.M.
9 HOURS, 23 MINUTES

The firing stopped and for a second the world went quiet. Nothing but the spatter of rain coming down on the roof.

Grey dawn light broke in through the bullet-riddled front door, gleaming down across our faces. I pushed up from the ground, disentangling myself from Reeve, then froze as the light began to move. A shadow rose up over the carpet. Someone was coming.

'I'd stay outside if I were you!' called Lazarro from the stairs, rifle still aimed down at the doorway. 'We got plenty of guns in here, and some guys too incompetent to know when to hold their fire.'

'Nice working with you too, mate,' said Chew from somewhere in the lounge room.

Lazarro turned to Reeve. 'I counted two out the front. Another one coming round the back. We've got the numbers for now, but –' He fired a short burst into the wall above the door. 'I said *get back!*'

A scream pierced the gunfire. 'Please – I'm unarmed!'

A woman's voice. Reeve sprung up from the ground like he'd been electrocuted. 'Katie!'

'*Matt!*' the voice called back.

'Stand down,' Reeve told Lazarro. 'Let her in.'

Lazarro didn't budge. 'It's a trap.'

'It's my *wife*,' said Reeve.

'Yeah,' said Lazarro. 'Just out for a walk, is she?' He barked into the lounge room: 'One of you clowns feel like getting out here and watching the back door?'

I jerked sideways as something vibrated at my leg.

Galton's phone. Someone was calling me.

Reeve started down the hall. 'Katie! Are you okay?'

'Enough!' snapped a voice from outside, stopping him dead. 'All of you, out the front door! Hands behind your heads!'

I dug my hand down into my pocket, shuffling out of the way as Chew and Wilson appeared in the hall, slipping out to the back of the house.

'That you, Justin?' Reeve called, his voice strained.

The guard hesitated. 'This isn't personal, Matt. I'm just doing my –'

'You have a gun on my wife!'

I stood, checking the caller ID.

Bruce Calvin.

'Matt, please,' Katie begged, 'you have to do what he says! They've got Lachlan!'

I slid the phone open. 'Luke!' said Jordan, and it was like something dead inside of me had come back to life.

'*Jordan,*' I hissed. 'We're surrounded. They've got Reeve's wife. They're using her to –'

Reeve took a step towards the door, and I lost my train of thought.

'Don't,' Lazarro warned. 'Don't do it, Matt. You know that doesn't end the way you want it to.'

'I'll give you thirty seconds, Matt,' called the guard. 'Tell your men to stand down and get their arses out here or I shoot your wife and we start again with the kid.'

Katie let out a desperate wail.

I turned my attention back to the phone call. 'Jordan?'

No answer. I heard rain, frantic voices, the rumble of an engine.

'Listen to yourself!' Reeve shouted back through the door, voice cracking. 'Listen to what you're saying! He's a *kid*, Justin. He's three. Are you seriously going to –?'

'This – this isn't about me, Matt,' said the guard. 'It's just orders. Twenty seconds.'

'Jordan!' I hissed. 'What's –?'

'Luke,' said a stony voice at the other end of the line.

Sweat prickled at the back of my neck. It was Calvin.

'Ten seconds,' said the guard.

'Turn on your speakerphone,' Calvin ordered.

'Nine.'

'*Why?*' I said.

'Eight.'

'Do it, Luke!' Jordan called in the background.

'Seven.'

I pulled the phone away from my ear.

'Six.'

Scanned the keypad, trying to figure out where the speakerphone button even *was*.

'Five.'

Reeve lurched towards the door.

'Four.'

Lazarro dived, thrusting a hand between the railings on the stairs.

'Three.'

He grabbed at Reeve, fist clenching on his collar.

'Two.'

I ducked under his outstretched arm, thumb finally coming down on the right button.

'One –'

'– DOWN!' Calvin roared, managing to sound loud and commanding even over the tinny speaker. 'REPEAT: STAND DOWN!'

Stunned silence, broken only by muffled sobbing from outside. I crept to the door, cranking up the volume as high as it would go.

Finally, the guard called Justin spoke up. 'Chief …?'

'I'm sending Luke Hunter out with the phone,' said Calvin. 'Ensure that he is not harmed.'

'Jordan?' I whispered, switching off the speakerphone for a second and holding the phone to my ear.

There was a pause as Calvin handed the phone back.

'It's okay,' said Jordan, clearly trying to sound more convinced than she actually was. 'Do what he says.'

I looked back at Reeve, still in Lazarro's clutches, tears streaming down his face. He nodded.

'O-okay,' I said, steeling myself, turning the speaker back on. 'Okay, I'm coming out. Nobody shoot anyone.'

I shoved the wreck of the door aside and stepped into the doorway. A woman with dark, curly hair stared back at me, red-eyed, white-faced, shaking in the grip of a heavy-set guy with a pistol jammed up under her chin. Two more guards stood out in the rain, aiming rifles through the lounge-room window.

'Matt!' Katie screamed, catching sight of Reeve. 'Don't let them –'

'SILENCE!' Calvin demanded.

I scanned the street. So far, it was just the three of them (plus maybe one more around the back), but the gunfire would attract others.

'Sir,' said the guard holding Reeve's wife, 'Officer Collins speaking. Shackleton's orders were to find these men and return them to base for questioning.'

'Do you think this is news to me, Collins?' Calvin asked.

'No, sir,' said Collins quickly. 'I – I just didn't realise you were back on duty.'

'I am ordering an emergency meeting of all security personnel,' said Calvin. 'Return to the Shackleton Building immediately.'

Collins stared at me, bewildered. He wasn't an idiot. He could see that something about all this wasn't adding up, but he knew better than to question Calvin.

The two other guards edged closer to the house, straining to listen in.

I held my breath, waiting for it all to fall apart.

'Sir,' said Collins, 'I have Officer Reeve and a number of his fellow rebels here with me. If you would be willing to send in some additional forces –'

'Officer Collins,' said Calvin fiercely, 'if I find myself in need of your tactical advice, I will ask for it.'

'Y-yes, sir.' Collins glanced back at his companions. They shrugged back at him, confused and frustrated.

And then, just in case we didn't have enough men with guns around, I spotted three more figures in black emerging from a side street, over the road. Half a minute, and they'd be right –

BLAM!

The window shattered behind me, showering the verandah with glass.

Officer Collins staggered. Blood poured from the side of his head. He crumpled to the ground, pulling Katie down with him. I dived behind them as the guards on the lawn returned fire, their rifles pointed back up at the lounge room. Katie cried out in horror, crashing into me as she scrambled from the limp form of Officer Collins.

Calvin's voice was still bellowing out of the phone, but I couldn't make out a word of it. I twisted around, deafened by gunfire, and caught a blur of movement as a little metal canister came sailing out of the window. It bounced off the railing and clanked back down onto the verandah.

I cringed away, thinking it was a grenade or something, but the explosion never came. Instead, with a loud hissing sound, the thing started spewing out thick black smoke, rattling around on the ground with the force of its own spray. Smoke filled the verandah, spilling out in all directions, across the yard and through the house, pouring into my eyes and nose and mouth.

Someone was still firing. The noise ricocheted in my head, everywhere at once.

Katie brushed past me, already on her feet. 'Matt!'

I staggered up after her, blind, eyes streaming. But the upside to a town full of identical houses was that it was pretty easy to find your way through one in the dark. I ran inside, ducking for cover, and stumbled down the hallway.

'Everybody out!' bellowed Lazarro, still somewhere above me. 'Go! Go! Go!'

I kept going, through the house and out the already-open back door, almost tripping down the steps. Smoke billowed out after me, clouding the yard, but it was thinner here, a grey haze instead of total darkness.

A figure stalked through the murk at the other end of the yard. It turned, catching sight of me. I dropped onto all fours, just as –

BLAM! BLAM!

The bullets whooshed past, swirling the smoke above my head. There was a shout from the house and someone else returned fire. How could they even tell who they were shooting at?

I shrank down, crawling away through the long grass, not stopping until I reached the back fence. I looked back. Someone was coming. I jumped up, vaulted over the fence, and ran.

Chapter 22

JORDAN

THURSDAY, AUGUST 13, 7.58 A.M.
9 HOURS, 2 MINUTES

He's okay, I told myself, like thinking it could make it true. *He's okay. He got out.*

But the sound of gunfire still rattled in my head. Luke hadn't called back, and I hadn't called him for fear of giving up his hiding place, or running down the battery.

I trudged through the mud, trying to busy my mind with the work of carrying explosives.

The wall was bigger than I remembered. A massive expanse of concrete, stretching forever in both directions, towering over our heads. It encircled the town, a line marking out the reach of the fallout. Towering bush on this side, barren wasteland on the other.

Last time had been easy enough. We'd just climbed a tree and thrown a rope over the side. But now that the shield grid had come bursting out of the wall, electrified cords slashing and burning through any tree tall enough to get in their way, things were a bit more complicated.

The sun was brighter overhead now, the shield grid even more ominous for being able to see it properly. Dark lines crisscrossed the grey sky, making this whole place feel, if possible, even more like a prison. The rain had eased off a little bit, but we were all so soaked through by now that it didn't really make any difference.

I picked up another box of explosives, lugging it through the rain towards a pair of gleaming silver doors: the hidden access point Reeve and the others had used to run their patrols to the outside, back in the day.

Calvin crouched in front of the giant doors, mounting explosives and connecting wires. Once upon a time, he could've just keyed a code and popped the doors open automatically, but somewhere along the line, Shackleton had locked him in with the rest of us.

He took the box from my hands, and I felt a twinge of something that felt bizarrely like solidarity.

'Thanks,' I said. 'For trying to get them out of there. That was …'

Calvin nodded slowly and then got back to work. I went back to the skid for the last box, an unwelcome thought gnawing at me. I was starting to trust him. How was I starting to trust him?

Amy was in the driver's seat, taking care of Tobias. After the incident with the gun, Calvin had decided that that was the best place for her. Amy had been too shaken up by the whole thing to argue, and I was more than happy to actually get up and *do* something.

'How is he?' I asked, leaning in to check on Tobias.

'Yeah, fine,' said Amy. 'Sleeping.'

'Listen, thanks for –'

'What do you think he's going to have to do when we get out there?' Amy cut in. 'I mean, what *can* he do? *Sleep* Tabitha to death?'

'I don't know,' I said.

'But you really believe Calvin's going to show you.'

I grabbed the final box of explosives from the cage, flicking my head to shake back a stray dreadlock. 'I don't know.'

I returned to the wall, dropped off the last of the explosives, and watched as Calvin set them in place.

What if this really was all just wishful thinking? What if my desperation to get out there and save the world had blinded me to some crucial detail that might have let me in on what Calvin was *really* doing here?

Or what if it was even simpler than that? What if Shackleton was just running down the clock? With only hours left until the end, what if he'd just sent Calvin out here to keep me distracted until it was too late?

But if that was true, why *Calvin* of all people? And why even bother when he could have just shot me or taken me prisoner? What wasn't I seeing?

'We're going to have to leave her behind,' Calvin said, without looking up at me.

'What?'

'Amy,' he said. 'Once we get the doors open, we're –'

'No. We're not.' I crouched down, glancing back to make sure she hadn't heard. 'She's coming with us.'

Calvin bent down lower, plugging something into one of the wads of explosive. 'She's too unpredictable.'

'*She's* too unpredictable?'

'You and I have a job to do –'

'Right, that secret job you won't even –'

'– and we cannot afford to take unnecessary risks,' Calvin steamrolled on, finally stopping to look at me. 'I will not allow the integrity of this operation to be compromised by a reckless rogue element.'

'By someone who might shoot you, you mean?'

'And what if I *had* been shot?' Calvin snapped. 'What then?'

'You weren't,' I said. 'And you won't be. She was just trying to get your attention.'

'Are you sure of that? Are you willing to stake the lives of all humanity on her co-operation?'

I opened my mouth to defend her and found that I couldn't get the words out. How was it that I was having a conversation with Calvin about whether someone *else* could be trusted with the future of humanity?

'Do you think you're safe from this?' Calvin asked. 'Do you think your *family* is safe if we fail today? If the effects of the fallout have truly been undone, what does that say for your immunity to Tabitha?'

A chill ran through me, deeper than anything the rain or the cold could reach. The question had been there all along, but I'd mostly managed not to let myself think about it.

'I don't know,' I said.

'Neither do I,' said Calvin. 'And I would prefer not to find out.' His eyes were filling up with what looked amazingly like genuine compassion. 'Amy is as safe here as anywhere. We'll pick her up on our way back. And by then, with any luck …' He wiped his hands on his pants and stretched upright. 'Come on. We're ready here.'

He started back towards the skid, apparently assuming he'd talked me around. And maybe he had. I fell into step behind him, still conflicted, but no longer convinced he was wrong. I told myself it wasn't a question of loyalty. I'd back Amy over Calvin every single time. But as long as they were together, there'd be conflict. And Calvin was right: we couldn't afford it.

Amy got up from the driver's seat as we approached, handing Tobias back to me. Calvin jumped behind the wheel and threw the skid into reverse. 'Follow me. Everyone get back to a safe distance.'

I took one last look back at the wall and hurried after him.

Calvin parked the skid, leapt out, and bobbed down behind it, pulling out a little remote-control thing. I crouched behind one of the giant front tyres, draping Tobias's blanket over his face and crossing my arms around his back.

'Stay down,' Calvin warned, flipping a little cap up from the detonator.

He pushed the button, and the whole wall vanished in a hurricane of orange light. The explosion roared through the bush, fierce, bloodthirsty, devouring everything with churning flames and a rushing wind, scorching my rain-drenched skin and hammering me into the ground and rocking the skid so hard I thought it was going to roll over on top of us. Debris rained down, exploded trees and hunks of wet earth.

And then it was over.

I sat up, ash and dirt cascading from my body, and pulled back the blanket to check on Tobias. He just yawned at me, like he did this kind of thing all the time.

'You call that a safe distance?' Amy grumbled.

Calvin ducked away to see what was left of the wall. I brushed the worst of the dirt off Tobias and jogged to catch up.

Twenty metres in, we reached the clearing created by the explosion. Light glowed through the smoke as the trees around the edge crackled with flames. The ground was uneven, ripped apart by the blast. I tried to make out how much damage had been done to the shield grid, but everything I could see was still intact.

Calvin squinted at the smoke, which was finally beginning to clear. A gust of wind whipped by, clearing a path in front of us, and Calvin stepped back like he'd been slapped. He swore under his breath, and I felt dread crash through me with even more force than the explosion.

'No way ...' breathed Amy, coming up behind us.

The doors were still there. Scorched black, but still looming over us. Undamaged. Unmoved.

Nine hours until the end of the world, and our last hope of saving it had just gone up in smoke.

Chapter 23

LUKE

I stretched above the low line of the picket fence, risking a glance out at the bush, and then dropped back down again, heart pummelling my chest. The darkness was long gone now, and every movement I made felt like taunting death.

Mrs Weir knelt in the grass beside me. She was the only one I'd found since abandoning the house. I'd run into her behind the primary school and almost smashed her over the head with a tree branch.

Together, we'd made our way down to the south end of town, agonisingly slow as we dodged the pairs of guards who were combing the streets, rounding up escapees. That was definitely not good news. If security were free enough to start sending out search parties, then we had to be pretty much back to square one in the Shackleton Building.

Already, whatever resistance there'd been out across the town was now nearly stamped out, everyone lying low or escaped into the bush or recaptured or worse. I thought of Lauren and the others we'd left behind this morning. What would happen to them when security came knocking?

'We should never have left you,' murmured Mrs Weir, eyes to the ground.

I turned to look at her. A cold breeze swept through, rustling the grass around our shoulders.

Mrs Weir sniffled, the ratty nurse uniform she was wearing still sticking to her skin with the rain. 'The night at the medical centre,' she said, 'when Brian and I got ourselves captured. We *knew* Peter was sick. We knew he needed us, but we ran off on that fool's errand and look where it got us.'

My insides squirmed. What was I supposed to say to that? What words could possibly make any kind of difference to someone who'd just lost their kid?

Dad would know. Somehow, he always knew what to say in situations like this.

'You were trying to help,' I said. 'You were doing what you thought was best for all of us, *including* Peter.'

'It was reckless,' she said. 'Stupid. Trying to spy on Shackleton when our son was sick and imprisoned. If we'd just stayed behind, we could have …' She sank lower in the grass, eyes red.

'No,' I said. 'You couldn't – I know you love him. But even if you were there … No-one could've stopped what happened to Peter. And like I told you, he did get better. Before – before the end. He was better.'

I bobbed up again, no idea if she'd taken anything in. No idea if I'd actually said anything *worth* taking in.

Mrs Weir didn't move. She'd been like this the whole time. Dazed. Sluggish. One foot in reality, and the other one a thousand miles away.

'C'mon,' I said, sweat pricking the back of my neck. I pulled her up and we started into the bush, heading for Reeve's truck and whoever was still alive to meet us.

'How did it happen?' asked Mrs Weir. I could see her steeling herself for the answer. 'How did he …?'

She faltered, unable to finish, and the storm in my stomach intensified. There was no right answer. Nothing that would even come close to capturing the convoluted mess of the last twenty-four hours.

'He was brave,' I said, surprised by the sudden flare of emotion as I said the words. Whatever else he'd been, Peter had started out as a friend. 'He died trying to do what was right. He stood up to maybe his worst enemy in this whole place, and he was – he was killed. Murdered. But it wasn't for nothing.'

Mrs Weir nodded, a kind of miserable gratitude on her face.

'I know that's not a whole answer,' I said. 'It's all – I don't know if I'll ever be able to explain it all completely. But I'll try. When all this is over, I promise I'll answer as much as I can.'

I flinched as Galton's phone started buzzing in my pocket.

Bruce Calvin.

'Jordan?' I said, sliding the phone open.

A sigh of relief at the other end of the line. 'What *happened* back there?'

'Someone started shooting,' I said, the sound of her voice calming my nerves a bit. 'But we're out now. At least –'

'Is everyone okay?'

'I don't know. We got separated. I'm heading back now to see if I can find the others. Where are you guys?'

'We're at the wall,' she said. 'Calvin tried to blow open the exit, but it didn't work, and now –'

Calvin barked something at her, but I couldn't make it out over the sound of the engine behind them.

'Need to be quick,' said Jordan. 'Phone's going to die any minute.' Her voice was steady, but I'd learnt to hear when she was trying not to panic. 'We can't get through the wall. Calvin says the only way out is over. We need you to shut down the shield grid.'

I looked up at the sky, at that massive, kilometres-wide structure that could shred military aircraft into smoke and rubble. 'How exactly …?'

'Shackleton's the only one with access to the control systems,' said Jordan. 'You're going to need to get up onto the roof of the Shackleton Building and physically bring it down.'

'The roof of the Shackleton Building,' I repeated.

'I know. I know it's crazy, but –'

'It's all crazy,' I said. 'Yeah. I'll try.'

'Did Reeve's guys in the truck make it back to you?' asked Jordan. 'Have you got any explosives or anything?'

'I don't know,' I said. 'Probably.'

'Okay, good. Calvin says the only way to knock out the grid by force is to destroy that antenna on top of the Shackleton Building that holds all the cords togeth–'

The phone beeped in my ear. She was gone. Battery finally dead.

Mrs Weir glanced over at me with the closest thing to focus I'd seen since we met up. Then a shout up ahead ripped her attention away again.

'Jess!' Mr Weir charged out, almost knocking Mrs Weir over in a ferocious hug.

There were others milling around behind him, gathered together in a little clearing in the trees. Reeve had got his wife out. The two of them were deep in a hushed conversation with Lazarro. Chew and Wilson were here too, and Hamilton, Lauren's dad, plus two new faces – the guys who'd been back here guarding the truck, I guessed.

'Any sign of the others?' I asked Mr Weir. 'There should be like three more of us, right?'

'Not anymore,' he said darkly. He forced a smile, clapping a hand to my shoulder. 'Glad you're okay, mate.'

'Yeah. You too.'

I turned away, crossing the clearing to talk to Reeve. He saw me coming, whispered something to Lazarro and Katie, and they backed off, leaving us alone.

'Mate,' said Reeve, pulling me out of earshot of

everyone else. 'I need you to tell me exactly what's going on out there with Jordan and Calvin.' He stared at me with absolute focus, like hearing the answer was the most important thing in the whole world. Maybe it was.

'I don't know,' I said uneasily. 'I mean, they're trying to get out to the release station. Jordan says Calvin's trying to help them.'

'And you believe that?' said Reeve.

'No,' I said automatically. 'I mean, of course I don't. But –'

'But how else do you explain what happened back at the house?' Reeve finished. 'And how do you explain him letting our guys go free when he caught them out at the armoury?'

'Right,' I said. 'Wait. What?'

'Kirke's been telling me what happened out there,' said Reeve, nodding at one of the guards I hadn't met yet. 'Crazy story about Calvin ordering his men to stand down and let them go. Anyway, you were saying …'

'They're at the wall,' I said. 'Calvin tried to blast through, but I guess it didn't work. He needs us to take down the shield grid so they can get over the top.'

Reeve's gaze drifted up to the grid.

'We're going to do it, right?' I said. 'I mean, we have to. If Jordan doesn't get out there by five …'

Reeve frowned, dark shadows under his eyes. It had been way too long since any of us had slept. He caught Lazarro's eye, cocking his head out at the bush. Lazarro nodded and started rounding everyone up.

'My gut still says Calvin can't be trusted,' said Reeve finally, leading the way out of the clearing. 'But you're right. We're down to the wire here. We might not have the luxury of only working with people we know we can trust.'

We'd reached the truck. Reeve and Lazarro did a quick circuit to make sure we were alone, and then Kirke rolled open the back door of the truck.

I peered inside. The truck was pretty packed, but it was hard to make out what was in there past the skid unit parked inside the door. Reeve's eyes widened. He climbed inside and twisted past the skid, making his way into the back to take stock.

'Uh … question,' said Chew, raising an eyebrow. 'You know this skid unit you have here? This smaller, faster, more manoeuvrable vehicle with the handy cage at the back for transporting equipment? Any reason why you didn't just –?'

'Didn't have a whole lot of choice,' said Kirke, who apparently had about as much patience for Chew as Lazarro did. 'The boys at the armoury were suspicious enough when we showed up unannounced. Had to make things look as routine as possible.'

'Any more stupid questions?' Lazarro asked. 'Or shall we get to work?'

'Right,' said Reeve, reappearing from inside before the bickering could take off. 'We've eaten up too much time already.' He dropped down in front of the skid, legs dangling over the side of the truck, and clapped his hands together. 'Here's what we know: five o'clock tonight, Tabitha gets out and the whole world bites the dust. Maybe us as well. Shackleton knows we're out here, but he also knows there's nothing we can do about Tabitha while the shield grid's still up.'

'And nothing we can do about the shield grid while we're stuck out here,' I said.

'Exactly,' said Reeve. 'Which means smart money for him is on just hunkering down in the Shackleton Building and running out the clock.'

'So we're screwed,' Chew summarised. 'Yeah. We knew that already.'

Reeve rubbed his eyes. 'Not quite. Way I see it, we've got two shots left, and I reckon we've got to take them both at once. First, we get to the roof. Take out the shield grid. Free Jordan up to get out to the release station and deal with Tabitha.'

I shot him a grateful look. A few other glances fired around the circle too. We hadn't actually *told* the rest of Reeve's men that Jordan and Calvin were road tripping out to the release station together, but it looked like some of them were starting to fill in the blanks.

'Second,' Reeve pushed on, 'we go after Shackleton. Make him turn the countdown back himself.'

'You really think that's going to happen?' said Wilson.

'Not without a fight,' said Reeve, 'which is why we have to play it smart. Retake the loyalty room first.

Use that to leverage more support to our side. There's enough of us now, we should be able to hold it.'

'Hang on,' said Hamilton, 'where's the part where we rescue our families?'

'I've just told it to you,' said Reeve. 'Listen, we've all still got people we care about in there, but if we're going to do this, we need to do it right. Blindly running in and grabbing our families gets us nowhere unless we get the rest done first.'

'Okay, sure, but aren't we getting a bit ahead of ourselves here?' asked Chew. 'I mean, as much fun as all that sounds, how are we even planning on getting inside in the first place?'

'Calvin's locked down all the tunnels,' I said. 'We're not getting in that way again.'

Reeve nodded. 'I think we might be past taking the subtle approach. If we want to get in there, I'd say we're gonna need to be a little bit more direct this time. Straight in the front before they see us coming.'

'One more stupid question,' said Chew, raising his hand. 'As genius as walking in through the front doors might sound, isn't there an outside chance someone might think to shoot us full of holes on the way in?'

'Yep. That's why we won't be walking.' Reeve reached behind to pat the giant tyre of the skid unit. 'This time, we're taking the car.'

Chapter 24

JORDAN

I glared up at the wall, hands pressed against the wet concrete, shaking with the frustration and the cold, adrenaline charging inside of me with nowhere to go.

The others were behind me with Tobias, still in the skid. We'd driven around to what Calvin had decided was a safe distance from the site of the explosion, then pulled up to wait for Luke to knock out the shield grid.

Calvin had suggested that Amy could take the skid back into town to investigate his progress. Amy had suggested that Calvin could go screw himself. Since then, there'd been silence.

It had been hours. At least, it had *felt* like hours; Calvin's phone had been our last way of keeping track of time. I'd paced. I'd punched the wall. I'd climbed trees and watched the shield grid vaporise anything I threw into the gaps. Anything to work out the nervous energy, to keep pretending I still had some kind of control over the situation.

None of it helped. This was out of my hands, and I knew it.

And, worse than that, with the end of the fallout, I felt like I'd lost the one thing that had ever given me any kind of edge in this fight.

For so long now, I'd been carried along on the strength of the visions that the fallout had handed down to me. Visions that had seemed almost hand-picked to nudge us along in the right direction, to keep us crawling forward towards some kind of solution to all this.

The fallout was what had brought us all out here in the first place. If I had my time-travel paradoxes straight, the fallout had even brought *itself* out here, using the portal-creating abilities it had given me to disperse itself over Phoenix, way back in the beginning.

It was the fallout that had caused Calvin's (alleged) miraculous change of heart. And it was the fallout that had brought Tobias into the world six months ahead of schedule, holding him up as the cure against the end of humanity.

But now the fallout was gone. And all the freakish mutations it had created were gone with it.

Where did that leave us? Whatever Tobias was meant to do, could he even still do it?

I dug my nails into the concrete. A cable as thick as a tree branch arched over my head — one of the cords that made up the shield grid. You saw the hugeness of the thing in a whole new way at this distance.

Luke is dealing with it, I told myself. *We're going to*

get out there. We're meant *to get out there. Tobias is still the answer. He has to be.*

But if there really was some greater purpose at work here – something that, like Amy had said, wasn't neutral about how this all played out – then why had it let *any* of this happen in the first place? The only reason the world needed saving was that Shackleton had been drawn out here by the same fallout that had caused all the rest of it.

I started pacing again.

'Save your energy,' said Calvin from his perch on the skid. 'You'll need it if the grid comes down.'

'*When* the grid comes down,' I said. But I did what he told me, abandoning my march along the wall and coming over to take back Tobias.

He smiled as I picked him up and I felt my chest tighten with anxiety. Who *was* this kid?

How many hours had it been since Mum had fed him back at the Complex, and all this time he was just perfectly content with not being fed or changed or even properly shielded from the rain?

I sat down against the wall, knees bent, propping him up in front of me.

'He'll have to be killed,' said Calvin.

My head snapped up, terror exploding like a grenade.

'Shackleton,' Calvin clarified, seeing the panic on my face. 'Whatever else happens, if we succeed, Shackleton has to be taken care of.'

I let out a shaky breath.

'And what about you?' Amy asked, getting to her feet behind him. 'What should we do with *you* when this is all over?'

'Whatever you think best,' said Calvin, that mournful tone colouring his voice again. 'You're right, of course. I am every bit as guilty as he is. But I'm not talking about justice. I'm talking about ensuring that this doesn't happen again.'

He returned his gaze to me, like for some reason he thought I was going to be the one who'd be making that decision. 'You can't imprison Shackleton. He's too well-connected on the outside. A prison sentence might as well be an acquittal for all the time it would take him to free himself. And then he'll be back on his feet, ready to start all over again.'

'No he won't,' I said. 'I mean, even if all that's true ... Phoenix is a one-off, right? He can't recreate the fallout.'

'The fallout was a gift,' said Calvin. 'A shortcut. But Shackleton's dream of a better world stretches back far beyond his discovery of this place. That dream will not die here. Not unless he does.'

Amy leant over the side of the cage, face hidden under her streaming hair. 'Brilliant.'

It took a minute to even get my head around it. However impossible it had seemed that we might actually *succeed*, in our minds, the end of Tabitha had always been The End. It had never even entered my head that it could drag out beyond that.

But what should have plummeted me to a whole new depth of exhaustion and despair felt strangely like the best news Calvin had shared with us since we ran into him.

Because what if *that* was the answer to the question I'd just been asking? What if Shackleton's discovery of Phoenix was no accident? What if he was *meant* to find this place – *this* place, out of all the other places and plans he could have come up with – not so he could exterminate humanity, but so he could *fail?* So that *we* could beat him?

What if we really could still win this thing?

Tell me that makes some kind of sense, I thought, lifting Tobias up so we were face to face. *Tell me I'm not just going crazy.*

Tobias gazed blankly back at me.

I mean, apart from the bit where I'm trying to communicate telepathically with a baby.

Tobias stared at me for a moment longer, nose wrinkling as a raindrop splashed into his face. Then he yawned and closed his eyes, drifting off into sleep.

Chapter 25

LUKE

Thursday, August 13, 10.59 a.m.
6 hours, 1 minute

'This is insane,' said Chew.

'We've done insaner,' I said. Then I took another look at what we'd done to the skid unit. 'Actually, no we haven't.'

'It's kind of like the Trojan horse,' said Wilson.

'Right,' said Chew, 'because no-one's going to suspect a thing when this rolls up to the door.'

'You don't want to come?' said Lazarro. 'Feel free to stay back here and guard the trees.'

'Oh, I'm coming,' said Chew. 'I just want it on record that I think this is insane.'

'Noted,' said Reeve. 'Get in.'

We piled into the cage at the back of the skid. Ten of us: the Weirs, Reeve and Katie, Hamilton, Chew, Wilson, Lazarro, Saunders, and me. All armed with rifles and utility belts.

I felt the weight of the weapon in my hands. Reeve

502 — DOOMSDAY

had pulled me aside and showed me how to fire it, but even *holding* the thing felt wrong to me.

Could I do it? When the time came, when someone got between me and where I needed to be, could I actually pull the trigger on another life? And what did it say about me if I could?

I twisted sideways as Lazarro pressed in next to me, a black metal tube thing perched over his shoulder. It was the centrepiece of our plan: a shoulder-mounted missile launcher. Shackleton Co-operative designed, sleek and compact and hopefully just powerful enough to take down the shield grid.

'Oi!' said Chew, as the back of the launcher swung past. 'Careful, mate. You could put an eye out with that.'

Lazarro rolled his eyes. 'Don't tempt me, Chew.'

Bodies crushed in all around me, and I felt the skid dip under our collective weight. This was definitely not what this thing was built for.

Kirke slammed the back of the cage shut behind us. He came around the side, to where four large riot shields were leaning against the side of the skid.

'How come we've never seen the Co-operative use these before?' I asked, as Kirke started passing the shields into the cage.

'Never had a riot,' said Kirke. 'Not a smart move to bring these things out until you really need them. People see a bunch of guys suited up in riot gear, they tend to rise to the occasion.'

Reeve, Chew, Wilson and Hamilton held the

shields together above our heads, creating a kind of makeshift roof over the cage.

The rest of the skid was as well-protected as we could make it. We'd roped whatever bits of wood and metal we could scrounge to the sides of the cage, and mounted another riot shield to the front of the skid to protect Kirke as he drove.

The engine rumbled to life beneath my feet. We turned in a slow circle, struggling only slightly under the weight of its oversized cargo, and surged off in the direction of the road.

The rain might have eased up a bit by now, but the cold still reached all the way down to my bones. I held onto my rifle, everyone pressed in close around me, and watched the trees slide past overhead, warping out of shape through the plastic of the riot shields. I might have been crammed in here like a battery hen with all the others, but I felt more alone than I had in weeks. It felt so unnatural to be going into something like this without Jordan standing next to me. Like half of me was missing.

'You okay, mate?' asked Mr Weir behind me.

'Yeah,' I lied. 'You?'

'Not my best day ever,' he said, a rough edge to his voice.

The skid dipped, emerging onto the main road. Kirke slowly brought us around, pulling to a stop just short of the south end of town. My nerves were stretched to breaking point. I pictured myself edging to the top of that first enormous hill on a roller coaster. Nothing to do but hold on and wait for the drop.

Kirke glanced back, waiting for Reeve's okay.

'Stay together,' said Reeve, nodding at him. 'We stay together and we keep each other alive in there.'

'Friends forever,' said Chew. 'Got it.'

Kirke stomped on the accelerator and the skid lurched forward, engine roaring. We shot up the road, bushland melting into a green-grey smear, bodies crushing into each other as we were thrown to the back of the cage.

The town raced up to meet us. We rocketed over the threshold where the trees gave way to houses, straight up Phoenix's only asphalt road, town centre dead ahead.

Past my old street, past the house where Jordan and I had hidden out all those weeks ago, all of it blurring together the same way it did in my head. I held my breath, waiting for the first gunshots.

The park whooshed past on my left, and suddenly we were threading the gap between the medical centre and the exploded shell of Phoenix Mall, the Shackleton Building towering over all of it. Our skid bucked and swerved as Kirke dodged the worst of the wreckage and ploughed straight over the rest. Bits of debris kicked up from the tyres, bouncing off the riot shields.

The second we cleared the medical centre, rifle fire surged from somewhere out of sight. Hamilton cried out as the bullets sprayed across his shield, cracking the plastic right in front of his face.

'Hold!' Lazarro barked.

He was okay. The gunfire hadn't made it through. Not this time, anyway.

SMASH!

The skid charged straight into the razor-wire fence guarding the entrance to the Shackleton Building. My head jolted up, smacking into the thing on Lazarro's shoulder. More gunfire, from multiple shooters now. I heard gasps and screams, but we were too packed together to tell if anyone had actually been hurt.

The skid shuddered against the fence and then finally pushed through it, dragging down a whole section and rampaging over the top. Kirke swerved around the fountain on the other side and punched the accelerator, speeding us towards the steps of the Shackleton Building.

And finally, I caught a glimpse of one of Shackleton's men. He peered up from a garden bed at the bottom of the steps, lining us up with his rifle.

'Kirke!' Reeve shouted, spotting him. 'On your left!'

Kirke's head twitched to the side, but it was already too late to change course. Cracks splintered across the riot shield at the front of the skid as the guard pulled the trigger. Kirke jolted in his seat, but held the wheel steady. The skid's massive tyres hit the steps of the Shackleton Building and started roaring up them.

Then disaster. The guard fired again, attacking

from the side as we hurtled past him. Blood spattered
the inside of Kirke's shield. He slumped over the wheel.
The guard kept shooting, and the skid rocked violently
as a tyre exploded under my feet. Chew's riot shield
flew from his hands, disappearing behind us.

The automatic doors at the top of the steps slid
open as we approached, but didn't get ten centimetres
apart before they were smashed to pieces. Glass rained
down on us. The skid veered, tipping onto two wheels,
smashing through a table and a couple of benches and
crashing sideways into a row of portable toilets before
winding up on all fours again, still moving, spinning
out of control, until we finally crunched to a stop
against the wall.

'Out!' Reeve shouted, pushing open the back of the
cage. 'Everyone out!'

I looked up to the front of the skid. Kirke was
gone. Left behind somewhere in the crash.

I turned to get out, but then Chew shoved past me,
almost knocking me over. He leant out over the side of
the cage, raising his rifle.

The noise ripped through my ears.

Back at the entrance, a man fell to the ground,
dead. The guard who'd shot Kirke had been coming
back for the rest of us.

Chew looked ready to throw up. 'Harris, you dumb
bastard. What'd you make me do that for?'

He knew him, I thought, falling out of the cage,
shaky but miraculously uninjured. *Of course he did.*

Twenty-four hours ago, they might have been on duty together. They might have been friends.

I ducked next to Katie, but she didn't even register that I was there. She was too fixated on her husband, already weaving his way across the giant, high-ceilinged foyer-turned-concentration-camp, holding up his riot shield in one hand and unclipping something from his belt with the other. Wilson and Hamilton were right behind him, zig-zagging through the sea of tables and chairs that had all been quickly abandoned when the explosions started going off last night.

'No,' said Katie, as I stood to go after them. 'He said to wait here.'

'But –'

BANG!

At the far end of the foyer, a set of double doors flew open and a half-dozen guards leapt out. The sound of a terrified crowd spilled through the doorway behind them. The people of Phoenix, crammed together inside the town hall with who knew how many armed men keeping them under control.

Shackleton's guys spread out, opening fire. Reeve and the others kept moving, while Lazarro, Chew and Saunders all jumped up from behind the skid to help cover them.

There was a strangled cry from across the foyer and one of Shackleton's men collapsed, clutching his leg.

'Idiot!' Lazarro snapped at Chew. 'Any minute

now, we'll be asking them to *join* us. Don't shoot them unless –'

'Unless *what?*' said Chew. 'And it wasn't even me! It was Saund–'

He looked sideways just in time to see Saunders jolt back and crumple to the floor. I leapt out of the way as he fell, heart thumping into my throat. He was gone.

Lazarro swore. He fired again. Across the foyer, I saw Shackleton's guys digging in, taking positions behind whatever cover they could find.

Reeve stopped maybe twenty metres out from us. He dropped down behind a table, pulling his whole body in behind his barely-intact riot shield, and hurled a silver canister over his head at the guards. It was a smoke bomb, like the one they'd used back at the house. Hamilton and Wilson followed suit, and in seconds, a murky black cloud was spreading out across the foyer.

'GO!' Reeve shouted out of the darkness. 'GO! GO!'

'You heard him!' said Lazarro. 'MOVE!'

I jumped up, almost knocking over Mrs Weir, who was supporting Mr Weir over her shoulder. It looked like he'd twisted his ankle or something in the crash.

'More coming!' said Katie breathlessly, looking back at the front steps as the smoke began swirling over us.

'Get out of here,' Mr Weir grunted, shooing me away.

I ignored him, rushing to his other side and helping Mrs Weir steer him around the skid unit. I almost dropped him again as someone came charging through the smoke towards us.

It was Reeve. He dashed past, throwing an arm over Katie, covering her with the riot shield, then glanced at Mr Weir, taking in his injured leg. 'Are you guys –?'

'We're great,' said Mr Weir. 'C'mon, I'll race you.'

We hobbled as fast as we could, barely dodging tables and benches and random other obstacles as they loomed up out of the smoke. Reeve and Katie tried to hang back with us, but it wasn't long before we lost them.

Gunfire blazed around us, flashes of lightning in the swirling cloud. I flinched every time, expecting the bullets to come tearing through me, throwing me to the ground in a bloody heap, just like Kirke, and Saunders, and the guard across the foyer, and the one back at the school, and –

An agonised scream rang out across the room, then stopped. Another one. Gone.

'Keep going,' Mr Weir urged. I hadn't even realised I'd stopped.

We limped around the last couple of tables and either the smoke was thinning out or we were getting to the edge of it, because when the doors to the town hall burst open again and another armed guard came barrelling out in front of us, I had no trouble seeing him.

'Steve!' said Mr Weir, locking eyes with the guard. He straightened on his good leg, pulling his arm from my shoulder to reach for his rifle. Too slow. 'Steve – C'mon, mate. You don't want to –'

The guard raised his own rifle and Mr Weir froze.

He stared at us, stony-faced – then almost jumped out of his skin at a sudden burst of shrieks and gasps behind him.

A huge shape blurred through the doors, body-slamming the guard to the ground. The figure sprung back to his feet, grabbed Mr Weir, and threw him over his shoulder. Then he bolted along the back wall in the direction of the lift. 'This way!'

It was Mr Burke. Jordan's dad.

Mrs Weir and I stared at each other, still trying to work out what had just happened.

A flash of movement inside the hall snapped me out of it. More guards coming. I grabbed Mrs Weir's arm and sprinted for the lift.

Chapter 26

LUKE

'Come on, come on, come on, come on!' said Wilson as we tore up the last few metres to the lift. He and Reeve were standing at the doors, shields up to guard everyone inside. They split apart, letting us in, and then Reeve hammered the close button.

The lift slid shut, muffling the noise from the hall. From the sound of it, some of the other prisoners had taken Mr Burke's breakout as their cue to do the same.

Reeve hit another button and the lift jolted upwards. I did a quick head count. Ten of us, counting Mr Burke. We'd managed not to lose anyone else since the smoke bombs went off.

'Thanks for the lift, mate,' said Mr Weir, as Mr Burke lowered him to the floor. 'And listen, sorry for leaving without you last night. You know we would never have –'

'Of course,' said Mr Burke. 'Where are the others?'

'Most of us were captured,' I said, breathing hard. 'Taken down to Shackleton's bunker.'

'So that's where we're heading?' he said.

I hesitated, not wanting to be the one to tell him no. Mr Burke was the most gentle, kind-hearted guy you'd ever meet, but he was also huge and imposing and fiercely single-minded about the safety of his family.

'It's on the list,' Reeve jumped in. 'First we need to disable the shield grid, then we need to get to the loyalty room, *then* we can see about –'

'We should split up,' said Lazarro. 'While they're still reeling. Won't take them long to get the crowd back under control, but while they're doing it, we have an opportunity.'

'Up to the top first,' Reeve insisted. 'We need that shield down. Until we're sure we can –'

'I'm sorry,' Mr Burke broke in, sounding the complete opposite of sorry, 'but if you expect me to co-operate with a plan where my wife and kids are priority number *three* –'

He silenced himself as we slowed to a halt at what was allegedly the top floor. There was a clatter around the lift as everyone grabbed hold of their weapons. Reeve and Wilson hoisted their shields back up in front of the doors. I squeezed the handle of my rifle, just needing something to hold onto.

The lift doors opened to reveal the reception area. Wide hallways ran out to our left and right, leading off to offices for all of Shackleton's top guys. Everything was silent. Abandoned. Reeve and Hamilton stepped cautiously out onto the carpet, shields up.

'That way, right?' said Mr Burke in a whisper, getting out after them and pointing down the corridor to our right.

Katie nodded. She and Mr Weir had worked up here, back in the day.

The lift we'd been in only ran from here to the ground floor. To get up to the roof or down to the bunker, we'd need to take the *other* lift – the secret one outside Shackleton's office.

'We won't get to the bunker that way, though,' I breathed, knowing what Mr Burke was really asking. 'That lift was locked out from the basement level last night, so unless anything's changed since then …'

'Let's get the shield grid sorted first,' said Reeve, voice low. 'Once that's out of the way –'

'Doesn't take ten of us to navigate an empty corridor,' said Lazarro, joining them outside. 'Come on, Matt. Waste of time for us all to go up there.'

'You know what *else* is a waste of time?' said Chew, getting jittery. 'Standing around talking while –'

'I might be able to override the lift,' said Mr Weir. 'If I can get to a computer …'

'We'll need numbers to take the cafeteria later,' said Reeve, still talking to Lazarro.

'You need *soldiers*,' said Lazarro, rolling his shoulder under the weight of the missile launcher. 'Numbers are only good to you if they know their way around a gun. Look, I'll take these guys – Luke, the Weirs, and the Incredible Hulk, here. We'll deal with the grid, then see what we can do about getting into the bunker. Every chance Shackleton will be down there, anyway. You guys head for the cafeteria.'

Everyone shut up, waiting for Reeve's decision. Gunfire rattled up through the floor beneath our feet.

'Okay, yeah,' he said finally. 'Go.' He turned to his wife. 'Did you want to –?'

'No,' said Katie, eyes set. 'I'm with you.'

'Right,' said Reeve. He and the others stepped back into the lift, and the Weirs, Mr Burke and I started down the corridor with Lazarro. 'See you all soon.'

The doors slid closed. I felt a ripple of fear as they disappeared, knowing I might never see them again.

We headed towards the other lift, down the all-too-familiar corridor lined with the creepy red-brown abstract artworks Shackleton painted in his spare time.

'How did you get out?' whispered Mr Burke, running a hand through the tangle of dark, curly hair that had overtaken his formerly-shaven head. 'If the others were all captured …'

'Long story,' I said. Then, deciding it was going to come out soon enough anyway: 'Jordan got out too. She's gone out to the wall with –'

'Shh!' warned Lazarro, coming to a sudden stop.

Muffled voices, somewhere out behind us. I couldn't see anyone yet, but –

'In here!' hissed Mr Weir, pushing open the nearest

door. The word *PRYOR* was stencilled next to the handle.

The room was almost identical to Pryor's principal's office. Giant wooden desk with a computer in the corner, an ornate rug underneath – but this office had a huge oil painting of a phoenix in place of the tapestry she'd had back at school.

'Here, hold this,' murmured Lazarro, unstrapping the missile launcher from his shoulder and thrusting it into my hands. He stood back from the door, rifle raised, the scar on his cheek folding in as he smirked at the look on my face. 'Don't worry. Won't hurt you with the safety on.'

I stood to the side, hefting the launcher against my chest, straining to hear as the voices outside drew closer.

'Yes, sir,' said a nervous voice, 'I understand that. But those were his orders.'

'To lock down a facility you are not even authorised to access unaccompanied? To compromise our ability to navigate the town at this critical hour?'

The voice was sharp, aggressive and all too familiar. Ms Pryor. We had chosen the *wrong* office.

'Sir, you have to believe me,' said the first voice, closer now, and I realised it was Officer Cook, one of Calvin's guards from the Vattel Complex this morning. One of the guards who was *supposed* to be keeping Shackleton away from Mum and the others. 'I realise how it sounds. I had my own doubts about the orders, but –'

'But you still did what Calvin told you,' finished Pryor.

'Sir – It was *Calvin,*' said Cook, exasperated. 'If I'd kept arguing –'

I held my breath as the footsteps padded closer. There were more than just two of them. Whoever the others were, they weren't speaking. Probably more guards. I doubted Pryor would be going anywhere without an escort today.

My hands grew slippery against the missile launcher, my mind flashing down to the bunker. What was going on in there? If Cook was up here chatting with Pryor …

The footsteps stopped, just outside our door.

Mr and Mrs Weir raised their weapons. Mr Burke stood behind them, unarmed, but still just as menacing. None of it made me feel any better. They had at least as many guns as we did. We weren't getting out of here without a bloodbath.

'You are extremely fortunate that Mr Shackleton is too caught up at the medical centre to come after you for this,' said Pryor, in a voice that said she was feeling pretty fortunate about that herself.

'Y-yes, sir,' said Cook uncomfortably.

I felt a tiny trickle of relief. A bucket of water on a housefire. If Shackleton was across town in the medical centre, then at least he wasn't doing anything to hurt –

But then, what if that's exactly what he *was* doing? What if he'd hauled Mum or Mrs Burke or Georgia out there to interrogate them or experiment on them or …?

'Get back down there,' said Pryor. 'Keep the prisoners in line until he comes for them. Keep *Louisa* in line. Give Shackleton every reason to forget this morning's mistakes. And give me no reason to remind him.'

'Yes, sir. Understood,' said Cook, and I heard his footsteps fade back out the way we'd come.

I watched the door, waiting for it to move. Waiting for the tiny creak of the handle that would make this whole place erupt in fire and blood.

Instead, I heard more footsteps. They were fading. Continuing up the corridor towards Shackleton's office.

The corridor went quiet again.

I waited, still hardly daring to breathe, not ready to believe that they were really all gone. But the silence stretched out.

Finally, Mr Burke started towards the door.

'Give it a minute,' said Lazarro, holding out a hand.

Mr Burke glared down at him, obviously in no mood to be taking orders from a guy in a security uniform. But he backed off, rounding on me instead. 'You said Jordan was out at the wall. Why? What's going on out there?'

'She's with Calvin,' I whispered. 'And Tobias. They're –'

'With *Calvin?*'

'No, it's okay,' I said, hoping I was telling him the truth. 'He's helping her. Well, he seems to be. He hasn't hurt her, at least.'

'It does sound like he and Shackleton aren't on the

same page anymore, doesn't it?' said Mr Weir, jerking a thumb out at the corridor.

Mr Burke still looked far from convinced, but Mr Weir's reassurances seemed to sink in deeper than mine did. I guessed they'd formed a pretty tight bond after all those weeks trapped in the camp together.

'And this Tobias,' said Mr Burke stiffly. 'Who's he?'

I glanced sideways at the Weirs. I kept forgetting how long he'd been out of the loop. 'He's ... he's your son,' I said, and watched his face transform in a second. 'Mrs Burke had the baby last night, right before the guards found us. Jordan and I got out, and we brought Tobias with us, and ...' I paused, struggling to even get the words together. 'Mr Burke, we think Tobias can do something to stop Tabitha. That's why they're out there. Calvin says he knows what Tobias has to do.'

Mr Burke looked like he'd been hit by a truck. He stared at me, open-mouthed. Then slowly, he nodded. Not like he understood, but like it was all he could get his body to do.

'We should get moving,' said Mr Weir, glancing at the computer on Pryor's desk. 'I'll head down the hall and see if I can find a safer place to override the lift controls.'

'Ben More's office?' I suggested. 'He was killed last night. Shouldn't be anyone in there.'

We split up and I headed for the secret lift with the others, stopping at the big metal door opposite Mr Weir's old office. I shifted my grip on the missile launcher, which Lazarro still hadn't taken back, and swiped Bill's key card against the wall.

The door swung open. We stepped through, and I hit the button for the lift. The doors didn't open right away. Instead, I heard the heavy mechanical clunking of the lift coming down to meet us.

'It was upstairs,' said Lazarro in a low voice. 'There's someone up there.'

'Pryor,' I said, steeling myself, 'and the guards, or whoever was with her.'

'Hopefully too busy to notice us coming,' Lazarro said. 'Don't worry. We'll deal with them.'

The doors sprang open. We got inside and I hit the button for the basement, just to be sure we really were locked out.

The lift didn't move.

I pressed the button for the floor above us, and the doors slid shut.

'Here,' I told Mr Burke as we trundled upward, shrugging my shoulder to indicate that he should take my rifle. He was just pulling it away from me when the doors opened onto the secret top floor, a big open-plan office with floor-to-ceiling glass running along one side.

Lazarro opened fire as soon as the gap was wide enough. The noise roared around us, drowning the shouts of the security guards as they ducked for cover.

There were two of them. One was dead before he hit the ground. The other dived behind a desk, twisting around to return fire.

Behind them, Pryor abandoned the filing cabinet she'd been searching through and dropped to the floor.

I dived behind a desk and started crawling towards the door at the back of the room, dragging the missile launcher awkwardly along beside me.

The surviving guard fired his rifle, tearing up the wall behind me, and Mr Burke thumped heavily to the ground on my left. He rolled over, unhurt.

Lazarro was behind us. He fired again, blasting a giant hole in the glass wall. The wind swirled in, scattering paperwork and chilling the air.

A computer monitor exploded above my head. I hurried forward, throwing myself across a walkway between two desks.

And suddenly, there was the guard.

He turned, spotting me, whipped his weapon around in my direction – and then jerked backwards, shuddering with the impact of a dozen bullets from Lazarro's rifle. He collapsed against the wall behind him, streaking the glass with blood as he slid to the ground.

An eerie quiet swept through the office, broken only by Lazarro's cautious footsteps and the rustle of paper in the wind. Where was Pryor?

Lazarro crept up to join us, rifle sweeping through the air ahead of him. 'Stay behind me,' he muttered.

I kept low to the ground, my eyes jittering around the room. Where *was* she?

'This it?' said Mr Burke as we reached a locked door in the back corner of the office. I nodded, and he jumped up, smashing the door handle to the ground with the butt of his rifle. Then he flinched and dropped to the floor again, just as –

BLAM! BLAM!

Two neat holes pierced the door, right where his head had been.

'GO!' said Lazarro, returning fire. 'Get up there!'

I grabbed the bottom of the door, yanked it wide and scrambled through, finding a flight of steep metal stairs on the other side. I started climbing, still heaving the missile launcher.

More gunshots. Two from Pryor's pistol, and then a burst from Lazarro's rifle. A shrill scream cut through the air.

Lazarro came racing up the stairs behind me, followed by Mr Burke.

'Hurry!' said Mr Burke. 'I don't –'

BLAM!

He cried out, and I heard a dull thud as he hit the stairs.

Lazarro swore. 'No!' he shouted as I turned to look. 'Go! Keep going!'

He fired back down the stairs.

I kept staggering up until I came to another door. Unlocked. I pushed it open and an icy wind blasted me in the face.

Lazarro caught up again, practically throwing me out onto the roof. 'Quick!' he said, shrugging off his rifle. 'Take this. Give me the –'

BLAM!

Lazarro fell silent. His mouth opened and closed, a trickle of blood spilling down the side of his chin.

He fell to the ground.

Chapter 27

LUKE

Clank. Clank. Clank.

The footsteps were heavy and uneven. Pryor was still coming, but she wasn't having an easy time of it.

I stood there, stunned, unable to drag my eyes away from Lazarro's body. Twelve hours ago, I could barely have told you who he was, but now ...

Clank. Clank. Clank.

The wind was ridiculous up here. It blasted into me like a cannon, spraying me with rain, almost knocking me off my feet.

Clank. Clank.

The panic finally overtook my paralysis and I stumbled backwards, away from the door. I broke into a run, lugging the missile launcher across the giant expanse of the roof, but where was there to go? Those stairs were the only way down.

The only way down you could survive, anyway.

The antenna loomed over me, so much bigger than

it seemed from the ground, thicker than the oldest trees in the bush and impossibly tall. I circuited around it, ducking out of sight just as Pryor emerged at the top of the stairs.

Antenna in front of me. Edge of the building behind, way too close for comfort.

The missile launcher shifted in my hands, slippery with rain. I hoisted it onto my shoulder, staggering sideways as a particularly savage gust of wind blew past, realising what I was going to have to do.

My hands found the twin grips on the underside of the launcher, one index finger slipping around the trigger. My eyes twitched between the antenna and the edge of the roof behind me and the single bulbous missile sticking out of the front of the launcher. I had one shot. One chance to knock out the shield grid. And about ten seconds to make that shot before Pryor came and finished me off.

I edged backwards, putting as much distance as I could between me and the antenna. There was a little plastic targeting thing half-hanging from the launcher. I pulled it down and stared through the crosshairs.

What are you doing? I thought, body screaming at me to run. *You don't know how to fire this thing! You're going to blow yourself off the side of the building!*

I shoved it aside. No other choice. I had about five hours left anyway if the grid didn't come down, and failing now meant dooming everyone else in the world with me.

No way was I going out like that. If this really was a one-way trip, then I was at least going to make sure the ending counted for something.

I dropped to one knee, feeling the bone scrape against the concrete as I angled the launcher up at the antenna. A bizarre sense of calm fell over me.

Maybe Jordan was right after all. Maybe there really was a bigger picture here, even if it wasn't the one I would have painted. Maybe I hadn't been saved from getting murdered just so I could run off into some happily-ever-after.

Maybe I'd been saved for *this*.

I aimed high, pointing the crosshairs to the top of the antenna. With any luck, it would take out the electrified cords without –

A breathless grunt from behind me shattered my focus. I whipped the launcher around and the sights locked onto a pale and bleeding Pryor.

'Drop it,' she coughed, staggering out from the antenna, one hand pressed against her bloody side.

I panicked, pulling the trigger on the missile launcher. *Click.*

Nothing happened.

Pryor smiled weakly and took another lunging step.

The safety, I realised. How did you –?

Pryor raised a shaky hand, pointing her pistol at my head. She swayed, almost losing her balance in the wind, and then –

Whump.

I had barely registered the sound of running footsteps before the blurred figure of a man in black threw himself into Pryor, knocking her off her feet.

BLAM!

The gunshot went wide as they flew through the air together, crashing down precariously close to the edge of the roof.

Time slowed. They were still moving, rolling over each other. The guard's face came into view and I realised it was Lazarro, still alive, and with enough energy left to –

No.

He latched onto Pryor, and together they rolled over the side.

I dropped the launcher, stretching over the edge on my hands and knees just in time to see them thump down against the Shackleton Building's front steps. It was surprisingly quiet.

Pryor tumbled limply down the stairs, rolling to rest on the footpath. Lazarro lay sprawled on his back, gazing up at the sky. Both of them just bodies now. I started retching, hacking violently, as shouts echoed on the ground. Shackleton's men rushing over to see what had happened.

When my gag reflex subsided, I backed off from the edge, fumbling for the missile launcher. I dragged myself back to the other side of the antenna, looking the launcher over, trying to figure out where the safety was. My eyes landed on a little switch above the trigger.

I flipped it, and lifted the launcher back over my shoulder.

Then came the voices. Reinforcements arriving downstairs. Discovering the mess and the bodies in the office. Spotting the open door up to the roof ...

I readjusted the little targeting lens, crosshairs back up on the antenna.

And I hesitated.

It wasn't just the antenna that looked bigger from up here. The crisscrossing cords of the shield grid were enormous too, thick as my arm and rippling with electricity. What was going to happen when I brought them all crashing down on top of us?

Clank-clank-clank-clank.

The sound echoed up the stairwell behind me. Boots on metal.

Now or never.

Clank-clank-clank-clank.

I dropped down on one knee again.

Clenched my fists, struggling to keep the launcher steady.

Clank-clank-clank-clank.

I aimed high. Fixed the crosshairs up where the lowest cords converged on the antenna.

Felt for the trigger. Felt it give slightly under the weight of my finger.

Clank-clank-clank-clank.

'HEY!' demanded a voice behind me. 'DROP –!'

I closed my eyes and fired.

Chapter 28

JORDAN

Bright orange light exploded in my peripheral vision.

I whirled around, almost losing my balance on the tree branch. I was climbing again. Not because I thought it was going to get me anywhere. Mostly just because I couldn't keep still. And because from up in this tree, level with the top of the wall, I could see the top of the Shackleton Building peeking up between the treetops.

My heart was already pounding before my brain had time to catch up with what was going on. An explosion. Something had just detonated in the air above the Shackleton Building.

A huge fireball rose up from the roof, brilliant against the grey sky. I squinted into Calvin's binoculars, but it was all too far away. In seconds, what little I could see had been enveloped in a cloud of roiling charcoal smoke.

'Guys!' I shouted, fists tight on the branches as I peered down at the others. 'I think –'

But the rest was choked out by a gasp as the shield grid began to shudder above my head, sending sparks raining on top of me. I dropped down a couple of metres, half-climbing, half-falling through the branches.

They'd done it.

The thundering above me grew more violent, the whole grid rolling like someone shaking out a blanket. I looked up, grabbing a branch above my head and leaning out to see better.

'Keep moving!' Calvin called up. 'Get down here!'

The grid creaked and hissed, sparks still cascading down all around me. I dropped down to the next branch, losing my footing in the wet and only just catching myself in time to avoid falling the rest of the way.

And then a new sound. A low, echoing rumble that seemed to come from somewhere deep inside the wall itself. I turned back and saw the cord nearest to me slithering back into the top of the wall, like a power cable getting sucked up into a vacuum cleaner.

The grid was coming down – but not *straight* down. The cords were shrinking away again, unlacing from each other, retracting the way they'd come.

It was a safety mechanism. Of course. Shackleton was cocky, but he wasn't stupid. He'd clearly put a lot of faith in his shield grid, but if it *did* come down, he couldn't have it crushing his precious town. As usual, he had a contingency in place.

I looked down. Still maybe five metres to the ground. The cords might have left the town untouched, but they weren't going to do the same to the treetops. I could already hear them rustling back through the branches, flailing like the tentacles of some hideous sea monster.

Amy screamed as the cord above me suddenly crashed down into the tree, whipping past only centimetres over my head. I ducked, slipping from branch to branch, falling again, jarring my shoulder as I shot out an arm to catch myself, the whole tree shaking with the writhing of the cord. I caught a glimpse of the end of it, ragged and frayed from the explosion, snaking towards my tree.

'Jump!' Amy yelled.

I hesitated, judging the distance, and took her advice. I dropped to the ground, bending my knees to absorb the impact but still jarring both legs. I landed awkwardly on my back just as the cord pulled clear of the tree and out of sight.

For a few seconds, everything was silent. A hand shot out in front of my face. Calvin, coming to help me up. I grabbed on, skin still crawling a bit at his touch, and he hoisted me to my feet.

'He did it,' said Calvin with just the hint of a smile.

I looked up at the sky, wide open again.

'Here,' said Amy, handing Tobias back as soon as I was upright. She'd rearranged his blanket while I was up the tree, tying the corners together to create a little sling. 'For the climb.'

Calvin turned on her. 'You're not coming.'

Amy took a couple of steps back.

'She's coming,' I said.

'We can't trust her,' said Calvin. 'When we reach the release station –'

'We can't trust *me*?' said Amy. 'I'm sorry, but –'

'Yes, well done, you've noticed the irony. Be that as it may,' said Calvin, pulling a coil of rope from the back of the skid, 'I cannot allow you to jeopardise the success of this mission. You are staying here.'

'If you think you're just going to tie me up and –'

'I don't,' said Calvin, slinging the rope over his shoulder. He tracked across to the wall, sizing up nearby trees, picking one out not far from the tree I'd just been climbing. He reached up, hoisting himself up off the ground, and got to his feet on one of the lower branches. 'This is as far as I climb until Amy agrees to remain behind. If the two of you believe you can stop Tabitha without my help, then by all means, continue on without me. If not …'

He let the sentence hang in the air, a look of infuriating calm on his face. He had me, and he knew it. And so did Amy.

I reached out to her. 'Listen –'

'It's *fine*,' said Amy.

'It's not,' I said. 'None of this is fine. But if we want to have any shot at stopping –'

'Yeah,' she said, shrugging my hand off her shoulder. 'I get it.' But then her expression softened a little. 'Sorry. I just … It's been kind of a big day.'

She peered down at Tobias. He stared back at her,

smiling. 'I think he can do it,' she said. 'I mean, I don't know *what* I even think he can do, but – I don't think we're wrong about Tobias. I really think he can fix this. Don't trust Calvin. Not for a second. But if you can get Tobias out there ...'

Again, my mind shook with images of Tobias's grisly death. And again, I pushed it all aside.

'I'll get him out there.' I reached out to hug her, and this time she didn't pull away. 'You just stay safe until we get back. Keep hidden. They're sure to come looking for us, now that the shield's down.'

'Yeah,' she said as I released her. 'And listen, if they have a Coke machine at the release station ...'

I half-smiled, stomach grumbling at the thought of some actual food and drink. 'Back soon.'

I checked Tobias's sling to make sure he was fastened as securely as he could be, and then grabbed hold of the first branch, following Calvin up into the tree.

LUKE

Thursday, August 13, 11.45 a.m.
5 hours, 15 minutes

BOOM!

I'd barely even felt my finger come down on the trigger before the missile exploded away from me, setting the sky on fire. The launcher slammed against my shoulder, but not nearly as hard as I'd worried it would. Fire and smoke blasted out behind me and I staggered, somehow managing to stay upright.

The explosion swelled, blinding, deafening, drowning me in its heat, filling my nostrils with the smell of my own singed hair. Gravel-sized bits of exploded antenna rained down on top of me.

With a terrified glance out at the edge, I lurched to my feet, eyes readjusting as the explosion passed.

There were guards at my back, but they didn't seem to be in a hurry to grab me. They looked on, stunned as I was, as a massive section of the antenna came plummeting out of the smoke.

I ducked pointlessly as it tumbled overhead, staggeringly huge, catching the corner of the building on its way down, smashing through the concrete and sending shockwaves across the roof. I lost my footing, landing hard on my hands and knees.

Somewhere far below, the giant bit of antenna hammered into the ground with an earth-shattering crunch.

I'd done it.

I hung there, head between my arms, struggling to even process it. The whole scene seemed to drag to a stop, everyone frozen in place, until the sound of someone else climbing the stairs woke me up again. He paused at the top, let loose with a long string of expletives, then snapped at the guards. 'What are you doing? *Grab* him, you idiots!'

The two guards latched onto me from behind,

hauling me to my feet, and I saw who was handing out their orders. Arthur van Pelt, the weedy little guy who used to run Phoenix Mall. I'd only ever seen him once or twice, but I knew he was another one of Shackleton's inner circle.

'This is a disaster,' he muttered, pushing his glasses back up onto his nose. He stared through the clearing smoke at the shield grid, which was collapsing rapidly. Not down onto the town, but back out to the wall, like it had just been switched off rather than blown up.

The guards dragged me towards the stairs, and again, I felt that weird sense of calm drift over me. If they were going to kill me, there was nothing I could do about it. And if they weren't …

Then I might just have found myself a way into the bunker. From there, I could find Shackleton and –

'Where's Melinda?' van Pelt demanded, suddenly up in my face. 'Ms Pryor. Your principal. Where is she?'

'She's dead,' I told him, and watched his face turn pale.

He spun away from me, barking at his guards. 'Quickly! Take them away!'

Them? I wondered, as the guard shoved me down the stairs ahead of them. But then a shout from downstairs answered my question.

My heart lifted. It was Jordan's dad. He was alive.

I stumbled back out into the office and saw Mr Burke glaring darkly at two very nervous-looking guards as they cuffed his hands together behind his back. His right sleeve glistened red with blood.

'I know what you're thinking,' said van Pelt, slipping into the room behind us. He advanced on Mr Burke, jabbing a finger at his chest. 'But let me warn you, an escape attempt would be unwise. We've been ordered to keep your friend,' he jerked a thumb at me, 'alive for questioning. We've received no such orders for –'

Van Pelt swore as Mr Burke landed a sharp kick between his legs.

'Oi!' snapped a guard behind Mr Burke, tugging backwards on his enormous arms. Mr Burke gasped at the strain on his wounded shoulder.

One of the guards pushed past me, drawing his pistol.

'No!' I shouted. 'Leave him!'

'Not –' van Pelt winced, grabbing himself as he leant against a desk. 'Not yet. Take him down with the others. If he wants to see his family again, he'll be sure to co-operate.' He limped determinedly up to Mr Burke. 'Won't you, Abraham?'

Mr Burke sneered but didn't bite back, and the guards hauled us through the mess of our gunfight to the lift. As we passed the giant, shattered window, I looked down at the fallen antenna stretched out across the street, cracked concrete snaking out around it.

The shield grid had completely retracted by now. Nothing but cloudy sky all around.

As we squeezed into the lift, one of van Pelt's men

hammered the bunker button. 'Bloody lockdown,' he muttered, when the lift wouldn't budge. 'Sir, I thought Shackleton got inside already. Can't you just call and ask him to let us down this way?'

'Would *you* like to call him?' said van Pelt, pulling a phone from his jacket. 'He's only working furiously to save all of our lives. I'm sure he wouldn't mind hearing from an insolent security officer with a complaint about his orders.'

The guard's eyes flickered. 'Why don't we just take the long way around?

'Yes,' said van Pelt, returning the phone to his pocket. 'Why don't we?'

The lift brought us down to the floor with all the Co-operative heads' offices. The two guards on Mr Burke shoved him outside, steering him towards the other lift. I moved to follow him, but van Pelt clamped a hand down on my shoulder. 'I'm afraid not, Mr Hunter. We've made other arrangements for you.'

He nodded at the two remaining guards, and they started dragging me off in the opposite direction.

Mr Burke twisted around to see where they were taking me. His two guards freaked out, shoving him into the wall, shattering a painting of some rust-red animal. Mr Burke cried out at the pain in his arm. He jerked back his good elbow, catching one of them in the face.

'Get him under control, will you?' van Pelt snapped, straightening his glasses again, and my two guards ran off to help. But before I could even think about making a run for it, I felt the cold muzzle of van Pelt's pistol pressing between my shoulder blades. 'This way, Mr Hunter.'

He marched me up to the end of the corridor. I realised where we were headed seconds before we got close enough for me to read the name on the door. The noise of Mr Burke's scuffle with the guards seemed to fade into the distance. My legs went numb, stumbling to a stop, like they'd suddenly lost their connection to my brain.

'*Move*,' snarled van Pelt, pushing me forward again.

My eyes hovered over the name on the door and whatever warmth my body had left drained away.

'Oh, don't worry,' said van Pelt, stretching up to whisper into my ear. 'I know I said he was busy, but I'm sure Mr Shackleton will be *extremely* pleased to see you.'

Chapter 29

JORDAN

'What if they find her?' I said, as we jogged up the gentle slope through the rocks. 'We *know* they'll be coming after us – How could they not? And she's just sitting out there, waiting for –'

'Yes Jordan, I do understand the situation,' said Calvin impatiently. 'Whatever else I might be, I'm not a fool. And as I've already said, she's far safer there than we are here. Whoever Shackleton sends after us, they won't come climbing over the wall. They'll go through the gates. They won't get within half a kilometre of her.'

'Unless they see the rope we used to get over the wall,' I said.

Calvin stopped, catching his breath. 'Jordan, please, try to keep this in perspective. We are out here in an attempt to *save the world*. Amy may be your friend, but I will not stake the lives of billions on –'

'Who are *you* to decide what happens to the lives of billions?' I spat bitterly. 'You're the one who –!'

'I'm the one who can show you how to save them,' said Calvin. He turned his back on me and continued up the slope.

It was just over an hour since we'd touched down on the outside of the wall. It had been terrifying scaling the side with Tobias, but we'd both reached the ground in one piece.

The wasteland stretched all around us. Just rock and dirt and the occasional scraggly plant. Still no sign of the release station.

We'd made it far enough from Phoenix now that I could see the curvature of the wall and the wasteland stretching out behind it on both sides. It was so weird to be *outside* it all – to see all of the past hundred days, everything we'd been through, sealed off in its own little world within a world.

'What about me?' I asked Calvin, holding my side as we reached the top of the rise. 'If you're so worried about *rogue elements*, then what am *I* doing here? Why didn't you just take Tobias and do it all yourself?'

'Because I *can't*,' said Calvin, voice cracking. He slowed again, gazing down the hill. 'I cannot do this on my own. I need you here with me in case ...'

'In case what?' I said, but something about the sudden shift in his body language made the fire drain out of my voice.

'I did plan to come alone, at first,' said Calvin, slipping back into creepy-introspective mode. 'Last night, when Shackleton first learned of your whereabouts, my priority was to extract your brother and bring him here as quickly as possible. And I almost managed it. But then I was attacked by – by the man you call Crazy Bill.'

'But you *had* us,' I said, pushing aside sudden, swirling images of Peter. 'When you ambushed Amy and me out at the skid, you could have just –'

'I couldn't,' said Calvin, voice even softer now. 'I couldn't take him. After everything I'd already inflicted on you …' He sighed deeply, staring out into the distance again. 'I am not accustomed to making emotional decisions. But I made one then. I felt you deserved the opportunity to come out here and see this through for yourself. But then you informed me of the apparent disappearance of the fallout. And however I might have responded at the time …'

I looked up, ready to prod him to continue, and was startled to see tears welling in his eyes. And it was more than just sadness or regret or whatever. I could see it all over his face: he was scared.

'The fallout was –' Calvin swallowed hard. He wiped his eyes, pulling himself together, and tried again. 'Whatever change you see in me – Whatever *good* you see … This is not something I chose. I did not summon up this change of heart from some deeply hidden store of my own inner goodness. You of all people know what I was before. I was dead. The fallout dragged me out of that. It gave me back my humanity.'

He stared down at hands, still covered up by the same

Phoenix-red gloves he'd found to keep from soaking up everyone else's emotions.

'And now the fallout's gone,' I said, feeling suddenly cold, 'and you don't know what the rules are anymore. You're worried that it's all going to go away again. So you've brought me out here to – to make sure you actually see this through.'

Calvin drew his pistol, holding it out to me. 'And for as long as I am able to, I'll do the same for you.'

I took the gun.

It was so unnerving, seeing him like this. An actual human with actual vulnerabilities. But even worse was the thought that he might just lose all that and revert to his same old evil self.

'Okay,' I said, sticking the pistol down into the back of my jeans, 'okay, but look, if we're doing this, then you need to *tell* me what we're actually out here to do.'

'I will. When we get there.'

'Calvin, if you're that worried about me flipping out and –'

'Shh!' he said, dropping behind a boulder, eyes back out the way we'd come. He rested his rifle on top of the rock.

I crouched behind him, one hand on Tobias, and whipped out the binoculars. I could hear it too, now. The hum of an engine, faint, but getting louder.

I swept the binoculars back in the direction of the wall. *There.* A pillar of dust, trailing out from the oversized tyres of a skid unit as it streaked across the wasteland towards us. One guy in the driver's seat, and a few more hanging on at the back.

I jumped as Calvin suddenly let loose with his rifle, opening fire right next to my ear. Tobias flinched. I honed in on the skid again just in time to see it crunch down on its side in a cloud of dust and smoke.

I stared at Calvin. 'How on *earth* did you do that from all the way up here?'

'That was not my first time firing a weapon,' he said, getting up from the rock, looking uncharacteristically shaken by what he'd just done. He started walking again, down the far side of the hill.

'They'll keep coming,' he warned. 'The ones who still can. Today more than ever, they know what Shackleton will do if they fail him.'

I hurried after him. 'It's too late though, right? They're not going to catch up to us on foot.'

Calvin nodded. 'Not far to go now.'

I trod carefully down the slope, both arms tight around Tobias, my mind running back over what Calvin had said about the fallout.

I tried to reassure myself. Whatever other fears he had, he still believed Tobias could do what he needed to do out here. That, or he was just clinging desperately to the same shred of hope that I was.

'What I don't get,' I said, more to fill the silence than anything else, 'is how you guys were *expecting* all this to go. I mean, if you knew about the fallout, then surely you must have known what it was going to *do* to us. Did you really think people would just turn a blind eye when their neighbours started randomly developing superpowers?'

'Of course we didn't,' said Calvin, who for all his apparent changed ways was still weirdly defensive of the solidness of the Co-operative's plans. 'Do you honestly think we would have bothered to construct the whole elaborate facade of the town if we'd *known* these things were going to happen?'

'But that was the whole point!' I said. 'I mean, wasn't it? Wasn't the fallout *supposed* to change us? Isn't that why we were all chosen in the first place? Isn't that what a genetic candidate *is?*'

'The point,' said Calvin, 'was to create a society that could survive the release of Tabitha. And to that end, yes, candidates were selected for their genetic susceptibility to the effects of the fallout. Over the course of one hundred days' exposure, we knew the fallout would render such candidates immune to Tabitha. We were also aware that the fallout would boost your immune systems and accelerate your bodies' natural healing abilities. What we did not expect were the *other* side effects.'

'How could you not have expected them?' I said, picking up my pace as the ground levelled out again. 'What about Bill? What about *Galton?*'

'We learnt about Bill's abnormalities at the same time you did. The night out at the airport. His *outburst* –' Calvin winced at the memory, '– was our first indication that the fallout was doing more than we'd anticipated. We didn't know about Galton's powers until days after –'

'But she's Shackleton's *daughter!* How could you not have known she was …?'

Calvin narrowed his eyes, like he thought I was messing with him. 'What?'

'Are you serious?' I said.

'Galton isn't Shackleton's daughter.'

'She is! She lived here as a kid with the Vattel Complex people! Shackleton adopted her when the Complex was destroyed because he *knew* something was up with her. She's how he discovered the fallout in the first place!'

Calvin shook his head, taking it all in. 'If that's true,' he said slowly, 'then why was Shackleton as surprised as the rest of us when he found out about her telekinesis?'

I thought back to our first real run-in with Dr Galton, under the medical centre. She'd strode into the room with complete calm, lifting up furniture and people and hurling them at the walls, every movement so smooth and perfect. So controlled. Definitely not the first time she'd used her powers.

And in that vision I'd had last week … A teenage Dr Galton, out in the bush with a ten-years-younger Shackleton. She'd got all antsy as soon as he'd started talking about what the fallout had done to her body, and then weirdly relieved when –

When she realised he was just only talking about the small stuff.

She was hiding the rest of it, I realised. *She knew she had other abilities. Way back then, she knew. But she was keeping them from him.*

And she'd kept *on* keeping them from him. All this time. All through their plotting and planning for the end of the world. Right up until – when? The day Dr Montag started blood-testing everyone in town?

'Just up here,' said Calvin, apparently taking my silence as an admission that I'd been wrong about Galton.

I looked where he was pointing, but all I could see was more rocks and dirt.

Movement against my chest. Tobias was stirring in the sling. I brought up an arm to cradle him through the blanket, thoughts still wandering back to Dr Galton.

Why hadn't she told him?

Shackleton had obviously brainwashed her enough to help him with his plan for world domination. Tabitha might have been his idea, but Galton had been the one who'd created it, and she'd never been anything but fully committed to the cause.

Or had she? Was there some part of her that still clung to that old resentment, that knowledge that Shackleton wasn't her true father, that he was just using her the way he used everyone else? Had she *wanted* him to fail?

Or was she too scared of what he might do to her if he knew she could throw him across the room with her brain?

Calvin stopped in front of me.

'What's wrong?' I asked. We'd come to the top of a little hill. Not even a hill. Just a slight rise in the ground, low and circular, like the top of a giant ball poking up from the dirt. Still nothing but wasteland all around.

Calvin crouched at the top of the rise. He pulled off his gloves and started clawing at the ground with both hands, scratching away the dirt. There was something under there. Gleaming silver, like Shackleton's tunnels under the town.

I looked back out over the rise we were standing on and couldn't believe I'd missed it: the perfect, symmetrical roundness; the complete absence of rocks and plants. This wasn't a hill. It was a bunker.

Calvin continued brushing away the dirt, revealing a square panel set into the metal. He slid back the dirt-encrusted cover to reveal a single silver button beside a little round hole.

Out of nowhere, Tobias started squirming against me, like he was trying to fight his way out of the blankets.

Calvin pulled his gloves back on. His hand slipped into his pocket, coming back with a plastic vial filled with what looked horribly like blood.

He looked up, smiling grimly. 'We're here.'

Chapter 30

LUKE

I waited.

Hunched over, hands cuffed around one arm of an enormous wooden chair that looked like it had been swiped from a museum. I was wrung out. Sick with fear. Dripping sweat. Beyond exhausted, beyond anything but the nightmarish visions of what Shackleton was going to do when he finally came for me.

His office was immaculate, everything just as creepily neat and tidy as Shackleton himself. A giant desk stretched out in front of me, empty except for a computer and a little stack of journals topped with a fountain pen. Behind the desk hung another one of Shackleton's paintings. The same weird, abstract brushstrokes, like finger painting almost. The same dull red.

The walls on either side of me were lined with books – history, poetry, philosophy, art – all painstakingly arranged and ordered. I realised that every one of them was authored by someone who was either dead or about to be.

A clock ticked loudly, somewhere out of sight. Like Shackleton had hidden it there, just to torture me with the noise of it.

How long had it been now? An hour? More?

I hadn't heard a gunshot in ages. I hadn't heard *anything* except the clock and the murmuring of the guards outside and the low hum of Shackleton's air conditioner blasting the room with an oppressive, unnatural heat.

Where were Reeve and the others? If they'd taken back the loyalty room, then why hadn't anyone come for me? And if they hadn't taken it back …

Then the quiet outside was not a good sign.

I looked down to where I'd tried to saw through the arm of the chair with my handcuffs. I'd kept it up for about twenty seconds before the guard came in and told me to knock it off, and in that time I'd done a whole lot more damage to my wrists than I had to the chair.

What if this was it?

What if he just never came?

What if I just sat here cuffed to this fancy chair until Tabitha swept in and twisted me inside out?

No. It couldn't end like that. Even trapped here in Shackleton's office, I couldn't believe the world was just going to fall apart without me even fighting it.

Jordan was still out there. She was probably halfway to the release station by now.

Jordan, Calvin, and a magic baby.

What could possibly go wrong?

I tensed, my wrists jarring painfully against the handcuffs as the door suddenly burst open.

Shackleton came striding into the office, as dressed-down as I'd ever seen him. He was still wearing his usual shirt and suit pants, but his jacket and tie were gone, his top button undone, his sleeves rolled up to the elbow. Red splotches spattered his white shirt and stained his hands and forearms.

I felt a cold surge of adrenaline. Whose blood was that?

'Please,' Shackleton grinned, staring down at my raw wrists, 'don't get up.'

He was back. Whatever little blip of fear or uncertainty I'd heard on the phone before had disappeared without a trace, covered over again by his usual smiling calm. And something else: a kind of gleeful anticipation on his face, like whatever was coming next, he was planning on enjoying it.

Shackleton padded across to a little side table and poured himself a glass of water from a silver jug. He crossed back to his desk, taking the seat behind it as though this was just another business meeting. He held the glass to his thin lips, took a tiny sip of water, and then sighed loudly, pulling a coaster from somewhere under the desk and setting the glass on it.

'I tell you,' he said, arms crossed in front of him, 'I've had quite a time this morning. These things never seem to work out quite as cleanly as one imagines at the outset, do they, Mr Hunter?'

He paused, giving me room to respond, then pushed on, just as happy to carry the conversation by himself. 'The disappearance of the fallout on today of all days!' he said, like it was all one giddy adventure. 'It gave us quite a scare. Imagine, making it this far in, only to have it all come to nothing in the final few hours.'

My eyes dropped to Shackleton's water glass, smudged red where his fingers had pressed against it. His hand slipped down, picking it up again.

'Thankfully,' he went on after another sip, 'it appears our fears were unjustified. Dr Galton and I took a small sample group to the medical centre this morning. The fallout may have dissipated but, evidently, the protection it afforded our candidates has not.' He lifted the glass up to eye level, frowning at the smudge marks. 'The same, I am sorry to say, does not apply to their healing abilities.'

I clenched my fists together, shaking but trying not to show it. *A small sample group.* Like our guys in the bunker? Was that Mum's blood splashed across his –?

No. The bunker had still been locked down when I'd called.

But that was hours ago now. Anything could have happened since then.

Shackleton smiled again, guessing what I was thinking but not giving anything away. His gaze slipped up over my shoulder, and the ticking of the clock seemed to swell to fill the room.

How long left until the end?

Shackleton's eyes returned to mine, piercing through any attempt to cover up the terror flashing through me. I stared back, forcing myself not to look away. Sweat slithered across my skin, sticking my clothes to my back.

Shackleton chuckled and took another mouthful of his drink. 'I'm almost disappointed you won't be around to see it,' he mused, running his finger in a slow circle around the rim of the glass. 'You're an intelligent young man, Luke. I know in time even you would have seen the beauty of what we are about to accomplish here.'

'Right,' I said, finally taking the bait, 'because slaughtering humanity is exactly my idea of –'

'*Salvaging* humanity,' Shackleton corrected, like I'd said the wrong word by accident. 'Grasping hold of what little is left before the whole enterprise disintegrates completely. Or would you have us continue down the path of blind self-destruction until we tear ourselves to pieces entirely?'

'You *want* to tear everyone to pieces!' I said, handcuffs grinding into my wrists again. 'That's your exact plan!'

Shackleton shook his head patiently. 'Not everyone. And not because I take any joy in it. I am no monster, Luke. However, one need take only the most cursory survey of the history of the human race to discern the trajectory on which we are currently travelling.'

He looked like a kid at Christmas.

'The present humanity is a cancer. A hulking, self-destructive scourge, unguided and ungoverned, stubbornly incapable of rising above its primordial origins. Its only hope,' he paused, leaning forward, 'is leadership. The singular vision of a guiding force with the courage to see the crisis for what it is and the prescience to set a course toward true human flourishing.'

'By *murdering* us all?' I said. 'How is that –?'

Shackleton chuckled darkly. 'As if you were not already accomplishing as much on your own! The entire planet teeters on the precipice of complete environmental collapse and still you forge merrily onward, gorging yourselves into oblivion as if the next generation were an enemy to be slaughtered. You make a sport of inequity and waste, turning a third of your own food production into landfill, while every two seconds another child dies of starvation.'

The clock ticked loudly overhead.

'Meanwhile, not content with the two hundred and thirty-one million butchered in the insipid wars of the past century, you continue the proliferation of weapons powerful enough to render this entire planet uninhabitable and obliterate whatever slender hope of recovery you might delude yourselves into believing you have left. How long before it all boils over, Luke? How long before the last threads snap and the whole human enterprise vanishes into the darkness of a blind, indifferent universe?'

I opened my mouth and closed it again.

'You could not be setting yourselves a more exacting

course towards self-annihilation if you were doing it on purpose,' said Shackleton. 'Humanity does not need my help to die, Mr Hunter. That much is well in hand already. Humanity needs my help to *live*.'

'Yeah, well, no offence,' I said, finding my voice, 'but I vote *not you* for that job.'

'Oh?' said Shackleton, eyes glinting again. 'Go on, then. Tell me I'm wrong. Plead humanity's case. After countless centuries of chaos and depravity, tell me with a straight face that *yours* is the generation that will spontaneously pull itself up by its bootstraps.'

I sat back in my chair, caught off-guard by the question and, worse, by a fresh jolt of the same nagging feeling that had gripped me in the depths of Mum and Dad's divorce: that if humanity was the best the universe had to offer, then maybe we really *were* all screwed.

'Mm,' Shackleton nodded, before I had time to answer. 'So you admit –'

'No! I don't – That's not the point!' I exploded, reeling but still convinced I was right. 'Who are *you* to decide any of this? What gives you the right to –?

'The right?' said Shackleton, excruciatingly calm, the smile back on his lips. 'Right is what we make it, Luke.'

'That's crap!' I said. You don't just get to *decide* –'

'And in any case,' he pressed, holding up a hand, 'the matter is now closed. Your second attempt at a coup has proven even more ill-conceived than the first, and your reckless destruction of my shield grid has gained you nothing. Even if Officer Calvin had not been eliminated at the armoury this morning, and even if you were somehow able to penetrate the release station without my being present – which, let me be clear, you cannot – the dissipation of the fallout certainly does not bode well for an infant's chances of besting the most sophisticated weapon ever devised.'

Shackleton studied me intently, waiting for a reaction. But instead of caving under the weight of such a comprehensive list of all the ways we were done for, my brain latched onto the one chink in Shackleton's armour. Calvin hadn't been *eliminated*. Not at the armoury, anyway. Where was Shackleton getting this from?

'You didn't know?' said Shackleton, misreading the confusion on my face. 'Yes, I'm terribly sorry. And just when you might have found yourselves an ally with some hope of assisting you,' he shrugged, face twisting in false sympathy. 'Your dear friend Jordan and her newborn brother – Tobias, is it? – were apparently not with Officer Calvin at the time, or else my men at the armoury might have made a clean job of it.

'Not to worry,' he said with a slight grunt as he pushed back to his feet. 'I have dispatched a team to address the situation. The two of them will, I expect, not live out the hour. All that to say,' he continued, sliding his chair under the desk, shrugging off murdering a baby like it was no worse than butchering a pig, 'that despite today's unforeseen obstacles, despite any lingering philosophical objections, and despite your *incessant* efforts to the contrary, Phoenix will survive.'

I wanted to shout back at him, to kick and curse and rattle my chains, but what would be the point of any of it? He had me. And he knew it. And any reaction I gave would only be another victory for him.

'So what am I doing here?' I asked, as Shackleton paced across the room again, disappearing somewhere out behind me. 'If you've already won – If I'm just going to get vaporised in a few hours anyway –'

'I read a fascinating study earlier this week,' said Shackleton casually, as though he hadn't even noticed I was speaking. 'A pair of Dutch researchers, investigating the human experience of pain.'

I shifted, trying to see what he was doing, but the stupid high-backed chair blocked him from view.

'The study sought to apply a numerical value to the intensity and severity of various causes of pain,' said Shackleton, in a voice like an English teacher trying to get me excited about a new class novel. 'The idea being that one could then rank those experiences against one another.'

I heard a *clack* of wood on wood, and another little grunt as Shackleton bent to lift something.

'The finer details of their research methodology were a little over my head,' said Shackleton, moving back into view. 'I must ask Victoria to step me through it all sometime. But some of the findings were truly eye-opening.'

He stopped on my side of the desk, snapping open the thing in his hands. An easel, holding up a blank white canvas.

'There was one particular pain experience that stood out to me,' said Shackleton, pulling open another drawer. 'An experience the study ranked far higher than I ever would have thought, higher even than *childbirth*. You'll never guess what it was.'

He leant forward, both hands on his desk, like he was actually expecting me to guess.

I stared back at him, at the blood splattered across his shirt. It had still been wet when he came in here, but in the sweltering heat of the office, it was quickly drying out, turning the same dull rust colour as –

Cold realisation washed over me as Shackleton reached into the open drawer and pulled out a glinting, silver-handled knife.

'Accidentally severing a finger,' he said, advancing on me, 'ranked as one of the top *five* pain experiences measured by the study.' He grinned incredulously. 'Can you believe that? I understand it has something to do with the usually high concentration of nerve endings in that part of the body.'

I shuddered audibly, finally unable to contain the fear.

Shackleton's smile broadened. He stopped at the easel, tracing his free hand along the top of the canvas. 'This is a momentous day, Mr Hunter. You may not survive to see the end of it, but have no fear.' He rolled the knife handle slowly between his fingers. 'I will not let you disappear without leaving your mark.'

Chapter 31

JORDAN

THURSDAY, AUGUST 13, 1.24 P.M.
3 HOURS, 36 MINUTES

'Whose blood is that?' I asked, holding Tobias with both hands while he wriggled around like there were bugs on him.

'Shackleton's,' said Calvin, giving the vial a little shake and then pulling the cap off. 'He and Galton are the only ones who still have access.'

I lifted Tobias up against my chest, finally giving up on keeping him in the sling, and crouched beside Calvin. Tobias kept squirming, like he was trying to flip himself over and see what Calvin was doing. A squeak of frustration escaped his throat and, feeling somewhere between stupid and terrified, I spun him to face the ground.

Calvin's hands hovered over the little panel in the dirt. 'If this doesn't work ...'

'*Make* it work.'

He pressed the button. Something blurred out of the little hole next to it and then back in again. A needle. Calvin upended the vial, sending Shackleton's blood dribbling down into the hole.

'Trust him to make this as disgusting as possible,' I muttered, as the excess liquid bubbled up over the side.

'Careful,' said Calvin holding out his arm. 'Don't –'

The ground jolted under my feet and I lurched into him. He got up, dragging me back from the square-metre section of the bunker that had started sinking into the ground. A trapdoor, like the ones under the town. Light shone up from inside.

'Thanks,' I said, shaking Calvin off and readjusting my hold on Tobias, who seemed to have calmed down a bit now that he could see what was going on.

The trapdoor rolled aside, revealing a set of shimmering silver steps. Calvin sighed heavily as he stepped inside, and I felt my breath catch in my throat. I looked back at Phoenix, the top of the wall peeking up over the rise behind us. 'There'll be more, right? More than just the guards from that skid. If Shackleton knows we're out here, he'll throw everything he's got at us, won't he?'

Calvin paused on the stairs. 'If Officer Reynolds has done his job, Shackleton thinks I'm dead already. He will be far less concerned than he should be.'

'But Reynolds didn't even –' I broke off, figuring it out. 'You sent him back to tell Shackleton he'd killed you. But you had him wait until after we left.'

Calvin nodded. 'You doubted me enough as it was without seeing me order him back into town.'

'What about the explosion at the wall? Surely they must have seen that from town.'

'With any luck, Shackleton has assumed you were acting alone,' said Calvin, continuing inside. 'It certainly seems that way, judging by the half-hearted approach he's taken to coming after us.'

He slipped out of sight and I rushed down after him, into a narrow passageway, gleaming silver on all sides, as spotless and pristine as all the buildings back in town. As all the buildings back in town *used* to be, anyway.

Tobias squeezed his eyes shut against the light, and I raised a hand to shield his face.

As soon as the door hissed closed above overhead, the fear that had been pressing in since last night suddenly lunged at me, biting down like an animal. I was shocked by the force of it.

The stairs continued down and down, a lazier spiral than the one running down to the Vattel Complex, like we were circling around and around some giant structure in the middle.

'So,' I said, pulling myself together enough to get the words out, 'how about you tell me what happens when we get to the bottom of this thing?'

Calvin kept walking.

I sped up, closing the gap between us. 'Calvin –'

'Almost there,' he said.

I backed off, startled by the emotion in his voice.

Just keep going, I told myself over and over again as we plunged into the ground. *Whatever this is, Calvin*

*already told you Tobias isn't going to die. He can't. That's
not how this is meant to end.*

But then what was Calvin so freaked out about?

Finally, the stairs ran out and we emerged into a big
round room, almost completely empty. Every surface
was the same Shackleton Co-operative silver, glinting
under bright white lights.

In the centre was an enormous pillar, maybe three
metres across. The pillar ran straight up for about ten
metres, then spread out like a giant kitchen funnel until
it was as wide as the room itself.

Mounted to the side of the pillar at head height
was a monitor like the one I'd seen last night, up on
the top floor of the Shackleton Building. Two digital
countdown clocks:

Final Lockdown Procedures
00:00:00:00
Tabitha Release
00:03:29:57

'Come here,' said Calvin, pulling a biohazard suit
from a cupboard built into the wall. 'Put this on.'

I took the suit from him, willing my hand to keep
steady. 'What's this for?'

'Just in case,' said Calvin, taking down a second suit
for himself.

'In case *what?*' I said. 'I thought you knew what was
down here!'

Calvin gestured at Tobias. 'Make sure he's in too.'

I squeezed my eyes shut, letting it go, lowering Tobias back into the sling. He kept still this time, like he somehow knew this was important. I pulled the biohazard suit on over the two of us, one arm in the sleeve and the other one guarding Tobias.

Calvin finished zipping up his suit and pulled what looked like a toolkit out of the cupboard. He pushed the door shut and the cupboard disappeared into the wall again.

I jumped as his voice crackled through a speaker in my ear. 'This way.'

Go, I thought, turning after him. *See it through. What else is there?*

I followed Calvin clumsily out across the huge open floor, still getting used to moving in the suit, which felt somehow too big and too small at the same time.

It was freezing in here. Or maybe that was just my nerves kicking into overdrive. Tobias started wriggling against me, his agitation rising again after the momentary lapse.

We reached the pillar. Calvin circled around to the far side and crouched down. He opened his toolkit, pulled out a screwdriver, and started undoing one of the silver panels.

I stood back, expecting an alarm to start blaring or something. Instead, as soon as the panel came loose, there was a deep, echoing hiss, and the air around Calvin began to distort, like heat rising off a hot road.

Calvin froze. It was some kind of gas, almost invisible. I held my breath as it swam up around my head.

Tobias tensed against me, a tiny groan escaping his throat. I looked down, but all I could see was the little bulge of his body inside our suit.

The hissing sound cut out. Slowly, the gas began to dissipate.

Calvin breathed again, the sound rasping in my ear.

I stared down at him. 'Was that ...?'

'No. Not Tabitha. A last line of defence. At least, we should hope it is the last.' Calvin leant in with the screwdriver again, returning to work. 'Tabitha is still inside, housed within a containment capsule at the core. All automated access was locked down the moment the hundred-day countdown was initiated. I'll need to get inside and remove the capsule manually.' Calvin said all this without looking at me, like he was trying to distance himself from whatever was coming next.

'And then what?' I asked.

The last screw clattered to the ground and Calvin pulled the panel away. The opening was as wide as a doorway and half as high – big enough for Calvin to squeeze through in his suit.

I don't know what I'd expected to see inside. A computer console, maybe, or a mess of circuitry. Not this.

The pillar was completely hollow. Empty, except for a set of metal rungs on the far wall, running up towards the roof and down into the darkness below.

'Wait here,' said Calvin, moving to crawl inside.

I grabbed the back of his suit. 'No. No further. Not until you tell me what happens next.'

Finally, he turned to look at me. The face staring out from behind the glass of his helmet was more real than I'd ever seen it before.

'Wait here,' he said again, 'and I'll tell you.'

I released him, clenching my teeth to stop the chattering. He crawled inside and started down the ladder, taking himself even deeper into the ground.

I slipped my other arm into the chest of the suit, cradling Tobias against me. 'Start talking.'

Calvin took a couple of heavy breaths, already out of sight but coming in loud and clear through the speaker in my helmet. 'The Co-operative has known about Tobias for some time now. Not by that name, of course, but we caught our first glimpse of your brother's true nature at the same time you did.'

'The night at the Shackleton Building,' I said, shivering at the memory. 'When we broke in to contact Luke's dad.'

It was the first of many narrow escapes from being murdered by Calvin. We'd made it out alive, only to find Mum and Dad stumbling to the medical centre in the dead of night, crying out for help, their unexpected pregnancy suddenly a whole lot more unexpected.

Dad's voice rang in my head. *There's something wrong with the baby!*

'Exactly,' said Calvin, snapping me out of it, voice punctuated by the steady *clank, clank, clank* of footsteps as he continued down the ladder. 'Over the days that followed, we began to understand how your brother's condition fit into the bigger picture of all the *other* changes befalling the residents of Phoenix. We identified as many cases as we could and brought them into the medical centre for testing.'

'You kidnapped my family, you mean?'

Calvin was silent for a long moment. When he spoke again, I could hear the tears in his voice. 'Jordan, when this is all over, I promise you, I will sit down and confess to every crime I have ever committed here. I will make whatever amends I can, and accept whatever punishment is handed down to me. But cataloguing the full extent of my guilt will be a lengthier process than even you can imagine, and right now we do not have the time. You have asked for an explanation. May I continue to give it to you?'

I didn't answer.

After a few seconds, the clanking of Calvin's footsteps echoed in my helmet again. Slower now. Quieter. He'd reached the bottom of the pillar.

'You and your friends managed to break into the medical centre and free your captured family members before we could complete our research,' he pushed on. 'But afterwards, we began to realise just how significant Tobias was.'

'Significant how?' I asked, staring out across the huge empty space around me.

He grunted, and I heard a sound like splintering

glass. 'Your brother isn't merely a candidate like the rest of us. His life *began* here. He has been immersed in the fallout throughout the entire course of his development. We believe that the last one hundred days have shaped Tobias in ways that are completely unique.'

Calvin's footsteps returned to their steady climbing rhythm. He was coming back up.

I paced back and forth in front of the pillar, bouncing Tobias inside the biohazard suit. 'So basically, you're saying that any baby who was –'

'No,' said Calvin. 'Obviously, our understanding of these developments is still limited, but your own experience should tell you that the fallout affects each person differently. When I tell you your brother is *uniquely* qualified to assist us, I am using the full meaning of the word.'

Calvin kept climbing, and now I could hear his footsteps outside my suit as well as through the speaker. He made a noise that sounded almost like it could have been laughter. 'In hindsight, the projected due date Dr Montag gave your parents might have given us a clue that Tobias was destined for some greater purpose in all of this. Though of course, Shackleton would dismiss such a thought out of hand even if it did occur to him.'

'Not you, though?' I asked.

Calvin's face reappeared. His eyes locked onto me, still streaked with tears. 'Jordan, I've just been dragged out of my death of an existence and handed an opportunity to save the world. How could I *not* believe there was something greater at work here?'

Calvin crawled back out of the pillar, a glass cylinder about the size of an energy drink can held carefully in one hand. It was capped with metal at both ends, with a bit of silver tubing hanging out the bottom where I guessed it had been disconnected from some machine. Sloshing around inside the cylinder was what could almost have been water but was just slightly too thick.

'All right,' Calvin sniffed, pulling himself upright. 'This is it.'

'What is?' I said stupidly, looking him over again, trying to work out what I'd missed. My eyes kept sliding back to the cylinder in Calvin's hand, but my brain refused to take it in. It was so small, so pathetic, so *unworthy* of all the anguish that had brought us here.

But at the same time, from somewhere deeper than reason, I *felt* it. The weight of this moment. The dread like a bruise. And the tiny shards of hope that maybe – *maybe* – we were actually going to undo it all.

'He'll need to come out of there,' said Calvin, looking at the baby-shaped bulge in the front of my suit. 'Don't worry, that gas should have dissipated by now.'

'*Should* have?' I said, focusing on that to avoid focusing on the thing in his hand, fighting to keep pushing back the tide of suspicion that had been rising against me all day, the relentless dread that there was only ever one way this could end.

Calvin reached back to unzip his suit. He took off

his helmet and sleeves, gently switching the cylinder from hand to hand as he did so, and let the top half of the suit fall to his waist. He waved an arm out, demonstrating that he was still alive.

I was already unzipping my own suit.

Calvin stepped forward, clutching the cylinder in one hand and the bit of silver tubing in the other, and all of my worst fears were confirmed in a heartbeat. But somehow my hands kept moving, trembling as they went, time slowing to an agonising crawl.

By the time I'd peeled back the suit from the top half of my body, Calvin was right in front of me, tube pointed at Tobias like he was going to spray him down with it.

'Here,' he said. 'Put this –'

Something snapped in my head. I couldn't do it. 'No! No – y-you're not –'

'Shackleton believes –'

I stumbled backwards, hitting the pillar, survival instinct obliterating everything else. 'I don't *care* what Shackleton –!'

'*Jordan*!' Calvin bore down on me, matching me step for step, face hard again. He stared at me with such intensity that, for a moment, I was paralysed.

Calvin took a breath, bringing his temper under control. 'Jordan, please understand the stakes here.'

'*You think I don't get –?*'

'Disconnecting Tabitha from the system has gained us nothing,' he said. 'We may slow the rate of dispersal, but there is no stopping Tabitha's release. Not without Tobias. Which, abhorrent as it may be, leaves you with a decision to make: either your brother consumes Tabitha –' Calvin lifted his hands, holding the transparent goop up in front of me, '– or Tabitha consumes everyone else.'

Chapter 32

LUKE

THURSDAY, AUGUST 13, 1.29 P.M.
3 HOURS, 31 MINUTES

'I know what you're thinking,' said Shackleton, gliding towards me, knife in hand. 'Blood. It does seem rather a limited medium, doesn't it?'

I squirmed in my chair, eyes flitting around the room. Searching for an exit. Something I'd missed.

'But the more I explore,' he went on, 'the more I realise just how versatile it is. As you'll see,' Shackleton cast a hand at the painting above his desk, 'the tonal range one can achieve with just a bit of practice is quite remarkable.'

My wrists rubbed painfully against the handcuffs, hands balling into fists. My legs were still free, but I wasn't dragging this chair anywhere in a hurry, and the guards would be on me at the first sign of a struggle.

'And of course, I need hardly mention the richness of the symbolism.' Shackleton circled around behind me, gesturing excitedly with his hands. 'Beauty wrought from pain. Life giving way to life. The human struggle for survival and significance, all enacted right there on the canvas.'

I hunched forward. I was going to throw up. Any second now, I was going to lose control of my stomach and empty it out into my lap.

Maybe he could make a painting out of that too.

Shackleton moved back into view. Circling. Soaking up the moment. Whatever else was going on in his twisted brain, this part was extremely simple.

He had me.

I'd been a stone in his shoe since the day I got here, and now, finally, it was just him and me, and I was going to pay for the frustration I'd caused him.

'You're not a great appreciator of the arts, are you, Mr Hunter?' Shackleton stopped behind me, leaning in to examine my bound hands. The blade of his knife gleamed in my peripheral vision.

'No matter. My belief is that great art transcends such limitations. The true artist cuts through the intellect and into something deeper. Something *visceral*.' Shackleton's spit flecked against my cheek. 'Above all else, I want my work to provoke a *reaction* –'

I jerked my head sideways, smashing it into Shackleton's. He reeled back, grunting, and I sprung up from the chair, still anchored by the handcuffs but manoeuvrable enough to throw a leg out at his stomach. Shackleton dodged, surprisingly agile for an old man who'd just been smashed in the head. My foot swung wide and I lost my balance, crying out as my wrists jerked against the cuffs.

The office door burst open and two black-sleeved arms dropped into view, dragging me roughly back up into the chair. My eyes blurred with tears. I blinked them away and saw a guard with a shaved head standing over me with a pistol. Shackleton stood behind him, smoothing his hair back into place.

'Thank you, Officer Lee.' Shackleton bent down, retrieving his knife from the carpet. 'While you're here, would you mind holding our guest still for me? His restlessness is stifling my creative process.'

Officer Lee glanced at the blank canvas. A glimmer of recognition passed across his face. He moved to the back of my chair, and I felt the cold muzzle of his pistol press against my temple. His right hand came down on my fist, pinning it to the arm of the chair.

'Please,' I whimpered, not daring to turn my head, 'don't let him do this.'

Shackleton crouched at my hand. I flinched as he reached for me, but Lee mashed his palm down harder, holding my hand in place.

'Lee!' I gasped. 'Lee, listen – We can stop him! We can stop *all* of this! Just –'

Lee knocked his pistol against my head. 'Quiet.'

Shackleton pursed his lips, prising my forefinger out from my clenched fist. 'Officer Lee,' he said slowly, without looking up, 'when we've finished here, would you mind putting in a call to maintenance for me? I suspect –' My knuckle cracked loudly as he pressed my finger down against the wood of the chair. '– that I may need to have the carpets redone.'

'No – no, no, no – no, please – *please* –!' I was trembling uncontrollably now, tears rolling down my cheeks.

Shackleton brought the knife gently down against the base of my finger, lining it up. He angled his hand, slowly increasing pressure, and I felt the blade pierce the skin. I gasped, head twisting away, pain spiking up my arm, small and sharp at first, and then –

THUMP. THUMP.

Two sharp impacts as something outside smashed violently against the door. I heard the guard in the corridor thud to the ground, and I realised that *something* had been his face.

I winced as Shackleton reared up, taking a little chunk of my finger with him. He glared furiously at the door, and then disappeared behind me.

Officer Lee let me go, rushing to the door. 'Sir, permission to –' He cocked his head. 'Sir …?'

A burst of compressed air hissed loudly behind me, followed by a mechanical clattering sound. I tried to swivel around to look, but –

THUMP.

My attention jerked to the door again. Officer Lee reeled back, grunting.

THUMP.

A rifle butt came down across his head again and he slumped to the carpet.

A rush of feet stepped over the bodies. I looked up and saw two faces I hadn't run into since before all this blew up last night: Tank and Officer Miller, both in security gear. Reeve and Katie flew in behind them.

Reeve dropped to one knee beside me, firing his pistol at whatever was making that clattering noise.

I turned again, finally catching a glimpse behind me, just in time to see a bookcase slide back into position against the wall. Another compressed air noise, and then silence. Shackleton was gone.

'Trapdoors under the rugs and secret bookcase doors,' said Miller, heading over to examine the back wall. 'Shackleton's a sucker for the classics, isn't he?'

'Where did he go?' asked Tank.

'Could be anywhere,' said Miller. 'Or still back there. It could just be a panic room.'

'Doubt it,' said Reeve, getting up again. 'Not really Shackleton's style to pin himself in a corner like that.'

'He's probably headed for the bunker,' I said. 'Safest place for him to be right now.'

Reeve glanced down at me like he'd only just taken in that I was here.

'Well, wherever he went, we're not following,' said Miller. He pointed at a little silver circle mounted to the wall. 'Thumbprint scanner.'

'Oi,' said Tank, standing over me, clutching a rifle. 'Move your hands.'

I flinched, still coming down from the terror of almost losing a finger. Then I realised what he was asking. I stretched my arms out, twisting them so the chain of my handcuffs stretched across the arm of the chair. With a grunt, Tank brought the butt of his rifle down against the chain, smashing it apart and freeing my hands.

'Thanks,' I said, sliding the cuffs up my wrists to check on the raw skin underneath.

Tank shrugged. He looked so much older in the uniform. A different person from the big, dumb school kid I'd met on my second day here.

'Here,' said Miller, handing me a handkerchief from his pocket to mop up the blood dribbling from the gash in my finger.

'Thanks,' I said again, then turned to Reeve. 'Where have you guys been?'

'Loyalty room,' said Reeve, as Miller moved to guard the door. 'They'd upped the number of guards on duty since last time. We – we lost Wilson on the way in.' His expression darkened. 'Took them about two minutes to disarm the rest of us. We've been twiddling our thumbs with the rest of the prisoners ever since.'

'So how did you get out?' I asked.

'Same way we got up here without getting shot,' said Reeve, indicating Miller and Tank. 'These two.'

'We've been hiding out in the building since last night,' said Miller. 'Keeping a low profile. I couldn't show my face after yesterday, but your mate here's been posing as a new recruit. And so far, with all the chaos going on, no-one's pulled him up on it.'

'Tank walked right into the loyalty room and convinced the guards to hand Katie and me over,' said Reeve. 'Told them Shackleton had ordered him to take us in for questioning.'

Tank beamed.

'Plan was to go back in and get the others,' said Miller, 'but I guess that's out the window now that Shackleton's seen us.'

'Speaking of which,' said Katie, 'shouldn't we be getting out of here?'

The question was barely out of her mouth when the sound of footsteps came racing up the hall. Miller leapt out, rifle raised.

'Whoa – hey!' said a frantic voice outside. 'Hey, don't shoot!'

Miller stood aside and Mr and Mrs Weir came barrelling into the room.

'Luke!' Mrs Weir's mouth fell open at the sight of my cuffed wrists and bleeding hand. She rushed over and put her hands on my shoulders. 'Oh Luke, we thought we heard something going on in here, but we had no idea it was –'

'It's fine,' I said. 'I'm fine.'

Mr Weir looked around, scanning the faces in the room, then rushed to Shackleton's desk. He pushed down on the top of it with both hands, and a section of the wood levered up like a laptop screen. I ran around the desk, crowding in with everybody else to see what he was doing.

Mr Weir's fingers were flying across the keyboard at the base of a monitor. 'Controls for the automated defences,' he explained, not looking up. 'I've been tinkering on old mate Ben More's computer for the last few hours. Couldn't access any of this from there, but I could see the pathway I needed to ...' He trailed off, focusing.

I stared at the screen, barely breathing, not a clue what I was looking at, but still completely transfixed.

And even though, from what Dad had said, the military weren't in any massive hurry to get here, I still couldn't totally push aside the image of all of them swarming in and tipping the balance back in our favour.

Don't, I ordered myself. *Three hours left. You're not saving humanity with wishful thinking.*

'Guys,' said Miller, over at the door, 'I know this is important, but I really think we need to –'

'Almost there ...' said Mr Weir.

'Can't save the world if we're dead,' said Miller.

'Yeah,' Mr Weir bristled. 'Which part of "almost there" didn't you –?'

A little chime sounded from the speaker above the screen. Mr Weir stepped back from the computer, fists flying into the air in a startlingly Peter-like expression of triumph.

'Only problem is he can still come in here and

reactivate it. If you give me a few minutes, I might be able to lock out the interface and –'

Miller pushed forward.

BLAM!

The computer screen exploded in a shower of shattered plastic.

'Or that,' said Mr Weir, as Miller lowered his pistol again. 'That'll work.'

'Great,' said Reeve. 'Time to go.'

'We need to get down to the bunker,' I said. 'Find Shackleton and –'

'Yeah,' said Miller. 'There's just that small matter of us being completely locked out.'

Mr Weir raised his hand. 'Actually …'

Every head turned to look at him.

'Like I said, I've been doing some digging on More's computer. And look, obviously there are no guarantees until we get in there and try, *but*,' Mr Weir's face twisted into a kind of half-smile, the same look he'd had when he got the transceiver working, 'I think I might have just bypassed Shackleton's lockdown.'

A ripple of noise ran through the group. My heart felt like it couldn't figure out whether to float into my chest or plummet into my stomach.

I looked around the circle. This was it. A handful of people, half of us barely able to hold a weapon the right way up, and no plan left but a blind attack on Shackleton's last stronghold. But we had only a few hours, and I wasn't about to spend them sitting around waiting to die.

I just hoped Jordan was having better luck than we were.

Mr Weir looked to me, like for some reason he thought the decision was mine to make. He nodded at the resolve on my face. 'What do you say we get down there and end this thing?'

Chapter 33

JORDAN

I reached behind me, heart pounding in my head, drawing Calvin's pistol and training it on his chest.

He took a half-step back.

'That's not going to fix this, Jordan. I drop this canister and it's over.' He held the thing out to me, liquid oozing around inside like it had a life of its own. 'Seven billion dead. You don't want to have that –'

'Don't you dare!' I shouted, moving shakily towards him. 'You sick bastard! Don't you *dare* try to put this on me!'

'Jordan –'

'He's a *baby!*'

'A baby who just *happened* to be brought into the world six months ahead of schedule by the very same force that turned me around and brought me here to help you? Can you honestly –?'

'I'm not going to kill him!' I screamed, and felt Tobias start writhing against me again. 'I don't care if –'

'You're *not* going to kill him,' said Calvin. 'The entire basis of Shackleton's concern is your brother's ability to *survive* Tabitha.'

'And what it he's *wrong?* What if –?'

But my rant was cut short as Tobias let loose an ear-splitting scream. He squirmed like a fish out of water, face red, mouth stretched like he was being tortured. I hesitated, glancing up at Calvin again, then stuck the pistol in my jeans and pulled Tobias from the sling.

Tobias kept screaming, and it was like he was draining the fight out of me. I held him to my shoulder, bouncing him up and down, making the closest I could come to a soothing noise, somehow knowing none of it was going to work.

'Can't you – can't you just *destroy* it?' I said desperately. 'Bury it underground or something?'

'Don't be an idiot,' he barked, in a voice that sounded terrifyingly like the old Calvin. 'Do you truly believe I need Tobias's assistance to *bury* this weapon?'

Tobias threw himself against my hands, gasping for breath, and screamed again.

Calvin hunched over. 'Tabitha will not be contained,' he said. 'It is no mere *weapon*. It is alive – or near enough. We *brought* it to life a hundred days ago when we activated the countdown. There is no turning back from that.'

'But this whole place –'

'This facility was set up to allow Tabitha to disperse with maximum efficiency. To minimise the window of opportunity for a retaliatory strike from the outside. But Tabitha doesn't *need* this place. When the countdown expires, Tabitha will either be released from the containment capsule or it will *burst* out of it. It will vaporise instantly, self-replicating with exponentially increasing speed until it completes the task for which it was designed. Humanity will be extinguished in a matter of days.'

I could barely hear him over Tobias's shrieking in my ears, and even the bits that did get through just turned to dust inside my head. It was too much to even begin to process. An endless sea, surging and swirling in my mind's eye, millions upon millions of nameless, faceless people destined to be tortured to death unless I stood here and fed poison to my terrified, day-old brother.

'Come on, Tobias,' I said, crying along with him now. 'Come on, shh-shh-shh-shh. You're okay. You're okay.'

But lying to a baby was about as comforting as lying to myself.

Visions of our family swam up out of the blur, Mum and Dad and Georgia, all trapped in the Shackleton Building, and Luke ...

Luke, on the run if he was lucky. Dead as soon as Tabitha got out.

'Jordan ...' said Calvin, edging forward again.

Tobias took a shuddering breath, face bright red from the effort, and cried out again. I held onto him, my arms trembling.

I imagined Shackleton in his office, prowling

around above it all, rubbing his hands together at his impending genocide, and the rage that had been simmering inside me boiled over again. My stomach churned with an overpowering disgust at that sick, self-righteous old man and his twisted self-made morals and his filthy lie of a town. With all the strength I had left, I hated this place and I hated *him*.

But more than anything else, I hated that it was all completely out of my control. A hundred days of fighting and it came down to this. A leap into the darkness.

No guarantees. No promises that this was going to turn out okay.

Just faith.

Faith that I hadn't been through all this for nothing, that those glimpses of a bigger picture weren't all just in my head, that somehow that picture was big enough to accommodate even *this*.

Calvin stared down at me, his face white. He looked tempted to just snatch Tobias out of my hands and do the thing himself. 'Jordan –'

'Give it to me!' I snapped, sitting down with my back against the pillar, my tears almost drowning the words out. I cradled Tobias in my lap, propped up against my knees. He twisted on his back, still wailing uncontrollably, his tiny fists balled up.

Calvin crouched next to me, holding out the little canister again. I held Tobias's head as steady as I could with one hand, and reached out with the other, taking hold of the tube dangling from the Tabitha canister. I could barely keep my fingers on it.

I held tight to the tube, trying to guide it down towards Tobias's mouth, but I couldn't do it. My mind gave the instruction, but my body refused to co-operate. I just sat there, gazing down at him, sobbing and shaking and sucking in ragged half-breaths.

Calvin's hand came down around mine, cold and strong. I stiffened, but didn't pull away. He held my hand steady, slowly guiding the canister towards Tobias's face.

'It's okay,' Calvin whispered, as close as I'd ever heard him to gentle. 'It's okay. Just a few minutes –'

Tobias's eyes snapped open. He gazed up at the tube. And immediately, he stopped screaming. He let out a squeaky gasp, lungs fighting for air, eyes locked onto Tabitha with the kind of focus a newborn baby should definitely not have been capable of.

I froze up again. Calvin's hand tensed on mine.

He kept moving, nudging my hand gently forward.

At the last second, I freaked out again. 'No, wait! Wait – I don't –'

Too late.

The end of the tube slipped into Tobias's mouth. Instantly, his lips clamped down around it and he started suckling furiously.

A cold shudder wracked my body. I cringed with disgust, expecting Tobias to spit the stuff back out, but he kept drinking like it was milk.

I pictured Mum and Dad standing over me,

watching on in horror as I poisoned their only son. Georgia crying, screaming, begging me to stop. Luke, white-faced, shaking his head, all his love for me curling up and dying.

'I'm sorry ...' I murmured, reality and unreality blurring into each other. 'I'm sorry ... I'm sorry ...'

Tobias kept drinking, little gurgling and swallowing sounds escaping his throat as he sucked the canister dry.

Calvin tightened his grip, holding me steady, but he might as well not have been there for all the notice I took. I sniffed, nose running, eyes blurring everything together. 'I'm s-sorry ... I'm sorry ...'

And still Tobias kept going, sucking ravenously, dragging the last tiny droplets down the sides of the capsule until finally – *finally* – all of it was gone.

Tobias squirmed against my knees again. He yawned deeply and the tube dropped out of his mouth.

I stopped moaning. Stopped breathing. Silence flooded the release station. Calvin slowly released his hold on me, pulling the canister out of my hand and laying it on the ground.

Tobias opened his eyes. He gazed up at me, face breaking into a smile, and I felt the air flood back into my lungs.

He was okay.

He was *alive*, and that meant –

I glanced at Calvin for confirmation, not daring to believe that it could really have worked, that all of this could really be over. He hovered over me, half-dazed, a smile pulling just slightly at the corners of his open mouth, and relief washed over me like nothing I'd ever felt in my life.

It was over.

We had done it.

I looked at Tobias again and burst out laughing, overwhelmed with a dizzying rush of elation. I got to my feet, hugging my brother to me, tears still pouring down my face.

And then Tobias began to shake.

At first, I thought it was just my own jittering. But then Tobias took a deep, heaving breath and started screaming like he was on fire.

'No ...' I breathed, holding him out in front of me, staggering as the weight came slamming back down onto my shoulders again. 'No, no, no, no ...'

Tobias convulsed in my hands, his eyes wide open and rolling to the back of his head. He screamed again, weaker this time, like his throat was closing over.

'No, no, no ...' My voice dissolved into wordless groaning, and I swayed, almost dropping him. Calvin's hands came down around me, cradling me and the baby, keeping us upright.

Tobias kept trembling and writhing like there was something alive inside him, but I could already feel him growing weaker, see his face turning from red to blue. He let a pitiful cry and tried to fill his lungs again. He couldn't do it. His eyes squeezed shut with the effort, lids closing over vacant white globes.

The visions of my family returned, wailing and screaming, reaching out to tear the baby away from me, but it was too late. Already far too late. A few more desperate, shallow gulps and his breathing gave out altogether, the shaking slowed to a stop and he fell silent, collapsing heavily into me.

I let out a cry of my own, harsh and guttural and spewing up from the depths of me. I searched him frantically for a pulse, a heartbeat, *anything*. But there was nothing there. Nothing but clammy, lifeless flesh.

Just a tiny body.

Adrenaline exploded inside me and I tore out of Calvin's grip, stumbling back from him. 'WHAT HAPPENED?'

Calvin didn't even lift his head to look at me. His eyes hovered over the lifeless form of my brother hanging limp in my arms, and a disbelieving gasp escaped his lips. 'It didn't work.'

Chapter 34

JORDAN

'IT DIDN'T WORK?' I stormed forward, Tobias's body sinking into my chest. So still. So *heavy*.

Calvin backed away from me. 'Jordan, I – We knew it was a possibility. With the disappearance of the fallout, we knew there was a chance this might –'

'NO! You said it would work! You said we were *meant* –' I ducked Calvin as he reached out in a deluded attempt to calm me down. 'Get away from me!'

His eyes were red, face stretched with pain. 'Jordan –'

'Shut up!' I snapped, fumbling behind me for the pistol. 'Shut up. Don't even –'

'We need to get back into town,' said Calvin cautiously, realising I might actually be unbalanced enough to pull the trigger this time. 'If the disappearance of the fallout has compromised our resistance to Tabitha, our only remaining hope of survival is to return to Phoenix and find Shackleton. He may know some other way to withstand –'

'You think you deserve to *survive* this?' I spat, my weapon trembling in my hand. 'The whole human race is about to be wiped out, and you think *you* –?'

'I am not concerned about me!' said Calvin. 'I am trying to save *your* life! You have a family back there who –'

'I JUST KILLED MY BROTHER!'

The words rang in my ears, and a suffocating dread swept over me, blotting out all the light in the room. The pistol slipped out of my grip, clattering noisily to the floor, and I clapped a hand to my mouth, overcome by the crushing horror of what I'd just done, like it had taken saying the words out loud for it to become real.

I stared down at Tobias's unmoving body, cradled in my other arm like he was still a person and not just an empty shell, and I was torn between wanting to hug him to me and wanting to throw his body to the ground. I don't remember consciously making the decision, but the next thing I knew, I'd lowered him back into the sling on my shoulder.

Calvin reached out to me again. 'You were doing what you thought –'

'It doesn't matter! It doesn't matter what I thought! He's *dead!*'

My brain fired with images of myself trudging up the steps to the Shackleton Building, delivering my baby brother's dead body back into the hands of my parents. I saw the looks on their faces, looks that refused to go away no matter how much I tried to explain myself. Because there *was* no explanation. No way in the world to justify what I'd done.

It didn't matter what happened after this. It was already over.

'You should –' Calvin began, then closed his eyes for a moment. 'We should leave Tobias here. When Tabitha – When the countdown expires, we want to be as far away from him as possible.'

'Who *cares?*' I said. 'Who *cares* what happens to us? In three hours, the whole world is dead! What difference could it possibly –?'

I cut myself short, seized by a sudden suspicion, and ducked to the ground, scrambling to retrieve the pistol.

I sprung up again, thrusting the weapon back on Calvin's chest. 'You *knew!*'

Calvin's hands flew out in front of him. 'No –'

'You *wanted* this to happen!' I spat, my guilt shifting into a hot fury that coursed through every part of me. 'You didn't bring Tobias out here for us! You brought him out here for you! For Shackleton! You needed Tobias to – to what? *Incubate* Tabitha? To activate it?'

'*No!*' said Calvin. 'Jordan, that isn't – How could Shackleton have built his whole plan around a child he didn't even know the fallout was capable of creating?'

'Someone could have told him! Someone from the Complex, from the future – Someone –' My head spun, trying to fit it together.

I was so desperate for this to be his fault, so desperate

for it to be something I'd been deceived or coerced or forced into, but I knew deep down that wasn't true.

I'd done this. I'd brought Tobias out here. I'd made the call.

And now he was gone. And Tabitha was still coming.

Calvin edged towards me, hands outstretched for my gun. Even though I was grieved out of my mind, I could see how distraught he looked. 'Jordan,' he croaked, pressing his hand around the pistol, 'I do not deny responsibility for what has happened here, but – but please believe that my only intention was to help you. I brought you out here because I truly believed your brother had the power to put things right. It was –' His eyes drifted to the sling, a tear spilling down his cheek. 'It was supposed to work.'

I released the gun. Calvin pulled it from my hands and stowed it away behind him. He laid his hands on my shoulders. 'I am truly, truly sorry.'

I couldn't breathe. I felt the evaporating warmth of my brother's corpse against my chest and the devastating weight of all that had happened, of all that *would* happen when the clock ran down to zero, and my resistance crumbled to pieces. I collapsed into him, sobbing.

Calvin's hands slipped around my back as my legs gave way again, and for a long moment it didn't matter who he was or what he'd done, only that he was here and real and holding me together as I cried and cried and cried.

Calvin lowered me to the ground, then stepped out of his biohazard suit. I lay on my side, still crying myself blind, my breath coming in wet, choking moans.

He crouched over me again. I hunched, crossing my arms over my chest as his hands hovered past Tobias. 'What are you –?'

Calvin slid his arms under me and hoisted me into the air, cradling me like a baby. He threw one last glance at the countdown screen behind us and then began hulking slowly towards the exit.

'There may be no hope left of saving the world,' he grunted. 'But that doesn't mean I can't save you.'

LUKE

Thursday, August 13, 1.49 p.m.
3 hours, 11 minutes

We slipped out of Shackleton's office, over the unconscious bodies of the fallen guards, and squeezed into the lift across the hall. Seven of us, all armed with either a pistol or a rifle or both.

'Okay,' said Mr Weir, hand drifting to the panel on the wall. 'Moment of truth.'

He hit the button. With a jolt and a clunk, the lift began sliding downwards. Nervous murmurs filled the tiny compartment. No turning back now.

'Duck for cover as soon as you can find it,' Reeve

said. 'Whoever's down there, we don't want to make it easy for them.'

He pushed forward, pistol raised at the doors. Miller and Tank took up positions on either side of him.

The lift crept down, torturously slow, like someone was making sure I had time for the last hundred days to flash before me while we travelled to the bottom.

And you're still here, I told myself. *All that misery and you're still here. Surely that has to count for something.*

I held tight to the spare pistol Tank had handed me, finger still throbbing and oozing blood where Shackleton had gouged it open. Would I do it? Would I shoot someone if it meant saving Mum or Georgia or one of the others?

The lift rolled slowly to a stop, and the sound of raised voices on the other side of the doors snapped me back into focus. There was a ripple of movement as everyone tensed and raised their weapons.

Finally, the doors slid open.

'– don't care *what* she did!' said a voice I couldn't place. 'If you touch her again –'

'What?' snarled a second voice. 'You'll shoot me?' That was van Pelt, the guy from the roof. 'What then, Louisa? What do you think happens when Shackleton finds out he's lost *another* member of his ruling council?'

I peered into the enormous bunker, its walls embedded with a circle of heavy doors leading off into the Co-operative's tunnel network. Shelves stacked with food and other supplies stretched out from the wall to our left, partially blocking the view, but I could still see where the argument was coming from.

In the centre were a couple of black leather couches with a coffee table between them. Cathryn was sitting at the foot of one of the couches, weeping into her hands, while van Pelt and a grey-haired woman stood over her, looking ready to tear each other apart.

'Idiot,' the woman snorted. 'Is *that* what he promised you? A place on some fictitious *council?* And I thought Aaron was gullible.'

It was Cathryn's mum, Louisa Hawking. Miraculously, in the heat of the argument, neither of them had heard the lift door open.

Reeve and Miller crept out towards them, Tank right behind. The rest of us spread out, taking up positions behind the storage shelves.

Cathryn let out a loud sob at her mum's feet.

'Quiet!' Hawking barked, then set her sights back on van Pelt. 'I think Shackleton might place a *slightly* higher value on a healthy sixteen-year-old candidate than a worn-out businessman, don't you, Arthur?'

Van Pelt shrank back from Hawking, his hand moving to the pistol on his hip. 'My contribution to this cause –'

'Was strictly financial,' she finished coldly, 'and has already been paid in full.'

I crouched behind one of the shelves, looking between the stacks of cans and beyond to the row of unmade beds on the other side, wondering if we should just wait here until they finished each other off.

But then, with a nauseous jolt, I saw them. Mum and the others. All still there, and still alive. Bunched up on one of the beds, with three guards standing around them in a circle – Officer Cook and two of his mates from the Complex this morning.

Mum was staring anxiously at Cathryn, a purple mark across her face where one of the guards had obviously struck her. Mr Burke, still handcuffed, one arm crudely bandaged, sat beside Mrs Burke. Georgia cowered in his lap, the three of them finally back together again after weeks apart. Soren was perched behind them all on the opposite side of the bed, rocking back and forth, still messed up from his interrogation last night.

Reeve spotted them too and took a hasty step back, out of the guards' line of sight. But their attention was flickering between the prisoners on the bed and the argument across the room.

'Get up,' Hawking snapped at Cathryn. She nodded at a bookshelf on the far wall. 'Find something to read. If I see you anywhere near the other prisoners again –'

'Find something to *read?*' Cathryn shrieked, standing up, finally taking her hands away from her face to reveal the deep gashes Peter had scratched into her cheeks the night before. 'Do you *seriously* think –?'

Her mouth fell open at the sight of Reeve and the others. My insides turned to stone.

Hawking and van Pelt whirled around. The guards at the bed followed suit, and in two seconds, everyone who could lay their hand on a weapon was pointing it across the bunker.

I dropped behind my wall of cans, bracing for the roar. But instead of erupting in gunfire, the whole bunker turned deathly silent.

Nobody moved.

One shot would plunge this place into a bloodbath, and it looked like no-one on Team Shackleton valued the cause more highly than they valued their own life.

Mum still hadn't spotted me. I saw her glance at Mr Burke, trying to catch his eye.

No! I thought. *Stop! You're going to get yourself* –

'You okay, Cat?' grunted Tank, ending the silence. He stood maybe two metres back from them, his rifle fixed squarely on Hawking.

'Please,' Cathryn begged, 'don't shoot her.'

'Don't want to shoot anyone,' said Tank.

'Then how about you all just back away nice and slow,' said van Pelt, sounding a lot less cocky than the last time I'd run into him, 'and we forget you ever came down here?'

'Where's Shackleton?' said Reeve.

'Not here,' said van Pelt. 'Now, unless you want –'

'Give us back our people,' said Reeve, not missing a

beat. 'You hand them over and it's done. We're out of your hair without any more –'

There was a shout across the room, and a blur of movement sprang from the bed.

Not Mum. Soren.

He threw himself at one of the guards, knocking him down to the floor and out of sight.

I heard screams from the bed. The other two guards reeled back as –

BLAM!

– either Soren or the guard fired a pistol blindly into the air.

Mrs Burke dived to the floor, dragging Georgia with her. Mr Burke sprang up, his hands still cuffed behind his back, and charged the nearest guard.

'STOP!' Hawking demanded, bringing her gun around. 'Stop or I'll –!'

Automatic weapons-fire exploded throughout the room and she hit the floor. Cathryn screamed.

Tank threw up his arms, horrified. 'It wasn't me! It wasn't me!'

A roar rose up from right beside me, and Mr and Mrs Weir suddenly burst out of hiding. Van Pelt panicked, diving behind one of the couches.

More gunfire. Georgia wailed in terror, somewhere out of sight. I looked back at the bed. Soren was on his feet, spinning in a circle like anyone could be a target. Mum was gone. I raced along the row of shelves, eyes sweeping through the gaps in the groceries, but she was nowhere –

Whump.

I slammed straight into someone running past in the opposite direction.

'*Luke!*'

'MUM!'

She threw her arms around me, weeping with relief, then went rigid again as another round of rifle-fire cut the air behind us.

Soren let out a gut-wrenching shriek.

'Quick!' said Mum, breaking away. 'We need –'

CLUNK.

The noise cut through everything else in the room. A deep, reverberating sound of metal on metal.

CLUNK.

Mum squeezed down on my hand.

I looked up, searching for the source of the noise.

CLUNK.

It was moving. Circling the room.

It seemed to be coming from inside the walls.

CLUNK.

The firing stopped, everyone else as mesmerised as we were.

CLUNK.

'The doors,' I breathed, turning to the wall as the sound boomed closer.

'It's like before,' said Mum. 'Someone's locking us –'

CLUNK.

The nearest door, almost behind us, shuddered like it had just been struck with a battering ram.

Then a new sound. A clattering, groaning noise.

My eyes swept along the wall and froze on the lift. A steel door, massive and handle-less like the others, had just rolled in front of it.

CLUNK.

The noise echoed and died.

And there, standing beside the door, still dressed in the same blood-spattered shirt, a pistol in one hand and a riot shield in the other, was Noah Shackleton.

'I wouldn't,' he warned, as weapons flew up at him. 'You would all suffocate long before anyone found a way to free you.'

He strode out across the bunker, surveying the scene with absolute calm, like he was completely oblivious to the sounds of anguish in the air all around him.

I was clenching my pistol now, rage and fear burning through me, chewing me up like acid.

'I understand that emotions are running high,' said Shackleton, glancing at Cathryn as she wept over her mother. 'However, I think it best that we forego any further action until after Tabitha's release this evening. We will have a far greater chance of coming to an understanding once that whole contentious business is behind us. Until then, I have taken the liberty of placing this facility under lockdown.'

'It doesn't matter!' I spat, barging out from behind the shelves before I even knew what was happening.

'They don't need us! Calvin's still alive! He and Jordan are out there right now with Tobias!'

I was just ranting. I had no idea if any of it was true anymore.

Shackleton lowered his shield, propping it against one of the couches. 'You are correct,' he smiled, not missing a beat. 'It most certainly *doesn't* matter. Whatever grand designs my former security chief may have concocted, your last slender hope of disrupting my work evaporated with the fallout. As of this morning, Tobias is nothing but an ordinary baby. If an attempt is made to use that child to neutralise Tabitha, he will fail, and he will die. Which leaves us –' Shackleton set his pistol on the coffee table and sank contentedly into the couch, '– with nothing to do but wait.'

Chapter 35

JORDAN

THURSDAY, AUGUST 13, 3.58 P.M.
1 HOUR, 2 MINUTES

I barely even noticed as the skid rolled to a stop. I just sat there in the back of the cage, staring with unfocused eyes out at the sky.

The sun edged down slowly towards the deserted houses. The fighting was over now, everything quiet and still. Like it was all dead already.

The last two hours were a hazy mess, but I'd somehow pulled myself together enough to walk. I had scattered memories of trudging through wasteland, of Calvin pulling me down behind some rocks as the guards from that other skid came searching for us.

How did we get back inside Phoenix? I racked my brains and dredged up a vision of Calvin dragging his way up the wall on the rope we'd used to get out. He must have pulled me up with him, because there was no way I was capable of scaling any walls.

A clank of metal stirred me out of my daze. Calvin

was standing over me, pulling open the back of the cage. He rested a hand on my shoulder.

I staggered out of the skid, Tobias's body still heavy against my chest. It was cold now.

Amy climbed out after me. Silent. I don't know how I'd been expecting her to react, but after a cry of shock at the sight of Tobias, she'd gone completely quiet for the rest of the journey back. Either that or I'd just been too out of it to hear her.

We were behind the medical centre. You couldn't see the full extent of the destruction in town from here, but there were still plenty of smashed windows and scorched walls, and the stench of smoke hung heavily in the air.

The rain had disappeared, and now sun streamed down cheerfully between the clouds in a mockery of the devastation on the ground.

Calvin pulled some keys from his belt and unlocked the same door to the medical centre that we'd broken through a month ago, on our way to free Mum and Georgia and the others. For all the good that had done.

'He'll be down in the bunker,' said Calvin, leading us through a little storeroom and out into a spotless white corridor. 'If we can get down there ...'

I trailed off. No end to that sentence. No plan.

We kept walking, out towards the front of the medical centre. I folded my arms under the sling, staring down at my brother's body again, shocked at how quickly the colour had drained out of it.

Not even a person anymore. Just a thing.

I dragged my eyes up towards Amy. She quickly looked away.

It would have been better if she'd just yelled at me. There was nothing left of me to tear down that I hadn't already demolished myself. I shuffled down the shadowy corridor, Mum and Dad and Georgia still condemning me over and over again inside my head.

We reached the front of the medical centre, and Calvin grabbed my arm, pulling me quickly across the reception area, past the smashed glass doors looking out on the carnage in the town centre. The Shackleton Building stood just across the street. All quiet. There must surely have still been a few people lying low in houses or getting lost out in the bush, but it wouldn't take the Co-operative long to round them up tomorrow.

Assuming there *was* a tomorrow, even for us. And there was a huge part of me that really hoped there wasn't, that Tabitha would just take us *all* out and be done with it. Better no humanity at all than a humanity with Shackleton in charge.

Calvin released my arm. We were back out of sight of the town centre now, moving down the corridor that led to the tunnel entrance.

My hand dropped to my pocket. There was a phone there. It took me a minute to figure out where it had come from.

It was Ketterley's. The one I'd lost in the skid crash this morning. Calvin had insisted on stopping to look for it on our way back.

Why? What were we going to do with it? Call Shackleton and ask him nicely to surrender?

I'd tried to phone Luke. I remembered now: the phone was still working despite all the rain, and I'd tried to call Luke, but the phone had just rung and rung, and I'd burst into tears in the back of the skid.

He was dead. Either gone already or he'd be twisted inside out when Tabitha came through in an hour's time. All our struggling to save him from Peter, and we'd only bought him a few more miserable hours.

'I'm sorry,' said Amy.

I jumped, the sound of her voice pulling me back out of myself, into the dim light of the medical centre.

'I'm sorry I wasn't more co-operative. I'm sorry I told you not to trust him.' Her eyes flickered with that faraway look of hers, like she was listening to a voice that no-one else could hear. 'You were right. You did the right thing. I know – I know it didn't turn out the way we wanted it to, but that doesn't mean ...'

Her brow furrowed as she searched for the words.

My feet crunched on broken glass. There was a huge hole in the window next to us, like a person had been shoved through it.

'Look,' said Amy, as we rounded another corner, 'just don't give up, okay? Don't stop hoping. I know that sounds like a stupid thing to say –'

'Don't stop *hoping?*' I shouted, something snapping inside me. 'Are you *insane?* Hope is what made me kill him! I murdered my brother because I *hoped* he was going to save us all! Because I was stupid enough to believe we were *meant* to stop this!'

'What if we still are?' said Amy.

'LOOK AT HIM!' I rounded on her, out of my mind, backing her up against the wall and ripping open Tobias's sling. *'DOES THIS LOOK LIKE A HAPPY ENDING TO YOU?'*

Amy cringed away, looking appalled.

Calvin's hand came down on my shoulder. 'Jordan …'

I twisted out from under him, shivering all over, no idea what I was even doing anymore, then stopped, seeing a gleaming silver door and realising where we were.

I spun back to Amy, delirious. She was still pressed up against the wall.

I lost my balance and collapsed, pain spiking through my kneecaps as they smashed into the cold floor. I thrust out my hands just in time to catch myself, chest heaving, throat clenching up, and there was a disgusting splatter as I emptied my stomach out onto the hospital floor. Not that there was anything much to empty.

I hung there, all pain and no vision, gagging and drooling and wishing I could just hurry up and black out, fingers clawing the ground as the world spun around me, Tobias suspended grotesquely from my chest, corpse swaying in the sling.

Hands came down on either side of me, keeping me from collapsing any further. When the feelings finally subsided, I was dragged to my feet, rested against the wall. My chest heaved, throat stinging with bile.

Amy's face blurred into my field of vision. 'Jordan …'

I couldn't even dredge up the will to focus my eyes.

'*Jordan*,' she snapped, grabbing my face with both hands. 'Listen, I – I don't pretend to understand why this has happened to us. But I know what I've seen. What *we've* seen. I know what the fallout gave me. And maybe I forgot all that for a while when I suddenly lost my powers, but that doesn't make it untrue. This wasn't all an accident. You know that. One way or another, this isn't – I don't think this is the end.'

'Tell that to my brother,' I said, stumbling towards the door. Calvin swiped a key card and the door clunked open, into a tiny room with a trapdoor set into the floor. I followed him inside.

Amy trailed after me. 'What if that's –? I mean, what if his death meant more than you think it did?'

'Fallout's gone now,' I said, bending down to activate the trapdoor. 'None of this *means* anything.'

'You say that,' said Amy, 'but you keep moving forward.'

A hiss of compressed air cut through the room, and a square of the floor sank down and rolled away. Calvin checked to make sure I was actually coming, then started down the stairs underneath.

'Don't give up,' said Amy, as we headed down after him. 'I know you want to, but –'

BLAM!

The sound blasted through the tiny room, so loud that for a second I was sure it was me who'd been shot. But then Calvin pitched forward, tumbling to the foot of the stairs.

Amy screamed, backing up. Not even close to fast enough.

BLAM!

She shrieked and fell down on top of Calvin, blood blossoming under her ribcage.

Adrenaline fired through me, blowing away the cloud over my mind. But instead of trying to escape, something kept me moving down the stairs, even when I saw the woman striding across the room to meet me.

Dr Galton, white with surprise, draped in a blood-stained lab coat. She raised a gun to my face with perfect precision.

BLAM!

I reeled back, but there was no pain. No blood.

What …?

Calvin had Galton down on the floor, arms wrapped around her legs. Blood pooled under him. Galton brought her pistol around again, aiming it down at Calvin's head.

'NO!' I cried, leaping down the last of the stairs.

Calvin thrust out his arm, too late to knock the weapon away.

BLAM!

He slumped down on top of her.

An animal roar exploded from my throat. Galton

dropped her hands to the ground, dragging herself free, but I was on her before she could get up, one hand at her throat and the other clamping down on her wrist.

Galton's pistol clunked to the floor. She snarled up at me. 'You think you can –?'

I spat in her face. 'Shut up.'

There was a whimpering moan behind me, and I glanced back to see Amy twisting around to face us. Blood glistened through the front of her jumper, no more fallout to stop the flow. But as her eyes locked on to mine, a smile spread across Amy's face.

Galton shifted under me, hijacking my attention. She shot me a smile of her own as she eyed the sling hanging down between us.

'What are you hoping to achieve here, Jordan?' she asked, nose wrinkling at the spit sliding down her cheek. 'If it's Shackleton you're looking for, you won't find him. He's locked himself in the bunker with your family and your boyfriend. He's not coming out.'

'Not even for his daughter?' said Amy weakly.

And for the first time ever, I saw fear flash behind Galton's eyes. 'Shackleton doesn't *have* –' she began, but she broke off into a grunt as I flipped her over, pinning her down on her face.

She was weak, I realised, reaching for her gun. Without her powers from the fallout, she was nothing. And with that realisation, a fierce energy welled up inside me.

Whatever happened tomorrow, whoever was still around to see it, I knew there was no place for me there. Not anymore. But until then, I had work to do. If there was another way to stop Tabitha, or to at least do something to keep my family safe, I couldn't just sit here and let it slip away.

Amy groaned again. I hesitated, but she shook her head as adamantly as she was still able to. 'Take her. Somewhere he can't send someone else to get you.'

'No, I'm not just –'

'What are you going to do?' gasped Amy. 'Drag me upstairs and operate? Go!'

I faltered for just a few seconds longer before finally pulling away.

'Come on,' I grunted, yanking Galton to her feet and digging her weapon into her back. 'Your dad thinks it's fun to screw with people's families? How about we go find out how much *he* likes it.'

Chapter 36

LUKE

'Luke,' said Shackleton, waving me over to the couch. 'Come and take a look at this.'

I glanced up from my seat on the bed and felt Mum's arm tighten around me. We were huddled together in a little group with Reeve, Katie and the Burkes, keeping as far as from Shackleton and his goons as we could.

The two guards who'd survived our initial firefight stood watch on either side of Shackleton, rifles raised. The other one lay on the bed at the end of the row with a sheet pulled over his head. Soren and Miller were stretched out on the beds next to him, both drifting in and out of consciousness, their makeshift bandages slowly darkening with blood.

Hawking was still alive. Not happy, but alive. We'd hoisted her onto the couch opposite Shackleton and done what we could to stop the bleeding. Cathryn hadn't left her side since. Tank was perched next to her, a hand on her shoulder. For the past hour, he'd been moving back and forth between our side and theirs, split between his loyalty to her and his loyalty to Reeve.

And through it all, Shackleton had just sat there on the couch, smiling around at us, like this was all just something mildly interesting he was watching on TV. He'd sent van Pelt across the room a few minutes ago to pull out a laptop, and was now hunched over the coffee table, attention flashing every few seconds to whatever was on the screen.

I kept waiting for something to happen, for some new terror to sweep in and shake everything up again. But I guessed we were past that. The cards had all been dealt now and everyone was just hanging here in this weird limbo, waiting for the end.

I couldn't even find the energy to freak out about it. I mean, obviously I didn't *want* to die, but after everything with Peter this morning, the idea of doing it all again just seemed painful. I was so exhausted already. Too burnt out to even process anything properly. If this really was the end, then I just wanted it to be *done*.

'Come now, Luke,' said Shackleton again, his voice a tiny bit harder this time, 'there's no need to be childish. I have good news. I believe I have located your father.'

Mum's grip tightened again. 'Luke, don't …'

But I was already pulling to my feet, frustrated at being so easily manipulated but unable to pass up what might be my last chance to catch a glimpse of my dad. I guessed I still had energy to spare for *some* things.

'Drop the weapon,' snarled Officer Cook, eyeing Tank's pistol, still heavy in my hand.

'Oh, let him keep it.' Shackleton waved the threat away like it was nothing. Like I was just a dog who'd got into something he wasn't meant to be eating. He gestured at the laptop screen as I approached. 'What do you think, Luke? Is it him? How desperately does your father wish to see you again before this is all over?'

Cook stepped aside as I approached. Shackleton patted the cushion next to his. I ignored him, snatching up the computer.

It was some kind of satellite map, with Phoenix in the middle and the wide expanse of wasteland stretching out all around. A little huddle of triangles were edging slowly in from the top of the screen.

Aircraft.

A rescue party.

For one flickering moment, hope sparked inside me. And then it was gone again, snuffed out by another thought. Whoever was out there, they were as dead as the rest of humanity. Mr Weir may have deactivated the automated defences, but even if they made it to Phoenix, Tabitha was going to shred them alive before the hour was out.

Unless Shackleton was wrong about Tobias. Or unless he was more of a threat than Shackleton was letting on. But would Shackleton really just be kicking back in his bunker if he thought there was even a *chance* that Jordan might succeed?

'Yes,' Shackleton nodded at the resignation on my face. 'Too little, too late, I'm afraid. They'll drop out of the sky a good half-hour before they reach us. Still,' he shrugged, 'you certainly have to admire their –'

He paused, raising an eyebrow as a burst of classical music rang out from his pocket. An even deeper hush seemed to fall over the room as Shackleton drew out his phone. Over his shoulder, I saw the name on the screen.

Aaron Ketterley.

Jordan.

I lunged, heart exploding against my ribcage.

'HEY!' Cook's fist balled up around the scruff of my neck, yanking me backwards, and Shackleton pirouetted to his feet.

'Manners, Luke,' he said, holding up an admonishing finger. He answered the call, tapping the speakerphone button. 'Hello?'

'JORDAN!' I yelled.

Loud, shaky breathing on the other end of the line.

Mr Burke jolted to his feet, snatching the rifle from Katie's lap. Reeve and the Weirs jumped up behind him. Cook shoved me aside and swung his rifle around, the other guard following suit. I could see on their faces how little they liked their chances.

Shackleton ignored them all, focus set on the phone in his hands.

'Jordan,' he said calmly. 'Is there something I can –?'

'I've got your daughter,' she growled, finding her voice.

The contented look on Shackleton's face wavered just for a moment before the mask went back up again, but it was enough for me to see that the threat had hit home. Whatever warped mockery of affection Shackleton was actually capable of showing another human being, he was showing it to Galton.

There was someone in this world that he actually cared about. And that made him vulnerable.

Hawking and van Pelt's heads snapped up at Shackleton, wearing matching looks of incredulity. Apparently not even they knew about him and Galton.

Shackleton stared back at them, calculating. 'Let me speak to her,' he said finally.

'Fine,' said Jordan. 'Come out of your bunker and –'

'*Now*, Jordan,' Shackleton ordered. 'I'll remind you, you are not the only one with a hostage.'

'We've got him outnumbered!' I shouted at the phone. 'If we have to, we can –'

'No, Luke,' Shackleton ducked down, snatching up his pistol and stabbing it at me, 'you cannot. Kill me, and you kill everyone else in this room.'

'Anyone else starting to think maybe that's not such a bad idea?' said Mr Weir.

'NO!' screamed Jordan, and I heard what sounded like a strangled gasp from Galton on the other end of the line. 'Nobody –!'

'Let her go, Jordan,' said Shackleton, the veneer beginning to crack again.

'*Let my family out of there!*'

Shackleton turned slowly, bringing his gun around to face Mr Weir. 'I understand your anger, Jordan. Truly, I do. But we both know you're not a murderer. You're not going to –'

'*I just killed my brother!*' Jordan roared, with a fury that startled even Shackleton. '*You don't know what I'll do!*'

A stunned, breathless silence swept out across the bunker. Mr Burke spun to face Mrs Burke, still huddled with Georgia on the bed, then back to me, searching for an explanation. And whatever fear I'd been nursing as we'd sat trapped in this place, it had nothing on the mutilating despair that crashed over me now. I stared around the room and saw the same thing mirrored on the faces of the others. Defeat.

'Jordan ...' her dad began shakily.

'No!' sobbed Georgia, breaking away from Mrs Burke, her tiny voice swelling to fill the room. 'No, no, no, he's not meant to die! He's meant to *win!* He told me!' She crumpled on the floor. 'He *told* me!'

Shackleton glanced down at her, and a new look passed over his face. Again, just a flicker, unreadable, then gone.

'If that's so,' he said, lifting the phone closer to his face, 'if your brother is dead, then you must already know you have failed. The question you should now –'

'FINE!' shouted Jordan, hysterical now. 'Fine! I've failed! Now what about you? You want to see your daughter again or not?'

And in a rush, I felt tears surging up into my eyes. What had Calvin *done* to her out there?

'Let me speak to her,' said Shackleton again.

'No! You don't get to –!'

'Either you let me speak to my daughter or this conversation ends here.'

A moment's pause, and then Jordan let out a frustrated growl. There was a scuffle of movement and, from slightly further away now, Jordan snapped, '*Talk.*'

Shackleton, turned again, like he was trying to find somewhere where no-one could see his face. He quickly gave up. 'Tori?'

'I'm here.'

'Will she do it?' Shackleton asked.

'I –' Galton broke off into a spluttering cough. 'I don't know. I think she might.'

Shackleton glanced up at me, both of us thrown off-balance by the fear in her voice. I spent a horrible moment wondering what Jordan could possibly have done to Galton to get that kind of reaction before my mind clicked to the other side of the equation: Galton wasn't a superhero anymore. Almost her whole life, she'd been just a thought away from crushing anyone who got in her path. Suddenly, all of that was gone. Of course she was terrified.

'Where are you?' Shackleton asked.

There was another burst of shuffling as Jordan snatched the phone away again.

'Okay,' she said, between shallow breaths, 'you've

talked to her. Now here's what you're going to do. You let my family out of there, and then Luke and my dad are going to bring you to the top floor of the Shackleton Building. You're going to tell us how to stop Tabitha, or your daughter is going to die.'

I glanced back at Jordan's mum, my stomach turning at the pain on her face.

'Noah!' Galton shouted. 'We're up on the med–'

She broke off with a grunt as Jordan barked, 'Quiet!'

'Enough!' said Mr Weir, pushing past Jordan's dad. 'Either you do what she says or –'

'Not your father,' said Shackleton into the phone. 'He stays. If you wish to meet, it will be just Luke and myself, both of us unarmed.'

He knows I'm dead when the time runs out, I thought. *All he needs to do is run down the clock and then he can call for backup.*

No response from Jordan. I could hear her crying into the receiver.

'That is my final offer, Jordan,' said Shackleton.

I wiped my eyes, looking to Mr Burke again. He was a wreck. We all were. Hanging in suspense, transfixed by the tinny speaker in Shackleton's hand as Jordan gasped for breath, steadying herself to speak.

When she finally did, it was low and fierce, more animal than human.

'Get up here.'

Chapter 37

LUKE

THURSDAY, AUGUST 13, 4.43 P.M.
17 MINUTES

Shackleton snapped the phone shut. 'Back on the beds,' he said, gun still fixed on Mr Weir. 'All of you.'

'Not happening,' Mr Weir snarled.

'Brian ...' said Mrs Weir, lowering her weapon to reach for him.

He shrugged off her touch. 'You want to let him lock us up again?'

'Boss?' said Tank, standing up, looking to Reeve for instructions.

'Don't think we have much of a choice,' said Reeve. 'Clock's ticking. If there's a hope left, it's with Jordan, not us.'

'I think it would be best if we all relinquished our weapons,' said Shackleton. He set his pistol down on the coffee table, like maybe we needed a demonstration.

I came around and put my gun down with his. Then I grabbed Shackleton by the back of the collar, snatching the phone from his hand.

Reeve shrugged off his rifle, and Tank followed his example. One by one, the others reluctantly laid down their weapons, until only van Pelt, Cook and the other guard were still armed.

'Don't kill anyone unless you have to,' Shackleton told them. 'I want to hold onto them until tomorrow morning's coronation ceremony.'

'Yeah, brilliant, wouldn't want to miss that,' Mr Weir muttered, leading his wife back to the beds. Reeve and Mr Burke trailed after them, whispering, while Tank pulled a wailing Cathryn to her feet.

Van Pelt nodded at the guards, and they closed in on the beds.

I glanced at Mum, barely able to hold my eyes on her agonised face. Probably only fifteen minutes left now. Chances were this was the last time we would ever –

She sprinted across the bunker towards me. I lost my grip on Shackleton, sure one of the guards were going to pull the trigger on her, but they held their fire. She almost knocked me over as she threw her arms around my neck. 'Oh, Luke …' she breathed. 'I'm –'

'Mum, stop,' I said, pulling back enough to look at her, knowing that if I started properly crying now, I'd be in no shape to take Shackleton anywhere. 'I know. I love you too. But –'

She dragged me to her again, kissing me on the forehead.

'When you're ready,' said Shackleton in an undertone.

Mum spun away from me, arms out at Shackleton like she was going to strangle him, but then she caught sight of van Pelt storming over to break them up and she shrank away, back to her place on the bed.

I looked at them all, one last time, then took Shackleton's shirt in my fists and pulled him across to the giant door he'd rolled over the lift. 'Open it.'

He bent slightly, holding down the lift button and speaking into a tiny hole above it that I'd never noticed before. *'Igne natura renovatur integra.'*

CLUNK.

The giant deadbolt inside the wall hauled itself apart and the barricade rumbled open, groaning under its own massive bulk. More thundering clunks rang out around the room as the lockdown was reset.

I glanced back and saw Reeve leaning in close to Jordan's dad, still whispering.

I cringed. *Please, please, don't do anything stupid.*

Shackleton released the button and the lift doors sprang open. I pushed him roughly inside, hitting the button to take us upstairs, and the doors closed again.

As soon as the bunker was blocked from view, I heard a shout from the other side of the doors. The shouting turned into screaming, which was overtaken almost immediately by a deafening barrage of rifle fire.

I cried out, abandoning Shackleton and throwing myself at the doors, but it was already too late. The lift jerked upwards, pulling us away from the noise.

I rested my head and hands against the doors,

forcing myself to breathe. Surely the guards hadn't just killed them all. Not after Shackleton specifically ordered them not to.

I straightened up again, turning to catch Shackleton's reaction, but it was like he hadn't even heard the shots. He just stared straight ahead, straight through me, his attention locked on the doors. The mask of unconcern was completely gone now, replaced by a look of absolute focus.

We'd lost. He knew that much.

But we could still keep him from winning.

'You have no idea how much it will please me to watch you writhe in agony,' he said tonelessly.

I jerked him backwards. 'I think I can imagine.'

But as the lift kept rising, a new voice sounded in the back of my mind, hardly audible over the whirlwind of terror and anger, but still making itself heard. A still, small voice, waking me to the reality of what I was doing, quietly questioning whether this was really how I wanted to go out.

Because whatever the stakes, whatever the extenuating circumstances, I was still dragging an old man into a hostage situation to barter for the life of his daughter – and that felt a little too much like *his* tactics for me to actually be okay with it.

Shackleton was as close as I could imagine to pure, unblemished evil. He was a monster. He *deserved* to pay for what he'd done.

But what about me?

If it really was all over, if humanity was doomed and I was going to be unceremoniously torn apart in only a few minutes …

Was I going to spend that time letting myself get dragged down into Shackleton's twisted new reality, or *fighting* it?

The doors opened, and I led Shackleton out onto the scene of destruction left behind by our earlier firefight. It was eerily quiet, the whole place cast in an orange glow by the setting sun outside. Cold wind blew in through the broken windows, rustling papers and raising the hair on the back of my neck.

I jolted, a sudden vibration shooting up my arm as Shackleton's phone began to ring again. I fumbled, almost dropping it, then jerked it to my ear. 'Jordan?'

She didn't speak, but I could hear her breathing, even unsteadier than before.

'Where are you?' I asked, dragging Shackleton across the room. 'We're here.'

Galton growled something I couldn't make out.

'The window,' Jordan choked. 'We're outside, but –'

'Coming,' I said, a chill snaking through me. 'Almost there.'

'Luke, *wait*,' said Jordan. 'Galton –'

She broke off as I reached the broken window, and I felt my heart splinter into a thousand tiny shards.

They were down on the roof of the medical centre. Jordan was kneeling on the concrete, muddy and trembling, a wet blanket slung over her shoulder. Galton stood over her, pressing a pistol to her head.

Shackleton peered down, face still fixed with that cold, emotionless focus.

'Well,' he said, in barely more than a whisper, 'doesn't that change things?'

Chapter 38

JORDAN

THURSDAY, AUGUST 13, 4.47 P.M.
13 MINUTES

I couldn't do it.

For all my screaming fury, when the time came, I just stood there, frozen, unable to channel any of it into action. I'd got Galton all the way up to the roof, pinned her down, made the call to Shackleton, and then –

I don't even know what happened next.

But suddenly she was darting out from under me, spinning to attack, and the gun was right there in my hand, ready to shoot her in the leg or something, but I couldn't do it, and that moment's hesitation was all Galton needed. She might not have had her powers anymore, but twenty years of hiding them from her father had turned her into a creature of absolute poise and precision. In a single, fluid motion, she'd kicked my knees out from under me and sent me crashing in a heap to the concrete, still trying in vain to protect my brother's dead body.

And just like that, the whole world went spinning back out of my control.

Galton released the fistful of my hair she was holding and tore the phone away from my ear. She glared up across the street at Luke. 'Release him.'

Luke stepped away from Shackleton, arms spread wide. But instead of disappearing back into the building, Shackleton stayed right where he was.

He wants to see it, I thought, barely keeping my head up enough to look at him. *He wants to watch us die.*

Shackleton reached out to Luke, who handed over the phone.

'Yes,' said Galton above me, clearly shaken. 'Yes, I'm fine. What do you want me to do with her?'

I stared at the figure in the window. What would give Shackleton more satisfaction? Seeing Luke's reaction as Galton put a bullet through my head, or forcing me to watch as Luke got torn up by Tabitha?

The moment stretched out, and I wanted to be stoical, to go to my death full of rage and defiance, but my gaze drifted to Luke and all of that disintegrated and I slumped down, shuddering for breath, nose and eyes running streams down my face. We were finished.

Tobias's body hung in the sling, cold as frost against my chest. I stared down at our shadows, stretched out across the roof in the setting sun, the dark bulge of the sling protruding from my stomach in a sick parody of a pregnant woman. I turned away, hugging him against my chest, and a roar rose up from the depths of me.

WHY? WHY DID YOU DO THIS TO ME? WHAT WAS THE POINT? WHAT WAS THE POINT OF ANY OF IT?

'Here,' snapped Galton. She shoved the phone against the side of my head and I heard Luke gasp into my ear.

'Jordan!'

'Luke!' I croaked, dragging myself up to look at him, lifting my hand to take the phone. 'I'm so, so sorry. I didn't –'

'Don't,' he said. 'Don't be stupid. You have *nothing* to –'

'I killed him, Luke!'

'I know that's not true.'

'Luke, you weren't –'

'It doesn't matter!' he said, voice cracking. 'I don't care *what* happened out there. You didn't kill him. They did.'

And though I knew he was wrong, hearing him even defend me was like a shot of life back into my veins.

'Listen to me,' said Luke. 'I know this didn't work out the way we wanted it to, but I want you to –'

His voice fell away. Back up at the window, I saw Shackleton snatch the phone out of Luke's hands.

'Thank you, Jordan,' he hissed in my ear. 'I believe that will be sufficient. Just enough to ensure that your voice is fresh in his mind as he watches you die.'

He spoke in a cold, grey monotone, completely different to his normal voice. This wasn't wide-eyed, gleeful, surface-level Shackleton. This was the real deal.

'Now,' he said, the words turning darker still, 'hand back the phone.'

I couldn't move. I just knelt there, frozen in place.

Shackleton's silhouette leant towards the window. 'VICTORIA!' he shouted, loud enough to be heard at a distance, and Galton clawed the phone from my hands. She paused, listening to Shackleton, the cold muzzle of her weapon digging into the back of my head again.

'Really?' she said, with the hint of a sneer. 'Are you sure you wouldn't like to stand here and listen to them chat a bit longer?'

She glanced up at the window, listening again. Then a ragged shout rang out from across the street and she started, smacking me in the head with her gun.

It was Luke. He'd just launched himself at Shackleton, knocking him over, the two of them rolling to the ground, perilously close to the shattered window.

And from nowhere, some secret store of adrenaline charged through me and I whirled around, diving into Galton's legs. She thumped to the ground, losing hold of the phone but not her pistol, right arm already outstretched to –

BANG.

I tumbled to the ground, sure I was dead, rolling over in time to catch a glimpse of the hulking figure exploding through the doorway. He barrelled out onto the roof, and I felt relief burn through me like wildfire.

'Dad!'

Galton scrambled to her feet, aiming her weapon

again. Fast, but not fast enough. Dad grabbed her arm, tearing the gun away, throwing it to the concrete.

He lifted up a massive hand and pounded her into the ground.

LUKE

'*Oof!*' Shackleton grunted, coughing old man smell into my face as I slammed him down by the shoulders again.

We were right at the edge now, jagged glass rising up from the ground on my right and scattered across the floor beneath us. Icy wind lashed at my face, spraying me with rain that had apparently decided *now* was a good time to start coming down again.

I glanced through the haze of wet glass, my heart rocketing as I saw Jordan's dad send Galton sprawling. He pinned her down with one knee, dragging her hands around behind her back.

Shackleton bucked under me with strength too big for his ageing body. He lunged with his head, trying to smash it up into mine. I ducked and he used the momentum to roll us over.

I slammed into the low wall of cracked glass rising up from the edge of the carpet and heard a sickening *creak* as it shifted under our weight. I pushed off with my feet, and a huge shard of it snapped away, tumbling

out of sight through the rain. But it was enough.
I was back on top again, kneeling now, a hand to
Shackleton's throat to keep him from struggling.

Across the street, I saw Jordan fumbling to pick
something up from the roof. She raced over to her dad,
one hand still clutched to the bulge at her chest.

Shackleton snarled up at me. 'You're dead, Luke.'

I cocked my head at the medical centre. 'She's not.'

Down on the roof, Jordan raised a hand to her ear,
and another blast of music rang out from Shackleton's
phone. It vibrated across the carpet, just out of reach.

I took a hand off Shackleton and lunged. He
pushed up from under me, trying to free himself, but
my knees kept him down just long enough to grab the
phone and pull it open.

'Hey,' I grunted, putting the phone on speaker and
dropping it on Shackleton's chest, freeing my hands to
pin down his throat again. 'You okay?'

'Can you see him, Jordan?' Shackleton gasped,
before she had a chance to answer. 'How long do we
have left now, do you think? Five minutes? Six? Your
view might not be quite as good as mine when this
pestilential blight finally meets his end, but I hate the
thought of you missing –'

'Jordan, listen,' I said, squeezing down on his throat
to silence him, 'you need to get out of here, okay? Take
your dad. Get your family out.'

'*No*,' she choked. 'No – I'm not just going to *leave* –'

'I'm dead, Jordan! A few minutes and I'm gone.

But I can at least hold Shackleton long enough for you to –'

'Luke,' Mr Burke cut in, 'Reeve told us to wait here. He's gone down to the labs under –'

Shackleton's eyes widened.

With a burst of energy, he wrenched his body, throwing me off balance. I flew to the ground, one hand still clawing at his throat, and the phone somehow wound up underneath me, digging into my back.

Shackleton drove a bony fist into my face, and my vision blacked out for a second. By the time the blur cleared, he was back on his feet. A muffled voice screamed up from the phone. 'Luke!'

Pain shot through my ribcage as Shackleton delivered a vicious kick to my side, and I rolled towards the glass again. Rain hammered into my face.

'Jordan, listen to me,' said Shackleton in a rush, snatching up the phone. 'I am prepared to negotiate a prisoner exchange – Luke's life for my daughter's – but only if –'

'No!' I groaned, spitting blood out of my mouth and scrambling back from the edge. 'I'm dead anyway! What's the point of –?'

'I can save him,' said Shackleton, still speaking to Jordan instead of me. 'There is a way. But you must follow my instructions precisely.'

'He's lying!' I shouted, pulling myself upright on the nearest desk, fingers slipping in the wet. But even as I said it, I felt a little spark of doubt.

Could there be another way for me to survive this?

'His parents too,' said Jordan, voice still thick with tears. 'You have to –'

'His mother,' said Shackleton. 'I can't save his father.'

And even though it wasn't new information, hearing him write off my dad like that was like a sledgehammer to the gut.

I staggered towards Shackleton, hazy doubt forcing its way to the front of my mind. This was wrong. Why were we even having this conversation? What had happened to Shackleton's ecstasy at watching me die?

'You have thirty seconds to return my daughter's weapon and release her down the stairs behind you,' Shackleton pushed on when Jordan didn't respond. 'And the phone,' he added as an afterthought. 'You will surrender Ketterley's phone to her as well.'

'Something's wrong,' I said leaning in. There was a frenetic energy in Shackleton's expression that I'd never seen before. 'He's worried all of a sudden. I don't know why, but –'

Shackleton drove his elbow sharply back into my chest and I heaved back, grunting.

'Twenty seconds,' he said. 'Release her and I will show you how to save Luke.'

Jordan's voice gasped out of the speaker. 'How do I know you're even –?'

'*Fail* to do so,' said Shackleton, venom in every word, 'and I will call down to the bunker and have your family executed.'

I grabbed hold of him again. 'You think I'm just going to let you –?'

'He can't,' said Mr Burke, sounding less than certain. 'The bunker is ours now.'

'Is it still?' asked Shackleton. 'Fifteen seconds.'

I moved back to the window, dragging Shackleton with me. A gust of wind swept through and I almost overbalanced.

Mr Burke was still perched on top of Galton, her pistol aimed down at her with one hand. He and Jordan stared at each other, neither of them speaking.

'Ten seconds,' said Shackleton. His voice was icy as ever, but I could feel him shaking. 'Nine. Eight.'

Jordan jerked around, looking up at us. Even from here, I could see the agony on her face.

'Seven. Six –'

'Do it!' said Jordan, snapping. 'Let her go! Dad, come on, we can't just –!'

'Five –'

'He's bluffing!' I said. 'Don't –!'

'Four –'

'*Dad!*' Jordan screamed, pulling at him with both hands.

'Three –'

'Okay!' said Mr Burke, getting up. He spun to face us, hands in the air, and Galton struggled to her feet.

'The pistol,' Shackleton ordered.

'No!' I said. 'Guys, this isn't –'

Mr Burke threw out his hand, sending the pistol

skittering across the ground towards the stairwell. Galton snatched the phone from Jordan and hurried over to pick the weapon up.

Jordan raced after her, yelling at the phone. 'Shackleton!'

Galton whirled around, pointing the pistol at her, and Jordan fell silent.

Shackleton nodded in approval and my stomach lurched again.

Right into his hand.

But how else had they thought it would go? There was no saving me. Of course there wasn't.

Galton raised the phone to her mouth and started moving backwards towards the stairs, careful to keep Jordan between herself and Mr Burke. 'Noah?'

'Victoria,' said Shackleton urgently. 'Get downstairs. I need you to find Matthew Reeve and –'

With a feral grunt, I smashed my fist into the back of Shackleton's head, and the phone sailed out of his grip. He fell perilously close to the edge of the window, but his hands clenched on air and the phone went tumbling away through the rain.

Shackleton spun, barely missing a beat, and aimed another fist at my face. I ducked, glancing past him to see Galton disappearing down the stairs. Whatever Shackleton had been trying to tell her, it seemed like she'd got the message.

Mr Burke bolted past Jordan to give chase. Jordan hovered on the spot, torn between going after them and staying here where she could see Shackleton and me.

'GO!' I shouted down at her, moving in to grab Shackleton again. 'Get out of here!'

Shackleton stepped back. Too far. His boot crunched down on the glass sticking up from the edge of floor and he slipped backwards, spinning his arms in a vain attempt to regain his balance.

Instinctively, I reached out to grab him, like I'd blanked out for a second and forgotten who he was. My hand came down around the front of his shirt before I'd even realised what I was doing.

Shackleton glared into my eyes with a look of absolute disdain. He kept falling, feet teetering on the edge. My arm jerked out, straining under his weight but somehow still not letting go.

The wind and rain drove at us from all sides. My shoes skidded on the glass-strewn carpet and I felt my whole body pulled closer to the edge. But just as the signal finally got through from my brain to let go of him and save myself, Shackleton's hands came clamping down around my arm. His fingers dug into me, clawing up my sleeve like it was a rope.

BLAM! BLAM! BLAM!

Gunshots echoed up from across the street. Jordan screamed, and I felt my guts turn to liquid inside me.

'*What was that?*' I demanded, neck straining to see past him.

'That,' said Shackleton, a grim smile stretching across his face, 'was the end of you.'

He flung himself forward, head-butting me in the face. I screamed, crashing to my knees as he dealt a savage blow to my stomach.

'Luke Hunter,' he said between breathless gasps.

I opened my eyes and saw him standing over me, legs planted firmly apart against the wind.

'You will never know how very close you may have just come to –' He broke off, his whole body shuddering, as a roar of machine gunfire rose up from somewhere out of sight.

Something wet splashed across my face.

Shackleton's eyes bulged in surprise. He unclenched his jaw, like he wanted to finish his sentence, but all that came out was a mouthful of blood. His body arched backwards, legs slowly folding, like he was jumping off a high-dive. Then he finally tumbled out of sight, crashing down to earth with the rain.

Chapter 39

JORDAN

The whole world slowed to the pace of a dream as I watched Shackleton fall. His body sank through the air, limbs splayed, head-first by the time it disappeared from view.

A dull thump floated up through the rain, followed by a high streaking sound, like a hand dragging across glass.

Time quickened again, and I knelt at the ledge, needing to know I hadn't just imagined it. I stared over the side of the building, scanning the warzone below.

The shield grid antenna was still stretched out across the street like a barricade. Shackleton had landed right on top of it, then slipped down the side to the ground. He lay face-down on the cracked concrete, legs still propped up against the antenna, blood pooling out beneath him.

Dead.

I stood up again, trembling, leaving the scene behind. And only then did I wonder where the shooting had come from.

I turned around and saw Officer Reeve stretching slowly to his feet at the top of the stairs, fists tight around his rifle. He looked stunned. As unsure as I'd been that what had just happened was real.

Footsteps hammered up the stairwell behind him. Reeve barely had time to look back before my dad charged past him, running to meet me.

Tobias's weight seemed suddenly to double. I stumbled towards my dad, all the relief I *wanted* to feel drowned out in the dread of what he was going to do when he reached me.

But then his arms came crashing down around me, wrapping me into himself for the first time in weeks and weeks, and I knew that somehow the love was still there, big enough to cover even this. He pulled my head into his shoulder, grunting with the pain of some awful injury, stroking my filthy hair, and I broke down all over again, the cold lump of Tobias's body caught up awkwardly between us.

'I killed him ...' I sobbed. 'He was supposed to save us, and I –'

'Shh,' he breathed, choking back his own tears. 'Shh ... It's okay. It's all going to be okay.'

'Jordan.' Reeve put a hand on my shoulder, suddenly right behind me.

Dad loosened his grip and I twisted around. 'Where's Galton?'

'Bottom of the stairs,' said Reeve. 'Unconscious.'

He held something up into my field of vision and I flinched, thinking it was another gun. On second glance, I realised it was some kind of injection device, pistol-shaped, but with a syringe in place of the barrel and a vial of orange-ish liquid where the chamber would have been.

Reeve pulled on my shoulder, eyes down on the sling at my chest. 'I need you to –'

I reeled back, stumbling away from both him and Dad. 'What are you doing? What is that?'

'It's –' Reeve faltered, closing the gap again. 'It's me. My healing power. Galton was working on a way to extract it. To make it something you could use on –'

'No!' I said. 'No – No more – I'm not putting anything else –'

'Jordan, please,' said Reeve, 'you saw the state I was in after Shackleton put that Tabitha prototype into me. I was a mess. No way could I have survived without –'

'He's not a *mess!*' I said, hugging the body defensively. 'He's *dead!*'

Reeve hesitated, absorbing this, like he thought maybe I'd just been exaggerating before. 'Okay. Okay, but –'

He faltered again as Dad took a sudden step towards us. He held up Ketterley's phone to show the time.

4.56 p.m.

Four minutes.

'Do it,' said Dad. 'Try. It's not going to …'

I filled in the blank on my own. *It's not going to make him any deader.*

I looked away from both of them, gaze drifting back to the other side of the street. Where was Luke when I needed him?

Dad moved closer, arms outstretched to take Tobias.

'No!' I said, backing off again. Then, as calmly as I could: 'No. Let me do it.'

I'd already killed him. If anyone was going to bear the weight of further mutilating his body, it should be me.

I reached into the sling with shaky hands, the pain in my chest redoubling as my fingers slid down over his cold skin. A miserable gasp escaped from my throat as I slowly lifted him free of the blanket, and Dad couldn't hide his distress as he got his first proper look at his baby son.

'I'm sorry,' I choked, staring down at the pale, life-less thing in my arms and wondering at the stupidity of anyone who ever described a dead person as looking like they were just sleeping.

Tobias wasn't sleeping. He was gone.

Dad steadied himself enough to put an arm around me, but the warmth of his body only made Tobias feel even colder. I shifted him into one arm, and Reeve slid the injector thing into my free hand, and it was so much like the release station all over again that my legs began to buckle.

BANG.

The door at the top of the stairs burst open again, and Luke came pounding out across the roof. He stopped right in front of me, almost falling, doubled over with exhaustion. 'Do it,' he said, nodding at the thing in my hand. 'He was – Something just had Shackleton really freaked out. I think …'

He trailed off, looking right into my eyes, seeing all the anguish there, and I watched his face fill with a deep sadness that cut straight through the whole ugly mess.

He understood.

He saw it all, and he understood what I was going through. And even in the face of his own death, he still had empathy to spare for me.

I lifted the injector, needle hovering over Tobias's rain-soaked body.

'You just – stick it in his arm and pull the trigger,' said Luke, the urgency slipping back into his voice.

I brought the needle to rest against Tobias's skin, fist clenched to fight the shakes. Dad's arm tightened around me.

I glanced up at Luke again. If there was even a chance this could save him …

I pushed.

The skin gave under the pressure, and I guided the needle down into the flesh of his arm. I held my breath, pulled the trigger, and the liquid in the vial drained out into Tobias.

Luke looked on, face stretched with nerves.

Please, I begged inside my own head. *I know it's impossible, but please ...*

I eased the needle out again, dropping the injector to the ground.

The rain beat down on us, heavier now, but we just stood there, huddled around Tobias. Waiting.

And nothing.

Nothing.

No change.

'Just – just give it a minute,' said Reeve feebly, glancing at Luke. 'Give it a chance to ...'

But he couldn't even bring himself to finish the sentence.

Silence fell again. Nothing but the patter of rain.

The seconds ticked past, and I felt what little hope I had left tearing away from me. I started shaking again, almost losing my grip on Tobias. Dad pulled me closer into him, but it did no good.

Finally, the last lingering thread of hope snapped inside of me, and I wrenched myself away from him, shoving Tobias into his arms and staggering out of the circle, a furious scream bursting out from deep inside of me.

'Jordan ...' Dad choked, but I barely even heard it.

Luke was by my side in a second, arms around me, fighting my attempt to pull away from him.

'*Jordan,*' he said. 'Come on. You're *not* to blame for – Jordan, *please*. Please listen to me.'

I stopped struggling and looked at him, seeing the

bitter disappointment etched across his face. He swallowed hard, pushing it aside, tears welling in his eyes.

'Keep fighting,' he said fiercely. 'Shackleton's gone now. Most of them are gone. You guys need to take charge. Make sure the world that's left is a world worth –'

'I *can't!*' I wept. 'I can't do this without you!'

'Yes you *can*,' he said. 'Don't be stupid. Of course you can. You don't need me.'

'It was supposed to work!' I sobbed. 'He was supposed to *save* you!' I slumped down, head on his shoulder, clinging to him for as long as I still could.

'I – I know. I know he was, but listen –' He lifted my head again. '*Listen* to me, okay? Whatever happens after this – Don't let today be the end of *your* life. You did everything you could today. You – you were amazing. Don't you dare blame yourself.'

I tried to answer him, but the words wouldn't come.

He leant in to kiss me and I stretched to meet him, still sobbing, raking my fingers through his knotted hair. I closed my eyes, fighting back the sickening visions of him tearing apart in my arms, refusing to let my own mind drive me away from him before Tabitha did.

'I love you,' he breathed, breaking away, forehead resting against mine. 'You're –'

Luke jolted back, eyes wide, as a noise pierced the air behind me. A tiny croaking sound, almost like …

I whirled around, heart thundering.

Dad was staring down into his arms, his brow furrowed in –

In *what?*

Fear? Confusion?

What had he just seen?

Whatever it was, Reeve had seen it too.

I looked down at Tobias. His lips were parted. Just a fraction, but his mouth had definitely not been open before.

And his face. Surely I wasn't just imagining that. It was darker than it had been, like the colour was seeping back into the skin.

'Did –?' I faltered, terrified of the warmth flickering to life inside of me, bracing for reality to crash in and snuff it out. 'Did he just –?'

And then Tobias's whole body tensed, and his face screwed up, and he let out a scream so loud that I swear they must have heard it all the way down in the bunker.

It was the most incredible sound I'd ever heard in my life.

We stood there dumbly for a long moment, listening to him scream, too stunned to move or breathe or say anything. Then Dad's face lit up with a joy I hadn't seen since we'd touched down here. He gaped over at me, lifting Tobias up into the air, then held him to his shoulder, gently bouncing him, straight into Dad mode.

The phone tumbled out of his hand and I dived to catch it, that flicker of warmth flaring up into a firestorm. My fingers scrambled on the phone, lighting it up again just as the time ticked over.

5.00 p.m.

The end of the countdown.

My eyes locked onto Luke, breath catching in my throat. I spun the phone around, showing him the time. For a long moment, neither of us moved, still too scared to believe it was all really over.

Luke caved first. He leapt forward, crashing into me, spinning me off my feet. I squeezed him back, and he was real and solid and still alive. Time stretched out and out and out, and my brain slowly began to allow the possibility that he wasn't going to disappear on me.

Dad stepped in, throwing one big arm around the both of us. Tobias had stopped crying by now. He smiled at me, the colour flooding back into his face, and I felt tears stinging my eyes again. I lifted him up, holding him against me. He wriggled in my hands, warm despite the rain. Really alive.

'We should get down there,' said Reeve, coming up behind us. 'Make sure the others are all okay. Let them know it's over.'

'Right,' I said, handing Tobias back to Dad and clearing the rain out of my face.

Luke took my hand, fingers lacing between mine, and we started towards the stairs.

'So,' he said, gazing down into a sunset he'd never expected to see, voice lighter than I'd heard it in months, 'what do you guys want to do tomorrow?'

Chapter 40

LUKE

It was chaos when the military arrived.

Not gun chaos – most of the guards laid down their arms as soon as the first choppers landed. People chaos. The giddy blur of a town set free after weeks of imprisonment and terror.

Not all of it was happy. Some people took one look at this *new* group of people with guns and freaked out all over again. Others started smashing windows and benches, looking for a way to vent, or maybe just needing to play some small part in bringing this place down. A little gang of kids ran off to trash the school, and came back disappointed that the fire had beat them to it. More than a few people found places to just sit and weep, mourning lost loved ones or simply overwhelmed by it all.

But none of that could shake the wild, unrestrained joy that coursed through the air all around us. It was like those photos of the end of World War II: people hugging and kissing and shouting from the windows and dancing in the rubble.

Day turned to night without anyone noticing. A couple of guys found some secret wine cellar or something in one of the Co-operative leaders' houses and came trundling into town with a shopping trolley full of bottles to rapturous applause.

Jordan didn't leave my side the whole night. We and the others kept to the edges of all the partying, as euphoric as anyone but with less energy to show it. A few kids from school came up to thank us or whatever, but mostly people just left alone, either oblivious to everything we'd done or too caught up in their own celebrations to even notice we were there.

Sometime after midnight, the military guys made a half-hearted attempt to get everyone back into the Shackleton Building for the night, but that fizzled out pretty quickly, and they settled for keeping us contained to the town centre.

I'm pretty sure we were the only ones in town who felt like sleeping.

FRIDAY, AUGUST 14, 2.32 P.M.

'Crazy how it all works together,' said Reeve, cross-legged on the grass with his son in his lap. 'I mean, even the stuff you'd think was completely irredeemable. Like that serum – If I hadn't been captured and half-killed by the Co-operative, it never would've been made. We would've been sunk right there at the finish.'

I nodded lazily, soaking up the feeling of the sun on my face, of Jordan's head on my shoulder, of clean, dry clothes against my skin and a properly full stomach for the first time in weeks, my heart swelling with an overwhelming sense of gratitude for the life that had been given back to me.

'Not saying it didn't cost us plenty,' Reeve added quickly, glancing at the Weirs, 'but ...' He sighed, shaking his head. 'I don't know. I don't pretend to understand it. But I have to believe that somehow it all becomes worth it.'

Mr and Mrs Weir smiled weakly at him, at least *wanting* to believe it. Jordan and I had spent an exhausting couple of hours this morning, piecing everything together with them. I was sure nothing could make losing your kid feel worth it, but the fact that Peter had died making sure we all knew about Tobias had at least given them something solid to hold onto.

We were sitting together in the park – Jordan and her family, Mr and Mrs Weir, the Reeves, my mum and me – one of dozens of little huddles spread out all across the grass. They'd moved us out here when the sun came up. Easier to keep us contained, I guess.

There were still a bunch of people missing from the fighting yesterday, and it would be a while before everyone was accounted for. Once that was done, they were taking us all back to the 'facility' where Dad and

Kara had been yesterday for what was sure to be a long debrief.

Jordan smiled as Georgia got up from her lunch and started climbing her dad's back, perching herself on his shoulders. She stared around the park, then back down at Mr Burke, ruffling his hair with both hands. 'Okay, come on, it's time to get up and play.'

'Soon,' said Mr Burke wearily. 'Wait until everyone's finished eating.'

Georgia sighed dramatically. 'We *have* finished!'

'Your brother hasn't,' said Mr Burke, waving a hand at Mrs Burke, who was feeding Tobias.

'He's not *eating*,' said Georgia impatiently. 'He's *drinking*. Anyway, he doesn't even know how to play. He's just a baby.' She started kicking her legs, digging her heels into Mr Burke's chest like she was spurring on a horse. 'Come on! Giddy up!'

'Georgia, Dad's very tired today,' said Mrs Burke. 'Just give him a few more minutes to rest, okay? I'm sure he'll be ready soon.'

Jordan stirred next to me. 'It's okay,' she yawned. 'I'll take her.'

Georgia clambered down from her dad and ran over. I got up too, not ready to let Jordan out of my sight.

I bent down to kiss Mum on the cheek. 'Back soon.'

She smiled. 'Love you, sweetheart.'

'This is all so weird,' said Jordan, as we trekked across the grass. 'All these people, just sitting around having a picnic. I mean, I know it's over. I know it in my head, anyway. But it still doesn't *feel* over, you know? Like, I keep expecting some new, awful thing to come crashing in on us.'

I nodded. 'I think it'll be better when they finally fly us out of here.'

'Yeah,' Jordan sighed. 'Whenever that is.'

Georgia dragged on her hand. 'Hurry *up*. You're being so *boring*.'

I smirked, wishing I could just leave it all behind as easily as she could.

'Sorry, Georgia,' said Jordan. 'Almost –'

'Hey,' called a familiar voice from down on the grass. It was Amy, completely uninjured, finally reunited with her parents. She got to her feet, giving Jordan a hug. 'Thanks again.'

'Yeah,' she said. 'You too.'

There'd been more vials of whatever they'd pulled from Reeve in a fridge back down in the medical centre. We'd used one of them to bring Amy back from the brink. We'd tried the serum on Calvin too, but nothing had happened. Whatever that stuff was, it could heal the wounded, but it couldn't raise the dead.

So what did that say about Tobias?

The playground stood not far from the big taped-off area the military had marked out as a makeshift landing pad for their helicopters. It was vacant at the moment, but I could already hear another chopper thundering towards us.

As soon as we reached the playground, Georgia

broke away from Jordan and sprinted up to a little boy her age who was sitting on one of the swings. 'Hi Max!'

The boy jumped off the swing and gave her a big hug. 'Hi Georgia! Where have you been all this time? I couldn't find you anywhere!'

'That's Hamilton's kid,' said Jordan, looking around. 'Lauren's brother.'

Hamilton was standing at the edge of the playground, with a serious-looking women who I guessed was his wife. Officer Chew was with them.

'Hey,' said Jordan, walking over, suddenly concerned. 'Where's Lauren?'

Hamilton rolled his eyes and pointed across the park to where Lauren and Jeremy were awkwardly making out behind a tree. If they were trying to be secretive, they were doing a terrible job of it.

'Nice to have you back, Lauren!' Hamilton called. 'Love you!'

Jeremy jumped bolt upright. His pale face went bright red. Lauren shot her dad a filthy look and dragged him back behind the tree.

Chew snorted at Hamilton. 'Jerk.'

'Are you kidding?' he grinned. 'What's the point of having my daughter back if I can't at least torment her a little bit?'

By the time the fighting had ended, Hawking, Galton and van Pelt were the only members of the Shackleton Co-operative still left alive. The military had worked out who they were and quickly whisked them away.

Those three were the easy ones.

For now at least, most of Shackleton's security guys had been released back to their families. But what was going to happen, once they got us all out of here? They couldn't just arrest those three and forget the rest ever happened. It was going to take months to untangle it all.

I glanced back and saw Reeve and Katie coming over to join us, swinging Lachlan between their arms. Behind them, Mum and the others were getting up too.

We'd been doing that all day. Gravitating towards each other. Keeping the group together, almost without thinking.

My eyes darted up between the trees as the chopper I'd heard before came swooping in for a landing. It was different to the others that had been coming in and out today. Less aggressive-looking.

'Transport helicopter,' Hamilton commented over the noise of the engine. 'Maybe they're finally going to start letting some of us out of here.'

It was hard to even get my head around the idea of an *outside* anymore. That stuff was all so distant now, like the whole world beyond the wall was just an endless grey fog with my dad standing somewhere in the middle. But whatever it was, it was better than here.

The chopper touched down, and I watched the blades spin slower and slower, head full of the last hundred days, ten lifetimes of insanity and terror, crammed into the space of a few short months. And somehow, we'd made it through to the other side.

'Reeve's right,' I said, turning back to Jordan. '*You* were right. I don't think we did this on our own. Like, I don't think it's an accident we won. This place didn't just *happen* to spit out a baby who could fight off Tabitha.'

Jordan smiled, apparently amused that I was finally switching onto this thing she'd been trying to tell me for weeks and weeks. 'So what *did* happen?'

'Don't look at me,' I said. 'You're the one –'

'*Luke!*' she gasped, clutching my arm and dragging me back around to face the landing pad.

A door at the back of the helicopter had just opened, and an officer had dropped down to the grass, followed by a man and a woman in civilian clothes.

'DAD!' I shouted, breaking into a sprint, straight under the boundary tape, ignoring the shouts of the military people, both of us in tears before we even made contact.

He grabbed hold of me, crushing me into him, and then Kara practically wrenched us apart.

'Where's Soren?' she demanded.

'I – I don't know,' I said. The last I'd seen, he'd been eating alone in a corner of the park, looking as sullen as ever. 'But Kara –'

She broke away from me, racing off in the direction of the playground, and I felt a lurch in the pit of my stomach. Those two had a lot of difficult conversations ahead of them. After all Soren had done, I couldn't help thinking that even Mr and Mrs Weir had it easier than Kara did.

'How are you holding up?' Dad asked, pulling me close again. 'These guys treating you okay?'

'Yeah, fine,' I said, wiping my eyes clear, dragging him to rejoin the others. 'How did you get them to bring you here? Everyone I spoke to said they weren't going to let you in.'

'That was before I became useful,' he said sourly, with a sideways glance at the officer who'd come out of the chopper with them. 'You guys are first in line to be brought back to base for questioning, and I managed to convince them you'd be more likely to co-operate if I was part of the welcome party.'

'Of course,' I said, 'because without you, we might've all just decided to stay here.'

'Right,' said Dad, ducking under the barrier. 'See? It was all very tactical.'

As soon as he was through, Jordan barrelled into him. Reeve came up too, and patted him on the back. 'Good to see you, mate.'

'You're back!' said Georgia, appearing from the playground to latch onto his leg. 'I'm glad you didn't die!'

'Me too!' Dad smiled. He spotted Mum hovering at the edge of the group and went over to meet her, pulling her into what had to be the least awkward hug they'd had since before they separated. 'Hey, Em. Thanks for looking after him.'

The guy from the chopper cleared his throat. 'Your attention please, ladies and gentlemen. I've got a list here of persons of special interest to the –'

'Yep. Thanks mate,' said Dad, holding up a hand. 'This is them.'

The guy scowled.

Dad clapped me on the shoulder and turned to the others, stretching a hand back in the direction of the chopper. 'Any of you guys feel like getting out of here?'

Twenty minutes later, we were strapped in and ready to go. 'Everyone okay?' asked Dad, as the pilot came through for a final check.

Weary nods from around the cabin.

Jordan slipped her hand into mine as the whine of the engine was slowly drowned out by the *whump-whump-whump* of the blades above our heads. The chopper lifted off the ground – no screaming, nobody firing on it – and we gazed out the window, watching the town of Phoenix fall slowly away from us.

We rose up over the park, over the little huddles of people who had almost become the last of humanity, and then banked sideways, drifting above the broken wreck of the town centre. Shackleton's nightmare vision of a better world, burned to the ground and staying there.

I closed my eyes, concentrating on the warmth of Jordan's hand, not knowing where I was going, but knowing who I was going with. Trusting that whatever lay ahead was better than what we were leaving behind.

We'd come this far. We'd survived.

I had a feeling we were going to be okay.

THE END

Acknowledgements

Thanks to Hilary Rogers for taking a chance on an upstart twenty-something's wacky idea for a sci-fi series; to Marisa Pintado for all the incredible work you've put into dragging it out of my head and onto the page; and to Jennifer Kean, publicist extraordinaire, for patiently reminding me what day it is and what city I'm in, and for listening to me tell the same stories about myself more times than anyone else on this planet.

Huge thanks to everyone at Hardie Grant Egmont and my wonderful overseas publishers for getting behind this series and pushing it out there into the world, and to all the awesome librarians and book-sellers who've helped people find it (especially Shearer's Bookshop, my not-so-secret favourite).

Thanks to Rowan McAuley for being an amazing first reader and creative collaborator, and for introducing me to that Zac Power kid. Keep on putting my writing to shame with yours!

Thanks to Ben for all the technical advice about guns and bombs and helicopters.

Thanks to Rev Dave for being such an awesome pastor, mentor and friend (and for accidentally being rude from the pulpit); and to my second family at Abbotsford Presbyterian Church. It is an honour and a privilege to journey with you guys.

Shout-out to the A-Team. You know who you are. (Also Moose and Jr Moose.)

Thanks to everyone at PLC Sydney. You guys are the greatest. Turns out writing is only the second-best job in the world.

Thanks to Kerryn, Sarah, Claire, Phil, Mute and Weezy, all of whom have suffered living with me through at least one deadline; to the Rusbournes, Hardings, Thurstons, Barnetts and Doiners, who've been stuck with me for pretty much my whole life; and to the many, many other friends who've read, critiqued, encouraged, and told me to get on with it.

Thanks to Katie. Best brother-sister combo ever. (It's in print now, Kerryn! Beat that!)

Mum and Dad: I have no possible way of thanking you enough for your constant love, encouragement and support – and most of all, for showing me the true story that shapes all the others.

Finally, to all of you who've stuck with me all the way to the end of this book, THANK YOU. I hope I've given you an ending worth hanging on for. (If not, I'm sure I'll hear about it!) Looking forward to doing it all again with something new!

Chris Morphew was born in Sydney in 1985. His experiences as a qualified primary school teacher, combined with his own formative high school years, have resulted in unintentional invaluable research for his writing.

Life in the Flames is the third of the three new volumes of his best-selling series *The Phoenix Files*. *Man in the Shadows* and *Blood in the Ashes* were published in 2015. His current project sees him teaming up with another *Zac Power* contributor David Harding and best-selling *Go Girl* contributor Rowan McAuley, as Cerberus Jones, bringing us an exciting new sci-fi series for younger readers, *The Gateway*.

Chris still lives in Sydney and continues to divide his time between writing and teaching.